His Inexperienced Mistress

MICHELLE CONDER
SARA CRAVEN
CHANTELLE SHAW

D0994262

All rights reserved including the right of reproduction in whole or in part in any form. This edition is published by arrangement with Harlequin Books S.A.

This is a work of fiction. Names, characters, places, locations and incidents are purely fictional and bear no relationship to any real life individuals, living or dead, or to any actual places, business establishments, locations, events or incidents. Any resemblance is entirely coincidental.

This book is sold subject to the condition that it shall not, by way of trade or otherwise, be lent, resold, hired out or otherwise circulated without the prior consent of the publisher in any form of binding or cover other than that in which it is published and without a similar condition including this condition being imposed on the subsequent purchaser.

® and ™ are trademarks owned and used by the trademark owner and/or its licensee. Trademarks marked with ® are registered with the United Kingdom Patent Office and/or the Office for Harmonisation in the Internal Market and in other countries.

Published in Great Britain 2015
by Mills & Boon, an imprint of Harlequin (UK) Limited,
Eton House, 18-24 Paradise Road, Richmond, Surrey, TW9 1SR

HIS INEXPERIENCED MISTRESS © 2015 Harlequin Books S.A.

Girl Behind the Scandalous Reputation, The End of Her Innocence and *Ruthless Russian, Lost Innocence* were first published in Great Britain by Harlequin (UK) Limited.

Girl Behind the Scandalous Reputation © 2012 Michelle Conder
The End of Her Innocence © 2012 Sara Craven
Ruthless Russian, Lost Innocence © 2010 Chantelle Shaw

ISBN: 978-0-263-25224-8
eBook ISBN: 978-1-474-00403-9

05-0815

Harlequin (UK) Limited's policy is to use papers that are natural, renewable and recyclable products and made from wood grown in sustainable forests. The logging and manufacturing processes conform to the legal environmental regulations of the country of origin.

Printed and bound in Spain
by CPI, Barcelona

GIRL BEHIND THE SCANDALOUS REPUTATION

BY
MICHELLE CONDER

From as far back as she can remember **Michelle Conder** dreamed of being a writer. She penned the first chapter of a romance novel just out of high school, but it took much study, many (varied) jobs, one ultra-understanding husband and three very patient children before she finally sat down to turn that dream into a reality.

Michelle lives in Australia, and when she isn't busy plotting she loves to read, ride horses, travel and practise yoga.

For Paul, who always takes the kids—even when it means missing a surf—for my kids, who so graciously accept when Mummy is busy, for Laurel, who tirelessly reads my dodgy first drafts, and for Mum, who is always there when I need her most. And for Flo for her keen insights and endless encouragement. Thank you all.

CHAPTER ONE

'IS THIS your idea of a joke, Jordana?' Tristan Garrett turned away from the view of the Thames outside his tenth-storey office window to stare incredulously at his baby sister. She sat in one of the navy tub chairs on the visitors' side of his desk, legs crossed, immaculately groomed, and looking not at all like a crazy person sailing three sheets to the wind—as she sounded.

'As if I would joke about something so serious!' Jordana exclaimed, gazing at him, her jade-green eyes, the exact shade of his own, wide and etched with worry. 'I know it sounds unbelievable but it's true, and we have to help her.'

Actually, her story didn't sound unbelievable at all, but Tristan knew his sanguine sister had a tendency to see goodness in people when there was none to see at all.

He turned back to stare at the pedestrians lining the Thames and better able to enjoy the September sunshine than he was. He couldn't stand seeing his sister so upset, and he cursed the so-called friend who was responsible for putting these fresh tears in her eyes.

When she came to stand beside him he slung his arm around her shoulders, drawing her close. What could he say to placate her? That the friend she wanted to help wasn't worth it? That anyone stupid enough to try and smuggle drugs out of Thailand deserved to get caught?

Normally he would help his sister in a heartbeat, but no way was he getting involved in this fiasco—and nor was she. He gave her an affectionate squeeze, but he didn't try to contain the edge of steel in his voice when he spoke. 'Jo, this is not your problem and you are not getting involved.'

'I—'

Tristan held up his hand to cut off her immediate objection, his solid-gold cufflinks glinting in the downlights. 'If what you say is true then the girl made her bed and she'll have to lie in it. And may I remind you that you're eight days away from the wedding of the year. Not only will Oliver not want you getting involved, but I doubt the Prince of Greece will want to sit beside a known drug-user—no matter how beautiful.'

Jordana's mouth tightened. 'Oliver will want me to do what's right,' she objected. 'And I don't care what my wedding guests think. I'm going to help Lily and that's that.'

Tristan shook his head. 'Why would you risk it?'

'She's my best friend and I promised I would.'

That surprised him. He'd thought their friendship had died down years ago. But if that was the case then why was Lily to be maid of honour at Jo's wedding? Maid of honour to *his* best man! And why hadn't he thought to ask that question two weeks earlier, when he'd found out Lily was coming to the wedding?

He frowned, but decided to push that issue aside for the more pressing problem at hand. 'When did you speak to her?'

'I didn't. A customs officer called on her behalf. Lily wanted to let me know why she couldn't meet me, and— Oh, Tristan, if we don't help her she'll probably go to jail.'

Tristan pushed back the thick lock of hair that had fallen over his forehead and made a mental note to book a haircut.

Much as he didn't want to, he could see that he needed to get tough with his sister. 'Which is probably the best place for her.' He scowled. 'She'll be able to get help there.'

'You don't mean that!'

Didn't he? He didn't know. But what he did know was that his morning had been a lot better before Jordana had rushed into his office, bringing to mind a girl he'd rather strip from it altogether.

Honey Blossom Lily Wild.

Currently voted one of the sexiest women on the planet, and a talented actress to boot. He didn't follow films but he'd seen her first one—some art-house twaddle made by a precocious upstart of a director about the end of the world. Tristan couldn't remember the plot. What man could? It had Lily naked, save for a white oversized singlet and a pair of cotton panties masquerading as shorts, in almost every scene. The movie had signified to him that as a culture they were heading backwards—and people like Lily Wild were half the reason for that.

He and his father had tolerated the girls' teenage friendship because it had made Jordana happy—and neither man would ever have jeopardised that—but Tristan had disliked Lily on sight when he'd first come across her as a gangly fourteen-year-old, hiding drugs under his sister's dormitory mattress. She'd been haughty beyond her years that day, and if he had his time again he'd suggest his sister be relocated to another boarding school quick-smart.

Tristan heaved a sigh and returned to the smooth curve of his walnut desk, stroking his computer mouse to get rid of the screen saver. 'Jo, I'm busy. I have an important meeting in half an hour. I'm sorry, but I can't help.'

'Tristan, I know you have a thing about drug-users, but Lily is innocent.'

'And you know this how, exactly?' he queried, deciding that humouring his sister might expedite her leaving.

'Because I know Lily, and I know she doesn't take drugs. She hates them.'

Tristan raised an eyebrow. Was his sister for real?

'Have you conveniently forgotten the fallout from your eighteenth birthday party? How I caught her hiding a joint when she was fourteen? Not to mention the various press photos of her completely wasted in between.'

Jordana frowned and shook her head. 'Most of those photos were fakes. Lily's been hounded by the press her whole life because of who her parents were—and, anyway, she's far too sensible and level-headed to get involved in something as destructive as drugs.'

'And that would be why there was the scandal at your eighteenth? Because Lily is *so* level-headed?'

Jordana glanced at the ceiling before returning resigned eyes to his. 'Tristan, that night was so not what it seemed. One dodgy photo—'

'One dodgy photo?' he all but shouted. 'One dodgy photo that could have destroyed your reputation if I hadn't intervened!'

'You mean if you hadn't made Lily take the blame!'

'Lily *was* to blame!' Tristan could feel the old anger of six years ago welling up inside him. But it wasn't like him to let his temper override common sense and he controlled it with effort. 'Maybe if I had contacted her stepfather when I caught her with marijuana the first time she wouldn't be in the colossal mess she is now.'

Jordana briefly lowered her eyes before meeting his again. 'Tristan, you've never let me properly explain about any of this. What if the marijuana you found Lily hiding when we were fourteen wasn't hers? Would you be so disappointed if it was mine?'

Tristan expelled a breath. He really didn't have time for this. He got up and rounded his desk to enfold Jordana in his arms. He knew what she was trying to do and he loved her for it— even if the little bimbo she was trying to protect didn't deserve her loyalty.

'I know you're trying to take the blame for her, Jo. You've always protected her. But the fact still remains that she's trouble. She always has been. Surely her stepfather or stepsisters can help her?'

Jordana sniffed against his chest and pushed away a little. 'They've never been very close, and anyway I think they're holidaying in France. Please, Tristan! The officer I spoke to this morning said she might be deported back to Thailand. And, no matter what you think, I can't let that happen.'

Tristan swore under his breath. He had to admit he didn't want to imagine the gorgeous Lily Wild wasting away in a Thai prison cell either. 'Jo, my specialty is corporate law, and this will fall under the criminal jurisdiction.'

'But surely you can do *something*!' she implored.

Tristan released his sister and stalked over to the floor-to-ceiling windows again.

Unwelcome images of Lily as he'd last seen her crowded in and he forcibly held them back. She had been intruding on his thoughts and dreams for years now, but more so of late. Ever since Jordana had mentioned she was coming to the wedding, in fact, and to say that he resented her for it was putting it mildly.

He closed his eyes, the better to control the physical reaction he always seemed to have when he pictured her, but that only made it worse. Now he could not only visualise her, he could almost scent her as well.

Jordana touched his arm, and for a split second he imagined it *was* Lily.

Tristan muttered another curse under his breath. 'Jo, forget Lily Wild and concentrate on your wedding,' he growled, feeling like a heel when his sister flinched back from him.

'If Lily's not going to be there I might not even *have* a wedding.'

'Now you're being melodramatic.'

'And you're being horrible. Lily's been unfairly targeted…'

'Jordana, the woman wasn't targeted. She was caught redhanded!'

Jordana looked at him with the kind of pain he hadn't seen in her eyes since the day they had buried their mother. He'd vowed then that he'd do anything to protect her in the future and safeguard her happiness, and wasn't what he was doing now the opposite?

But what she was asking was impossible…

'Tristan, I know you hate drugs because of Mum, but Lily

isn't like that. And you usually jump at the chance to help a worthy cause.'

Tristan stared at Jordana. Her words brought back memories of the past he'd much rather leave dead and buried. And maybe it was somewhat illogical but he blamed Lily for that as well—because without her latest antics he wouldn't be having this conversation with his sister at all!

He turned back to face Jo and unclenched his jaw. 'Jordana, the key word in this situation is *worthy*. And as far as I'm concerned a drug-addicted actress who has hit the skids does not a worthy cause make.'

Jordana stared at him as if he'd just kicked a dog, and in that instant Tristan knew he was defeated. No way could he let his sister think so badly of him—and on top of that an image of Lily in a Thai prison cell kept swimming into his consciousness and twisting his gut.

He shook his head. 'This is a big mistake,' he warned, ignoring the little glow of relief he felt when Jordana's face lit up with unconcealed gratitude. 'And don't look at me like that. I might not be able to do anything. It's not like she shoplifted a bar of soap from the local chemist.'

'Oh, Tristan, you are the best brother in the world. Shall I wait and come with you?' Jordana was so happy she was practically singing.

Tristan looked up blankly, his mind already turning over to how he would approach the problem. When her words sank in his eyebrows shot skywards. 'Absolutely not.' The last thing he needed was his interfering sister getting in the way. 'I'll call you when I know something. Now, go. Do wedding stuff, or something, and leave me to sort through this mess you're so determined to get us in the middle of.'

He barely registered it when she kissed his cheek and let herself out of his office, already issuing orders down the phone to his secretary. 'Kate, reschedule all my meetings for the afternoon and tell Stuart Macintyre I want him in my office five minutes ago.'

He eased back in his chair and blew out a breath.

Was he completely crazy to get involved with this?

Lily Wild was trouble, and if seeing her bent over his father's prized nineteenth-century Dickens desk snorting cocaine at Jo's eighteenth party wasn't proof enough of that, then surely her attempt to smuggle drugs through Heathrow today was.

Not that Lily had ever admitted to taking drugs the night of his sister's party. She'd just given him a phoney, imperious smile that had incited his temper to boiling and after that he hadn't wanted to hear any excuses. Why bother? In his experience all users were supposedly as innocent as Carmelite nuns.

And what had made him even more irate was that earlier that night Lily had looked at him with those violet-coloured doe eyes of hers as if he was the only man in the world for her. And, fool that he was, he'd very nearly bought it!

Up until that point she had been nothing more than an irritation, occasionally taking his sister to her stepfather's industry parties when they were too young, and running away from him whenever he had come across her at the family estate during school holidays.

But she hadn't run away from him at the party. Quite the opposite in fact.

Forget it, he told himself severely as his mind zeroed in on the potent memory of how he had danced with her that night. Touched her. Kissed her.

The realisation that he'd very nearly lost control with her still rankled. But she had tasted pure and sweet, and so hot and…

Tristan shook his head and swore violently. Instead of reliving a moment that should never have happened in the first place he should be remembering how he had come upon her in his father's private study with a group of social misfits, his beloved sister, and about half a kilo of cocaine.

It had taken ten minutes to have Security dispense with everyone but his sister, and twenty-four hours to shut down the internet photos of Jordana that had been taken on a guest's mobile phone.

The taste of Lily, unfortunately, had taken a little longer to shift.

Lily Wild squirmed uncomfortably on the hard metal chair she had been sitting in for the last four hours and seventeen minutes and wondered when this nightmare she was trapped in would end. She was presently alone in a small featureless room that would make any director on a cop show proud.

Earlier today she had been equal parts nervous and excited at the prospect of returning to England, her home, for the first time in six years.

She had been lined up at border control for ages, and had just made it to the passport-check booth when the official behind the partition had directed her to a row of officers with sniffer dogs. She hadn't been concerned as she'd seen she was just one of many being checked over. Instead her mind had been on Jordana, hoping she would like the wedding present she'd bought for her and Oliver in Thailand, and also on how much she was looking forward to her long-overdue break.

Then one of the attending officers had lifted a medium-sized plastic bag out of her tote and asked if it belonged to her. She honestly hadn't been able to remember.

'I don't know,' she'd answered.

'Then you'll have to step this way.' He'd indicated a long, over-bright hallway and sweat had immediately prickled on her palms—like the heat rash she'd once developed while filming in Brazil.

Now, looking around the small featureless room, she wondered where the two customs officials had gone. Not that she missed them—particularly the smarmy younger one, who spoke almost exclusively to her chest and threatened to deport her to Thailand if she didn't start co-operating.

Which was a laugh in itself, because all she had done since they'd detained her was co-operate!

Yes, the multicoloured tote bag was hers. No, she hadn't left it unattended at any time. Yes, a friend had been in her hotel room the night she'd packed. No, she didn't think he'd gone near her personal belongings. And doubly no, the small plastic vials filled with ecstasy and cocaine were not hers! She'd nearly had a heart attack at the question, sure they must have made a mistake.

'No mistake, ma'am,' the nicer of the two officials had said, and the prickle of sweat had made its way to her armpits and dripped down the back of her neck like a leaky tap.

They'd then questioned her for hours about her movements at Suvarnabhumi Airport and her reasons for being in Thailand until she was completely exhausted and couldn't remember what she'd told them. They'd left after that. No doubt to confer with those watching behind the two-way mirror.

Lily knew they suspected Jonah Loft, one of the guys working on the film she had just wrapped, but only because he had been in her room just before she had left for the airport. She felt terrible for him.

She had met Jonah at the New York rehabilitation centre she volunteered at, and it wouldn't take the authorities long to discover that he had once had a drug problem.

Fortunately he was over that now, but Lily knew from her work with addicts that if anything could set off a relapse it was people not believing in them. Which was why Lily had got him a job on the film in the first place. She had wanted to give him a second chance, but she supposed when they found out she had been the instigator of having him work on the film it would reflect badly on both of them.

And yet she knew he wouldn't have done this to her. He'd been too grateful—and hopeful of staying clean.

Lily sighed. Four hours and twenty-eight minutes.

Her bottom was numb and she stretched in the chair, wondering if she was allowed to get up and walk around. So far she hadn't, and her thigh muscles felt as if they had been petrified. She rubbed her temples to try and ease her aching head.

She hoped Jordana had been contacted so she wouldn't be concerned about why she hadn't made it through the arrival gate. Though, as to that, Jo would likely be more worried if she *did* know what was holding her up. Lily just prayed she didn't contact her overbearing brother for help.

The last thing she needed was the deliciously gorgeous but painfully autocratic Tristan Garrett finding out about her predicament. She knew he was supposed to be one of the best lawyers alive, but Lily had only ever had acrimonious dealings with Tristan—apart from ten unbelievably magic minutes on a dance floor at Jordana's eighteenth birthday party. Lily knew he hated the sight of her now.

He'd devastated her—first by kissing her in a way that had transported her to another world, and then by ignoring her for the rest of the night as if she hadn't even existed. As if they hadn't just kissed like soul mates…

And just when she'd thought her teenage heart couldn't break any more he'd come across her in his father's study trying to clean up a private party Jordana should never have been involved in, and jumped completely to the wrong conclusion.

He'd blamed Lily—and her 'kind'—and thrown her out of his home. In hindsight she supposed she should have been thankful that he'd taken the time to organise his chauffer to drive her the two hours back to London, but she hadn't been. She'd been crushed—and so had her stupid girlhood fantasy that he just might be the love of her life.

Looking back now, she couldn't imagine what had possessed her even to think that in the first place. They were from different worlds and she knew he had never approved of her. Had always been as disgusted as she was herself at her being the only offspring of two notoriously drugged-out hippy celebrities who had died—*in flagrante*—of a drug overdose.

Not that she'd ever let him see that. She did have some pride—not to mention her late father's wise words running through her head.

'Never let 'em know you care, Honeybee,' he'd always said.

Of course he'd been referring mostly to rock music reviews, but she had never forgotten. And it had held her in good stead when she'd had to face down more than her fair share of speculation and scandal, thanks to her parents and, sometimes, to her own actions.

The hard scrape of the metal door snapped Lily back to the present and she glanced up as the smarmy customs official swaggered back into the room, a condescending smile expanding his fleshy lips.

He sat opposite her and cocked an eyebrow. 'You are one lucky lady, Miss Wild,' he said in his heavy cockney brogue. 'It seems you're to be released.'

Lily stared at him impassively, blinking against the harsh fluorescent light and giving nothing away as to how she was feeling.

The official sprawled back in the chair and rhythmically tapped the table with what looked like a typed report, staring at her chest. Men like him—men who thought that because she was blonde and had a nice face and reasonable body shape she was easy—were a dime a dozen.

This guy was a marine wannabe, with a flat-top haircut that, instead of adding an air of menace, made him look as if he should be in the circus. But even if he'd had the polish of some latter-day Prince Charming, Lily wouldn't have been interested. She might make movies about love and happy-ever-after but she wasn't interested in the fairy tale for herself. Not after her mother's experiences with Johnny Wild, and the humiliating sting of Tristan's rejection of her all those years ago.

'That's right,' Marine-man finally sneered when she remained silent. 'You celebrities always seem to know someone who knows someone, and then it's all peaches an' cream again. Personally, I would 'ave sent you back to Thailand to face the music. But lucky for you it ain't up to me.'

And thank heavens for that, Lily thought, trying not to react to his leering scrutiny.

'Sign these.' He shoved the stapled document across the table at her, all business for once.

'What is it?'

'Conditions of your release.'

Release? She really was being released? Heart thudding, and as if in slow motion, Lily took the sheets of paper, not daring to believe it was true. She bent forward, letting her long wavy hair swing forward to shield her face from his prying eyes. She was shaking so badly the words appeared blurry on the page.

When the door scraped open a second time she didn't bother to look up, assuming it was the other official, returning to oversee her signature. Then a prickly sensation raised the hairs on the back of her neck, and a deeply masculine and very annoyed voice shattered her concentration and stole the breath from her lungs.

'You'll find it's all in order, Honey, so just sign the damned release so we can get out of here.'

Lily squeezed her eyes shut and felt the throbbing in her head escalate. She'd recognise that chocolate-covered voice anywhere, and waited for the dots to clear behind her eyes before peering up to confirm that not only was her nightmare of a day not over, but it had just taken a distinct turn for the worst.

Fortunately Jordana had received the message about her delay, but unfortunately she'd done exactly what Lily had feared: she'd gone to her big brother for help.

CHAPTER TWO

LORD Garrett, Viscount Hadley, the future twelfth Duke of Greythorn, stood before her, with enough tension emanating from his body to fire a rocket to the moon.

'Tristan,' she breathed unnecessarily, her mind at once accepting that he was the most sublimely handsome male she had ever seen and rejecting that fact at the same time. He seemed taller and more powerful than she remembered, his lean, muscular physique highlighted by the precise cut of his tailor-made charcoal suit.

His chestnut hair was long, and lent him an untamed appeal he really didn't need, framing his olive complexion, flawlessly chiselled jaw and aristocratic nose to perfection. Her gaze skimmed up over the masculine curve of his lips and settled on cold, pale green eyes ringed with grey that were boldly assessing her in return.

His wide-legged no-nonsense stance set her heartbeat racing, and without thinking she snuck out her tongue to moisten lips that felt dryer than the paper she held between her fingers.

His eyes narrowed as they followed the movement, and Lily quickly cast her eyes downwards.

She pinched the bridge of her nose to ease the flash of pain that hammered behind her eyes, and blinked uncomprehendingly when a Mont Blanc pen was thrust in front of her face.

'Hurry up, Honey. I don't have all day.'

Lily wanted to remind him that she preferred Lily, but her throat was so tight she could barely swallow, let alone speak.

She grabbed the pen, flinching as her clumsy fingers collided with his, and scrawled her signature next to where he stabbed at the paper. Before she knew it the pages were whisked away, Tristan had grabbed her tote bag from Marine-man and he was ushering her out through the door with a firm guiding hand in the small of her back.

Lily stiffened away from the contact and rubbed her arms. He was well over six feet and seemed to dwarf her own five-foot-ten frame.

'If you're cold you should try wearing more clothing,' he snapped, hard eyes raking her body as if she were a foul piece of garbage.

Lily looked down at her white T-shirt, black leggings and black ballet flats.

'Ever heard of a bra, Honey?' His voice was silky, condescending, and Lily felt her breasts tighten as his gaze rested a little too long on her chest, her nipples firming against the fabric in a way she'd do anything to stop.

Lily was taken aback by his hostility, and it was all she could do not to cross her arms protectively over her body. She really wasn't up to dealing with any more animosity right now.

But she didn't say that. Instead she stared at the Windsor knot of his red tie and rubbed at the goosebumps that dotted her arms.

Tristan muttered something under his breath, shrugged out of his jacket, and draped it around her shoulders. She wanted to tell him she was fine, but before she could say anything he reached for her upper arm and propelled her down the long corridor, his clean, masculine scent blanketing her mind like a thick fog.

Tension bunched her stiff muscles, but she could hardly tell him to slow down when all she wanted to do was get as far away from the airport as possible. When he paused at the entrance to the duty-free hall Lily glanced up, feeling like an errant schoolgirl being dragged around by an enraged parent. She tried to loosen his grip, put some distance between them, but he ignored her attempt, tightening his hold before marching her through the throng of passengers. It reminded her of a couple of occasions in the past when he'd stormed into nightclubs and goose-stepped herself and Jordana out. It had been mostly at her stepfather Frank Murphy's parties, and in hindsight Tristan had done the right thing making them leave at their age, but at the time Lily had been hopping mad.

She noticed the large steel doors leading to the arrivals hall and breathed a sigh of relief. Hopefully Jordana was waiting on the other side, and once through Lily could thank Tristan for his help and bid him farewell until the wedding.

Her nerves were shot, but the relief that washed through her at the thought of freedom was suddenly cut short as Tristan veered left and led her into one of the small, dimly lit bars that lined the cavernous concourse.

The bar was long and narrow, with booths lining one wall and a polished wooden bar with red padded bar stools along the other. Except for two business types, deep in conversation, and an elderly gent who looked as if he might tumble into his early-afternoon schooner, the place was empty.

Lily waited to find out what they were doing, and was surprised when Tristan ordered two whiskys, watching as he glared at the bartender, whose eyes had lingered a little too long in her direction.

As soon as he'd moved off to get their drinks Tristan turned to her, and Lily nearly recoiled at the feral anger icing his eyes.

'What the hell are you doing back in my sister's life?' he demanded, his voice harsh as he lowered it so only she could hear.

Lily did recoil then and stared at him mutely.

Six years just seemed to evaporate before her eyes, and they might have been standing in his father's study again, where he'd accused her of something she hadn't done and called her a cheap slut.

Lily's eyes fell to his sensual mouth, now flattened into a thin line, and she quickly lowered them down the thick column of his tanned neck to rest once again on his silk tie. Looking at his mouth brought that devastating kiss to mind. She instantly reminded herself of his equally devastating rejection of her in an attempt to marshal her body's unexpected leap of excitement. How could she still feel so quivery over someone who had treated her so appallingly?

Tristan's tense silence seemed to envelop her, and she realised he was still waiting for her to respond to his rude question.

In all her mental imaginings of how this meeting between them would go this had not featured.

In one scenario she'd imagined they might be able to put the past behind them and become friends. Laugh over her silly teenage crush and his mistaken belief that she had set up the private party that had been splashed all over the internet. In that particular daydream she had raised her hand and said, *Please—don't give it another thought. It's over. It's in the past.*

But she didn't think that would play so well in this situation, and stupidly—so it now seemed—she had forgotten to prepare the whole busted-for-drugs-at-Heathrow scenario.

How remiss of her!

Now she had to ad lib, using a brain that wanted to drool over him like a beginner art student viewing her first Rodin nude.

Only she was no longer an impressionable girl caught in the throes of her first crush, Lily reminded herself firmly. She was a mature woman in charge of her own life. And wasn't one of her goals on this trip to meet Tristan as an equal? To look at him, talk to him, and put the juvenile attraction that had plagued her so often in the company of other men to bed? Metaphorically speaking, of course.

'I was invited to the wedding,' she said as politely as possible, given that his harsh question had evoked exactly the opposite response.

'And what an error of judgement *that* was,' he sneered, 'I can't imagine what my sister was thinking.'

Lily frowned and glanced at the bartender, pouring whisky into two glasses, so that she wouldn't have to look at Tristan. Perhaps the best thing at this point would be to apologise for inconveniencing him and leave quick-smart.

She watched as Tristan picked up his glass and swallowed down the contents with a slight flick of his wrist; his brows drawing together when she made no attempt to do the same.

'Drink it. You look like you need it.'

'What I need is a soft bed,' she murmured, only realising how he'd taken her innocent comment when his eyebrows arched.

'If that's an invitation you can forget it,' he dismissed.

Invitation!

Lily expelled a rushed breath, and then inhaled just as hastily, wishing she hadn't as Tristan's virile and somehow familiar scent wound its way into her sinuses. She felt the shock of it curl through her body and suddenly felt too warm.

Her heart rate picked up, and before she could change the direction of her thoughts she was back at the kiss she had been trying so hard not to think about.

He'd been lean and muscle-packed where she'd pressed against him, impossibly hard, and hot colour stole into her face as she remembered her youthful eagerness in his embrace. Lord, perhaps she had even instigated it! How mortifying... Especially in light of the fact that she couldn't recall any other man's kisses quite so readily.

Calling herself every type of fool for indulging in such useless memories, she swiftly removed his jacket and handed it back to him.

Then she sat her tote bag on the stool behind her and pulled out her favourite oversized black knit cardigan. She put it on. Found her black-and-white Yankees baseball cap and pulled that on too. Turning back, she couldn't see much beyond Tristan's broad shoulders, but the last thing she wanted was to be stopped on the way out by fans or—heaven forbid—any lurking paparazzi.

She noticed his condescending glance and decided to ignore it.

She was getting more and more agitated by her own memories and his snippy attitude. Logically she knew he had every reason to be put out, but she hadn't done anything wrong. Would it really hurt him to be civil? After all, it wasn't as if *he* had just been interrogated for hours on end over something he hadn't done!

Lily tried to smile as she hoisted her bag onto her shoulder. 'So, anyway, thanks for helping today. I can see that you didn't really want to, but I appreciate it all the same.'

'I don't give a toss what you appreciate,' he grated. 'I can't believe you would have the gall to try something like this, given your history. What were you thinking? That you could go braless and swish that golden mane around and no one would care what you had in your bag?'

Lily's eyes flew to his. Did he seriously think she was guilty? 'Of course I wasn't thinking that!'

'Well, whatever you *were* thinking it didn't work.'

'How dare you?' Lily felt angry tears spring into her eyes at the injustice of his comment and blinked them back. 'I didn't know that stuff was in my bag, and I've already told you these are my travel clothes and I look perfectly respectable.'

His eyebrows arched. 'That's debatable. But I suppose I should be thankful you're not displaying as much skin as you usually do on your billboards.'

Lily didn't pretend to misunderstand him. Movie billboards were often more provocative than they needed to be, and most of her fellow actresses found it just as frustrating as she did.

Not that Tristan would believe that. It was clear he still thought the worst of her, just as he always had, and the sooner she was on her way the better.

She looked up to suggest exactly that, but was startled when he leaned in close, invading her space.

'Tell me, little Honey Blossom, have you ever been in a movie that required you to actually keep your clothes *on*?'

Lily bristled. She hadn't been called Honey Blossom since she was seven, and she'd been fully clothed in all but her first film. 'My name is Lily, as you well know, and your comments are not only insulting and incorrect, but completely outrageous.'

He cast her a bored smile and Lily's blood boiled. Of all the rude, insensitive—

'Just finish the damned drink, would you? I have work to do.'

Lily felt so tense her toes curled into her boots until they hurt. Enough was enough. Thankful or not, she didn't have to put up with his offensive remarks.

'I don't want your *damned* drink,' she returned icily, angling her chin and readjusting her cap. 'And I don't need your odious presence in my life for a second longer. Thank you for your assistance with my...unfortunate incident, but don't bother coming to say hello at the wedding. I assure you I won't be in the least offended.'

Lily gripped her bag tightly, and would have marched out with her head held high if Tristan hadn't made a slight move to block her.

She hesitated and looked at him uneasily.

'Pretty speech,' he drawled, 'but your *unfortunate incident* has landed you in my custody, and I give the orders now—not you.'

Lily's eyebrows shot up. 'Your *custody*?' She nearly laughed at the thought.

He evidently didn't like her response, because he leaned in even closer, his voice deadly soft. 'What? Did you think I would just ignore the conditions of your release and let you waltz out of here by yourself? You don't know me very well if you did.'

Lily edged back and felt the bar stool behind her thighs, a tremor of unease bumping down her spine. She hadn't read the release form at all, and had a feeling she was about to regret that.

'I didn't read it,' she admitted, sucking on the soft flesh of her upper lip—a nervous childhood gesture she'd never been able to master.

Tristan frowned down at her, and then must have realised she was serious because he had the gall to laugh. 'You're kidding.'

'I'm glad you find it funny,' she snapped, staring him down when his grim smile turned into a snarl.

'Now, *funny* is probably the last thing I think about this situation—and here's why. You just signed documents that place you under my protective custody until you're either released—' his tone implied that was about as likely as buying property on another planet '—or charged with possession of narcotics.'

Lily felt dizzy and leaned heavily on the bar stool at her back. 'I don't understand…' She shook her head.

'What? You thought the evidence might up and magically disappear? I'm good, Honey, but I'm not that good.'

'No.' She waved her hand in front of her and briefly closed her eyes. 'The custody bit.'

'It's a form of house arrest.'

'I didn't know.'

'Now you do. And now I'm ready to leave.'

'No!' Her hand hovered between them and her voice quavered. 'Wait. Please. I… What does that mean, exactly?'

He looked at her as if she was a simpleton. 'It means that we're stuck with each other 24/7 for the foreseeable future, that's what it means.'

Lily blinked. 24/7 with this gorgeous, angry man…? No way. She pressed her fingertips to her aching forehead and ordered herself to think. Surely there was another solution.

'I can't stay with *you*!' She blurted out before her thoughts were properly in order.

His eyes sparkled into hers, as hard as polished gemstones. 'Believe me, the thought couldn't be more abhorrent to you than it is to me.'

'But you should have told me!'

'You should have read the paperwork,' he dismissed.

He was right, and she hated that. Only it was because of him that she hadn't read it in the first place.

'You crowded me and told me to hurry.'

'So now it's my fault?' he snapped.

'I wasn't blaming you.' She swiped a hand across her brow. This was terrible. 'But if you had warned me about what I was signing I wouldn't have done so!'

He went still, his over-long tawny mane and square jaw giving the impression of a fully grown male lion that had just scented danger.

'Warned you?'

Too late Lily realised he'd taken her comment as an insult.

'And what exactly would you have done, hmm? Do tell.'

Lily pressed her lips together at his snide tone and tried not to notice how imposing he was, with his hands on his hips drawing his shoulders even wider. If she'd thought he hated her six years ago it was nothing compared to the contempt he clearly felt for her now.

And she wasn't so much looking to put the past behind her any more as she was in burying it in a six-foot-deep hole! 'I—I would have looked for an alternative,' she stuttered. 'Brainstormed other options.'

'Brainstormed other options?' He snorted and shook his head, as if the very notion was ludicrous. 'We're not in a movie rehearsal now, Honey!'

Lily's heart thudded heavily in her chest. If he called her Honey one more time she might actually hit him. She took a deep, steadying breath and tried to remember that he felt he had a right to be angry, and that maybe, if their situations were reversed, she would feel the same way.

No, she wouldn't. She'd be too worried for the other person to treat them so—so…indignantly.

'Listen—' she began, only to have her words cut off when he pushed off his bar stool and crowded her back against her own.

'No. *You* listen,' he bit out softly. 'You don't have a choice here. You're no longer in charge. I am. And if you don't like it I'll give you another option. It's called a prison cell. You want it—it's back that way.' He jerked his chin towards the entrance of the bar, his eyes never leaving hers.

Lily blanched. Lord, he was arrogant.

'I didn't do it,' she enunciated, trying to keep her voice low.

'Tell it to the judge, sweetheart, because I'm not interested in hearing your protestations of innocence.'

'Don't patronise me, Tristan. I'm not a child.'

'Then stop acting like one.'

'Damn you, I have rights.'

'No, you *had* rights.' His tone was soft, but merciless. 'You gave up those rights the minute you waltzed through Heathrow carrying a bag full of narcotics. Your rights belong to me now, and when I say jump I expect you to ask how high.'

Lily froze. He had some nerve. 'In your dreams,' she scoffed, now just as angry as he was.

CHAPTER THREE

No, Tristan thought disgustedly, when he dreamt of her she was not jumping up and down; she was usually naked, her lithe body spread out over his bed, and her soft mouth was begging him to take her. But this was no dream, and right now making love to her couldn't be further from his mind.

Kissing that insolent curl from her luscious mouth—now, *that* was closer. But completely giving in to the insane desire that still uncomfortably rode his back—no. Not in this lifetime.

Not that he was at all surprised to find himself still attracted to her. Hell, she looked even better now than she had six years ago—if that was actually possible.

Even the bartender was having trouble keeping his distance—and not just because he'd probably recognised her face. Tristan doubted he'd be ogling any other actress with his tongue hanging out of his mouth, and there were many far more worthy of a second glance than this sexy little troublemaker.

No, the bartender was staring because Lily Wild looked like every man's secret fantasy come to life—even with those dark smudges beneath those wide purple eyes. But she damned well wasn't his. Not this time.

He should have just said no to Jordana, he realised distractedly. Should have made up a story about how it couldn't be done.

But he had too much integrity to lie, and in the end a close friend who specialised in criminal law had pulled a rabbit from a hat and here they were. But only by the grace of some clapped-out piece of nineteenth-century legislation that he would recommend be amended at the next parliamentary sitting.

'Did you hear me, Tristan?' she prompted, her glorious eyes flashing with unconcealed irritation. 'I won't let you bully me like you did once before.'

Tristan cast her the withering glance that he usually reserved for the seediest of his courtroom opponents.

Oh, he'd heard her all right, but she had no choice in the matter, and the sooner she got that through her thick, beautiful skull the better.

'Don't push me, Lily,' he grated warningly, and saw her teeth clench.

Her hands were fisted by her sides and he knew she probably wanted to thump him. Despite himself he admired her temerity. Most women in her position—hell, most *men*—would be grovelling or backing away, or both. Instead this little spitfire was arguing the toss, as if she might actually choose jail over him.

'Then don't push *me*!' she returned hotly.

He looked at her and tried to remind himself that he was a first-rate lawyer who never let emotion govern his actions. 'You signed the contract. Deal with it,' he said curtly.

She slapped her hands on her hips, the movement dragging her oversized cardigan open and bringing his attention back to her full, unbound breasts. 'I told you—I didn't know what I was signing,' she declared, as if that might actually make a difference.

Yeah, yeah—just as she didn't know how the drugs ended up in her bag. He had yet to come across a criminal who actually admitted any form of guilt, and her vehement denial was boringly predictable.

He noticed that the two businessmen who earlier had been deep in conversation were now stealing surreptitious glances at her. Not that he couldn't appreciate what they were looking at: tousled pearl-blond hair, soft, kissable lips, a mouthwatering silhouette, and legs that went all the way into next week.

They'd looked even longer coming down his parents' staircase at Jo's eighteenth party, in a tiny dress and designer heels. And just like that he was back at Hillesden Abbey, the family estate, at the precise moment she had approached him.

'Hey, wanna dance?' she'd invited, standing before him in a silver mini-dress that clung in all the right places, hip cocked, bee-stung pout covered in war paint.

He'd declined, of course. Just looking at her had stirred up a dark lust inside him that, at seventeen, she had been way too young to handle.

'But you danced with Jordana,' she'd complained, fluttering ridiculously long eyelashes like a woman on the make. 'And the girl with the blue dress.'

'That's right.' His friend Gabriel had elbowed him. 'You did.'

'So? What about it?' Lily had shifted her weight to her other hip, her dress riding up just that tiny bit more, head tilted in artful provocation.

He'd been about to refuse again, but Gabriel had interrupted and said *he'd* dance with her if Tristan wouldn't, and for some reason that had got his back up.

He'd thrown his friend a baleful glare before focusing on Lily. 'Let's go.'

She'd smiled her now famous million dollar smile at Gabriel and Tristan had gritted his teeth and followed her onto the dance floor.

As if on cue the music had turned dreamy and he'd almost changed his mind. Then she'd turned that million dollar number his way, stepped into his arms, and he'd no longer had a mind to change.

'It's a great party, isn't it?' she'd murmured.

'Yes,' he'd agreed.

'This is nice,' she'd prompted.

'Yes,' he'd agreed.

'Are you having a good time?'

Not any more; not with his self-control unravelling with each breathy little question.

He remembered he'd been so focused on not pulling her in close that he failed to notice when *she* had moved in on *him*. Then he'd felt the slide of her bare thigh between his jean-clad legs and the thrust of her pert breasts against the wall of his chest and self-control had become a foreign concept.

His hand had tightened on her hip to push her back, but she'd gripped his shoulder and looked at him with such unguarded innocence his heart had skipped a beat, and almost of its own accord his hand had slid around to the sweet indentation at the small of her back.

Her breath had hitched and when she'd stumbled he'd caught her against him. Her body had instantly moulded to his as if she was unable to hold herself upright. And he'd been unable to hide his physical reaction from her. His body had been gripped in a fever of desire: heart pounding, body aching and warning bells clanging so loudly in his head it was a wonder he'd been able to think at all.

He'd stupidly danced her into a secluded corner, with every intention of reprimanding her and telling her he didn't *do* girls barely out of nappies, but she'd quivered in the circle of his arms, lips delicately parted, and he'd fused his mouth with hers before he'd even known what he was about.

The bolt of pure heat that had hit his groin at the contact had almost unmanned him.

Before he'd known it he'd had one hand tangled in her golden mane, the other curved over her bottom and his tongue deep in her mouth, his lips demanding a response she had been more than happy to give.

He'd completely lost all sense of where he was, and hours could have flown by before a hand had circumspectly tapped him on the shoulder.

Thomas, the family butler, had stood behind him, seemingly

mesmerised by the imported mirror balls suspended above the dance floor.

Apparently his father required his presence most urgently.

For a second Lily's dazed disappointment had only been outweighed by his own. Then he'd realised what he'd nearly done and been appalled at himself. She was his little sister's friend, and the erotic images playing through his mind were highly inappropriate.

He remembered he'd abruptly released her and curtly told her not to bother him again, that he wasn't interested in babies. And then she'd punished him by attaching herself to some Armani suit for the rest of the night like ivy on a brick wall.

One of the businessmen hooted a laugh, and the sound broke Tristan's unwanted reverie.

He closed his eyes briefly to recompose himself, and then made the mistake of glancing into the mirror behind the bar—where his gaze collided with Lily's.

For a split second something hot and primal arced between them, and then the pink tip of her tongue snuck out to douse her full lower lip and just like that he was hard again.

Damn. Had she done that on purpose? Had she known what he'd been thinking about?

He blinked slowly and turned his gaze as hard as his groin. He wasn't an idiot, and he wasn't going to let her use that comehither look she'd probably learned in the cradle to manipulate him. The sooner she figured that out, the better for the both of them.

'I don't care what you did or didn't know. You signed the forms and now we're leaving.'

'Wait.' She put her hand out to touch him and then snatched it back just as quickly.

His jaw clenched. 'What now?'

'We need to sort this out.'

He picked his jacket up off the stool and shrugged into it. 'It's sorted. I'm in charge. You're not. So let's go.'

'Look, I know you're angry—'

'Is that what I am?' he mocked.

'But,' she continued determinedly, 'I didn't know I had that...stuff in my bag.' Her voice was barely above a whisper. 'And I'm not going with you until I know what happens next.'

Tristan glanced at the ceiling, hoping some divine force would penetrate it and put him out of his misery. He knew she had a headache. He'd known the minute he'd seen her. And now she was giving him one.

'You've got to be kidding me,' he groaned.

'No, I'm not. I mean it, Tristan; I won't let you push me around like you did six years ago. Back then—'

'Oh, cut the theatrics, Honey. There's no camera to turn it on for here.'

'Lily.'

He stared at her for a beat.

'And I'm not—'

Tristan glared at her and cut her off. 'You think I like this any more than you do? You think I didn't rack my brain to come up with an alternative? I have just involved a good friend of mine to get you out of this mess and all you can do is act the injured innocent. *You* broke the law, not me, so stop behaving like I'm the bad guy here.'

Lily seemed to lose a little steam over that. 'A friend?' she whispered.

'What? You thought I could just stroll up here myself and demand your release? I'm flattered you think I have that much power.'

Tristan glanced around the bar and saw that more passengers had entered. They were getting far more attention than he was comfortable with.

'He won't go to the press, will he?' she asked.

Tristan shook his head. 'So typical of you to be worried about yourself.'

'I wasn't worrying about myself,' she snapped. 'I was thinking about how this might impact Jordana's wedding if it gets out.'

'A bit late to think about that now. But, no, he won't say anything. He has discretion and integrity—words you'd need to look up in a dictionary to learn the meaning of.' He shook his head at the improbability of the whole situation. 'For God's sake, it's not as if you couldn't get a fix here if you were so desperate.'

She looked at him from under her cap. 'Whatever happened to being innocent in this country until proven guilty?'

'Being caught with drugs in your bag sort of makes that a moot point,' he scoffed.

Lily's chin jutted forward. 'Aren't lawyers supposed to be a little more objective with their clients?'

'I'm not your lawyer.'

'What are you, then? My white knight?'

A muscle ticked in his jaw. 'I'm doing Jordana a favour.'

'Ah, yes. The big brother routine,' she mocked. 'I seem to recall you really enjoy that. It must have made you feel valued—rescuing Jordana from my disreputable company all those years ago.'

She wrapped her arms around her torso in a defensive gesture that pinched something inside him, but he refused to soften towards her. He had no respect for people who created a demand for drugs and hurt those around them by using, and all today had done was confirm his father's view that Lily Wild was bad news just waiting to happen.

'It's just a pity I didn't nip your friendship in the bud sooner. I could have saved my family a lot of embarrassment.'

That seemed to take the wind out of her sails and he almost felt bad when her shoulders slumped.

'So what happens now? Where will I be staying?' she asked.

Tristan pulled a wad of notes from his pocket and threw some on the bar. 'We'll discuss the ground rules later.'

'I'd like to talk about them now.'

He turned to her, what little patience he'd started with completely gone. 'If I have to pick you up and cart you out of here I will,' he warned softly.

Her eyes widened. 'You wouldn't dare.'

Tristan crowded her back against the bar stool again. 'Try me.'

She inhaled a shaky breath and put her hand up between them. 'Don't touch me.'

Touch her? He hadn't really intended to, but now, as his gaze swept down her curvy body, he realised that he wanted to. Badly. He wanted to push aside that cardigan, slide his hand around her waist and pull her up against him until there was no sign of daylight between them. Until she melted into him as she had done six years ago.

'Then co-operate,' he snarled, crowding even closer and perversely enjoying her agitated backwards movement. It wouldn't hurt her to be a little afraid of him. Might make sure she kept her distance this time.

'I'm trying to.'

Her eyes flashed, and the leather creaked as she shifted as far back on the stool as she could, her monstrosity of a bag perched on her lap between them.

Tristan leaned forward and hooked his foot on her bar stool, jerking it forward so she was forced back into his space. He caught her off guard, and his bicep flexed as she threw her hand out to balance herself. Her breath caught and her eyes flew to his.

'No, you're not. You're trying to bug me.' He watched as colour winged into her face, his eyes narrowing as she snatched her hand back from his arm. 'And it's working.'

She raised her chin. 'I don't like your controlling attitude.'

He stilled, and their eyes locked in a battle of wills: hers bright and belligerent, his surprised but determined. His nostrils flared as he breathed her in deep. She smelled of roses and springtime and he had to fight the instinct to keep inhaling her.

They were so close he could see the flawless, luminescent quality of her skin—a gift from her Nordic heritage—and her thick, sooty lashes, as long as a spider's legs, nearly touching her arched brow. His eyes turned hot before he was able to blank them out, and her breath stalled as she caught the heat.

He stopped breathing himself and felt the blood throb powerfully through his body. For a split second he forgot what they were doing here. Time stood still. But before he could wrap his hand around her slender neck and bring her mouth to his she blinked and lowered her eyes.

Tristan exhaled, his anger all the stronger because of the unwanted sexual tension that lay between them like a living thing.

'Do you really think I care?' he snapped. 'When I first heard you were coming to Jo's wedding I didn't even intend to say hello. Now I find that hello is the least of my problems, and I can assure you I will *not* spend the next eight days arguing every single point with you. So if—'

'Fine.' She cupped her hand over her forehead and winced.

He knew what she meant, but he was insulted by her attitude and wanted to hear her say it.

'Fine what? Fine, you want to come with me? Or fine, you want me to take you back to Customs?'

She raised her head and he waited. The smudges under her eyes looked darker, and her skin had lost even more colour.

'Oh, to hell with it.' He straightened and held his hand out to her. She took it, without argument, and he realised that the shock of the morning was finally starting to set in—or maybe she'd been in shock the whole time.

Her fingers were icy in his, and he shrugged out of his jacket once again and pulled it around her. She squirmed as if to push it off, and her eyes jerked to his when he grabbed her upper arms and dragged her close.

'Co-operate,' he growled, pleased when she stilled.

'You never say please.' She sniffed.

Hell, she was still trying to call the shots. He kept his eyes locked on hers, because if they dropped to her mouth he knew he'd taste her. He was hard and he was angry, and the adrenaline pumping through his veins was pushing his self-control to its outer limits.

'Please,' he grated after a long, tense pause. 'Now, can you walk?'

'Of course.' She gripped her bag and swayed when he released his hold on her.

He knew it would be a mistake on so many levels, but before he could think twice he scooped her into his arms and strode out of the bar.

She started against him, but he'd had enough. 'Don't say a goddamned word and don't look around. The last thing I need is for someone else to recognise you.'

And just like that she relaxed and turned her head into his shoulder, her sweet scent filling his every breath.

The cool breeze was a welcome relief as he exited the terminal and headed down the rank of dark cars until he found Bert.

His chauffer nodded and held the rear door open, but just as Tristan was about to toss Lily inside she laid the flat of her hand against his chest and looked up through sleepy eyes.

'My luggage…' she murmured.

Tristan's chest contracted against the hot brand of her touch.

'Taken care of,' he growled, wishing the unbearable physical attraction he still felt for this woman could be just as easily dealt with.

CHAPTER FOUR

LILY collapsed back against the luxuriant leather car seat and closed her eyes, trying to equalise her pounding heart rate. Her head hurt and she felt shivery all over. She didn't know if it was remembering her previous attraction to Tristan that had brought it screaming to the fore, or the man himself, but she was unable to deny the sweet feeling of desire that had pooled low in her pelvis when he'd held her in his arms and looked at her as if he wanted to kiss her.

Kiss her? *Ha!* Shake her, more like it. Especially given how much he still disliked her.

As she did him.

Actually, now that she thought about it, her physical response was probably due to emotional tiredness and stress making her super-sensitive to her surroundings and nothing to do with Tristan at all. How could it be when he immediately assumed that she was guilty? When he clearly thought she was lower than dirt?

His cold arrogance fired her blood and made her want to fall back on all her juvenile responses to criticism. Responses that had seen her play up to the negative attention her celebrity lineage provoked by flipping the press the bird, wearing either provocative or grungy clothing, depending on her mood, and pretending she was drunk when she wasn't.

Nowadays she preferred to ignore any bad press or unfair comparisons with her parents' hedonistic lifestyles, and just live her life according to her own expectations rather than other people's. It worked better, to a certain extent, although she knew she'd never truly be able to outrun the shadow of who her parents had been.

Hanny Forsberg, her mother, had arrived in England poor and beautiful and on Page Three before she had found a place to live, and Johnny Wild, her father, had been a rough Norfolk lad with a raw musical talent and a hunger for success and women in equal measure.

Both had thrived on their fame and the attention it engendered, and after Lily was born they had just added her to their lifestyle—palming her off on whichever one wasn't working and treating her like a fashion accessory long before it had become hip to do so.

The camera flashes and constant attention had scared her as a child, and even now Lily hated that she always felt as if she was living under the sullied banner of her parents' combined notoriety. But none of that had been enough to put her off when her own creativity and natural talent had led her down the acting career path. Lily just tried as best she could to take roles that didn't immediately provoke comparisons between herself and her parents—though as to that she could play a cross-dressing homosexual male and probably still be compared to her mother!

Sighing heavily, and wishing that one of her directors was going to call 'cut' on a day from hell, Lily turned to stare out at the passing landscape she hadn't seen for so long.

Unfortunately the rows of shop fronts and Victorian terraces soon made her head throb, and she was forced to close her eyes and listen to the sound of Tristan texting on his smartphone instead. A thousand questions were winging through her mind—none of which, she knew, Tristan would feel inclined to answer.

For a moment she contemplated pulling the script she had promised to read from her bag, but that would no doubt make the headache worse so she left it there.

No great hardship, since she didn't want to read it anyway.

She had no interest in starring in a theatrical production about her parents, no matter how talented the writer-director was.

She'd nearly scoffed out loud at the notion.

As if she'd feed the gossipmongers and provoke more annoying comparisons to her mother by actually *playing* her in a drama. Lord, she'd never hear the end of it. The only reason she was pretending to consider the idea was a favour to a friend.

Her mouth twisted as she imagined the look on Tristan's face if he knew about the role. No doubt he'd think her perfect to play a lost, drug-addled model craving love and attention from a man who had probably put the word *playboy* in the dictionary.

In fact it was ironic, really, that the only man Lily had ever thought herself to be in love with was almost as big a playboy as her father! Not that she'd fully comprehended Tristan's reputation as a seventeen-year-old. Back then she'd known only that women fell for him like pebbles tossed into a pond, but she hadn't given it much thought.

Now she was almost glad that he'd rejected her gauche overtures, because if he hadn't she'd surely have become just another notch on his bedpost. And if she *was* anything like her mother that would have meant she'd have fallen for him all the harder.

Lily removed her cap and rubbed her forehead, glancing briefly at Tristan, slashing his red pen through a document he was reading. If she tried to interrupt him now to discuss her house arrest he'd no doubt bite her head off. Still…

'I take it you won't be put out if I don't feel up to making conversation right now?' she queried innocuously, smiling brightly when he looked at her as if she had two heads. 'Thought not,' she mumbled.

Suddenly she was feeling drained, and not up to fighting with him anyway, so it was a good thing he'd ignored her taunt. A taunt she shouldn't have made in the first place. Never prod a sleeping tiger…wasn't that the adage? Especially when you were in the same cage as him!

Lily leaned back against the plush leather headrest and closed her eyes. The manly scent from Tristan's jacket imbued her with a delicious and oddly peaceful lassitude, and she tried to pretend none of this was happening.

Cheeky minx! She knew he didn't want to talk. He couldn't have made it any plainer. He slashed another line through the report he was reading and realised he'd marked up the wrong section. Damn her.

She sighed, and he wondered if she knew the effect she was having on his concentration, but when he glanced up it was to find she'd fallen asleep.

She looked so fragile, swamped in his jacket, her blonde hair spilling over the dark fabric like a silvery web.

He knew when he got it back it would smell like something from his late mother's garden, and made a mental note to have his housekeeper immediately launder it. Then he realised the direction of his thoughts and frowned.

He was supposed to be focused on work. Not contemplating Lily and her hurt expression when he'd cut off her attempts to explain her situation earlier.

He didn't want to get caught up in her lies, and he had taken the view that the less she said the better for both of them. She had a way of getting under his skin, and for an insanely brief moment back in the bar, when her eyes had teared up, he'd wanted to reach out and tell her that everything would be all right. Which was ridiculous.

It wasn't his job to fix her situation. His job—if you could call it that—was to keep her out of trouble until Jordana's wedding and find out any relevant information that might lead to her—or someone else's—arrest.

It was not to make friends with her, or to make empty promises. And it certainly wasn't to kiss her as he had wanted to do. He shook his head. Maybe he really had taken leave of his senses getting involved with this. Stuart, the friend and colleague who had helped him find the loophole in the law that had placed her into his custody, had seemed to think so.

'Are you sure you know what you're doing, Chief?' he'd asked, after the deal had been sealed.

'When have you ever needed to ask me that?'

His friend had raised an eyebrow at his surly tone and Tristan had known what was coming.

'Never. But if she's guilty and people question your involvement it could ruin your legal career. Not to mention drag your family name through the mud again.'

'I know what I'm doing,' he'd said. But he didn't. Not really.

What he *did* know was that he was still as strongly attracted to her as he had been six years ago. Not that he was going to do anything about it. He would never get involved with a drug-user.

His mother had been one—although not a recreational user, like Lily and her ilk. His mother had taken a plethora of prescription meds for everything from dieting to depression, but the effect was the same: personality changes, mood swings, and eventually death when she had driven her car into a tree.

She had never been an easy woman to love. A shop girl with her eye on the big prize, she had married his father for his title and, from what Tristan could tell, had spent most of their life together complaining on the one hand that he worked too hard and on the other that the Abbey was too old for her tastes. His father had done his best, but in the end it hadn't been enough, and she'd left after a blazing row Tristan still wished he hadn't overheard. His father had been gutted, and for a while lost to his children, and Tristan had vowed then that he would never fall that deeply under a woman's spell.

He expelled a harsh breath. He was thirty-two years old and in the prime of his life. He had an international law firm and a property portfolio that spanned four continents, good friends and enough money to last several lifetimes—even with the amount he gave away to charity. His personal life had become a little mundane lately, it was true, but he didn't really know what to do about that.

Jordana thought it was because he chose unsuitable women most of the time, and if he did date someone 'worthy' he ended the relationship before it began. Which was true enough. Experience had taught him that after a certain time a woman started expecting more from a man. Started wanting to talk about love and commitment. And after one particularly virulent model had sold her story to the tabloids he had made sure his affairs remained short and sweet. Very sweet and very short.

He knew he'd probably marry one day, because it was expected, but love wouldn't play a part in his choice of a wife. When he was ready—if he ever was—he'd choose someone from his world, who understood the demands of his lifestyle. Someone logical and pragmatic like he was.

Lily made a noise in her sleep and Tristan flicked a glance at her, wincing as her head dropped sideways and butted up against the glass window. Someone the opposite of this woman.

She whimpered and jerked upright in her sleep, but didn't waken, and Tristan watched the cycle start to repeat itself. That couldn't be good for her headache.

Not that he cared. He didn't. She was the reason memories from the past were crowding in and clouding his normally clear thinking, and he resented the hell out of her for it.

But just as her head was about to bump the window again he cursed and moved to her side, to move her along the seat. She flopped against his shoulder and snuggled into his arm, her silky hair brushing against his cheek, giving him pause. He felt the warmth of her breath through his shirt and went still when she made a soft, almost purring sound in the back of her throat; his traitorous body responded predictably.

If he were to move back to his side now she might wake up and, frankly, he could do without her peppering him with the questions he'd seen hovering on her lips while he'd been trying to work.

She made another pained whimper and he looked down to see a frown marring her pale forehead.

Oh, for the love of God.

He blew out a breath and lifted his free hand to her hairline, stroked her brow. The frown eased instantly from her forehead and transferred to his own. If he wasn't careful this whole situation could get seriously out of hand. He could just feel it.

Five minutes. He'd give her five minutes and then he'd move. Get back to the waiting e-mails on his smartphone.

Twenty minutes later, just as he was about to ease his fingers from her tangled tresses, his chauffeur announced that the car had stopped. Well, of course he'd noticed.

'Drive us to the rear entrance, Bert,' he said, trying to rouse Lily. She rubbed her soft cheek against his palm in such a trusting gesture his chest tightened.

God, she really was a stunning woman.

How could someone born looking like she did throw it all away on drugs? He knew she must have struggled, losing both her parents at a young age, but still—they all had their crosses to bear. What made some people rise above the cards life dealt them while others sank into the mire?

According to Jordana, Lily was sensible, reserved and down to earth. Yeah, and he was the Wizard of Oz.

'You okay, Boss?' Bert asked, concern shadowing his voice.

Great. He hadn't noticed the car had pulled up again. He had to stop thinking of Lily as a desirable woman before it was no longer important that he neither liked nor respected her.

'Never better.' He exhaled, manoeuvring himself out of the car and effortlessly lifting the comatose woman into his arms. She stirred, but instantly resettled against him. No doubt a combination of shock and jet lag was laying her out cold.

A security guard opened the glass-plated door to his building, looking for all the world as if there was nothing out of place in his boss carrying an unconscious woman towards the service lift.

'Nice afternoon, sir.'

Tristan grunted in return, flexing his arms under Lily's dead weight.

He exited the lift and strode towards his office throwing a 'don't ask' look at his ever-efficient secretary as she hurried around her desk to push his door open for him.

'Hold all my calls,' he instructed Kate, before kicking the door closed with his heel.

He tumbled Lily gently down onto the white leather sofa in his office and she immediately curled into a fetal position, pulling his jacket more tightly around her body while she slept.

Scratch laundering it, he thought. He'd just throw the bloody thing away.

CHAPTER FIVE

LILY was hot. Too hot. And something was tugging on her. Pulling her down. Jonah?

She blinked and tried to focus, and found herself lying in an unfamiliar room.

'Missing your boyfriend already, Honey?' An aggravated male voice she instantly recognised drawled from far away.

Lily tentatively raised herself up on her elbow to find Tristan seated behind a large desk strewn with leatherbound books and reams of paper.

For a moment she just stared at him in a daze, unconsciously registering his dark frown. Then the events of the morning started replaying through her mind like a silent movie on fast forward.

The flight, the drugs, the interrogation, Tristan—

'You called his name,' he prompted. 'A number of times.'

Whose name?

Lily didn't know what he was talking about. She didn't have a lover and never had. She smoothed her fingers over her flushed face and wiped the edges of her mouth. It felt suspiciously as if she had drooled. *Urgh!* She was grimy and sweaty, as if she'd been asleep for days. Of course she hadn't been—had she?

Lily peered at Tristan more closely and noticed the same white shirt he'd worn earlier, the sleeves now rolled to reveal muscular bronzed forearms. The same red tie hanging loosely around his neck and the top button of his shirt was undone.

Okay, still Friday. Thank heavens. She glanced around his impressively large and impressively messy office.

For some reason she had expected someone so controlling to be a neat freak, but his desk was barely visible behind small towers of black, green and red legal tomes and spiral-bound notebooks. A set of inlaid bookcases lined half of one wall, with books stacked vertically and horizontally in a slapdash manner, and what looked like an original Klimt dominated another.

And that surprised her as well. Klimt had a soft, almost magical quality to his work, and that didn't fit her image of Tristan at all.

'It's an investment,' he said, as if he could read her mind. 'So who is he to you?' Tristan repeated, pulling her eyes back to his.

'Gustav Klimt?'

Tristan made an impatient sound. 'The loser whose name you were chanting in your sleep.'

Lily shook her head, realising one of the reasons she felt so hot was because she still wore Tristan's jacket. Removing it quickly, she placed it on the seat beside her and met his scornful gaze. 'I don't know who you're— Oh, Jonah!'

'He'd no doubt be upset to find himself so easily dismissed from your memory. But then with so many lovers on the go how can a modern girl be expected to keep up?'

Lily's brow pleated as she gazed at him. No improvement in his mood, then. Wonderful.

And as for his disparaging comments about her so-called lovers—the press reported she was in a relationship every time she so much as shared a taxi with a member of the opposite sex, so really he could be talking about any number of men.

She was just about to tell him she didn't appreciate his sarcasm when he held up a manila folder, a look of contempt crossing his face.

'I've had a report done on you.'

Of course he had.

'Ever considered going directly to the source?' she suggested sweetly. 'Probably save you a lot in investigators' fees.'

Tristan tapped his pen against his desk. 'I find investigators far more enlightening than "the source".'

'How nice for you.'

'For example, you're currently living with Cliff Harris…'

A dear friend who had moved into her spare room due to financial problems.

'A lovely man.' She smiled thinly.

'…while you've been photographed cosying up to that effeminate sculptor Piers Bond.'

Lily had been to a few gallery openings with Piers, and Tristan was right—he was effeminate.

'A very talented artist,' she commented.

'And presumably sleeping with that dolly boy in Thailand behind both their backs?'

Lily suppressed her usually slow to rise temper and threw him her best Mona Lisa smile. A smile she had perfected long ago that said everything and nothing all at the same time.

'Grip,' she corrected with forced pleasantness. 'He's called a dolly grip.'

'He's also called a junkie.'

'Jonah *once* had a drug problem; he doesn't any more.'

'Well, you should know. You've been photographed going in and out of that New York rehab clinic with him enough times.'

Also true. She volunteered there when she could, which was how she'd met Jonah. She just hoped Tristan didn't know about the director's marriage she was supposed to have broken up while working on a film the year before. But since it had been all through the papers…

'And Guy Jeffrey's marriage? Or is that so far back you can't remember your part in that particular melodrama?'

Great. He probably knew her shoe size as well.

'My, your man *is* thorough,' she complimented dryly. 'But do you think I might visit the bathroom before you remind me about the rest of my debauched lifestyle? I don't think I can hang on till tomorrow.'

Tristan scowled at her from beneath straight brows, and if the situation hadn't been so awful she might have laughed. Might have.

She picked up her tote bag from the floor and grimaced as she realised she felt as if she was requesting a permission slip from the school principal when she had to ask for directions to the bathroom.

Tristan nodded towards a door at the rear of his office. 'Leave the bag,' he ordered, returning his focus to his computer screen.

'Why?'

'Because I said so.'

Rude, horrible, insufferable... He raised his eyes and locked them with hers. His gave nothing away about how he was feeling while she knew hers were shooting daggers.

She suspected she knew why he wanted her to leave it. She suspected he was trying to show her who was boss. Either that or he thought she'd been able to magic some more drugs into her bag after it had been searched by Customs. But, whatever his reasoning, he'd now succeeded in making her angry again.

She planted her hands on her hips, prepared to stare him down. 'There's nothing in it.'

He leaned back in his chair and regarded her as a predator might regard lunch, and goosebumps rose up along her arms. 'Then you won't mind leaving it.'

Lily felt her mouth tighten. No, but she wouldn't mind braining him with it either—and damn him if he didn't know it.

She stalked towards him, her narrowed eyes holding his, and before she could think better of it upended the entire contents of her tote onto his desk. He couldn't hide his start of surprise, and Lily felt inordinately pleased at having knocked him off his arrogant perch.

'Careful.' She cast him her best Hollywood smile before

swinging round towards the bathroom. 'I left a King Cobra in there somewhere, and it's trained to attack obnoxious lawyers.'

As parting shots went she thought it was rather good, but his unexpected chuckle set her teeth on edge. And if she was honest she was a bit worried she'd never find her favourite lipstick again in amongst all the rubble on his desk.

His bathroom was state-of-the-art, with slate-grey tiles and an enormous plate-glass shower stall. Lily would almost kill for a shower, but the thought of putting on her smelly travel clothes afterwards was not appealing. Plus Tristan was in the other room, and she didn't want to risk that he might walk in on her. She didn't think she could cope.

A sudden image of him naked and soapy, with water streaming off the lean angles and hard planes of his body, crowding her back against the slippery tiles pervaded her senses and made her feel light-headed. She wondered if he had an all-over tan, and then pulled a face at the image of male perfection that bombarded her. He probably had a very small penis, she thought, grinning at her wan complexion. It would only be fair.

But then she recalled the feel of his hard body pressed into hers in the secluded corner of that long-ago dance floor and knew he wasn't small. Far from it.

She wouldn't ruin her mood by thinking about that. Somehow tipping her bag upside down on Tristan's desk had alleviated her anger and lifted her spirits considerably.

She splashed cold water on her cheeks and poked at the dark circles under her eyes. She looked a mess. And her hair was unusually knotty around her temples. A vague memory of soothing fingers stroking her scalp came to mind and she realised at the same time that her headache was gone. Had he stroked her? Soothed her?

The comforting gesture didn't fit his harsh attitude, but she was secretly thrilled that he might have done it.

Thrilled? No. She shook her head at her reflection. Thoughts like that led to nothing but trouble, and hadn't he already made it completely clear that he detested every minute he had to spend with her? And didn't she feel exactly the same way? The man was rude, arrogant and obnoxious, to say the least.

She blew out a noisy breath and pulled her hair into a rough ponytail, securing it with the band she kept around her wrist for just such purposes—a habit that made Jordana shudder. But Lily had never been one for fashion and clothing, like Jordana. Which was probably why Jordana was a buyer for women's wear at a leading department store and Lily wore just about anything she recommended.

Lily turned towards the door and paused with her hand on the brass knob. She was almost afraid to return to the lion's den.

Then she chastised herself for her feebleness.

No doubt Tristan was just planning to lay down the law. Tell her he wanted absolute silence and co-operation again. And if he did she wouldn't argue. The less they had to do with each other the better.

Sure, she had questions, but perhaps it was better to try and stifle them. She'd soon find out what was going to happen, and as much as the thought of being at his mercy made her skin crawl what choice did she really have right now?

Yes, that would be the approach to take. Polite, but aloof. Mind her own business and hope he minded his as well.

Tristan regarded Lily coolly as she walked back into his office. She'd put her hair up, which made her look more unkempt than when she'd first woken up—and incredibly cute. A fact he found hard to believe when he usually preferred women well-mannered, well-bred and well-groomed.

He was still smarting from having lowered himself to question her about her lovers before, like some jealous boyfriend, and wouldn't have minded if she'd spent the rest of the afternoon in the bathroom. All the better for him to get some actual work done.

But she hadn't, and now her eyes alighted on the refreshments his secretary had just placed on his desk. He knew she must be hungry, because he doubted the customs officers had made it a priority to feed her earlier today.

He suppressed a grin when he saw her glance surreptitiously around for her bag. Much as he hated to admit it, he admired her spunk.

'No, I didn't bin it,' he said conversationally. 'Although there wasn't much in there worth keeping apart from a miniature pair of black panties.'

Her eyes flew to his and he had to wonder why he'd said that. It had gone totally against his intention to direct her to the sofa and tell her to keep quiet.

Her mouth gaped with embarrassment and he almost felt sorry for her. She'd obviously forgotten they were in there.

Then she recovered and sauntered across the room. 'I'm not sure they're your size, but you're welcome to keep them.'

'I generally like to take them off women, not put them on,' he purred, enjoying the way her eyes widened before lancing him with a knowing look.

'So I've heard,' she rejoined. 'But I was referring to your personal use, not...' Her pouty lips tightened and she looked flustered, dropping her gaze to the assortment of cups in front of her. 'Never mind. I take it one of these is mine?'

'Yes. Take your pick. I didn't know if you preferred coffee or tea so I ordered both.'

She looked at him as if she thought such thoughtfulness was beyond him and his mouth compressed. He could be thoughtful when the moment called for it.

'And I know what you were referring to.'

She didn't respond but sipped pleasurably at the tea she'd just poured. He watched the way her mouth pursed daintily around the edge of the cup. It hadn't been quite so dainty when it had opened under his six years ago, and no matter how hard he tried he couldn't seem to stop thinking about that.

It had been six years, for heaven's sake. He couldn't even remember the colour of his last lover's hair let alone how she'd

tasted, and yet just looking at Lily Wild brought her unique flavour to mind. Her generous curves. Her responsiveness… Ah,
the sweetness of a response that had most likely been fuelled
by chemical enhancers. Or had it? It was a question that had
kept him up late on more than one occasion.

'I feel like I'm on an episode of *This is Your Life.*' She
smiled from behind her cup, the incongruous comment thankfully pulling his attention away from her mouth. 'Only the host
usually smiles, and I would have expected at least one or two
guests to have turned up by now.'

Tristan scowled—both at the flippant remark and his unquestionable hunger for somebody he didn't even like.

'Okay.' She sighed, completely oblivious to the tumultuous
thoughts playing out in his head. 'I'm presuming you don't
want my shoe size, so why don't you tell me what happens next
and—?'

'No, I don't want your shoe size,' he agreed, cutting her off
mid-sentence and leaning back in his chair. Some devil on his
shoulder wanted to throw her as off-balance as he felt. 'I already know it. Along with your jeans size, your bra size, and
of course what type of panties you like to wear.'

'That's an invasion of privacy,' she snapped.

'So sue me,' he drawled, unaccountably pleased to see her
affable expression fade and her eyes flash purple sparks. Her
watery attempt at friendship had annoyed him. He didn't want
that from her. In fact he didn't want anything at all from her!

Lily pressed her lips together and tried to hold on to her temper.
How dared he? Lounging back in his executive chair like King
Tut. She took a deep breath and willed herself to remain calm.
Polite and aloof…

*Just imagine he's a difficult director you have to put up with
for a short while. You've done that before.*

She was trying to think of some way to regain her equilibrium when Tristan's mobile rang and thankfully he picked it
up. He didn't even acknowledge her as he pushed away from

his desk and presented her with his back as he walked to stand in the vee of the floor to ceiling windows that partially lined two walls of his corner office.

Lily started reeling through every foul name she could think of to call him, and then her eyes wandered to the view outside his window. London only had a handful of luxury skyscrapers and Tristan owned one of them. It wasn't the tallest, from what she could see, but it was certainly located on prime real estate near the heart of the city. Lily could see Big Ben, Westminster Abbey and the London Eye, and she hadn't had to pay a penny for the privilege.

Without even being aware of it she shifted her gaze from outside the window to the man standing in front of it, legs apart and one hand in his trouser pocket, pulling the fabric of his trousers tight across his taut backside.

Her eyes drifted down over his long legs and up again to the wide sweep of his shoulders, to the ripple of muscle evident beneath his close-fitting shirt. He really was an impressive male and, given his sedentary job, he must work out all the time to stay as fit as he looked.

As if sensing her too-intimate regard, Tristan glanced over his shoulder and pierced her with his green eyes.

The air between them seemed to thicken. Lily's breath caught and her body hummed with a vibrant awareness. Then a dismissive expression flitted across his face, and Lily released a long, steadying breath when he swung his gaze back to the window.

She heard him speaking rapidly to the caller about some EU presentation, effortlessly switching between English and a language she couldn't place. His keen intelligence was evident in the incisive timbre of his voice.

Lily's stomach growled, and she picked up a sandwich from the plate and forced herself to chew it. It was beyond her that she should feel such a strong physical reaction to someone who clearly couldn't stand the sight of her. And it was getting a bit hard to put it down to stress and anxiety. But surely the brain had some input when it came to sexual attraction?

Tristan ended his call, dropped the phone into his pocket and stalked to his desk, gripping the high back of his chair as he studied her with relentless intensity.

'I must say you seem remarkably composed for a woman who's potentially facing at least twenty years in the slammer,' he scorned, leaving Lily stunned by his coldness when minutes earlier there had been such heat.

'I trust the universe will work everything out.' She said, wincing inwardly at her prim tone and refusing to react as he raised a condescending eyebrow.

'The universe? As in the moon, the stars and Mother Earth?'

'No.' Lily tried not to roll her eyes. 'At least not in the way you mean. The universe is like a forcefield—an energy that we create for ourselves and others. Sort of like if we all think positive thoughts then good will always prevail.'

Tristan cocked his head as if he was seriously considering her view, but of course that was a fool's notion. 'Well, I'd say your universe was either out for lunch when you tried walking through Customs today, or it's working perfectly and you're as guilty as hell.'

Lily folded her arms and bit into her top lip.

How was it possible for someone to be so devastatingly attractive one minute and so perversely irritating the next?

'I also have great faith that the authorities know what they're doing,' she said waspishly.

'The authorities want someone to put behind bars.'

Lily angled her chin. 'Are you trying to frighten me?'

'I'm not even sure the Grim Reaper knocking on your door could do that. Perhaps you're not smart enough to see the danger.'

'You're very good with the lofty insults, Lord Garrett, but I believe that right *will* win out in the end.'

Tristan shook his head. 'I'm sure if some of those corpses

buried at Tower Hill could speak they'd suggest that was a little whimsical.'

Lily was sure that if some of those corpses could talk they'd tell him they were relatives of hers—and not the blue-blooded ones!

'Are you implying that I'm being unrealistic?'

'Actually, I thought I was doing more than *implying* it.'

Lily sniffed. 'I wouldn't expect someone like you to understand.'

'Someone like me?'

'Someone who thinks everything is either black or white. Someone who requires tangible proof before they'll believe anything.'

'It's called dealing in the real world,' he jibed.

'But sometimes the real world isn't always as it seems.'

Tristan made a scoffing sound. 'I thought I told you I didn't want to hear any of your protestations of innocence.'

Lily's eyes narrowed at his bored tone, and she breathed in deeply through her nose.

Never let 'em know you care, Honeybee.

She exhaled slowly. This would all be a lot easier if he'd just talk to her, instead of snapping off pithy comments here and there.

'And, as *pleasant* as this conversation is,' he continued, 'I have work to do. So I'd prefer you finish your tea and sandwiches over on the sofa.' He sat down and turned to his computer, dismissing her like some servant girl.

Oh, she'd just bet he'd prefer that. And she would have happily done so if he'd been a little nicer, but now…

'Actually, accusations and criticisms do not add up to a conversation. And would it really hurt you to be a little more civil?' she demanded, throwing the whole idea of polite and aloof out of one of his ultra-clean windows.

'To what end?'

He didn't bother looking up from his computer screen and that incensed her. 'To…to… I don't know. Just to be *nice*.'

'I don't do nice.'

Lily nearly laughed.

As if she hadn't worked that one out for herself! 'You know, for someone whose job it is to communicate with others you're not very good at it.'

That got his attention. 'My job is about justice, not communication. And you better be careful because I'm really good at it.'

Lily shook her head. The man needed to learn some home truths. 'You might be hot stuff in the courtroom, Lord Garrett, but personally you're an avoider. You'd rather shut me up than try to have a constructive conversation with me.'

'That's because I don't *want* to have a conversation with you—constructive or otherwise.'

Lily raised her eyebrows. 'That's a fine way to solve a problem.'

'I don't have... No—wait.' He tapped his pen impatiently on his desk. 'I *do* have a problem. She's blonde, five-foot-ten and won't stop jabbering on at me as if I care.'

Lily's mouth gaped, and she stuck her tongue against the back of her front teeth to prevent herself from telling him just what she thought of his rude comments and hurtful attitude.

'You really think you've got me all sussed out, don't you, Tristan?' Her voice was husky with raw emotion. 'I'm just some no-good dumb celebrity who takes drugs and uses the casting couch to get her roles as far as you're concerned.'

'Well, not if you're screwing the dolly boy. I can't imagine *he* can win you too many roles.' He leaned back in his chair and folded his arms behind his head.

Arrogant jerk.

Lily narrowed her eyes and stabbed her finger in his direction. 'You might have some two-bit report on your desk, but let me tell you—you know nothing about me. Absolutely nothing.'

'I know all I need to know,' he confirmed.

Lily shook her head. She was wasting her breath trying to

talk to him. He'd made up his mind about her a long time ago and there was nothing she could do to sway it. In fact, when the police found out who the real drug smuggler was he'd probably accuse her of sleeping with the whole police force to get the result.

She gave a slight shake of her head. When she'd left England six years ago she'd instigated a policy never to rise to people's bad opinion of her again, but for some reason she couldn't seem to help herself with Tristan. For some reason his condescending attitude hurt more than everybody else's put together—and she hated that.

Lily folded her arms across her chest and decided to give up all attempts to change his opinion. Let him think what he wanted.

'You know it's a good thing you're not my lawyer because I'd fire you.'

'Fire me?' He gave a harsh burst of laughter. 'Sweetheart, I wouldn't touch this case if it came gold-plated.' He sat straighter and looked down his aristocratic nose at her. 'Because I know what you are, Honey Blossom Lily Wild—or have you conveniently forgotten what happened at Jordana's eighteenth?'

Lily stiffened at the ominously quiet question. Here was the basis of his true hatred of her. The presumed ruination of his little sister because of her association with big, bad Lily Wild. He'd judged her on circumstantial evidence at least twice before, and she hated that he had never once given her the benefit of the doubt.

'You know—you know,' she spat, ignoring the inner voice that told her to calm down. 'I could make a movie about what you *don't* know, you ignorant jerk, and it would be an instant classic.'

'Ignorant jerk?'

That seemed to rile him, and it startled her when his chair shot back, nearly tipping over with the force of his movement. He circled his desk, a predatory intent in every silent step, and

Lily's heart bumped behind her ribs. She didn't think he'd hurt her, but still, the instinct to run was nearly overwhelming.

He stopped just in front of her, his hands balled on his hips, his green eyes ablaze with suppressed emotion.

'Let's see,' he snarled, leaning over her and caging her in with his hands on the armrests of her chair. 'You tried to hide a joint under my sister's mattress when you were fourteen, you took her to sleazy parties in the city—*underage*—you caused an outrageous scandal the night of her eighteenth, snorting cocaine from the glass front of my father's *seven-hundred-year-old* Giotto painting, and today you cart a truckload of charlie and disco biscuits into Heathrow.' He leaned in closer. The pronounced muscles in his forearms bunched. 'Tell me, Honey, how am I doing so far with what I *don't* know about you?'

Lily felt the back of the chair hard against her spine and ran her tongue over her dry lips. She could explain every one of those things—but he wasn't looking for an explanation, and frankly she was getting so sick of his rudeness she almost wanted him to dig a hole so she could bury him in it.

She remained tight-lipped, and his mocking expression said it all.

'What? No comment all of a sudden? No further explanation as to why I walked into my father's study and found a group of wasted idiots—my sister being one of them—and you leaning over the desk holding a rolled fifty-pound note, with some Armani-clad idiot standing behind you like he was getting ready to take you? What a surprise.'

Lily blushed profusely at his bluntness. That wasn't how it had been at all—but had it really looked like that? And how could he think she'd even been interested in that guy after the kisses they had shared?

'For heaven's sake, why would I kiss you if I—? Oh.' She stopped abruptly and nodded. 'You think I just went from you to him. Hence the cheap slut reference.' She shook her head as if she was truly stupid. 'Sorry, I'm a slow learner. Maybe you can add dumb blonde to my list of credentials? That's if you haven't done it already, of course.'

Tristan moved as quickly as a striking snake and reached down to pull her to her feet. 'Stop. Trying. To. Garner. My. Sympathies. You took a chance. It didn't come off. Now, deal with it.'

Lily tried to pull her hands free, and then stopped when she realised it was a futile waste of energy. Her eyes blazed into his. 'I don't know what ever made me think I could reason with you,' she bit out, adrenaline coursing through her veins. 'You know what? Go to hell. All you do is judge me and I've had it. You've never wanted the truth where I'm concerned and— oof!'

The air left her body as Tristan pulled her hard up against him and covered her mouth with his own. She tasted anger and frustration—and something else. Something that called to her. Something that left her mind reeling. After a token struggle she felt her resistance ebb away. Her brain simply shut down, leaving her body and her heart firmly in charge, and both, it seemed, craved his touch more than air.

Tristan knew it was a mistake as soon as he did it—but, seriously, just how much self-control did she think he possessed? Did she never give up? Standing there, glorious in her anger, her eyes sparkling like cabochon amethysts.

She shoved against him and tried to twist her mouth away, but Tristan wound her ponytail around his fist and held her head fast. Some distant part of his brain tried reminding him that he didn't behave like this. That he didn't shut women up with his mouth like some Neolithic cave dweller.

But it was too late. He'd been hungry for the taste of her all day, and something far more primitive than logic and civility was riding him now.

She moaned, her hands pushing against his shoulders, and he immediately gentled the pressure of his mouth. A voice in his head was telling him to stop. That now he was behaving like a jerk. That he hated this woman whose mouth felt like hot velvet under his.

She represented everything wrong with mankind. She took drugs, she partied hard, she was self-centered, self-absorbed—like his mother. Just when he might have had a chance of pulling away her fingernails curled into his shoulders, no longer pushing him away but drawing him closer, and he was lost.

He eased the hand in her hair and pressed his other one to her lower back, to bring her into firmer contact with his body, and delighted in her responsive quiver.

Right now he didn't give a damn about parties and drugs. Right now he was satisfying an urge that had started six years ago and got a whole lot worse today. He felt a groan rise up from his chest as her lips moved almost shyly beneath his. He wanted her. Hell, his body was aching with it. And he knew by the way her fingers clutched at his shirt that she felt the feral chemistry between them as intensely as he did.

He softened his lips even more and felt hers cling.

'Open your mouth, Honey,' he urged. 'I need to taste you.'

She obeyed instantly, and his tongue slid home and drank from her as if she was the finest wine. Only she tasted better. Sweeter than he remembered. He nearly expired at the shocking pleasure that jack-knifed through his body. She was like ambrosia to his senses, and he was once again reminded how men could start wars over a woman. And then he lost the ability to think at all as her tongue snuck into his mouth and she raised herself onto her toes to deepen the contact between them.

It was all the encouragement Tristan needed, and he widened his stance to take more of her weight, burning up when she rubbed her full breasts against his chest. Her soft, breathy whimpers incited him never to stop this crazy dance. His hands were unsteady as they skimmed down her torso, skating over her breasts and pulling her restless hips more firmly against his almost painful arousal.

She gasped and pressed even closer, buried her hands in his over-long hair.

Tristan couldn't contain another groan, and his hands rose up to push her cumbersome cardigan aside so that he could palm her breasts with both hands. She arched into him and his thumbs flicked over her peaked nipples. His senses revelled in her soft cries of pleasure. His lips drifted down over her neck as he dragged oxygen into his starved lungs, and he slid one hand down to delve underneath the elastic waistband of her tight leggings to cup her bottom. Her skin felt gloriously smooth and hot, and there was no thought of stopping now. He'd wanted this for too long, and he knew when he touched between her legs she'd be wet and wanting…

The strident buzz of his intercom resounded through the room like a death knell, and Tristan sprang back from Lily as if he'd been kicked.

'Tristan, I know you said no interruptions, but Jordana is on line one and threatening legal action if you don't take her call.' His secretary's humorous voice rang out clear, despite the blood roaring in his ears.

Hell. Everyone was a comedian all of a sudden.

'Tristan?'

'Fine,' he snapped. 'Tell her I'll be a minute.'

He watched Lily blink a couple of times, her hands on her heaving chest, her eyes hidden as she contemplated the foot of black carpet between them as if it was a seething pit of snakes. Her lips were deeply pink and swollen from his kisses.

He shook his head at his own stupidity.

He wasn't some hotheaded youth at the mercy of his untried hormones. What had he been thinking?

He noted the rise of hot colour that started at her neck and swept into her face. He didn't know if it was from embarrassment or desire.

'Hell,' he seethed, stalking back round to his side of the desk, raking his fingers through his hair. He willed his body to calm down. 'We are *not* going to do this. You are *not* going to look at me with that come-hither sexiness. You want to know what happens next? I'll tell you. You sit over there on that sofa and you don't move. You don't talk and you don't whine. The only thing you're allowed to do without me is go to the bathroom, and if I think you're up to no good in there you'll lose that privilege as well. Is that clear enough for you?'

'Crystal,' she snapped, straightening her clothing and pulling her cardigan tightly around her body.

She touched her tongue to her lips and another shaft of desire shot into his aching groin. Then she raised her chin and looked at him with over-bright eyes, and once again he felt like the jerk she'd called him earlier.

'You know,' she began softly, 'Jordana thinks you're one of the good guys. Boy, does she have *that* wrong.'

CHAPTER SIX

TRISTAN sat opposite his sister at one of London's most exclusive eateries and tried not to brood over Lily's earlier comment. Because Jordana was right, damn it. He *was* one of the good guys, and he didn't know why he was letting the two-bit actress beside him, laughing over Oliver's unfunny jokes, make him question that.

Maybe because he'd kissed her the way a man kissed a woman he planned to sleep with and then blamed her for it. As if this maddening desire he felt for her was a deliberate spell she had cast over him... Which, come to think of it, was a much better explanation than the alternative—that he just couldn't keep his hands off her.

Which was not the case at all. What had happened in his office earlier was the result of extreme stress boiling over. Nothing more, nothing less.

Tristan prided himself on his emotional objectivity when it came to the fairer sex, and really this constant analysis of what had happened earlier was ludicrous. Yes, he was a man who liked his '*i*'s dotted and his '*t*'s crossed, but Lily was just an anomaly. An outlier on an otherwise predictable curve.

So what if his reaction to her was at the extreme end of the scale? It happened. Not often to *him* before, granted, but...once she was gone and his world had returned to normal he'd forget about her—as he had done the last time.

As he had done every other woman who had graced his bed. Only Lily hadn't graced his bed, and maybe that went some way to explaining his almost obsessive thoughts about her. He'd never had her. Had, in fact, made her off-limits to himself. And he wanted her. No point denying the obvious. Maybe if he had her—*no!* Forget it. Not going to happen.

But that didn't change the fact that now that his ferocious anger at being caught up in her situation had abated, and now he'd had a chance to observe her with Oliver and his sister all night, he had to admit he was starting to question his earlier assessment of her.

There was something so earthy and genuine about her. Something so lacking in artifice. He'd noticed it when she had engaged in a conversation with his PA and three of his paralegal secretaries.

She hadn't tried to brush them off, or spoken down to them. She'd been warm and friendly and called them by name. Something he would not have expected a drug-addicted diva to remember, let alone do.

He couldn't comprehend that he might have been wrong about her—but nor could he ignore the sixth sense that told him that something didn't add up.

Especially since the police believed that the haul found in Lily's bag, although small, had been intended for resale purposes. Lily just didn't strike him as the type who worked for a drug cartel, and nor did she appear to need money. Which left the possibility that she was innocent, had been framed, or had been an unknowing drug mule.

Or she'd brought the drugs in for a lover.

In his business Tristan had come across people who did far worse things for love, and he told himself the only reason he cared about this possibility was because he felt sorry for her. If she was so in love with some jerk she'd committed a crime for him she would definitely do jail-time. Lots of jail-time.

As if all that wasn't bad enough, the langoustines poached in miso—Élan's signature dish, which he had enjoyed many times before—had failed to get the taste of her out of his mouth. And that was just damned annoying.

Lily shifted on the black leather bench seat beside him and for the millionth time he wished she'd just sit still. They had been given a corner booth, overlooking Hyde Park, and whenever she so much as blinked, or turned to take in the view, his mind thought it was a good idea to let him know about it.

He glanced around at the *über*-modern, low-lit interior and recognised some of the more celebrated restaurant clientele, who all seemed to be having a better time of it than him. Laughter and perfume wafted through the air, along with the sound of flatware on Limoges china, but none of it could distract him from his unhealthy awareness of her.

He reached for his glass and took a long pull of classic 1956 Mouton Rothschild Medoc, forcing his attention from the spoon Lily was trying to lick the last morsel of ice cream from, as if it was thousand-pound-an-ounce caviar, and back to Oliver's discourse about his barbaric Scottish ancestors and some battle he'd no doubt claim they had won against the English.

God, his friend could talk. Had he known that about him?

Lily leaned forward and laughed, and Tristan refused to look at the way her low-cut silk blouse dipped invitingly, wondering where her tent-like cardigan had disappeared to.

When they had arrived at Jordana's prior to dinner the two girls had cried and hugged for an eternity. Then Jordana had whisked Lily away to shower and change, berating him for not thinking of it himself. Tristan hadn't told her that the last thing he needed was to have Lily Wild naked in his shower!

Now she was dressed in a red gypsy blouse, fitted denims and ankle boots, all provided by his sister. Her hair was brushed and fell in shiny waves down her back and she'd put on a bra. Pink. Demi-cup. Though he'd be a lot happier not knowing that. Because she had fabulous breasts and he couldn't help wondering what they would look like naked.

'It was love at first sight.'

Jordana's words sounded overly loud to his ears, and brought his awareness sharply back to the conversation.

What was?

Tristan looked at his sister, who was thankfully gazing at her fiancé and not at him, and released a breath he hadn't even realised he was holding.

'That's rubbish,' Oliver grouched. 'It took a month of haranguing you to help me find the perfect anniversary present for my parents before you even agreed to a real date.'

'I wasn't talking about me!' Jordana giggled pointedly, and then squealed when Oliver grabbed her leg under the table.

Lily laughed at their antics—a soft, musical sound that curled through Tristan's abdomen like a witch's spell.

'Steady on,' he said, as much to himself as to Oliver. 'She's still my baby sister, you know.'

'Stop your whining, you great plonker,' Oliver retorted. 'You're just jealous because you can't find someone who'll have you.'

'Ah, but haven't you heard, my good friend?' Tristan drawled. 'A man doesn't know what real happiness is until he's married. And by then it's too late!'

Jordana pulled a face. 'Oh, ha-ha. You'll fall in love one day. Once you get your head out of those legal bibles and stop dating women who are entirely unsuitable.'

'That swimwear model didn't look too unsuitable to me.' Oliver grinned.

'That swimwear model looked like a bobby pin.' Jordana said archly. 'Or should I say *booby* pin?'

'Lady Sutton, then?' Oliver offered.

'Hmmm, right pedigree, but—'

'I *am* still here, you know,' Tristan grumbled, 'and I'll thank you both for staying out of my personal affairs. There's nothing worse than two people who think love conquers all trying to talk perfectly happy singles into jumping off the same cliff.'

Not to mention the fact that he had no plans to relinquish his freedom to such a fickle and painful emotion as love.

But that reminded him that now would be a good time to find out who Lily could be so in love with she'd risk everything to please him.

And he had a right to know. He'd stuck his neck out for her, and he'd be damned if he'd risk getting it cut off because she'd done some idiot's bidding.

'What about you, Lily? Ever been in love?' he asked, smiling benignly as she shot him a look that would have felled a tree.

Now, what on earth had made Tristan ask her that? He'd ignored her all night, and when he did speak to her it was to ask something she had no intention of answering. Not seriously anyway…

'Oh, gosh, how long have you got?' Lily jested lightly, trying to think of a feasible way to change the subject. She'd rather talk about money than love!

'As long as it takes,' Tristan replied amiably.

She cast him a frosty look and murmured her thanks as a waiter discreetly refilled her water glass just before she picked it up.

Tristan scowled at him, but Lily appreciated his attentiveness. As she did the 'no cameras' policy the restaurant insisted on. No doubt the main reason the place was so well-attended by the super rich. Although, as to that, this restaurant exuded a class all of its own.

Eating out had been the last thing Lily had felt like doing, especially after the incident in Tristan's office, but she'd have done anything not to be alone with him. Which she would be once they left the restaurant.

And now he wanted to discuss her love-life as if they were best friends!

She didn't think so.

There was no way she would tell him that, yes, she had thought herself silly enough to be in love once.

With *him*!

Especially not when she had returned those kisses in his office a few hours earlier as if she still *was* in love with him.

Unbelievably, her body had gone off on a tangent completely at odds with her mind, and she was still shocked by her behaviour.

And his.

Although she shouldn't be. Tristan had been angry and had shut her up in the most primitive way possible. It didn't make it right—in fact it was downright wrong—but then so had been her response. She should have slapped him, not kissed him back. All she'd done was confirm his view that she was easy. A view she already knew would be impossible to reverse, so why even try? It wasn't as if he would believe the truth anyway.

'Well, let's see…' Lily paused, avoiding Jordana's interested gaze and counting on her fingers. 'First there was Clem Watkins, and then Joel Meaghan. Then—'

'Joel Major, you mean? And Clem? The guy from the gym squad?' Jordana scoffed. 'He had a nose that looked like he'd gone ten rounds with a hockey stick and he thought the ozone layer was a computer game.'

Lily pasted on a smile. 'He had good teeth, and he realised his mistake about the ozone layer almost straight away.'

'After everyone laughed. How could you have been in love with them? You didn't date either one.'

And that, Lily thought as she tried to ignore Jordana's frowning visage, was one of the problems with ad-libbing. Or telling white lies. You made mistakes.

Like forgetting that your closest friend was also at the dinner table and knew almost all of your teenage secrets.

'I'm not interested in your high-school dalliances, Lily.' Tristan cut in scathingly, his voice rising over the sounds of laughter in the background. 'I do want to get home tonight. Let's talk about *men* you've been in love with.'

Ha!

'Let's not,' Lily said, dismissing him with one of her enigmatic smiles. 'You'd be bored silly.'

'Humour me,' he insisted, his tone intimate as he shifted

his hand along the back of the velvet seat. 'Who's the current love of your life?'

His thumb grazed one of her shoulderblades and the heat of his touch burned through her thin blouse like dry ice.

Lily jerked forward and pretended she had been about to place her water glass back on the table.

He had done that deliberately, and if she hadn't agreed to put on a united front for Jordana and Oliver she'd happily tell him where to go.

Looking at the sexy little smile curving his lips, she knew he knew it. Which only fuelled her ire. If he thought he had the upper hand in this situation he had another thing coming.

'Oh, don't be silly,' she cooed, reaching across and placing her hand a little too high on his thigh, and patting him as one might a family pet. 'You already know everything there is to know about me. Remember?'

She felt a spurt of pleasure when Tristan looked taken aback by her action.

'I thought it was your contention that I didn't?' He replied lazily, smiling a devil's smile and clamping his larger hand over hers, effectively imprisoning her palm against his muscular thigh. 'I've always believed it's better to go directly to the source when you want to find something out.'

Lily's smile froze as his steely thigh muscles contracted beneath her palm. Her fingernails automatically curled into his trousers and she gave serious consideration to piercing through the heavy fabric to the flesh beneath.

Heat surged through her body as he squeezed her hand and locked his darkly amused eyes with hers. Lily shifted her gaze to the twinkling lights of the park through the unadorned windows before managing to recover her equilibrium enough to flick her dismissive gaze back over him.

'How very open-minded of you,' she purred pointedly, digging her nails into his thigh once more before dragging her hand away.

Lily had wanted to put Tristan in his place, but instead he

threw his head back and laughed—a delightfully masculine sound that was like fingernails down a chalkboard to her highly strung emotions.

She could see Jordana and Oliver looking perplexed, and then Tristan smiled at her. 'That's just the kind of guy I am,' he said, picking up his wine glass and holding her gaze as he stroked his thumb over the stem.

'I take it that was an in-joke?' Jordana offered, jolting Lily's attention away from Tristan.

'I don't know.' Lily sniffed. 'I didn't find it funny at all.'

'Well, regardless, now I'm even more confused.' Jordana tilted her head. 'Are you seeing someone, Lil, or not?'

Lily saw the open curiosity in her friend's face and wished she could rewind the last few minutes—because Jordana was far too nosy and would no doubt start hassling her about how hard she worked and how she needed to get out more.

'No.' She sighed, and then, feeling herself observed by Tristan's sceptical gaze, added, 'No one of any importance, that is.'

Let him make of that what he would!

'Well, good,' Jordana surprised her by saying. 'Because like Tristan, you've gone for completely the wrong partners so far. But—' she raised her index finger as Lily was about to intercede '—as you're my best friend I've decided to help you out.'

'How?' There was nothing scarier than Jordana on a love mission.

'Ah, not telling. Let's just say I have a little surprise for you during the wedding celebrations.' Jordana cast Oliver a conspiratorial glance from behind her crystal wine glass.

Lily didn't even try to smile.

'Jordana, what are you up to?'

'Now, don't be like that,' Jordana admonished her. 'I know how hard you've worked the past couple of years and it's time you cut loose a little bit. Look around, Lil.' She waved her glass towards the row of white tabletops. 'Have some fun, like your peers.'

Lily gave her friend what she hoped was a good-natured grimace. Jordana was sounding more and more like her old therapist, and that was just plain scary. 'Jordana, you're starting to scare me, and—much as I hate to agree with Tristan—I think you're so loved-up at the minute you're blinkered. I'm very happy as I am. I don't want a relationship. I like being single.'

'I'm just loading the gun, Lil, you don't have to fire the bullets,' Jordana returned innocently. 'Now, how about a pot of tea to finish off?'

'We really should be going,' Tristan said. 'Lily's tired.'

Lily looked at him, surprised he'd noticed. She *was* tired, but she'd do anything to prolong the time before being alone with him.

'No, I'm not.' She smiled brightly. 'And I never finish a meal without a cup of peppermint tea.'

'I'll have one too,' Jordana said.

Tristan and Oliver both raised their hands to signal the waiter at the same time, and Lily couldn't help laughing. Clearly Jordana had found herself an alpha male top dog to stand up to her overbearing brother.

The waiter took their order and Lily excused herself to use the bathroom.

Tristan frowned at her as she stood up, and she knew exactly what he was thinking. 'Be a dear and mind my handbag, would you?' she said to him, tilting the smaller satchel she had brought along in place of her tote precariously towards him and enjoying the way his eyes flared at her provocative move.

Serve him right for asking her such a personal question before, and trapping her hand against his thigh.

'Lily! Hi.'

Lily looked up into the mirror above the handbasin into the gorgeous face of a previous co-star she had shot a film with two years ago.

'I thought it was you. Summer Berkley—we worked together on *Honeymooner*.'

'Yes, I remember.' Lily wiped her hands.

Summer was a quintessential LA actress, with the tan, the boobs, no hips whatsoever and the hair just so. But she had a good heart, and a genuine talent which would eventually take her further than all the rest combined.

They swapped stories for a few minutes, and when Lily couldn't stall in the bathroom any more without drawing attention to the fact that she was doing so, she reluctantly preceded Summer into the dimly lit corridor—and almost straight into Tristan, leaning indolently against the opposite wall, arms folded, legs crossed at the ankles.

'Oh, *hello*,' Summer breathed behind her, and Lily mentally rolled her eyes. 'Are you waiting for us?'

'In a manner of speaking.' Tristan smiled at the redheaded Summer with bemused interest.

Lily decided there was no way she was standing around to watch Tristan hit on another woman, but when she moved to sidestep him he deliberately snagged his hand around her waist to waylay her.

Lily stiffened, and couldn't miss Summer's disappointed pout before she strutted suggestively past Tristan, who looked designer casual with the top buttons of his shirt undone and a five o'clock shadow darkening his chiselled jaw.

'I'm sorry, Lord Garrett. Did I take more than my allotted thirty seconds?' Lily murmured, stepping away from his touch.

Tristan let her go and held up his mobile phone. 'I had to take a call. But, yes, as a matter of fact, you did. And deliberately, I have no doubt.'

'Now, why would I do that?'

'Oh, I don't know.' His smile didn't reach his eyes. 'Because you like bugging me?'

'Hardly,' Lily denied, looking down her nose at him. 'Do you mind?' She looked pointedly towards the restaurant's dining room.

'Why don't you want me to know who your current lover is?' he asked.

Lily stared at the stubble on his chin and wondered absurdly if it was hard or soft. 'If I ignore you will you go away?' she queried hopefully.

'Nope.'

She sighed. 'How about because it's none of your business, then?'

'Is he famous?'

'No.'

She had to step closer to Tristan to allow two women to walk past, but quickly stepped back again.

'Married?'

'No!'

'Do I know him?'

Lily let out a breath. She couldn't understand why he was pushing this. He was starting to sound like a jealous beau. But that was ridiculous. He didn't even *like* her, did he?

'I don't see that it's any of your business,' she said again with icy politeness, folding her hands across her chest.

'Unfortunately for you everything about you right now is very much my business.'

Lily shook her head. 'I don't see how. You're not my lawyer, and the question is irrele—'

She broke off with a squeak as Tristan grabbed her elbow again, to avoid more diners heading to the bathroom and marched her around a short corner, stopping in front of a closed door.

They were close enough now that Lily could feel heat—and anger—emanating from his muscular frame.

'If you brought those drugs into the country for someone else,' he began scathingly, 'and you get approached by the moron while you're in my custody I could be implicated. Not only could my reputation and legal practice go down the drain but, depending on how it played out, I could be charged along with you.' His voice never lost its tenor, and the message was clear. 'So, whether you think my questions are relevant or not is completely *irrelevant* to me.'

Lily's heart beat heavily in her chest. So that was what was behind his earlier probing. She had been right. He wasn't interested in her as a person. She hated the fact that for a brief moment she had toyed with the idea that he might actually like her. Talk about living in a dream world.

She swallowed, not wanting to dwell on the way that made her feel—because she couldn't—wouldn't—continue to be disappointed by his low opinion of her.

She looked furtively around the small space and realised she was trapped between some sort of cupboard and Tristan and would need to push past him to return to the dining room.

For a minute she considered ignoring him, but she knew how well that would go down. And nobody had ever benefited from pulling a tiger's tail that she knew of...

'I wasn't anyone's drug mule and I don't know who the drugs belong to or how they ended up in my bag. And, contrary to *popular* belief, I don't have a lover right now. Sorry to disappoint you on that score.'

His brooding gaze held hers, and Lily resisted the urge to slick her tongue across her lips. He looked annoyed and intimidating, and a lot like he had when he'd thrown her out of his family home six years ago.

'What happened in my father's study six years ago?' he asked suddenly, and Lily wondered if maybe he really was a mind reader!

'You threw me out of your home and told me not to contact Jo again,' she said immediately.

'Which you ignored.'

Her eyes widened. 'Did you really expect me to cut myself off from her?'

His lips curved up slightly, as if he found the question amusing, but his eyes remained hard. 'Of course I expected it. But there's nothing I can do about that now. And that's not what I was asking about and you know it.'

If he was asking about the private party he had interrupted at Jo's eighteenth that was his problem. If Jordana hadn't already told him that *she* had instigated the party then Lily wouldn't do it either. It wouldn't serve any purpose but to make him think poorly of Jo, and Lily had no intention of ruining relations between them so close to the wedding by being some sort of tattle-tale after the event.

'I see no point in rehashing the past,' she said.

'Well, that's too bad, because I do.'

Lily unconsciously squared her shoulders. 'Actually, it's too bad for you, because I don't.'

Tristan's eyes narrowed dangerously. 'You were keen enough to talk earlier.'

'And you pointed out what a terrible idea that was, and now I'm agreeing with you.'

'Careful, Lily. That's twice you've agreed with me… Don't want to make a habit of it.'

Lily leaned forward and balled her hands on her hips. 'Well, here's something else I agree with you about—we need to set some ground rules before we go any further, and your macho "I'm in charge" routine just isn't going to cut it. Especially in public.'

'Really?'

'Yes, really.' Lily angled her chin up, ignoring the mocking glint in his eyes. 'And the first rule is that what happened back in your office is never to be repeated.'

'Now, how did I know you were going to say that?' he murmured silkily.

'I don't know. Putting that off-the-scale IQ of yours to good use for once?' she quipped, a sense of her own control making her reckless.

'Don't pretend you didn't want it,' he grated. 'You've been eating me up with your eyes ever since I picked you up today.'

'Oh!' Lily forgot about the fact that they were in a public space. 'You are something else!'

'So I've been told.'

'I just bet you have. You have quite the reputation as a ladies' man, but if you think I want to join their lowly ranks you can think again.'

'That's not how you played it six years ago,' he sneered.

'Six years ago I was too young to know any better—and don't forget I was high as a kite,' she lied. Why not *really* play up to his nasty opinion of her? Answering honestly before hadn't done much to change his opinion of her.

'Well, that might be.' His eyes flashed in response to her taunt. 'But you weren't high back in my office, and the way you tried to crawl up my body you wouldn't have stopped until I was deep inside you and you were completely sated.'

Lily gasped. His words conjured up a sensual image that caused her pelvis to clench alarmingly. 'You're delusional if you think that,' Lily spat breathlessly.

The cupboard's doorknob poked into her back as she instinctively moved back when Tristan closed the small space between them.

His eyes glittered dangerously into hers. 'A challenge, Honey?'

'No!'

'Oh, yes.'

He placed a hand either side of her head and leaned in, his mouth so close she could feel his warm breath on her lips, smell the coffee and wine he'd consumed.

Lily's heart sounded as loud as a road train in her ears, and her pelvis continued to clench in wicked anticipation of his kiss. Try as she might, she couldn't seem to find the will to resist his animal magnetism that was pulling her under.

Tristan's gaze held hers for a lifetime. 'Oh, yes,' he whispered again. 'Definitely a challenge.' He straightened away from her and dropped his arms, his expression closed. 'But, as gorgeous as you undoubtedly are, I'm not interested—so go play your games somewhere else.'

CHAPTER SEVEN

THE ride to Tristan's home was tense, to say the least. Lily was still fuming over the humiliation of nearly embarrassing herself before, when she had almost reached up and pulled Tristan's taunting mouth to hers. Something she hadn't even been aware she was about to do until he'd pulled back.

Until *he'd* pulled back.

She swallowed a moan of distress and watched one neon sign become another as Tristan steered his silver Mercedes through the streets from Park Lane to Hampstead Heath—one of London's most prestigious addresses.

How dared he tell her that he wasn't interested in her? As if she would care! How about the fact that *she* wasn't interested in *him*?

And he'd certainly been a little more than interested back in his office. Interested in sex, anyway. Not that she would have let it get that far. But deep down she knew what he was trying to say. She wasn't his type. He thought her attractive, but nothing more.

Frank Murphy, her stepfather, had warned her about men like Tristan. 'They'll take one look at that face and figure and, believe me, they won't care about your personality. You give them what they want and you'll get a reputation for being easy.' *Like your mother.* The unspoken words had hung between them and Lily shifted uncomfortably at the memory.

Her mother had been ruled by her desires. Or, more specifically, her desire for Johnny Wild, but Lily wasn't like that.

Which was one of the reasons she resented this attraction she still felt for Tristan. She'd sworn never to fall for an unattainable man, and here she was all but salivating over one.

Dammit, Tristan was right. She had wanted him earlier in his office. Had, in fact, been completely enthralled by the sensations and emotions his touch had evoked.

The memory made her cheeks heat with shame. Hadn't she learned anything from his first rejection of her? Was she just a glutton for punishment?

Lily sighed and leaned her head back against the butter-soft leather seat, wishing she hadn't decided to come back to England after all this time. She should never have told Jordana she could make her wedding. Would be *in* her wedding!

It seemed that the stars had aligned and no matter which way she looked she was being sent a message that she wasn't as ready to come home as she had thought. And maybe she never would be.

Thankfully her morose thoughts halted when Tristan's powerful car pulled up and waited for the ten-metre-high wrought-iron gates to open. Lily glanced at the towering stone mansion softly lit by discreet exterior lights that made it seem as if it touched the skyline.

The car inched forward and down into an underground car park that held a motorbike, a four-wheel drive, and a gleaming red sports car.

A sense of entrapment suffused her, and Lily felt so tense she jumped out of the car before it had come to a complete stop. Then wished she hadn't as she swayed and had to grab hold of the roof to steady herself.

Tristan's mouth tightened, but he didn't say anything as she followed him to a lift.

A *lift*!

'The house belonged to an elderly couple before I bought it,' he said, noticing her surprised reaction.

Lily didn't respond; emotional exhaustion and jet lag were weighing her down as effectively as a giant bag of sand. She calculated that it was about 5:00 a.m. in Bangkok, which meant that she'd been up all night, and the effort it took to work that out made her nearly trip over her own feet when the lift doors opened.

Tristan cursed and reached for her, and cursed again when she stumbled trying to avoid him.

'Don't be a fool,' he ground out as she wrenched her elbow out of his reach.

'I don't want you touching me,' she snapped, wedging herself into the far corner of the panelled lift and staring at his shoes.

'Fine—fall over, then,' he mocked, moving to the opposite side of the small space.

Tristan had briefly considered arguing with her, but if she wanted to deny the sexual chemistry between them then that was her prerogative. He should probably take a leaf out of her book and do the same thing. It had been silly, goading her in the restaurant, rising to her challenge. A challenge, he'd sensed from her awkwardness afterwards, that had been more innocent than intentional.

And maybe he'd have more success ignoring the chemistry between them if she'd stop flinching every time he came within spitting distance of her? Because that just made a primitive part of him want to pursue her even more.

'You need to stop doing that,' he said.

She raised her eyes from his feet all the way up his body and looked at him from under pitch-black lashes. 'Breathing?' she quipped, folding her arms across her chest as he mimicked her leisurely scrutiny.

He barely resisted the urge to smile. *Yeah, that would help.*

She glanced away and worried her top lip and he wished she'd stop doing that as well.

The lift doors opened and Tristan strode out and dumped his keys on the small hallway table, walking through the vast foyer and up the marble staircase. He noticed her glance around at the pristine surroundings and the priceless artwork on the walls as she trailed behind.

His home was modern and elegant, with eclectic pieces he'd picked up from his travels here and there, and he wondered what she thought of it. And then wondered why he cared.

He stopped outside the room he'd asked his housekeeper to allocate to her. 'This is your room. Mine's at the end of the hall.'

He opened the door and stood back to let her precede him inside. When her scent hit him between the eyes he steeled himself against what he was about to do.

'As you can see, your suitcases are already inside the dressing room and the *en suite* bathroom is through there.' He flicked open another door and hit the light switch. 'My housekeeper was instructed to make the room ready, so you should have everything you need.'

She didn't say anything, just stood beside the silk-covered queen-sized bed clutching her bag.

'I'll need to see the bag before I go,' he said evenly.

'What for?' She snapped her eyes to his.

Because after she had spent so long in the bathroom at the restaurant with that redhead with the fake lips he had wondered if she hadn't slipped Lily a little something. Of course Lily might have already taken it, but he hadn't seen any evidence of that when he'd backed her up against the cupboard in the restaurant. All he'd seen then was a heady desire that matched his own.

He knew the chances of the woman giving Lily something were slim to none, but with a Scotland Yard detective due to interview her in the morning he wasn't prepared to take that chance.

'The bag.'

She narrowed her eyes. 'You already know what's in it. Remember?'

'That was before you visited with your friend in the restaurant bathroom.'

'Oh, come on. It's not like I planned to run into her.' Lily's tone was incredulous.

Tristan held out his hand and Lily lobbed her bag at him as if it was a missile. 'Have it—and good luck to you.'

Tristan walked closer to her and upended the contents onto the bed. There wasn't much to see but cosmetics and a purse. He checked the purse and then dropped it back on the bed.

'Now you.'

She didn't move, and he clenched his jaw when he saw understanding dawn across her stunning face.

'Tell me you're kidding.'

He sincerely wished he could. 'The way I see it we can do this one of two ways. Either I search you or you strip.'

She made a small sound and then slapped her hands on her hips. Her eyes, when they met his, were glacial. 'Is this how you get your kicks? Trying to frighten innocent women into doing what you want?'

'I didn't ask for this,' he grated, his eyes drawn to the little gap at the centre of her blouse where the red ribbon tied in a bow. 'But it's my house. My rules. So—arms out.'

He stepped towards her and she stepped backwards—and came up against the bedside table.

Her gaze flitted between him and the bedroom door, as if she was contemplating making a run for it. 'I'm clean. I promise you I am.'

'Don't make this harder than it has to be.' He stopped just in front of her.

The colour was high on her cheekbones and the pulse-point in her neck looked as if it was trying to break free. Just when he thought he'd have to consider force she surprised him by suddenly opening her arms wide.

'Go ahead. You don't scare me.'

Tristan stepped forward. Impudent witch. He might be as hard as stone at the thought of touching her but he actually resented having to touch her like this. No matter how much he tried to deny it to himself, he knew that he would much prefer her willing and wanting. And he'd lied to her before. He *was* interested. Too interested.

Wanting to get this over with as quickly as possible Tristan circled her tiny wrists and ran both his hands up the long sleeves of her blouse at the same time.

'My stepfather warned me about men like you,' she said, her voice a breathy caress in the otherwise silent room.

'Is that right?' His hands rounded her shoulders and then ran lightly under the heavy cascade of her hair and across her back. He felt her shiver and swallowed hard.

'That's right—*oh*!' She gasped as his hands skimmed around her ribcage and rose to cup her breasts. Her nipples peaked against his palms and made it nearly impossible for him to leave that tiny bow done up.

'Keep talking,' he growled, his hands skimming back down over her torso. It was easier to ignore the feel of her if she kept annoying him. 'You were saying something about men like me?'

He knelt at her feet and unzipped one of her boots.

'Yes,' she said, and her voice was only a touch uneven. 'Men who only want one thing from a woman and then discard them when they're finished.'

'That "one thing" being sex, I take it?' He put the boot aside and set to work on the other one.

'Yes, I'm sure you do,' she bit out scornfully. 'Take it, that is.'

He looked up to find her studying the ceiling. 'This is hardly *taking it*, Lily,' he retorted gruffly. 'And let's just say I'm not enjoying this either—but I don't usually entertain possible drug felons, so you'll have to excuse my current *modus operandi*.'

'I'll excuse nothing,' she spat.

'And—' he stopped, completely losing his train of thought when he found his face on a level with that part of her body he'd love to touch. To taste.

Was she as aroused as he was? Wet even?

Hell, don't go there. Just don't go there.

He blanked his mind as much as possible as he ran both hands up over one long, lean leg, finally remembering what he was about to say. 'And I've never had a woman complain.'

'That's not true.'

He stopped and looked at her.

'I remember reading about that girl. A model who said that you tricked her into thinking you cared. That you wouldn't know love if it...if it hit—no, knocked you on the head.'

Tristan paused. 'She's entitled to her opinion, but it wasn't my fault she fell in love with me. She knew exactly what type of relationship she was getting into, and love was never part of the deal.'

'Silly girl.' Lily folded her arms across her chest and stared anywhere but at him. 'She doesn't know how lucky she was. Personally, I don't know any woman in her right mind who could ever imagine being in love with you.'

He shifted to her other leg.

'Unfortunately it happens. But women fall in love with many things, and it's rarely the man they see in front of them.' And in him, he knew, they saw a title and a life of privilege. Like his mother had with his father. *Shopping, champagne and chauffeurs,* he'd heard her brag to more than one friend.

'You should be thankful they want something at all. It's not like you can rely on your charming personality,' she scorned.

Tristan laughed—a hard sound in the deathly silent room. 'I'm not looking for love.' He rose and reached around to cup her bottom, closing his eyes as he slid both hands into her deep back pockets.

Lily's hands flew to his chest, as if to hold him back, but how easy would it be just to tug her forward and let her feel how much she aroused him?

'What happened?' She gasped breathlessly. 'Did a woman scorn you, Tristan?'

He knew she was deliberately trying to distract him, and that she was right to do so.

'No woman's ever got close enough to scorn me, Honey,' he

sneered, skating his hands along the inside of her waistband and then finally cupping between her legs.

'You bastard!' she seethed, her hand rising to slap his face.

He stopped her, but deep down he knew he deserved it. He let her go so she could stalk to the opposite side of the bed.

'I hope you're satisfied.'

Not by a long shot, sweetheart.

'That was necessary. Nothing else,' he said evenly.

'Keep telling yourself that. It might make you sleep better tonight,' she spat.

'I'll sleep just fine,' he lied.

'Well, you shouldn't. But I'm curious—is it just me you don't trust, or all women?'

'Don't go there.'

'Why not? Your attitude is abysmal for someone whose parents were happily married—'

'Actually, my parents weren't happily married.'

'They weren't?' She blinked in surprise.

'No. I don't think my mother ever really loved my father and he refused to see it. Which was to his detriment in the end, because as soon as she got a better offer she took off.'

'Oh, that's terrible.' Her automatic compassion was like a fist to his stomach.

'Yeah, well, that wasn't the worst of it. Love has a way of making fools of us all. Something to remember.'

He turned sharply on his heel and strode from her room before he did something stupid. Like throw her on the bed and give her what he knew they both wanted—no matter how much she tried to deny it.

Once in his room, Tristan shed his clothes and jumped into the shower, turning the mixer all the way to cold and dousing his head as if it was on fire. He let the freezing water wash over him for a minute and then reset the temperature to hot. God, that search… He blew out a breath. The more he tried to control his physical reaction to her the more out of control it seemed to become.

This situation was seriously driving him crazy. *She* was seriously driving him crazy. And, worse, the memory of the day his mother had walked out on them wouldn't leave him alone.

Tristan had overheard his parents arguing. Overheard his mother telling his father that he had nothing she wanted. That her son, Tristan, had nothing she wanted either. And that had bitten deep, because every time she had spiralled downwards Tristan had always been there to try and help her. Tried to be there for her. So to have her only want Jordana...

The memory still chilled his blood. It had taken him a long time to realise that no one was good enough for her and that all those years of trying to win her love and approval had been for nothing.

He scrubbed his hand over his face and shut the mixer off. He pulled on silk boxer shorts and walked up the outdoor circular staircase to his rooftop balcony.

The night was cool, and he enjoyed the sting of air on his skin as he leaned on the wrought-iron railing and looked out over the dark mass that was the Heath and the twinkling coloured lights of London beyond. The cumulus clouds that hung over the city had a faint pinkish tinge due to the light pollution, but he barely noticed. His mind was focused on replaying the day's events in his head.

Which wasn't a good thing—because his head was full of more questions than answers.

He didn't know whether to believe Lily about her not having a current lover, but he was beginning to suspect that she was telling the truth about not knowing she'd had drugs in her bag. That was disconcerting, because it meant he'd been wrong about her. He couldn't remember the last time he'd been wrong about a person. Hated to think that he was now. Because if he was he owed her an apology.

Could she really be as genuine, as *untouched,* as she appeared? Or was he just a fool, being taken in by a beautiful and duplicitous woman? One whose job it was to pretend to be someone she wasn't.

Whatever she was, he desired her more than he'd desired any woman before—and that wasn't good.

He gripped the balustrade so tightly his palms hurt. He needed an outlet for all the pent-up energy whizzing through his blood, and the only thing he could think of to assuage his physical ache was totally off-limits.

Straightening, he clasped his hands behind his neck, twisting his body from side to side to ease the kinks in his back. A run usually helped clear the cobwebs away. And if he didn't have a suspect movie star sleeping next door he'd put on his joggers and do exactly that. But then, if he *didn't* have a suspect movie star sleeping next door he probably wouldn't need to go for a run at—he glanced at his watch—one in the morning.

Grimacing, he strode inside and flopped face down on his bed.

Given that he couldn't get rid of her in the short term, the only way he could think of to deal with this situation was with the detached professionalism he would offer any client and ignore the attraction between them.

He'd told her more than once today that he was in charge, and damn it if he wasn't going to start behaving as if he was tomorrow.

CHAPTER EIGHT

'A MOVIE premiere? Is this your idea of a joke?'

Tristan's PA flinched as she stood on the other side of his desk, and he realised he'd said almost those exact words to his sister at almost this exact time yesterday.

Again he'd been having a great morning, and again it was shot to—

Okay, so it hadn't been *that* great a morning, what with Lily waking up late and a police detective waiting around in his home until she did so, but it was definitely ruined now. He cut a hard look to Lily, who stared back impassively at him from the white sofa.

'Uh, n-no,' Kate stuttered.

He glanced back at his computer screen, at the images Kate had brought up of the legions of fans who had camped out overnight in Leicester Square to get a glimpse of Lily Wild at some premiere to be held that evening.

'Lily, tell me this is a joke.'

He watched Lily's throat work as she swallowed, and then he returned his eyes to his surprised PA, who didn't seem to know what to do with her hands. She'd never seen him on the verge of losing his temper before and she was clearly daunted.

'I wasn't going to say anything,' Lily informed him coolly, standing to walk over to his desk.

Only she wasn't so cool deep down, because she didn't seem to know what to do with her hands either, and nervously pleated the loose folds of her peasant skirt.

His eyes swept upwards over her clinging purple shirt and then into eyes almost the same shade. 'I'm sure you weren't,' he mocked.

'Only because I was going to cancel my attendance—not because I didn't want you to know about it.'

Cancel it? He doubted that very much. She'd set up her attendance long before now, and while she might be feeling apprehensive about her drug bust he doubted she seriously wanted to miss an opportunity in the limelight. She'd chosen that life, after all.

'Oh, you can't cancel!' Kate cried, trying very hard not to appear starstruck. 'The premiere was delayed until today so you could make it, and there are people who have camped out in the cold night to see you. They'll be so disappointed. Look.'

She pointed to the computer screen, but Tristan's eyes stayed locked on Lily's face.

Just as they did later that night, when he found himself in the back of his limousine being whisked through central London on his way to Leicester Square.

It wasn't quite sunset, but the sky was filled with leaden clouds that blocked the setting sun from view and made it darker than it otherwise would be. Light rain splattered the windows, and Tristan wondered if Lily looked so nervous because she was worried that the rain would ruin the look she and Jordana had come up with in his bathroom or something else.

Because she certainly looked nervous.

Her chest was rising and falling with each deep, almost meditative breath she took. Her hands were locked together in her lap, and with her eyes closed she looked like Marie Antoinette must have before being dragged to the guillotine. But he didn't think Marie Antoinette could have looked anywhere near as beautiful as Lily Wild did at this minute. As she did every damned minute.

Then the car rounded the final bend and he suspected he knew why she might be nervous.

The car pulled up kerbside, and the door was immediately opened by a burly security guard wearing a glow-in-the-dark red-and-yellow bomber jacket. A wide red carpet extended in front of them for miles, dividing the screaming mass of fans barely constrained behind waist-high barricades.

Men and women in suits trawled the carpet, and the fans went from wild to berserk, waving books and posters around like flags, as Lily alighted from the car into a pool of spotlights.

The stage lighting on nearby buildings and trees was no match for the sea of camera flashes that blinded Lily, and then himself, on both sides as Tristan followed Lily out of the car.

An official photographer rushed up and started snapping Lily from every angle, while a woman in a dark suit and clipboard motioned her along the carpet to sign autographs for the waiting fans.

Tristan felt as if he'd stepped into an alternative universe, and wasn't wholly comfortable when Lily approached one of the barricades and the fans surged forward as one, making the beefy security guards who could have moonlighted as linebackers for the New Zealand All Blacks square off menacingly.

Tristan felt sure the fans were about to break through the barricades, and his own muscles bunched in readiness to grab Lily and haul her behind him if that should happen.

In the surrounding sea of multiple colours and broad black umbrellas held aloft to ward off the fine rain falling from the sky Lily stood out with her cream-coloured dress, lightly golden skin and upswept silvery-blond hair.

When he had first seen her in the dress Jordana had produced earlier—a knee-length clinging sheath with a high neck—he'd known he was in trouble. Then she had turned to reveal that it had no back, and he'd nearly told her to go back and put on her blouse and peasant skirt. But then he'd have had to explain why, and he didn't like admitting why to himself let alone anyone else.

Now he could appreciate that Jordana had wrought a small miracle, and had made Lily look like a golden angel amid a sea of darkness.

Which, aesthetically, was wonderful, but was not so great for his personal comfort level—nor, he could safely say, that of any other man who happened to look upon her that night!

He watched her now, doing her thing with the fans, and thought back over the interminable day.

All day she had been a paragon of virtue. She'd done exactly as he wanted—sat on the white sofa in his office and acted as if she wasn't there. Which should have made it easier to ignore her but hadn't. Because while she had immersed herself in a script with all the verve of someone preparing to sit a final exam he had struggled to find one case that held his attention long enough for him to forget she was in the room.

When he'd tried to engage her in a conversation about what had happened the night of Jo's eighteenth birthday party she had clammed up, and he had to wonder why. Jordana had implied that he'd been wrong about Lily's involvement, but if so why would Lily remain tight-lipped and only throw him that phony smile of hers when he broached the topic?

A roar from the crowd snapped his head around as a tall, buff Latino heart-throb dressed in torn jeans and a crumpled shirt swaggered towards Lily, raising both hands to wave at the near-hysterical crowd as he went. Lily turned and swatted the man with her million-dollar smile and Tristan felt his insides clench. That smile was like the midday sun coming out from behind heavy clouds—bright and instantly warming. Seductive and impossible to ignore. And so genuine it made his jaw harden. She had yet to turn it his way again, and he realised that he wanted her to. Badly.

The heart-throb draped his arm around Lily's waist and leaned in to kiss her, smiling at her like some long-lost lover.

They looked good together, his dark hair a perfect foil for her blondeness, and Tristan's eyes narrowed as he watched them work the crowd. His initial instinct to leap forward and rip the actor's arm from its socket slowly abated as he calmed his senses and realised that the actor's light touches here and there were too tentative to be that of a lover.

If the guy had known her intimately he wouldn't be just placing his hand on her hip now and then for a photo. He'd be subtly spreading his fingers wide over the small of her back, which Tristan already knew was sensitive to a man's touch. He'd let his fingers trail the naked baby-soft skin there and smile into her eyes when she delicately shuddered in response. Maybe he'd even press lightly on her flesh to have her arch ever so slightly towards him. Maybe exert just enough pressure so that he could hear that soft hitch in her breath as her mouth parted—

Hell.

Tristan pulled his thoughts back from the brink and dug his hands into his pockets, calling himself an idiot and wondering how long he could continue like this.

The crowd gave a howl of complaint as Lily and the heart-throb walked back towards the red carpet. The actor's hand hovered behind her protectively, and even though Tristan knew they weren't lovers he could tell by the expression on the Latino's face that he'd probably give up that arm to become so.

He was immensely irritated by the man's proprietorial air—and by his own desire to possess her. Especially when she had done little to incite his attention. And why hadn't she?

Lily Wild was turning out to be an enigma, and he was not at all happy to find that he might have been guilty of stereotyping her just as much as the next person.

'I have to do the red carpet thing and answer a few questions from the press and then we can go in,' she murmured over the noise of the crowd.

He nodded, but his eyes were on the actor, and Tristan found himself deliberately stepping into Lily's personal space to let the heart-throb know she was off-limits.

Lily's eyes widened quizzically, but the actor got the message, throwing his chest forward in a display of machismo.

They took each other's measure for a beat, and then the actor gave a typically Mediterranean shrug.

'Hey, man, don't sweat it.' He laughed, backing down when it became obvious that Tristan wouldn't. 'I was just helping Angel, here. You know how she gets in crowds.'

Tristan didn't, but he nodded anyway and watched the heart-throb amble further along the line.

He put his hand on Lily's arm to stop her following. 'What was he talking about?'

Lily sniffed, and raised a hand to wave at her fans. 'Nothing.'

He tightened his grip as she made to shrug him off. 'How was he helping you?'

'Not by feeding me drugs, if that's what you're thinking.'

He hadn't been thinking that, and her comment ticked him off. 'Then tell me what he was talking about.'

'I can't explain here.' She nodded to a fellow actor who blew a hello kiss. 'I don't have time.'

'Make time.'

'Oh!' She huffed, and then leaned closer to him, her delicate perfume wafting into his sinuses. 'I used to have agoraphobia. Now can we go?'

Tristan frowned. 'Fear of open spaces?'

'Do you even know *how* to whisper?' she complained, clearly uncomfortable with the subject matter. 'Most people think of it as that, but in my case it's a fear of crowds and being trapped in a situation I can't control.'

'That's what the therapy was about?' he said.

She glanced at him sharply. 'How do you know...? Oh, your special investigator's report. Well, it's nice to know he got some things right.'

'How do you know it was a he?'

'Because from the little I know of what's in it he's made snap judgements on very little evidence at all—just like a man.'

Tristan bit back a response and refocused. 'How bad is your phobia?'

Lily sighed. 'It's not bad at all. Jordi Mantuso and I swapped stories on set and he was just being kind.'

Tristan was shocked by her revelation. 'And are you okay? Right now?'

She looked taken aback by the question and he gritted his teeth, realising that his behaviour towards her had given her a very negative impression of who he was.

'Y-yes. I'm okay. It's not like I can't go out in a crowd—it's more a fear of being trapped by them.'

'Like when you were a child and surrounded with your parents' crowds of fans?'

The softness that had come over her face at his concern disappeared, and she looked away before glancing back. 'Yes. They think that's where it started. But I haven't had an attack in years.'

One of the female minders approached, to find out what was delaying them, and Tristan watched Lily paste on a smile that didn't reach her eyes she walked towards the rows of paparazzi.

She answered questions and posed for photographs like the professional she was, and he couldn't help respecting the adversity she had learned to overcome in order to work in her chosen profession.

He could see her making moves to finish up, and then her body stiffened. Something was wrong. Was she having a panic attack?

'I don't do theatre,' she was saying firmly.

'But why not, Lily? You've been offered the role of a lifetime, playing your mum. Are you not even considering it?'

'No.' Polite, but definite.

'What's wrong with the U.K., Lily? Don't you like us?'

'Of course.' Another pretty smile that didn't quite reach her eyes. 'My schedule hasn't allowed me to return to England before now.'

'The roles you choose…' an oily voice spoke up from the rear and paused for effect '…they're very different women from your mother. Is that a deliberate decision on your part? Is that why you won't take the West End gig?'

Lily felt Tristan step closer, and the warmth from his body momentarily distracted her from the reporter's question. She hated this part of the proceedings. And she wouldn't take the part playing her mother if it was the last known acting role on the planet.

'I choose my roles according to what interests me. My current film, *Carried Away,* is a romantic comedy, and…I like happy endings…what else can I say?' Lily smiled and turned to answer another question about location, before the same reporter who had been taking potshots at her from the get-go piped up again.

'Do you ever worry about being thought of as like your mother?'

'No.' Lily's smile felt as if it was made of cardboard and she thought about making an exit.

'What's it like kissing Jordi Mantuso?'

'Divine.' Lily's smile was genuine, and the fans who had caught her words whooped.

But the oily guy was back. 'Miss Wild, I'm still not clear about the West End gig. We've heard the director is holding off signing another female lead, so is the reason you won't do it because you're worried about the theatre aspect or…something else?'

Oh, this guy was good. He was a top-of-the-line paparazzo with a nose for a juicy story, and Lily could feel some of that old panic from years ago—the panic she had just told Tristan was firmly under control—well up inside her.

It was being back in London that was doing it. The whole stigma of who her parents had been. And the paps here were relentless. She rarely had to face such insolence in other parts of the world.

The reporter's question had become jumbled in her head and she was struggling to swallow when she felt Tristan's hand snake around her lower back and rest possessively over her hip-bone; his fingers spread wide, almost stroking her through her the delicate fabric of her dress.

She felt a flush heat her face as her stomach muscles trembled, and fervently hoped he wouldn't notice either response.

She tried to turn and silently berate him, but his fingers held her in place. His breath stirred the wisps of hair coiling around her temple as he leaned in closer and stole the breath from her lungs.

'You've forgotten he's a slimeball and you're taking his question seriously. Just look up at me as if I've said something incredibly funny and ignore him.'

He let her half turn in the circle of his arms, but she couldn't force the response he'd suggested.

Her hand automatically came up between them and flattened against the black designer shirt Jordana had provided him with. Her fingers curled into the fabric. She didn't know if she was trying to hold him back or draw him closer, because her brain had frozen at the open hunger banked in his direct gaze.

The noise of the crowd, the cameras, the lights…everything faded as Lily felt suffused with warmth and a sexual need that was as debilitating as it was exciting.

She felt his swift indrawn breath as she held his gaze, and was powerless to look away when his eyes dropped to her mouth.

Dimly she became aware of the crowd chanting, 'Kiss! Kiss!' and as if in slow motion a soft smile curved Tristan's firm mouth.

He leaned in and gently touched his lips to hers. The soft contact was fleeting, but still her lips clung, and as he pulled back and looked at her she knew he'd felt her unbidden response. He stared at her as if he wanted more—and if he didn't the screaming fans certainly did.

Lily's fingernails flexed, and somehow she found the wherewithal to pull back, once again becoming aware of the whistles and wild catcalls of 'Who is he?' and 'Is that Lord Garrett?' from the press.

The camera flashes were relentless, and Lily knew that while Tristan's actions had been motivated purely to help her out of an awkward moment, hers had not.

And wishing it was otherwise wouldn't make it so.

CHAPTER NINE

'I ENJOYED the film,' Tristan said, breaking the heavy silence between them. Lily didn't look at him but continued to stare out of the window as his chauffeur drove them through the glistening London streets.

It was late, and after two hours of sitting beside Tristan in a darkened movie theatre she felt uptight and edgy. The awareness she had been trying to keep at bay by pretending to read that hateful play for most of the day had exploded the minute his lips had touched hers on the red carpet.

No doubt he'd felt sorry for her after her earlier disclosure, but that didn't stop her from wanting him to touch her because he wanted to, not out of some misplaced duty to look out for her.

And she didn't want to make polite small talk with him now. She just wanted to get to the safety of her room and go to bed. To sleep.

In hindsight she should have been more prepared for the intrusive questions of the U.K. press, and probably would have been if worry over her case and the tension between herself and Tristan wasn't taking up so much head space.

Of course that brief kiss would be headline news in the papers tomorrow. Would be on the internet right now in this era of instantaneous news reports!

She knew she shouldn't be angry about what he'd done. He'd only been trying to help. But her own response to his sensitivity both now and this morning, when he'd made a Scotland Yard detective wait two hours until she woke from an exhausted sleep, and yesterday when he'd eased her headache while she slept in the car, made it harder for her to keep ignoring her feelings for him.

Especially after his disclosure about his parents and the pain in his voice when he had referred to his mother. The knowledge that he'd been hurt as a child made Lily feel differently towards him. Made her want to soothe him. To find out what had been worse than his mother leaving. Feeling this way about him wasn't clever. It could only lead to heartache—her own!

She sighed heavily and felt his gaze linger on her. She really didn't want to have any reason to lessen the animosity between them. Without that it would be far too easy to fall back into her adolescent fantasy that he was her dream man. What she needed to remember was that deep down he was essentially a good person, but any solicitude he extended towards her didn't automatically cancel out what he really thought of her.

'No comment, Lily?'

And he was calling her Lily now, instead of Honey. Oh, she *really* didn't want him being nice to her.

'You shouldn't have done that before,' she berated him, letting her embarrassment and uncertainty at this whole situation between them take centre stage.

He glanced at her briefly. 'Tell you I enjoyed your film?'

'Divert attention away from that reporter on the red carpet by kissing me.'

His direct gaze made her nervous, so she focused on the darkened buildings as the big car sped along Finchley Road.

'You looked like you needed it,' he said softly.

'I didn't.' Lily knew she was being argumentative, but she couldn't seem to stop herself. 'And now your picture—*our* picture—is going to be splashed all over the papers tomorrow. They'll think we're lovers.'

The car pulled up outside his exclusive mansion and he turned to her before opening the door. 'They'd probably have assumed that anyway given that I accompanied you.'

Bert opened the door and Lily smiled her thanks to him before stalking after Tristan, annoyance at his cavalier attitude radiating through her. 'Assuming and confirming isn't the same thing,' she retorted. Realizing too late what her words implied, she hoped he wouldn't pick up on it.

Movement further up the street alerted them to a lurking photographer, and Lily allowed Tristan to usher her up the short walkway to the black double front doors that looked as if they shone with boot polish.

He pushed one open and she preceded him into the marble foyer, and then followed him through to the large dining room where he turned to face her.

'Interesting phrasing. But I'm not sure how I could have confirmed something that's not true?' he drawled, a dangerous gleam lighting his eyes.

'Oh, you know what I mean,' she said, flustered by the strength of her confusing emotions. 'I'm tired.'

'Is that your way of defending your Freudian slip?'

'It wasn't…' She noted his raised eyebrow and swore. 'Oh, go to hell,' Lily fired at him, walking ahead of him through to the vast sitting room, dominated by a king-sized sofa that faced plate-glass windows overlooking the city.

'You know, all this outraged indignation over my attempt to help you before seems a little excessive to me,' Tristan said from behind her.

Lily turned, her eyes drawn to his lean, muscular elegance as he propped up the doorway even though she was determined not to be drawn in by his brooding masculinity. 'Oh, really?'

Tristan leant against the doorjamb and studied Lily's defiant posture. Her face was flushed, and more wisps of hair had escaped her bun and were kissing her neck. Her lips were pouting, and he'd bet his life savings that she'd crossed her arms over her chest to hide her arousal from him. He knew why she was so angry. He knew she felt the sexual pull between them and was as enthralled by it as he was.

And, while she might be upset with the media fall-out from his actions on the red carpet, he hadn't missed the way her lips had clung to his and how her violet eyes had blazed with instantaneous desire when he'd kissed her.

'Yes, really. Want me to tell you what I think is behind it?' he asked benignly.

'Pure, unadulterated hatred.' She faked a yawn and he laughed.

'You know what they say about hatred, Lily.' Tristan stalked over to the drinks cabinet and threw a measure of whisky into a glass. Two days with her and he was beginning to feel like an alcoholic!

'Yes, it means you don't like someone. And my reaction to your behaviour is not excessive in the slightest. All you've done tonight is give the tabloids more fodder—and for your information I could have handled that reporter by myself.'

Tristan raised his glass and swallowed the fiery liquid in one go, welcoming the sharp bite of distraction from the turn the conversation had taken. All he'd done was compliment her performance!

'Was that before or after you had the panic attack?' he asked silkily.

'It wasn't a panic attack! And just because I tell you something personal it doesn't mean you get to take over. You're not God's gift—even though you clearly think you are.'

Tristan turned slowly and stared at her. He'd heard the clear note of challenge in her voice and he knew the reason for it. And, by God, if he didn't want to do something about it—regardless of everything that lay between them.

He wanted her, and he knew for damned sure she wanted him, and looking at her right now, with her legs slightly apart and her hands fisted on her hips, her chin thrust out, he knew she wanted him to do something about it too.

Not that she would admit it.

He let his eyes slide slowly down her body and then just as slowly all the way back up. The pulse-point in her throat leapt to life, but she made no attempt to run from the hunger he knew was burning holes in his retinas.

There was something interminably innocent about her provocative stance, almost as if she didn't know what she was about, and it pulled him up for a minute. But then he discounted the notion. She might not be the Jezebel he thought she was, but women like Lily Wild always knew what they were about. He'd had enough of the simmering tension between them, and knew just how to kill it dead.

'Okay, that's it,' he said softly, placing his empty glass on the antique sideboard with deliberate care. 'I'm giving you fair warning. I'm sick of the tension between us—and the reason for it. You've got exactly three seconds to get moving before I take up from what we started six years ago. But this time there'll be no stopping. You're not seventeen any more, and there's no secretary to interrupt us like yesterday. This time we're on our own, and I'm not in the mind to stop at one kiss. Neither, I suspect, are you.'

Lily didn't know what thrilled her more—his blunt words or the starkly masculine arousal stamped across his handsome face. Her heart took off at full gallop and her stomach pitched alarmingly.

Six years ago she had wanted him with the desperate yearning of a teenager in the throes of a first crush. The night of Jo's party she had dressed for him, watched him, noticed him watching her—and then, on the back of a couple of fortifying glasses of vintage champagne, she had asked him to dance… and melted into him. Loved the feel of his strong arms around her, the sense of rightness that would have led her to do anything with him that night. And right now she felt exactly the same way. Which just didn't make sense. None of this made sense.

Does it have to?

'One.'

She shook her head. 'Tristan, don't be ridiculous. There's no point to this.'

'I couldn't agree more, but we have unfinished business between us and denying it hasn't made it go away. Nor has trying to ignore it. In fact, I think that's only made the problem worse.'

'And you think acting on it will solve it?'

He raised that arrogant eyebrow. 'Got a better idea?'

No, she didn't, and right now her body yearned for his with a desperation that was all-consuming. Yearned to experience more of the pleasure he'd wrought on her body yesterday. Yearned for a completion that Lily was starting to suspect only this man could fulfil.

Jordana's provocative suggestion that she cut loose and have some fun returned to mock her.

Could she?

Would having sex with Tristan fall under that banner? It wasn't as if she was holding out for a marriage proposal or anything. The only reason she hadn't had sex before was because of the lack of opportunity and…enticement. She'd never felt the way Tristan made her feel just by looking at him. Why keep denying it?

And then there was the notion she'd had to meet him this trip as an equal. To put the attraction she had always felt for him to bed…

'Two.'

His soft voice cut through her ruminations and she realised her heart was pounding behind her ribcage.

She swallowed. He hadn't moved, and yet the room seemed smaller; he seemed closer. Her senses were entirely focused on him.

His hair had flopped forward and she could see he was breathing as unevenly as she was. She found it almost shockingly exciting to think she could arouse a man like him to such a state. Because he *was* aroused. She could see the unchecked desire glittering in his darkened eyes and feel the dangerous intensity of his tautly held body.

Her stomach clenched and she felt an answering hunger in herself at the thought of finally being able to touch all that roughly hewn muscle. So what was she waiting for? Armageddon?

Lily slicked her tongue over her arid lips, a nascent sense of her own feminine power heating her insides and making her breasts feel firmer, fuller.

He must have sensed her silent capitulation because he moved then, pacing towards her with the latent grace of a man who knew exactly what he was about, and any notions Lily had had of taking charge of their lovemaking flew out of the window. She felt like that inexperienced seventeen-year-old again in comparison to him and his wealth of sexual experience.

He stopped just short of touching her and Lily gazed into his face with nervous anticipation.

'Tristan…' Her voice was a whisper of uncertainty and for a second her inner voice told her she was mad. She couldn't possibly give this giant of a man what he needed.

Tristan reached out and curled his hand around the nape of her neck, angling her face to his. He stared at her for what felt like ages. 'Tell me you want this.'

His warm fingers sent shock waves of energy up and down her spine and Lily was breathing so hard she was almost hyperventilating.

Want it? Need it sounded closer to the mark.

'I do.' She ran her tongue over her dry lips. 'I do want this. You.'

She heard an almost pained sound come from Tristan's throat as he lifted her face to his and took her mouth in a searing kiss. No preliminaries required.

Both his hands spread wide either side of her face as he held her still beneath his plundering lips and tongue.

Lily felt a sob of pure need rise up in her throat and reached up to grip his broad shoulders, to hang on as she gave herself over to the sensation of his masterful kiss.

He tasted of whisky and heaven, and for a moment Lily's senses nearly shut down with the overload of sensation rioting through her.

She pulled back, gasping for breath as she realised the dizziness was from a lack of oxygen, hyperventilating for real now as he angled her head back and skated his lips across her jaw and down the smooth column of her neck.

'Oh, Lord…' Lily whimpered, her face nuzzling his to bring his mouth back to her own.

He gave a husky chuckle and acquiesced, kissing her with such unrestrained passion she thought she might faint. His big body moved in, pressing her into the wall behind her.

His kiss claimed her. Branded her. The hard wall was flat against her back as his equally hard chest moulded to her front.

She moved her hands into his hair and lifted herself to try and assuage the ache that had grown to almost painful proportions between her thighs.

One of his hands disentangled from her hair and found the naked skin at small of her back as he stumbled back slightly at her eager movements.

'Oh, Lily, you're killing me,' he groaned into her mouth, his hands not quite steady as he held her in place against him.

His touch seemed as if it was everywhere and nowhere, and Lily could feel all her old emotions for this man welling up inside her. She couldn't have stopped what was happening now even if she'd wanted to.

She shivered and arched into his caresses, moving restlessly against him as wanton pleasure consumed her. His touch was electric, but it wasn't enough. She wanted to feel him all around her, and inside that part of her that somehow felt soft and hollow and unbearably empty.

'Tristan, please…' Lily implored, her hands kneading the hard ridges of his upper back. He seemed to know what she needed because he brought his mouth back to hers, his tongue plunging inside as his leg pressed firmly between her thighs.

She felt a moment's relief—but her dress hampered him from putting more pressure where she wanted it most and she squirmed in frustration.

Keeping her upright with his thigh, Tristan brought both hands up to cup her breasts, and then higher to drag the shoulders of her dress down her arms, baring her to the waist. Lily held her breath as he pulled back an inch and looked at her with such heated desire she could have wept.

For the first time ever she truly felt like a goddess, and when his eyes met hers they were dark with barely checked need.

'Honey, I want to go slow, but...' His eyes dropped back to her breasts and he placed his hands either side of her ribcage, lifted her body to meet his mouth. 'You're exquisite,' he whispered, his hot breath skating across an aroused nipple just before his mouth opened and sucked her flesh into its moist cavern.

Her legs gave out and Tristan had to tighten the arm around her waist to hold her up. Damp heat flooded between her thighs and she could dimly hear someone panting Tristan's name in a litany. She realised it was her.

She stopped, tried to centre herself, and then he grazed her with his teeth and she felt her insides convulse.

'Don't stop,' he breathed urgently against her flesh. 'Say my name. Tell me what you like.'

Lily didn't know what she liked, except for everything he was doing to her, and she gave herself over to him as he shifted his attention to her other breast, digging her nails into her palms. Wanting, needing to touch him as he was touching her.

She tried to move her arms and gave a mew of frustration when she found they were trapped by the tight band of his arms and her dress.

'Help me...' she began, but he already was, pressing his thigh firmly against her and moving his arms so she could disentangle her hands.

Once free, she immediately set to work on the buttons of his dark shirt.

He was breathing just as hard as she was, and a fine sheen had broken out over the skin her jittery hands were having trouble exposing. Then he raised both hands to her breasts to tug at her nipples and Lily's fingers fumbled to a stop.

'That's not helping,' she groaned, involuntarily arching into his caress.

'Then allow me.' Tristan grabbed hold of his shirt and tore the rest of the buttons free, leaning in close before she was able to look her fill of his sculptured chest, his ridged abdomen. Then his chest hair scraped her sensitised nipples, and she forgot about looking as feeling took precedence.

'Oh, God…' Lily swayed and rocked against the rigid length of him pressed into her belly.

'Easy, Honey,' Tristan soothed, but Lily was beyond easy. She needed him to touch her between her legs. The ache there was now unbearable.

She groaned with relief when she felt his hands smooth over her thighs and ruch her dress up around her waist, her legs automatically widening to accommodate his seeking hand.

His movements seemed as unsteady as she felt, and it imbued her with a sense of power.

Unable to keep her mouth off him, she bent her head and licked along his neck, breathing in his earthy masculinity.

'Tristan, please, I need you,' Lily begged, her voice sounding hoarse. Another saner voice was telling her that later she'd be embarrassed by such uninhibited pleading. But her body couldn't care less about later on.

It was caught up in the most delicious lassitude and straining for something that seemed just out of reach.

Then his fingers whispered over the very tops of her upper thigh and the feeling came closer. A lot closer.

Lily's breath stalled and her body stilled, and when finally he slipped his fingers beneath the lacy edge of her barely there panties and stroked through the curls that guarded her femininity she nearly died, clinging to his broad shoulders. Her body was his to do with as he willed.

And he did. His fingers slipped easily over her flesh, unerringly finding the tight bud of her clitoris before pressing deeper. Stretching her with first one and then two fingers.

A groan that seemed to come from the very centre of his body tore from his mouth. 'Honey, you're so wet. So tight.' He seemed lost for a second, and then established a rhythm within her that created a rush of heat to the centre of her body. But suddenly he stopped.

'No, I want to be inside you when you come.' He pulled his hand free and Lily's nails dug into his shoulders in protest.

She heard the metallic sound of his belt buckle and the slide of his zipper and in seconds he was back.

Only her panties were in the way, and with a decisive movement they went the way of his shirt.

Lily followed an age-old instinct and rocked against him, her mouth on his neck, her hands in the thick lusciousness of his hair.

'Honey, you keep that up and this will be over before I'm even inside you,' he said hoarsely, stroking his tongue into her open mouth. He eased back, seeming to remember where they were. 'Not here though.'

'Yes, here.' Lily demanded against his mouth, an urgent excitement driving her beyond the edge of reason.

Her lower body felt as if it was contracting around thin air and she needed him inside her. Filling her.

Tristan sucked in an uneven breath and lowered both hands to cup her bottom, lifting her into him. 'Put your legs around my waist,' he instructed gruffly, and Lily blindly obeyed as the velveteen tip of his body nudged against the very centre of hers.

The back of his neck was taut and sweaty and Lily's head fell forward and she nipped at his salty skin. He must have liked it, because with a sound that was part pain, part pleasure, he tilted her body towards him and surged into her in one single, powerful thrust.

For a second the world stopped, and then Lily registered a harsh cry and realised she must have bitten down on Tristan's neck—hard—as her body initially resisted his vigorous invasion.

He swore viciously and instantly stilled, reefing his head back and cupping her face in one hand to pull her eyes to his.

'Honey, please tell me this isn't your first time.'

Lily felt the momentary sting pass as her body stretched to accommodate his fullness, and wrapped her arms tightly around his neck.

'Don't stop,' she breathed as her body completely surrendered to his and tiny sparks of pleasure returned between her thighs.

She shifted to try and elevate the feeling, but Tristan's fingers dug into her hips to keep her still. 'Wait. Let your body adjust to me.'

'It has,' she insisted, and felt his slightly damp hair brush her face as he shook his head.

'Please, Tristan, I need to—'

He rocked against her and Lily moaned the word *move* as if it had six syllables.

Tristan eased in and out of her body gently, and then with more urgency, and Lily's brain shut down. All she could do was feel as a thrilling tightness swept through her and urged her on. Then Tristan moved one hand up between their bodies and lightly stroked his thumb over her nipple, and Lily's world splintered apart as pleasure clamped her body to his.

Tristan swore again, and thrust into her with such force all Lily could do was wrap her arms around his neck and hang on as he claimed her body with his and reached his own nirvana.

After what felt like an hour Lily became conscious of how her uneven breathing was pressing her newly sensitised breasts into the soft hair on Tristan's chest, and also of how hard the wall was behind her—despite the fact that Tristan had curled his arm around her back to take the brunt of the pressure.

She was also conscious that Tristan still had his mouth buried against her neck, his lips pressed lightly against her skin as he tried to regulate his own breathing.

Her arms were slung laxly over his shoulders and a feeling of utter contentment enveloped her. A sense of euphoria was curling through her insides like warm chocolate syrup.

It was madness. This inexplicable feeling of completeness that swelled in her chest. But maybe it was because she'd had a life-changing experience. And she had. Nothing had prepared her for what had just happened. No song. No movie. No book. And she knew she'd remember this moment for ever.

But even through her high she could discern that Tristan wasn't feeling the same way. He was unnaturally still, his breathing too laboured, as if he was having trouble composing himself. She shifted then, and the hardness of the wall scraped her skin. The air was slightly chilly now, as the sweat started to dry on her body. She shivered, still supported by his strong arms. Muscles she'd never felt before contracted around his hardness, still buried deep inside her, and she flinched as he cursed.

He pulled out of her, gently lowering her to the parquetry floor, stepping back. A look of abject disgust lined his face.

The shock of it made Lily recoil, and she quickly dropped her eyes and dragged her crumpled dress into place.

She heard him readjust his own clothing, and a primeval survival instinct she had honed as a child took root inside as she blanked out the feeling of utter desolation that threatened to overwhelm her for the first time in years.

'Don't say anything,' she ordered, knowing that the best form of defence was attack, and was mildly surprised when shock replaced the revulsion she had seen on his face.

Good. She might not be as practised as he was in these post-sex matters, but pride demanded that she did not behave like the bumbling fool she now felt.

For him this was just run of the mill but for her it was—

'Don't say anything?' he all but bellowed. 'You should have told me you were a virgin.'

Never let 'em know you care, Honeybee.

She looked at him levelly. 'It slipped my mind.' In truth she had hoped he wouldn't notice. But that seemed like a stupid notion in hindsight, given his size. 'And you wouldn't have believed me anyway, would you?'

He glanced to the side and it was all the answer Lily needed. Of course he wouldn't have—when had he ever believed her? Something tight clutched in her chest and she toed on the shoe that had fallen off when her legs had been wrapped around his lean hips.

'I didn't use a condom,' he said, the bald statement bringing her eyes back to his.

She wasn't on the pill. Why would she be?

'I think it's a safe time,' she murmured automatically, trying to quell a sense of panic so she could think about when her last period had been.

He groaned and paced away from her, one hand raking the gleaming chestnut waves back from his head as if he might tear it out.

'Look, Tristan, this was a mistake,' she said with an airiness she didn't feel. 'But it's done now so there's no point moaning about it.'

He stopped pacing. 'And if you're pregnant?'

She turned from her study of an ancient Japanese wall hanging and wet her lips. 'I'll let you know.'

He placed his hands on his hips and she tried really hard not to stare at his muscular torso.

'Look, if it's all the same to you,' she continued casting around the floor for her discarded underwear, 'I could do without a post-mortem.'

She didn't look at his face but she heard his sharp inhalation.

'It's next to the cabinet,' he bit out, and Lily followed his line of vision to where her tiny nude-coloured thong lay crumpled in a corner. She marched over and snatched it up, balling it into her fist. No way was she going to inspect the state of it while he stood there towering over her like some Machiavellian warlord.

'Well, I'm going to bed,' she stated boldly, turning towards the back staircase and heading for the relative safety of her room.

He snagged her arm as she moved past him. 'Did I hurt you?' His voice low and rough, as if the concept was anathema to him.

Lily cleared her throat. 'Uh, no. It was… I'm fine.'

CHAPTER TEN

FINE.

She had been going to say *it* was fine, Tristan thought moodily the next morning as he stared out of his kitchen window at the grey London skyline. The colour reflected his dismal mood perfectly.

But last night hadn't been fine. It had been amazing, sensational, mind-blowing. The most intensely involved sexual experience of his life, in fact. And he hated that. Hated that he hadn't had the wherewithal to go slow, and hated that he hadn't been able to take her into his arms afterwards and carry her up to his bed. Make love to her again. Slowly this time. More carefully...

He released a pent-up breath and scrubbed his hand over his face, remembering how she had looked afterwards. Gloriously dishevelled. Her dress creased, her hair half up and half down where his hands had mussed it, her lips swollen from his kisses.

He could recall with bruising clarity the moment her body had sheathed his, her shocked stillness. And she had bitten him—marked him—because even though she had denied it he *had* hurt her. The thought made him feel sick. He should have been more gentle. *Would* have been if he'd known.

A virgin!

She had been a virgin, and afterwards he had been disgusted with himself for taking her with all the finesse of a rutting animal against a wall.

Damn.

If there had ever been a time he'd felt this badly he couldn't remember it. Maybe when he'd come across her in his father's study doing cocaine—or so he had thought at the time—with some loser she had just had sex with.

Correction: *hadn't* had sex with.

Damn.

His head was a mess, and last night, after the deed was done, he'd stood in front of her like some gauche schoolboy with no idea how to fix what had just happened. Which was a first. But what could he have said? *Hey, thanks. How about we use a bed next time?*

And what about her response? *Don't say anything,* she'd said, and, *I could do without a post-mortem.*

Damn.

He couldn't have been any more shocked by her off-handedness if she'd hit him over the head with a block of wood. On some level he knew it was a defence mechanism, but it was clear she also regretted what they'd done together and that had made him feel doubly guilty.

Not that it should. She was an adult and had wanted it just as much. Things had just come to a natural head with two people available and finding themselves attracted to each other.

So he would have gone about things a little differently if he'd guessed the extent of her inexperience? If she'd told him! But that hadn't happened, and he didn't do regrets.

Tristan rubbed at a spot between his brows.

He might not do regret, but he owed her one hell of an apology for his condescending behaviour of the last two days. As well as his readiness to accept all the garbage that was written about her.

But hadn't it been easier to accept she was an outrageous attention-seeker like his mother so he didn't have to face how she made him feel?

Which was what, exactly?

Confused? Off-balance?

He took a swill of his coffee and grimaced as cold liquid pooled in his mouth.

He put his cup in the sink and stopped to look again at the morning papers on his kitchen table.

An earlier perusal of the headlines on the internet had confirmed that Lily's concerns the previous night had been well founded. A photo of their kiss was plastered over every two-bit tabloid and interested blog in the Western world.

On top of that someone had snapped their photo at the airport right before he had put her in the back of his limousine that first day. She'd had her hand on his chest and the caption in that particular paper had read 'Lord Garrett picks up something Wild at Heathrow'.

Cute.

So what to do about her? Try and play it cool? Pretend he wasn't still burning up for her? And *why* was he? Once was often more than enough with a woman, because for him sex was just sex no matter which way you spun it.

But it hadn't felt like just sex with Lily, and that was one more reason to stay away from her.

The thought that this was more than just an attraction chilled him. He didn't do love either.

Damn. Who'd mentioned anything about love?

He blew out a breath and snatched the papers off the bench. One good deed. That was all he'd tried to do. And now his life was more complicated than a world-class Sudoku.

When Lily woke that morning she remembered everything that had happened the night before in minute detail. Every single thing. Every touch, every kiss, the scent of him, the feel of him...

She rolled onto her back and stared at the crystal chandelier above her bed. She loved that these perfect antiques were woven into the ultra-modern décor of his amazing home.

Part of her wanted to regret last night. The part that had been hurt by his obvious rejection straight afterwards. But another part told her to get over it. She'd had sex. Big deal. People did it every day. Granted, it probably wasn't the smartest thing to have sex with a playboy type who thought she belonged in a sewer…but at least she hadn't made her mother's grave error and fallen in love with him.

And in a way it had been necessary. Tristan had been right when he'd said there was unfinished business between them. As much as she'd tried to deny it there had been, and now it was gone. Finished—as it were.

It wasn't as if Tristan had promised her a happy-ever-after. And even if he had she didn't want one. So what was there to regret? Except having to face him again. That could be awkward. Oh, and the small matter of an unplanned pregnancy. She didn't know how that had slipped her mind. Not that she was worried. She trusted the universe too much to believe that was a possibility, and she was still in the early part of her cycle so that was safe—wasn't it? She'd never had to consider it before, and those sketchy high school lessons on the birds and bees weren't holding up very well ten years down the track.

Pushing aside her thoughts, she glanced around the elegant, tastefully decorated room. His whole house was like that. State-of-the-art and hideously expensive. Lots of wide open spaces, acres of polished surfaces, toe-curlingly soft carpets against contrasting art and antiquities. And it was neat. Super neat. But that was most likely his housekeeper's doing, because his office was another story altogether.

It made her wonder at the person he was. Because as much as she wanted to hate him she knew she didn't. Most of his actions, she knew, were driven by a deep-seated sense of responsibility and a desire to look out for his sister, and even though he had been harsh with her he'd also been incredibly tender. If she was being completely honest with herself, his sharp intellect and take-no-prisoners attitude had always excited her.

Lily felt herself soften, and swung her legs onto the boldly striped Tai Ping carpet and headed for the shower, her body tender from his powerful lovemaking.

She showered quickly and smoothed rosehip oil all over her face and arms, running a critical eye over herself. She knew her face was much lauded, but like anyone she had her problems. A tendency for her skin to look sallow, and dark circles that materialised under her eyes as soon as she even thought about not getting eight hours sleep a night. Right now they looked like bottomless craters, and she reached for her magic concealer pen to hide the damage of another night with very little sleep.

Discarding the towel she had wrapped around her body, she donned her silk robe and felt the flow of the fabric across her sensitised skin. Her breasts firmed and peaked, and just like that she was back in Tristan's living room with his mouth sweetly tugging on her flesh.

Stop thinking about it, she berated herself. She was an intelligent woman who paid her own bills and made her own bed, and yet the only bed she could think of at the minute was Tristan's—with both of them in it! And since he wasn't thinking the same thing why torture herself with fantasies? She should be thinking about how she was going to face him still feeling so…so aroused!

A knock on the outer door brought her head around and she turned sharply towards the bedroom. It would be Tristan because she knew it was still too early for his housekeeper to have arrived, and she berated herself for dithering in front of the mirror for so long. It would have been more prudent to meet him downstairs, fully clothed.

'Come in,' she called reluctantly, tightening the sash around her robe and crossing her arms over her chest.

He did. And he looked gorgeous and refreshed. Just how she wanted to feel.

He walked over and dropped a couple of newspapers on her bed, and then stood regarding her, his hands buried in his pockets. His hair, still damp, curled enticingly around the nape of his neck and his olive skin gleamed darkly against his pale blue shirt. But it was his guarded expression that eventually held her attention. A level of awkwardness about his stance that gave her pause.

'I owe you an apology.'

'For last night?' Her voice was sharp and she moistened her lips. 'That's not necessary.'

'Yes, it is.' His voice was that of a polite stranger. 'If I had known it was your first time I never would have let things go so far.'

Lily sighed. She had been trying not to feel bad about what had happened last night but his open regret wasn't helping. Nor was the way he paced back and forth. 'I think we should just forget it ever happened,' she said, not quite able to meet his eyes. Lord, was this worse than his rejection of her six years ago? 'As you already said, we had unfinished business—and now…now we don't.'

He stopped pacing. 'And you're okay with that?'

'Of course. Aren't you?'

'Of course.'

Lily nodded. Of course. What had she expected? A declaration of love? Even the thought was ludicrous, because she absolutely didn't want that.

'So…'

'I also want to apologise for my attitude towards you when I picked you up. For accusing you of using drugs and knowingly bringing them into the country,' he said.

Lily's eyebrows shot skyward. 'So because I was a virgin I'm innocent of drug smuggling as well? Gosh, if only I'd thought to tell the customs official it would have saved all this hassle.'

Tristan threw her a baleful look. 'Your virginity has nothing to do with my reasoning.'

'No?'

'No,' he said irritably. 'I had already worked out you weren't a user before then. And you'll be pleased to know I've fired my investigator.'

'Shooting the messenger you mean?' she jeered.

'His work was substandard—even with the limited time

frame he had to collate the information. Hell, I thought you'd be happy to hear that.'

'Happy that a man lost his job because he confirmed your view of me? He probably just gave you what you wanted, like everybody else does,' she said caustically.

'Don't push it, Lily. You weren't exactly forthcoming with the truth when I questioned you.'

'That's because I don't find it beneficial to bash my head against a brick wall.'

She saw a muscle tick in his jaw as he regarded her from under hooded eyes.

'Tell me why I found you hiding a joint under Jo's mattress when you were fourteen.'

'I thought you were apologizing?' she countered.

'I did.'

'It could use some work.'

Tristan said nothing, his expression coolly assessing. It was a look Lily had come to recognise. It meant that he fully intended to get his own way.

'Don't use your courtroom tactics with me, Tristan,' she said frostily. 'They won't work.'

'Would it help if I tell you Jordana has already admitted that it was hers?'

Lily tried to keep her surprise from showing. 'When?'

'The day of your apprehension at Heathrow. I didn't believe her at the time.'

Lily placed her hand against her chest with a flourish. 'Oh, and for a minute there I felt so special.'

She could see her sarcasm had irritated him, but he rubbed a hand across his eyes before piercing her with his gaze again.

'It's confession time, Lily. I know my sister hasn't been the saint I've wanted her to be, and I'm tired of the misunderstandings between us.'

Lily thought about arguing—but what was the point? He'd only get his own way in the end.

'If you remember, you visited our boarding school on a surprise birthday visit for Jo—only she saw you from the rec room. She called me on the internal phone and asked me to hide it. I hadn't expected you would walk in without knocking.'

'And the night of Jo's eighteenth? In my father's study? No evading the answer this time.'

'You should ask Jordana.'

'I'm asking *you*.'

Lily crossed the floor and sat on the striped Rein occasional chair in the corner. 'I don't know how the party in your dad's study got started. I was tipped off by a mutual friend, and by the time I got there it was in full swing. I felt responsible, because the guy who'd brought the drugs worked for my stepfather's company, but no one listened when I told them to clean it up. So I decided to step in and do it myself and—'

'I walked in, put two and two together, and came up with several hundred.'

'Something like that.'

'And you didn't think to defend yourself?' His tone was accusatory.

'You didn't exactly give me much of a chance, remember?' she felt stung into retorting.

Tristan shook his head and strode over to the window, pushing the heavy curtain aside to stare outside.

Lily shifted and tucked her legs under her on the chair, absently noting how the light from the incoming sun picked up the bronzed highlights in his hair.

Then he turned back, his expression guarded. 'I'm sorry.'

Did he *have* to look quite so good-looking?

She cleared her throat and shifted uncomfortably on her seat. If he was apologising why did she suddenly feel so nervous? 'It's fine; I shouldn't have invited that guy in the first place.'

He shrugged as if that were inconsequential. 'I shouldn't have jumped to conclusions. I…I wasn't quite myself that night.'

Lily's mind immediately spun back to the dance floor. The kiss. Had he not been himself then either? How embarrassing.

'Me either,' she lied.

He nodded, as if that solved everything, and Lily's heart sank a little. 'Was there something else?'

He shook his head and then glanced towards her bed.

'Actually, yes.' He pointed to the bed. 'I'm sorry to say that your premonition about the photos has come true.'

Lily rose and walked over to the bed. 'Oh.'

'I said a little more than that myself,' he acknowledged ruefully.

'I did too.' She glanced up briefly. 'Internally…'

She thought a momentary smile curved his mouth, but it might easily have been a trick of the light given how stiff and remote he seemed.

'I should go.'

'Yes,' Lily agreed, following him with her eyes as he walked to the door. Then he stopped abruptly.

'Are you…okay this morning?' His voice was rough and slightly aggressive and she knew what he was asking.

'I thought we'd just agreed to forget last night?'

'I'm allowed to check how you are, dammit. And don't say *fine.*'

She arched an eyebrow. 'Will great do?' she asked lightly.

His nostrils flared and she thought that maybe now was not a good time to aggravate him.

Tristan's mouth tightened. This situation was intolerable. He couldn't be in the same room with her and not want to touch her, but it was obvious by the proud tilt of her head that she wouldn't welcome his advances. He didn't know what he had expected from her this morning, but her suggestion that they forget last night had surprised him. And annoyed him. Because he wasn't sure he *could* forget it!

The phone in his pocket rang and he checked the caller ID before answering. Bert had been caught in a six-car pile-up on Rosslyn Hill. He didn't want another car. He'd call a cab—it would be quicker.

'What happened?'

'Bert's been caught in an accident.'

'Is he okay?' Her concern was genuine, and he was reminded of how yesterday she had given Bert unsolicited signed promotional pictures of herself when she found out his daughters were fans.

'It was minor, but he's wedged between two other cars. I'll arrange someone to help him out and call a cab.'

'I'll get dressed.'

Tristan's eyes drifted down over the dove-grey silk wrap she wore and he noted the delicate pink that swept into her face. Even with the shadows beneath her eyes she was quite simply the most beautiful woman he had ever seen.

'Good idea.'

Twenty minutes later Lily joined Tristan on a rear terrace that looked out over a sizable manicured garden flanked by a glassed-in pool and gymnasium, absently noting that it was hard to believe she was in the middle of one of the busiest cities in the world.

Tristan wore his suit jacket now, and she felt like a tourist in her simple jeans, white T-shirt and faithful black cardigan. She noticed him glance at her cardigan as he watched her approach, a bemused expression flitting across his face.

'What?'

'Nothing.' He shook his head. 'I would offer you tea, but I'd like to get going and check that Bert is okay.'

'Sure.' Lily followed him back through the house towards the front door.

'It seems traffic is particularly bad this morning. The cab driver has had to park up the road a way.'

'That's okay.' Lily smiled. 'I like walking. It's a New York pastime.'

'I suppose it is,' Tristan agreed, feeling awkward and out of sorts after her disclosures in her bedroom. His instincts warned him to keep his distance from her. After last night she was more dangerous to his emotional well-being than she had ever been, and in hindsight having sex with her had been a terrible idea.

Lily waited for him to open the front door and stepped out ahead of him—straight into the view of at least twenty members of the press, who had breached his security gates and were filling the normally pristine space of his forecourt, trampling grass and flowerbeds as they jostled for position.

They shouted an endless list of questions as camera flashes momentarily blinded them both.

It was like a scene from a bad movie, and after a split second of shocked inertia Tristan grabbed Lily around the waist and hauled her back inside.

'Oh, my gosh!'

'I'll call the police,' he stated grimly, slamming the door shut before he turned to her and grabbed her chin between his thumb and forefinger. 'Are you okay?' His eyes scanned her face for signs of distress, wondering if perhaps she might have a panic attack.

'I'm fine,' she confirmed. 'I told you, I rarely have attacks any more—and, anyway, you grabbed me so quickly I barely had time to register they were even there.'

She smiled and he trailed a finger down her cheek, noting the way her eyes widened and darkened. Tristan felt his body harden and tamped down on the response. He was supposed to be forgetting last night and keeping his distance.

He dropped his hand and stalked through the house until he reached the kitchen.

'I'm sorry. I should have expected this…' she said.

Tristan shook his head. Not sure if he was more agitated at himself, her, or the hyenas filling his front garden. 'I don't know how you live like this.'

She swallowed. 'It's not normally this bad. In New York you get followed sometimes, but it's different here.'

'It's disgusting.'

'I'm sorry.'

He swore, and Lily flinched.

'Stop apologising. It's not your fault,' he bit out. 'If anything it's mine.' He raked a hand through his hair and pulled his mobile out of his pocket. 'Make a coffee, or something. We might be a while.'

'Do you want one?'

'No, thanks.'

After a brief interlude in his study, Tristan strode out into his rear garden and found Lily sipping tea on a stone bench, studying one of the statues that dotted his garden.

'Plans have changed,' he said brusquely, not enjoying the way she seemed to fit so seamlessly into his home.

'Oh?' Lily replied, confused.

'We leave for Hillesden Abbey in an hour.'

'How?'

'Helicopter.'

'Helicop…? But I have a dress fitting today with Jo.'

'You *had* a dress fitting. The seamstress will travel to the Abbey during the week to meet with you.'

'But surely Chanel don't…?'

'Yeah, they do. Now, stop arguing. A car will be pulling up in ten minutes to take us onto the Heath.'

'Helicopters leave from the Heath?'

'Not as a general rule.'

Ten minutes later two police motorcycles escorted a stretch limousine along Hampstead Lane and pulled up near Kenwood House, where a bright red helicopter was waiting. A few curious onlookers watched as they alighted from the car—but no paparazzi, Tristan was pleased to note.

'Are you okay to fly in one of these?' Tristan raised his voice above the whir of the rotors.

'I don't know,' Lily yelled back. 'I never have.'

He helped her secure the safety harness and stowed their overnight bags behind her seat.

'I'm co-piloting today, but let me know if you feel sick.'

'I'll be fine.' She smiled tentatively and he realised she probably would be. She was a survivor, and quick to adapt to the circumstances around her.

He handed her a set of headphones and took his seat beside the pilot, not wanting to think about how that was just one more thing to admire about her.

He was looking forward to going home. His father was away on business until Friday, when Jordana would arrive to commence her wedding activities, but Tristan always felt rejuvenated in the country. And most importantly of all, the Abbey was *huge*. It had two hundred and twenty rooms, which should be more than enough space to put some physical distance between himself and Lily and still remain within the constraints of the custody order. He felt sure that if he didn't have her underfoot the chemistry between them would abate. Normalise. She'd just be another pretty face in a cast of thousands.

His chest felt tight as the ground fell away, and he berated himself for not thinking of the Abbey sooner.

CHAPTER ELEVEN

LILY closed the last page of the play and stared vacantly into the open fire Thomas, the family butler, had lit for her earlier that night. The writer had captured a side of her parents she hadn't known about. He had focused on their struggles and their hunger for fame and what had driven it, rather than just the consequence of it.

The result was an aspect of their lives Lily knew about from her mother's diaries but which the press rarely focused on. It was an aspect that always caused Lily to regret who they had become. She had expected that reading the play would imbue her with a renewed sense of disgust at their wasted lives—and it had, sort of—but what she hadn't expected was that it would fill her with a sense of yearning for them still to be around. For a chance to get to know them.

A log split in the grate and Lily rose to her feet and prodded at it with the cast-iron poker. Then she turned and wandered over to the carved wooden bookcases that lined the Abbey's vast library.

She had been in Tristan's ancestral home—a palatial three-storey stone Palladian mansion set amidst eleven thousand acres of parkland resplendent with manicured gardens, a deer forest, a polo field and a lake with swans and other birdlife—for four days now.

She'd taken long walks every day, as she and Jordana had done as teens, petted the horses in the stables, helped Jamie the gardener tend the manicured roses along the canopied stone arbour, and caught up with Mrs Cole, the housekeeper, who looked as if she'd stepped straight out of a Jane Austen novel.

In fact the whole experience of wandering around on her own and not being bothered by the busyness of her everyday life was like stepping back into another era, and the only thing that would have made her stay here better was if she'd been able to see Tristan more than just at the evening meal, where he was always unfailingly polite, and nothing more. It was as if they were complete strangers.

For four days he had studiously locked himself away in his study and, from what Lily could tell, rarely ventured out.

Lily paused beside the antique chessboard that was always set up in the library and sank into one of the bottle-green club chairs worn from years of use.

At first she had thought Tristan had flown them to the Abbey to avoid the constant threat of paparazzi, but it had soon become depressingly apparent that he'd relocated them so that he could avoid *her* as well!

And she couldn't deny that hurt. After his apology back in his London home she had thought maybe they could build a friendship, but clearly he didn't feel the same way. Clearly the chemistry he had felt for her had been laid to rest after just one time together. She only wished she felt the same way.

Unfortunately, consummating her desire for him that night had resurrected an inner sexuality only he seemed to bring out in her. And now that she had experienced the full force of his possession she craved it even more.

'Want a game?' a deep voice said softly from behind her chair, and Lily swung around to find Tristan regarding her from just inside the doorway. She'd been so deep in thought she hadn't heard him come in.

Her heart kicked against her ribs at the sight of him in black jeans and a pale green cashmere sweater the exact shade of his eyes. He looked casually elegant, while she was conscious that she had changed into old sweatpants and a top before coming downstairs to read.

'I... If you like,' Lily found herself answering, not sure that saying yes was the sanest answer, all things considered. The man hadn't said boo to her for four days and now he wanted to play chess...?

'Can I fix you a drink?'

'Sure,' she said, not sure that was the sanest idea either.

'I know you're not fond of Scotch, but my father has an excellent sherry.'

'Sure,' she parroted, ordering her brain to come online. Her body quickened as he walked slowly towards her, and she straightened the pawns on their squares to avoid having him see how pathetic she was.

'You start,' he offered.

Lily tilted her head. 'Is that because you're so sure you can win?'

He smiled a wolfish grin. 'Visitor's rules.'

'Oh.'

'But, yes, I'm sure I can win.' He flopped into a chair and chuckled at her sharp look.

He had no idea.

She regarded him with a poker face. 'Is that a challenge, Lord Garrett?'

'It certainly is, Miss Wild.'

'Then prepare to be defeated.' She smiled, knowing that she was actually a pretty good chess-player. It was one of the things she liked to do while sitting around waiting for scenes to be set up on location.

She leaned forward, her ponytail swinging over one shoulder, and rested her hands on her knees, concentrating on the chess instead of on him. Given his overriding confidence she guessed he'd be a master player—and she'd need all her wits about her.

'You're good,' Tristan complimented her an hour later, as she chewed on her lip and considered her next move.

So far he had countered every one of her attacks and she was fast running out of manoeuvres.

'Did you enjoy your swim this morning?' he asked, leaning back in his chair, his long legs sprawled out on either side of the low table.

His question made her glance at him sharply. 'How do you know I went swimming this morning?'

'I saw you.'

'But you weren't there.'

'Yes, I was.'

Something heavy curled between them and Lily cleared her throat. 'So why didn't you swim?'

'It's your move.'

Lily looked down at the board. Had he really been at the pool? And if so why hadn't he joined her? Mulling it over, she carefully moved her bishop across the board—and then watched as Tristan immediately confiscated it with his marauding rook.

'Oh!' Lily looked up to see a wicked glint in his eyes. 'Not fair! You were trying to distract me!'

'It worked.'

'That's cheating.'

'Not really. I did turn up for a swim.' His voice was low, deep, and an unexpected burst of warmth stole through her.

'Then I repeat: Why didn't you have one?' She lifted her chin challengingly, sure that he was just playing with her.

'Because I didn't trust myself to join you,' he said dulcetly.

Was he flirting with her?

Lily's heart raced and she quickly averted her eyes, not sure she wanted an answer. Her stomach fluttered alarmingly and she looked at the chessboard without really seeing it.

'Aren't you going to ask me why?' he murmured.

Lily looked up and, seeing the competitive glint in his eyes, realised what he was doing. 'No,' she said a little crossly, 'because you're only trying to put me off my game.' And she *wasn't* going to be disappointed by that.

He laughed softly and the deep sound trickled through her like melted chocolate.

They played for a short time more, and finally Lily threw up her hands when he cornered her king.

'Okay, you win.' She smiled, not totally surprised at the outcome. After the swimming comment she'd lost all concentration.

She wondered if now wouldn't be a good time to go to bed. A cosy ambience seemed to have descended, and with the crackling fire behind them it would be all too easy to forget that he was here, with her, under duress.

Tristan tried to ignore the heat in his groin as his eyes automatically dropped to that lethal smile of hers, before sliding lower to the tempting swell of her pert breasts beneath the loose T-shirt. Did the woman even *own* a bra?

Oh yeah, he remembered. A pink one… He felt his body grow even harder at the image of her standing before him in matching delicate lace underwear. He loved the thought of her in matching underwear—not that she was wearing any at the moment…

He got up to top up his drink and give his hands something to do.

He'd been avoiding her all week, only seeing her at mealtimes, where she'd been so coolly remote they'd barely spoken to each other.

But he'd seen her. Watched her take long walks in the park, listened to her musical laugh as she'd helped Jamie choose which roses would be cut for the house in preparation for Jordana's wedding in two days' time.

Before, he'd been honest about not trusting himself to join her in the pool that morning, but he could see she hadn't believed him. Which was probably just as well.

Because distance had not done a damn thing to dampen the need he had to touch her, or just to be with her—which in some ways was scarier than the other.

Emotions he'd never had any trouble keeping at bay threatened to take him by the bit and make him forget all his good intentions to avoid relationships of any sort. She was dangerous, he knew it, but he couldn't deny he was drawn to her flame. Some primal desire was overriding his superficial instincts to keep away.

And now, against his better judgement, he returned to her side, holding the decanter of sherry in his hand. 'Here, let me pour you another drink.'

'No, I should…go to bed.'

The words hung between them but he ignored her hesitancy until she raised her near-empty glass.

'One more won't hurt.'

He replaced the stopper and sat the decanter beside his chair. He wasn't sure what he was doing; he only knew he didn't want her to go yet.

'Mmmm, this is nice,' she murmured, sipping at her glass.

He leaned back and studied her. She looked beautiful, with her hair in a messy ponytail, no make-up and her legs tucked up under her. The space between them crackled like the logs in the fireplace and he knew from the high colour on her cheeks that she felt it too. At this moment she had never seemed more beautiful to him. Or more nervous. He wondered whether she would bolt if he described the scene playing out in his mind.

'I've noticed you going for walks every day,' he said, in an attempt to distract himself.

'Oh, yes.' Lily's enthusiasm lit up her face. 'It's such a beautiful space here. You're so lucky to have it.'

'What do you like about it?' he asked, curious despite himself.

'It's rejuvenating, peaceful—and so quiet. And I love that your family has left the forest untouched.'

All the things *he* loved!

'They used to hunt there, that's why.'

'Oh, don't spoil it.' Her mouth made a moue of disappointment and he laughed.

'Never fear, Bambi is safe from this generation of Garretts.'

She smiled and the almost shy look she cast from under her lashes caught him in the solar plexus.

'That's nice.'

'That's only because I'm not here all that often,' he teased.

'I don't believe you. And you're spoiling it again,' she scolded, picking up on the falseness behind his words.

'Come over by the fire?' he murmured, mentally rolling his eyes at the stupidity of that suggestion.

But she did, and he poked at the fire while she found a comfortable position on the Persian rug.

'What was it like growing up in your world?' she asked, watching him carefully as he sat down opposite her, his drink dangled over one knee.

Tristan didn't like talking about himself as a general rule, but he'd invited her to sit by the fire and couldn't very well ignore her question.

'Privileged. Boring at times. Not that much different from any other life, I expect, apart from the opportunities that come with the title—although that also comes with a duty of care.'

'What do you mean?'

He glanced at her, and then back at the fire. 'I take the view that being born into the nobility is about being a custodian of history. All this is grand and awe-inspiring, but it's not mine and it never will be. I'm fortunate enough to look after it, yes, but this house is a part of something much bigger and it belongs to everyone, really.'

'Is that why you open your home to the public?'

'Partly. People are naturally curious about the country's history, and my ancestors have accumulated a lot of important artefacts that deserve to be viewed by more than just a privileged few. Especially if those privileged few don't understand the importance of what they have.'

'Do you mean people who don't care about their heritage?'

Her softly voiced question brought his attention back to her, and he wondered at the looseness of his tongue and the need he suddenly felt to unburden himself of the weight of the less salubrious aspects of his history. He suspected, given Lily's dislike of the press, that she wouldn't run off and disclose his secrets—and really they weren't all that secret anyway.

'My grandfather was a heavy drinker and gambler, and he ran the property into quite a severe state of disrepair. My father had to work two jobs for a while to try and rebuild it, and while he was off working my mother thought a good little money-earner might be to sell off some of my father's most prized heirlooms.' He couldn't stop the note of bitterness from creeping into his voice.

'Oh, how terrible!' Lily cried. 'She must have been so unhappy to try and reach out that way.'

Tristan cut her a hard glance. *'Reach out?'*

'Yes. My mother did terrible things to get my father's attention, and—'

'My mother wasn't trying to get my father's attention,' he bit out. 'She was trying to get more money to fund her lifestyle.'

Something she'd talked about endlessly.

'I'm sorry.' Lily touched his arm and then drew her hand back when he looked at her sharply. 'And was your father able to recover them? The heirlooms?'

'No.' His tone was brittle even to his own ears. 'But I did.'

Lily paused and then said softly. 'You don't like her very much, do you?'

Tristan put another log on the fire and ran an agitated hand through his hair, realising too late that he'd said too much. How should he respond to that? Tell her that he would probably have forgiven his mother anything if she'd shown him a modicum of genuine affection as he'd been growing up? But she had, hadn't she? Sometimes.

'My mother wasn't the most maternal creature in the world, and as I matured I lost a lot of respect for her.' He spied the bound folio next to the stone hearth and realised it was the play Lily had been carrying around with her. 'What are you reading?' he asked, reaching for it.

Lily made a scoffing noise. 'Not a very subtle conversation

change, My Lord. And not a very good one either. It's a play about my parents.'

'The one that slimeball reporter asked you about?'

She shifted uncomfortably and he wondered about that.

'Yes.'

'But you don't want to do it?'

'No.'

He watched the way the firelight warmed her angelic features and wondered what was behind her reticence to do the play. 'Tell me about your life,' he surprised them both by saying.

She shook her head. '*Quid pro quo*, you mean.'

'Why do you call yourself Lily instead of Honey?' he queried, warming to the new topic but sensing her cool at the same time.

For a minute he didn't think she was going to answer and then she threw him one of those enigmatic smiles that told him she was avoiding something. 'My stepfather thought it would be a good idea for me to change it. You know—reinvent myself. Make a fresh start.' She laughed, as if it was funny, but the lightness in her tone was undermined by the sudden tautness of her shoulders.

'How old were you?'

'Seven.'

'Seven!'

'I was a bit traumatised at the time—wouldn't speak to anyone for six months after my parents died. Plus my parents weren't the most conventional creatures, so it was a good idea, really.'

'Jordana said you were named after your mother?'

'Sort of. She was Swedish and her name was Hanna—Hanny. When she moved to England her accent made it sound like she was saying honey—so everyone called her that. I guess my parents liked the name. Which was why it was such a good idea when Frank suggested I change it. It set me free to become my own person.' She stopped, more colour highlighting her cheeks.

Tristan didn't agree. He knew of Frank Murphy. His office had handled a complaint against the man some years back, and he had a reputation for being an egotistical schmuck.

Tristan knew the story about how Hanny Forsberg had married him in a whirlwind romance and then returned to her one true love a week later. Only to die in said lover's arms that very night. Tristan couldn't imagine Frank Murphy taking her defection well, and wondered if he had taken his anger out on Lily.

'I'm not sure that would have been his only motivation,' he commented darkly, swilling the last of his Scotch and placing his empty glass behind him.

'What do you mean?'

'I mean Frank Murphy is a self-interested swine who would have been looking out for his own interests before yours.'

'Frank's not like that,' she defended.

'Come on, Lily. Frank Murphy is a user. Everyone knows that. And the accolades he got from taking in Hanny's orphan were huge.'

'Maybe.'

Tristan hadn't missed the flash of pain in her eyes before she shifted position and moved closer to the fire, her hands outstretched towards the leaping flames. He wondered what was going through her mind and then shook his head.

'I've upset you.'

'No.'

'Yes. I didn't mean to imply that Frank didn't care for you. I'm sure he did.'

'No. He didn't. Not really.'

'Lily, it's a big responsibility to look after a child that's not your own. I'm sure—'

'There was no one else.'

'Sorry?'

'Nobody else wanted me.' She shrugged as if they were discussing nothing more important than the weather. 'When my parents died I had nowhere to go. I would have become a ward of the state if he hadn't stepped in.'

'What about your grandparents?'

'Johnny's had died and my mother's were old, and they'd disowned her after her first Page Three spread.'

'But Johnny had a brother, I recall.'

'Unfortunately he used to get more wasted than Johnny and looking after a seven-year-old was not high on his list of things to accomplish.'

'Your mother—'

'There was no one, okay? It's no big deal. I think I'll go to bed.'

'Wait!'

'For what?'

'You're upset,' he said gently.

Lily shivered as if a draught of cold air had caught her unawares, and for a minute she seemed lost.

'Did you know I found them?' She held her hands out to the fire again, as if seeking comfort. 'The police kept it quiet, to preserve my "delicate psychological state", but I found my parents' bodies. It was Sunday morning and they were supposed to make me blueberry pancakes and take me to the park. Johnny had promised it would be a family day. Instead I woke up and found my mother lying on the sofa with vomit pooled in her hair and my father slumped on the floor at her feet. It was like some sort of Greek tragedy. If my mother could have looked down on the scene she might have enjoyed the irony of finally having my father in such a supplicating pose.'

Lily gave a half laugh and for a minute he thought she had finished speaking, but then she continued.

'At first I tried to wake them, but even then I knew.' She shook her head at the pointlessness of such a gesture. 'There's something about the utter stillness of a dead body that even a small child can understand. I knew—I knew even though I didn't know what was wrong—I knew I would never see them again.'

She stared into the fire for a long moment and Tristan thought it was lucky her parents weren't here right now or he'd kill them all over again. Then Lily gave an exaggerated shiver and smiled brightly at him.

'Gosh, I haven't thought of that for years.'

Something of the anxiety he felt must have shown in his face because she turned back to the fire and sipped at the sherry she had barely touched. She was obviously upset and embarrassed, and Tristan felt heaviness lodge in his chest. He'd had no idea she'd suffered such a huge trauma at such a young age.

As if sensing his overwhelming need to comfort her she shot him a quelling look he'd seen before, but his mind couldn't place.

'I'm fine now,' she dismissed, but Tristan could see it was an effort for her to force her wide, shining eyes to his. 'Completely over it.'

No, she wasn't. Any fool could see that, and he didn't like that she was trying to make light of it with him. 'No, you're not. I think you hide behind your parents' controversial personas— the controversial persona you've also cultivated with the press. Almost as if you use your past as a shield so people don't get to see the real you.'

Lily stiffened, shock etched on her features, and then Tristan remembered where he'd seen that haughty look before. Right after they'd had sex that first time.

CHAPTER TWELVE

LILY stared at Tristan and willed the ground to open up and devour one of them. She'd been having such a nice time and now he'd gone and ruined it.

'You don't know what you're talking about,' she whispered, placing her glass carefully on the hearth and willing the lump in her throat to subside. She stared at the inlaid stonework around the fireplace and realised she was about to cry. Cry! She never cried, and she wasn't about to start in Tristan's presence.

'Lily…'

Lily quickly scrambled to her feet, holding her hands out in front of her as Tristan made to do the same. 'I'm…'

The words wouldn't come and she turned to flee, making it only as far as the upholstered French settee before Tristan caught her.

'I can't let you leave like this.' He spoke gruffly, swinging her around to face him and Lily promptly burst into tears.

She tried to push him away but he was like an immovable force and she pounded his chest instead. 'Let me go. Let me—' A sob cut off her distressed plea and Tristan gathered her closer.

'Lily, I'm sorry. I really am an insensitive fool, and you were right the other day. I don't know anything.'

Rather than making her feel better that only made it worse and she buried her face in her hands, unable to hold back her tears any more.

'Shh, Lily, shh,' Tristan urged, holding her tighter. 'Let me soothe you,' he husked, his voice thick with emotion.

Lily tried to resist, but somehow all the events of the week converged and rendered her a sobbing mess, unable to put up any resistance when Tristan sank down onto the settee and pulled her into his lap.

He continued to stroke her even after her tears had abated and Lily rested against him, her mind spinning.

Tristan was wrong when he said she hid behind her public image. It was just easier to let people think what they wanted. They would anyway, and really she didn't care a jot what anyone thought.

But if that were true then why had she turned her back on the country she loved and set herself up in America, where people judged her more on her actions than on her past? Why had she always tried to do what Frank expected of her? And why had Tristan's rejection of her hurt so much six years ago?

Lily drew in a long, shuddering breath and then released it, her body slowly relaxing in Tristan's warm embrace. Try as she might she couldn't find valid reasons for her actions. Valid reasons for why she let the press write what they wanted about her. It was easy to say that no one would believe her if she corrected them. But why not?

An image of her mother, wretched and crying, came to mind, and Lily squeezed her eyes against the devastating image.

But then other images crowded in. Happier ones. Her mother singing to her and towelling her off after a bath. Her father putting her on his shoulders as they strolled through Borough Market eating falafels and brownies. Visiting her mother's photo shoots and putting on make-up with her in front of her dressing-table mirror. Curling up with her father while he played around with his guitar.

Lily gulped in air and her heart caught. More unprecedented memories of her parents stumbled through her mind and she felt breathless with surprise.

She felt Tristan's arms tighten around her, one of his hands stroking from the top of her head to the base of her spine as one might soothe an upset child. As her mother had once soothed her.

Her father's mantra came to mind, trying to rescue her. But for once it didn't work. Because Tristan was right. She *did* care what people thought about her.

Slowly she lifted her head and peered up at him. She knew she must look an absolute fright, and was shocked when Tristan pulled the sleeve of his expensive cashmere sweater over his hand and wiped her eyes and nose.

'That's gross,' she grumbled, ducking her head self-consciously.

She felt him shrug. 'That's all I had.'

He chuckled, and Lily smiled into the curve of his neck. Being in his arms gave her a sense of security she hadn't felt since before her parents had died, and although part of her, the self-preservation part, told her to pull away, that she had embarrassed herself enough, that she was better off handling this alone, she couldn't get her limbs to obey. He was just so big and warm, and his rich scent was extraordinarily comforting.

But none of this is real, she reminded herself glumly.

'You can let me up now,' she said quietly, pushing back from him as those disturbing thoughts stole through her mind.

When Tristan made no move to release her completely she looked up at him. 'I said you can let me go now,' she repeated, in case he hadn't heard her.

'I heard.' He nodded, but didn't move.

'I think…I think I should go to my room and be alone with my misery.'

'Now, I was always told that misery preferred company,' Tristan jested.

'Tristan, please…' Embarrassment was overriding pain and Lily couldn't smile at his teasing words. 'I can't do this. You were right. I *am* a coward. I…I need time alone to think.'

Tristan curled his arm around her shoulders, preventing her from pulling further away.

'Thinking is probably the worst thing you can do right now. And I never said you were a coward.' He feathered her ponytail through his fingers as if learning its silky texture. 'You're one of the bravest people I know. And you're loyal and warm and smart. You've faced false drug allegations with dignity and you have a generous spirit. It's why people are so drawn to you.'

'People are drawn to me because of the way I look and because of who my parents were,' she argued.

He tapped her on the end of her shiny nose and she squirmed. 'You're too young to be cynical. And you're more than the sum of your parts, Lily Wild.'

Lily felt more tears well up at his kind words and buried her face against his shoulder again. 'You're a nice person. How come you don't show that side of yourself more often?'

He tensed momentarily. 'I already told you I'm not nice,' he said, his voice gruff. 'I'm just saying all this to make you feel better.'

'Oh.' Lily laughed as she was meant to. But he didn't fool her. He *was* nice. Too nice.

She shifted off his lap so she was sitting beside him, wanting to tell him what was going through her mind even though she'd revealed more about herself tonight than she had to anyone else.

'You were right before,' she began haltingly. 'I *have* used my past as a type of shield.'

'That's perfectly understandable, given your experiences.'

Lily paused. 'Maybe. But it's also helped me avoid recognising things like…like the fact that for years I've been so ashamed of who my parents were and how they died that I hated them. And I've let their destructive love for each other cloud the way I relate to people. You see, my mother kept diaries for years. Basically she and Johnny would binge on each other and then he'd go off with his groupies and my mother would cry and rail and swear off him—until he came back and the whole cycle would start over again.'

Tristan was quiet, and Lily's fingers absently pleated the soft wool of his sweater as she leaned against him and soaked up his strength and sureness.

'That sounds like the problem was less about how they felt about each other and more about how they felt about themselves.'

'What do you mean?' she queried, leaning back a little to look up at him, her eyes drinking in the patrician beauty of his face in the soft light.

He shrugged. 'I'm guessing Johnny Wild loved himself a little too much and your mother didn't love herself nearly enough.'

Lily digested his words and then blew out a noisy breath. 'Of course. Why did I never see that?'

'Too close to the trees, perhaps?'

She shook her head. 'You're really smart—you know that?'

No, if he was smart he'd get up and go to bed right now, instead of wondering what she would do if he reached up and released her silky mass of hair from the confines of her hair tie. If he was smart he'd be questioning this need to comfort her and touch her rather than just going along with it as if he had a right to do those things.

'Not always,' he acknowledged, feeling the air between them thicken as he tried to ignore her soft hands on his chest. 'You need to stop doing that.'

He heard the hitch in her breathing at his growled words and the sound sent a jolt of lust to his already hardened groin.

'Or…?'

He clenched his teeth against the invitation apparent in that one tiny word. 'There is no "or".'

'Why not?'

'Lily, your emotions are running high.'

She looked him square in the eye, her purple gaze luminous despite her reddened eyelids. 'And yours aren't running at all?'

He needed her to stop looking at him as if he was better than he was. 'That's not emotion, sweetheart—that's sex. And the two should never be confused.'

'Believe me, I know that.' She expelled a shaky breath but didn't remove her hand. Instead she slid it further up his chest and ran the tip of her finger underneath the crew neck of his sweater, along his clavicle.

'Lily—'

'I want to make love with you.'

Tristan wanted that too—but could he risk it?

She'd noticed his hesitation and her eyes had clouded over. 'Sorry. I— Look, if you don't want to I'll understand…'

'Don't want to!' His hands felt unsteady as they automatically reached out to stop her from getting up. 'Lily, you drive me crazy.'

She shot him a surprised look and he nearly laughed. Didn't she know the effect she had on him? Didn't she *know* why he had stayed away from her for four days? Why he should have stayed away tonight as well…?

'I do?'

'Oh, yeah.' His hot gaze swept down over her tear-smudged face, baggy T-shirt and worn sweatpants. 'Stir crazy…' he whispered.

He felt her tentative hands creep into his hair, and groaned when she leaned in and placed her soft, full mouth against his own. Oh, God, this was heaven—and he couldn't fight both of them.

He cupped her face briefly, deepening the kiss and sealing his mouth to hers. He flipped her over on the settee and shoved his hands under her T-shirt. She moaned and arched into his hands, and Tristan felt like a starving man being offered a king's dinner. He yanked her T-shirt up and fastened his lips on one pert breast, tugging at her sweet flesh, licking, sucking, drowning in the aroused perfume of her body.

'Tristan!'

Her loud gasp and uncontrolled writhing fed his urgent need, and he attacked her sweatpants and panties and drew them down her legs, frustrated when they became tangled.

He sat up and pulled them all the way off, and then knelt on the floor in front of her, not even caring that the floorboards were hard on his knees. He parted her thighs so that he could feast on her in a way that had kept him hard for more nights than he cared to count, but he stopped when he felt her stiffen.

'Tristan...'

Her voice was uncertain, and he remembered that she had been a virgin until a few nights ago and that maybe no one had ever done this for her before.

His hands instantly gentled on her inner thighs, and his fingers massaged her silken skin until he felt her muscles lose their rigidity.

'Take down your hair,' he whispered softly, gazing at her breasts rising beneath her T-shirt with her movement. A soft cloud of pure gold swirled around her shoulders and he inhaled deeply. 'Now the T-shirt.'

His thumbs kept stroking her inner thighs, slowly drawing them further apart, and he could feel tiny shivers of anticipation running along the surface of her skin. His own skin felt hot and tight, and it got even worse when she swept the grey T-shirt up over her head. Her breasts were standing proudly for his inspection, her nipples hardening into tight pink buds. Saliva pooled in his mouth at the thought of reaching up and capturing one, but he had other endeavours on his mind.

He glanced down at the soft nest of golden curls at the apex of her body, and then back up to her face.

'Let me,' he husked, desire beating like a fever in his blood. 'I've wanted you like this for ever.'

She wet her lips and arched involuntarily as his sure fingers moved higher up her softened thighs, bringing her closer to the edge of the settee as he delved between her damp curls.

She was slick and ready, and Tristan lowered his head and devoured her with his lips, his tongue, his fingers. She made the sexiest noises he'd ever heard, and when she came he thought he might too, lapping at her until he had fully sated himself with her taste. Then he rose, and felt like an emperor as he looked down upon her pliant flushed nudity.

His heart lurched, and desperation and need grabbed him

by the throat as he quickly divested himself of his clothing and rolled a condom over his now painful erection.

She sat up and reached for him, but Tristan shook his head. He'd wanted to take things slowly this time, and already slow had gone the way of the birds. If she touched him he doubted he'd even make it inside her body.

'Next time,' he promised hoarsely, picking her up and carrying her back in front of the fire. 'I need to be inside you now.'

'Oh, yes.' She held her hands out to him, and Tristan settled over her and drove deeply inside her body on one long, powerful thrust. Her body accepted him more easily this time, but still she was tight and he tried to give her a minute to adjust.

Only she didn't want that and immediately wrapped her legs around his hips. 'More,' she pleaded, trying to move under him.

Tristan couldn't resist the urgent request and drove into her over and over, while he brought them both to a shattering climax that took him to the stars and beyond.

CHAPTER THIRTEEN

'I'LL be back,' he murmured against her mouth, and Lily flopped back against her pillows as Tristan quietly closed the bedroom door behind him.

She'd almost felt sick earlier, when she'd woken in the early-morning light to find Tristan trying to slip out of her bed without waking her. He'd pulled on his jeans, a frown marring his perfect features, and then he'd noticed her watching him. He'd looked remote, but then his eyes had devoured her and he'd walked over and let his lips follow suit.

'I'm going to make you a cup of tea,' he'd whispered, and she'd smiled and trailed her hand down his naked chest.

She didn't really want tea, just him, but she was glad now of the momentary reprieve as she stared at the ceiling and memories of last night swept blissfully into her consciousness.

Last night he'd told her she drove him crazy, and a slow grin spread across her face as she recalled the tortured way he had gasped her name when he climaxed. She liked the idea of driving him crazy. She liked it a lot. Because she felt the same way. She only had to think of him walking into a room for her hormones to sit up and beg.

Last night he had made love to her in front of the open fire and afterwards carried her to bed, where she had promptly curled against him and fallen into the deepest sleep she'd had since arriving back in the country.

He'd promised her slow, but she had no complaints about their lovemaking. In fact she'd loved it! The urgency, the excitement…the way he'd touched her, cared for her. In fact she loved everything about him.

Lily put her fingers over her face.

She loved him.

Oh, Lord. Did she?

She tested the words out silently in her head. And her heart swelled to bursting.

No. She couldn't. But she did. Completely and utterly.

And it had been there all along. It was the reason she'd been so nervous about seeing him again. It was the reason she had been so upset when he'd thought she was guilty of carrying drugs into Heathrow. That he'd thought her guilty of being a drug addict.

It was the reason she had been so morose these last few days, and the reason she had allowed herself to be swept away in the library last night. No, had *wanted* to be swept away—by him.

Lily swallowed, her heart pounding. They had made love so reverently, and she had given everything to him and he had seemed to do the same back.

He'd told her she drove him crazy with desire, and although he hadn't said he loved her she couldn't believe he didn't have any feelings for her.

But even if he did what did that mean?

Nothing. Because he didn't do love. He'd made that clear enough. And he wouldn't want her to love him either. Only… what if he felt differently with *her*?

Right. And how many other women haven't wanted that to be true?

Oh, Lord, she was starting to go back and forth like an entry in her mother's diary. He loves me. He loves me not.

The man had just spent four days avoiding her—he was hardly likely to go down on bended knee after one night in bed with her.

Something she couldn't deny that she now wanted. Lily blew out a breath.

In admitting that she had fallen in love with Tristan it was as if a wall against all her secret hopes and dreams had come down. She wanted what Jo and Oliver had. She wanted somewhere to belong, someone to love her. She wanted something lasting.

She groaned audibly and rolled onto her stomach and grabbed her pillow. What did she do now?

Seriously she didn't expect him to declare his undying love for her, but she couldn't stop herself from wanting that. Yearning for it. But he hadn't looked pleased to see her this morning, had he? No. He'd seemed distracted. Troubled. She'd dismissed it after his ferocious kiss, but…

Enough! She raised a big red stop sign in her head. She wouldn't do this. Play mental ping-pong over a man. The best thing to do would be to wait. Because really she had no idea how Tristan was feeling, and until she asked him she was just making up stories in her head. Lovely, sugar-coated romantic stories. But stories nonetheless.

Deciding to stop mooching around, she checked the bedside clock and was shocked to see that it was already nine-thirty. And, even worse, it was Friday. Jordana was due at the Abbey this morning to start all her pre-wedding pampering treatments, followed by lunch with a couple of girlfriends, and then a rehearsal dinner for close family and friends!

Maybe she should have a quick shower before Tristan got back? Or maybe she should go and find him and remind him that Jordana was due.

But then her phone rang and took the dilemma of what to do next out of her hands.

Pushing the tangled sheet aside, she jumped out of bed and reached for her tote bag beside the dressing table. Fumbling around inside, she finally located her mobile and quickly checked the caller ID. It was the detective working on her case.

Her case! Somehow she'd forgotten all about it with thoughts of Tristan swamping her mind.

'Good morning, Detective.'

'Miss Wild.' His polite, modulated tones echoed down the

line. 'I apologise for not delivering this news in person, but due to workload issues I'm unable to travel to Hillesden Abbey today, and Lord Garrett was adamant that we inform you of any breakthrough in your case as soon as it came to light.'

Lily swallowed, her palms sweaty around the silver phone. 'And…have you had a breakthrough?' she asked breathlessly.

'Not just a breakthrough, Miss Wild. We've solved the case. Or should I say Lord Garrett has solved the case.'

'Tristan?' Lily shook her head.

'Lord Garrett contacted us two days ago, after finding a discrepancy between the personnel records we initially received from the airline and the records that had been e-mailed to him.'

Lily plopped down on the velvet ottoman in front of the dressing table and stared at a baroque wall plaque. 'I don't understand.'

'One of the attendants who worked on your flight was not on the personnel list we were given, and was therefore not interviewed and fingerprinted. We were unaware of the last-minute replacement because the person who dealt with the staff-change had forgotten to send the information through to payroll. As we were given the original payroll records the replacement flight attendant did not appear on our list and was therefore not part of our initial investigation.'

He went on to explain that when Tristan had started looking into the case he'd picked up on the discrepancy and immediately informed the police.

'But why did she do it?' Lily asked.

'The flight attendant was bringing a small amount of narcotics into the country to earn a few extra quid on the side. When she learned that sniffer dogs would be going through not only the passengers' belongings but also the flight crew's she panicked, and you were an easy target. She was aware of your parents' notoriety and hoped that would be enough to prevent her own capture.'

Lily remained silent, struggling to process the information. 'So what happens now?'

'You're free to go, Miss Wild.'

'And the custody order?'

'Will be repealed by the courts some time today.'

Lily thanked the detective and sat for a few moments, completely stunned.

She was free.

She clasped her phone to her chest, trying to make some sense of it all. The whole sordid mess seemed surreal, and what stood out for Lily now was how sorry she was that her parents were still mainly remembered for their drug-taking rather than their artistic talents. Previously she would have felt suffocated by that. Tainted by it. But after her conversation with Tristan last night she saw that her parents had been only human. They'd made mistakes, yes, and paid the ultimate price for those mistakes. But they had tried.

It didn't mean she had to agree with their lifestyle choices, but nor did it mean she had a right to condemn them either—as many had condemned her. Except the author of the play hadn't judged them. He'd written a funny, informative and ultimately tragic account of their lives in a beautiful and heartfelt manner. And if she were to play her mother it could be her gift to them. Her gift to herself.

Lily felt short of breath at the surge of emotion that swept through her body.

Tristan. She wanted to talk to him. Share this with him because she knew he would understand.

She was free! And he had believed in her. Had helped her.

Lily sprang off the ottoman and grabbed the first items of clothing she found on the floor.

She wanted to feel Tristan's arms around her as he held her to him while she told him her news. Or did he already know?

She didn't care. She wanted to drag him back upstairs and make love with him. Run her fingers over his morning stubble—run her hands over his chest and take him into her hands as he had stopped her from doing last night.

Her body quickened, clearly agreeing with the direction of her thoughts and—

What if he's been working on your case just so that he can be rid of you?

The ugly thought weaved through her mind like an evil spell but she immediately pushed it aside. No stories any more. Just facing her fears head-on.

'I couldn't believe it when Mrs Cole told me you were in the kitchen making a cup of tea. And why are you only half-dressed at nine-thirty? You're usually up with the birds.'

Tristan turned at the sound of his sister's voice. He was half-naked because he'd needed to get out of Lily's bedroom fast and had forgotten his sweater.

'What are you doing here?' he asked, a little more harshly than he'd intended.

'I have a little thing called a wedding at the local manor house tomorrow. Remember?'

Tristan rubbed his belly. 'I meant in the kitchen.'

'You didn't respond to Oliver's text last night about meeting him at the polo field at half-eleven, so when Mrs Cole mentioned you were in here I thought I'd remind you. What *are* you doing in here?'

'Fixing tea. What does it look like?'

He glanced away from his sister's too interested gaze and willed the kettle to boil.

'Who for?'

'Didn't you say you had somewhere to be?'

Jordana tilted her head, her eyes narrowed. 'Why is your hair all over the place? And what's that mark on your shoul—? Oh, God.' She clapped her hand over her mouth in a melodramatic show. 'You've got someone stashed upstairs!'

Tristan followed Jordana's gaze to his right shoulder and saw the imprint of Lily's fingernails from their lovemaking last night.

He'd woken this morning to find her curved in his arms,

his upper arm numb from where she had used it as a pillow all night and a boulder the size of Mount Kilimanjaro lodged in his chest. He'd never woken up having held a woman all night before. In fact he usually tried to find a plausible excuse not to wake up with one at all, and he didn't mind admitting that having Lily snuggled against him like a warm, sleepy kitten had scared the hell out of him.

As had the feeling of well-being he'd been unable to dislodge alongside the boulder. If he'd thought the first experience with her mind-blowing then last night had been indescribable. She'd been completely abandoned in his arms and he... Suffice it to say it had been the most complete, the most intimate experience he'd ever had with a woman—even more unsettling than making love to her five nights ago.

He'd tried to sneak out of bed, but she'd woken when he was halfway into his jeans. He'd turned when he heard the bedcovers rustling to find her leaning up on one elbow, the linen sheet clutched to her chest and her golden mane spilling over one shoulder.

Her soft smile had slipped when he'd hovered over the idea of just walking out, but he hadn't been able to. Not after all they'd shared last night. He wasn't that big a heel. So he'd kissed her. Devoured her. Sucked her tongue into his mouth and very nearly forgotten why he had to get away.

'So?' Jordana prompted, bringing his eyes back to hers.

'None of your business. And keep your voice down.' The kitchen staff weren't close, but still he didn't want them overhearing. He turned back to the boiled kettle and filled the teapot, wishing that he hadn't sent Mrs Cole off when she'd offered to make the tea for him.

'I'll find out. I mean, she has to come downstairs some time...'

Tristan scowled at her too happy face. He'd be glad when this damned wedding was over and his loved up sister would go back to normal. 'Leave it alone, Jo.'

'Why? She must be important. Someone special?'

He put the kettle back on the hob and ignored her.

'Maybe it's a guy?'

'Jordana!'

'Just joking, big brother. Jeez, Louise, where's your sense of humour?'

Tristan turned away and asked himself the same question. But her next inane remark sent him into panic mode.

'That's okay.' Jo leaned against the bench. 'I'll ask Lily. She'll know.'

Tristan banged a lone mug on the tray. No way would he be having tea in Lily's room with his sister on the warpath.

'You won't ask Lily anything. You'll keep your nose out of my private life.'

'Why so tetchy? I'm only teasing you.'

'I'm not in the mood.'

'Well, that's obvious. Where is Lily anyway?'

'In her room.'

'Really?' She raised her brows at him. 'How can you be so sure? And isn't that peppermint tea? Lily's favourite?'

'I said leave it alone, Jordana,' Tristan growled.

'Oh. My. God. It's *Lily*.' Both hands were clapped over Jordana's cheeks. 'You're sleeping with my best friend!'

'Jo—'

'I'm so excited. I told Oliver I thought there was something between the two of you at the restaurant. I knew it. This is great.'

'Jordana, it's not great.'

'It is. I think you love her. The way you were looking at her that night at dinner… I told Oliver I thought it was fated. Lily getting into trouble and you bailing her out. It was as if it was meant to be.'

Tristan recoiled as if she'd slapped him. He was *not* in love with Lily Wild.

'Jordana, you're a dreamer. If I did care for Lily Wild it would never be serious, so you can forget about taking your romantic fantasy to the next level.'

'Why?'

'Because I'm not ready to get married, and even if I was Lily is not one of *us*. Now, if you don't mind, I have to start my day.'

Jordana didn't move from where she'd stood in front of him. 'That's very snobbish of you.'

'You can look at it any way you want, but I have responsibilities to uphold—and if there's one thing I've learned from our parents it's that love fades. You might want to believe in for ever after but believe me that's the exception, not the rule. I have no intention of falling into Father's trap and marrying a woman who might or might not be looking for an entrance into our society. One who will run away when she finds out there's a lot more to the title of Duchess than champagne and shopping.'

'Lily's not like that,' Jordana protested.

Yeah, he knew that. But he needed to tell his sister something to get her off his back, and if he told her that what he felt for Lily scared the life out of him she'd want to wrap her arms around him and kiss him better.

Anyway, he enjoyed his freedom. He liked having sex with a variety of women and he liked his life the way it was. Didn't he?

Tristan shook away the disquieting question. 'I don't care. I don't need love and I don't love Lily Wild. She's special to you—not to me. Personally, I can't wait until this damn drug case is over and I can get on with my life again. And the sooner you get that through your head the happier I'll be. Here.' The tea tray clattered as he shoved it at Jordana's chest. 'Take this to her, will you? And tell her—tell her...' He shook his head. 'Tell her whatever you like.'

'Can I tell her I think you're afraid and letting the mistakes of our parents get in the way of your own happiness?' she asked softly.

Tristan cut her a withering glance and stalked out of the room. His sister had always been a child with stars in her eyes.

It was why he and his father had protected her so much after their mother had died. She was too dreamy and too easily led. He remembered how he and his father had thought Lily would lead her astray.

Only she hadn't. Lily had actually tried to protect her.

He gritted his teeth. Lily hadn't turned out to be at all what he had expected.

He marched out of the kitchen and took the stairs two at a time as he sought refuge in his own suite of rooms.

Lily wasn't trouble waiting to happen. She was beautiful inside and out. He should never have slept with her again last night. It had been hard enough getting her out of his head six years ago, after one innocent kiss, and he doubted he'd be able to get her out of his mind as quickly this time when she left the Abbey.

Left the Abbey? He braced his hands against the sink in his bathroom and stared at his dishevelled reflection, wondering why that thought filled him with dread.

Because he wasn't finished with her, that was why. And by the look in her eyes this morning she wasn't finished with him either. They had started something last night—nothing permanent, but something definitely worth pursuing for as long as it lasted.

Jo had just panicked him before. Made him think this was more than it really was. But Lily herself wasn't interested in relationships and for ever after. Hadn't she said as much at Élan the other night? So what was he so het-up about? He didn't have to end things so abruptly; he could just let them run their natural course.

Lily pressed herself back against the hallway wall as Tristan stormed out of the kitchen, her hands against her chest as if that would make her thin enough to be invisible.

But he didn't see her anyway. He was in too much of a rage.

She let her head gently fall back against the wall.

It wasn't a cliché that eavesdroppers rarely heard anything

good about themselves, and Lily was still trying to register exactly what she *had* heard. Something about her not being special. Not being one of them. That he didn't love her and couldn't wait for her case to be over so he could get his life back.

Jordana had said something after that, but her softer tones hadn't carried quite so clearly.

Lily felt the methodical beat of her heart as her thoughts coalesced.

She supposed she now wasn't left in any doubt as to how he had felt this morning. That frown had been real and the kiss he'd given her had not. What had it been, then? Pity?

Lily reeled sideways and then righted herself. She wished she could go back ten minutes and reverse her decision to come downstairs looking for him.

Or did she? Wasn't she better off knowing how he really felt? Better off knowing that if she'd jumped into his arms as she'd wanted to do she would have just embarrassed them both? Wasn't this part of facing her fears?

A shiver of misery snaked down her spine and she blinked to clear her vision. She heard a rattling sound from the kitchen, and then voices, and quickly turned to sprint up the staircase before Jordana headed out to deliver her tea.

She made it to her room unseen and leaned back against the door, her breathing laboured and her stomach churning. Tristan's angry words were parroting through her brain like a DVD on repeat mode. He didn't love her. Didn't want to love her and never would love her. And, worst of all, she wasn't good enough for him.

She blinked. The shower. She would jump in the shower so that Jordana didn't see how upset she was.

In all honesty she hadn't expected that Tristan would wake up in love with her, but did he seriously think she was interested in his *title*?

Right now she'd like to tell him where he could stick it— only then she'd have to admit she'd overheard his conversation with Jo and she couldn't go there. Not without breaking down altogether.

Like her mother used to do over Johnny. Her mother had always turned to alcohol when Johnny had turned to his groupies, and where once Lily had looked back in anger at her mother she now looked back in pity. Because finally she truly understood what it felt like to fall in love with a man who didn't love you in return.

Lily felt as if she had a claw stuck in her throat as she let the hot water beat down over her face. As much as she might understand her mother a little better now, she also realised that she truly wasn't anything like her. She was her own person, and she wouldn't cling to Tristan, or rant or beg. She'd hold her head up high, tell him it had been great, and walk away.

Oh, Lord. She sucked in a deep breath and felt tears form behind her eyes. She remembered the moment she'd found her parents had died, the moment her uncle had said he couldn't take her, the moment her mother's best friend said she couldn't take her, the moment Frank had sent her to boarding school because she didn't want to appear on his TV show any more, and the moment six years ago when Tristan had sent her away.

But none of that had felt anywhere near as painful as hearing Tristan say he didn't love her, and it was only Jordana calling her name from the other room that prevented her from sliding to the floor and dissolving into a puddle of misery.

CHAPTER FOURTEEN

WHERE the hell was she?

Tristan scowled as he leaned against one of the ornate oak sideboards in the main drawing room, sipping an aperitif and talking with one of Oliver's cousins while awaiting the remaining guests for the rehearsal dinner.

A waiter discreetly circulated amongst those already present, and Tristan glanced through the open double doors to where a lavish dining setting, resplendent with antique crystalware, awaited twenty-four of Jordana and Oliver's close friends and family for the rehearsal dinner.

From what he could tell the room was empty of everyone other than waiting staff. Which meant that Lily wasn't down yet.

Tristan knew he should have been in a better mood, given that his baby sister was marrying one of his oldest friends the following day, but he wasn't. After his run in with Jordana this morning his day had gone from bad to worse.

He'd been off his game during polo from the start, and then Oliver had informed him that Jordana's 'surprise' for Lily was to set her up with all three of his single cousins!

Tristan had left the field immediately after that and discreetly cornered Jordana, telling her in no uncertain terms to rearrange the evening's place settings so that Lily sat beside him. Only she'd floored him by telling him that Lily had already asked that the place settings remain as they were.

Then she'd apologised for her earlier behaviour. 'Lily set me straight this morning,' she'd said. 'She told me she was just taking my advice and "cutting loose" by having a harmless fling with you, and that it was now well and truly finished.' Which had been news to him. 'I was just a bit carried away by the excitement of my wedding. I'm truly sorry to have teased you the way I did.'

Tristan had reassured her it was fine, but really he hadn't heard much after 'harmless fling' and 'cutting loose'. His memories of last night certainly did not fit under either one of those banners! And as for things being finished...

Did that mean Lily actually *wanted* to be set up with one of Oliver's cousins? This mountain of a man he was currently attempting to converse with, perhaps? Tristan hoped not, because objectively speaking he was an attractive devil. If Lily went for brawny males—and she had certainly been admiring his own muscles last night—then Hamish Blackstone would be right up her alley.

He scoured the room again for Lily and tried to clear the scowl off his face. Where was she? Avoiding him?

He'd deliberately stayed away from her all day to give her a chance to do girlie stuff with Jordana, convincing himself that the last thing either woman wanted was a male hanging around. But really, if he was honest, he'd been upset to find Lily constantly in his thoughts, and after their unbelievable lovemaking last night he'd needed time to think.

And what he'd thought was that there was no way she was getting it on with one of Oliver's cousins this weekend. Or the next, for that matter, and... Where on earth *was* she?

He was just about to go in search of her when the hair stood up on the back of his neck and he knew she'd arrived.

He turned to see her poised to enter the room from the single side door leading in from the south corridor and his heart stopped. For maybe a minute.

Not enough time to kill him, but long enough that it had to beat triple time to oxygenate his brain again.

George Bernard Shaw was meant to have said, 'Beauty is

all very well at first sight; but who ever looks at it when it has been in the house three days?' Tristan could safely answer that he did! If anything, as he looked at her standing in the doorway wearing a powder-blue Grecian-style gown that left her arms and décolletage bare, with her glorious hair upswept, he didn't think he'd ever seen a more divine creature. And by the intake of breath of his drinking companion *he* hadn't either.

'That's Lily Wild,' Hamish Blackstone announced under his breath.

Tristan grunted and waited for Lily to make eye contact with him. But she didn't. Instead she stepped straight up to a group of women that included the bridesmaids and Oliver's mother, looking relaxed and composed and every inch the movie star that she was.

'She's taken,' he found himself telling Hamish.

'You're joshing me?' the Scot spluttered. 'Jordana said she was single. Who's the lucky guy? I'll deck him.'

Tristan looked him up and down and thought he just might with those tree trunk arms. 'Excuse me. I need to mingle.'

He needed to talk to her, that was what he needed to do, and he didn't care who knew it. She couldn't just ignore him after last night.

'Cutting loose' be damned!

Lily smiled politely and answered questions about acting and America and everything else in between.

When she had first walked into the drawing room she'd sensed Tristan's presence and deliberately hadn't looked for him. She didn't want to see him. She had her pride, and she'd decided earlier that she wasn't going to collapse as she had wanted to do in the shower. That had been shock, and she'd had all day to steel herself against seeing him again.

Maybe it wouldn't be so hard.

He hadn't tried to see her once throughout the day, and since Jordana had set up a mini-beauty salon upstairs in her wing of the house she hadn't had time to see him either. Not that she'd wanted to.

What she was secretly hoping was that he would be glad she was keeping her distance and not make a big deal of it. He might even be happy about it. The last thing a man like Tristan Garrett wanted was a woman to go all starry-eyed over him. Or, even worse, over his precious title!

Which reminded her of how Jordana had said that Tristan was to be partnered with Lady Amanda Sutton at the wedding. A woman Lily had met at lunch earlier that day, who was charming, titled, and completely enamoured of Jordana's brother. Something Tristan hadn't told her about last night while he'd been making love to *her*!

'What was that, dear?'

'Nothing.' Lily smiled pleasantly at Oliver's mother from behind her champagne flute.

Lily let her anger at Tristan's subterfuge course through her. Maybe it was illogical, and maybe even a little unfair seeing as how he wasn't actually dating Amanda Sutton but Lily didn't care. She didn't feel logical right now. Or fair. She felt hurt and stupid and…empty.

Tristan had been magnificent last night. Strong, gentle, masterful, funny—every woman's ideal man come to life. Only he wasn't…or at least he wasn't *her* ideal man. Not that her body seemed to be getting that message. Even now it yearned for her to turn, seek him out, as if he was truly hers to touch and talk with. To laugh with and…

Oh, stop mooning, Lily!

It was time to smile and behave like the perfect maid of honour during the evening's festivities, and to do that she'd clearly have to make sure that any interactions she had with Tristan were later rather than sooner.

Which, okay, wasn't exactly facing her fears head-on—but one step at a time. Come Sunday she'd fly home and lick her wounds. Regroup. Forget Tristan Garrett.

'Lady Grove, Sarah, Talia.' Tristan's deep voice resonated

directly behind her. 'Do you mind if I borrow the maid of honour for a moment?'

'Of course not,' Lady Grove murmured. 'I'm sure you both have final touches to go over before tomorrow.'

'Absolutely.' Tristan smiled. 'Lily?'

Okay, so sooner was probably a good thing. It would mean she could relax for the rest of the night. Or not, she thought as she turned towards Tristan and saw him dressed in a black tuxedo.

Oh, Lord, but he was sublime. And he'd had his hair cut. The mid-length layers framed his masculine features to perfection.

Lily couldn't suppress a shiver of awareness as he took her arm and led her across the polished marble floor to a far corner of the room. Fixing a pleasant smile on her face, she subtly broke free of his hold.

At least this was one scenario she'd had time to plan for. *No tears, no tantrums*, she reminded herself. No matter how much she felt as if she was falling apart inside.

She lifted her glass to her lips and glanced around the room at the other guests, as if she didn't have a care in the world. But Tristan squared off in front of her, his broad shoulders effectively blocking her view and giving her nowhere else to look but directly at him.

'If you think you're sitting next to Hamish Blackstone tonight you've got another thing coming,' he ground out between clenched teeth.

Lily blinked, wide-eyed at his fervent tone. She had no idea what he was talking about.

Tristan knew he had surprised Lily with the dark vehemence in his voice. Hell, he'd shocked himself.

He'd known as soon as he'd laid eyes on her that she was miffed, and he planned to find out what was bothering her and fix it.

He'd thought maybe she was upset that he hadn't brought her

tea up this morning. Or hadn't sought her out during the day. Both theories he'd have put money on, but now he knew she'd taken umbrage at his tone as well, and logically he couldn't blame her.

'Excuse me?' she said with icy disdain.

Yep, she was definitely annoyed with him.

'You heard.' No way was he backing down now. She had to know she wasn't sitting next to anyone but him tonight.

'But maybe *you* didn't,' she said stiffly. 'I'm no longer under your protective custody any more. You're free to get on with your own life. Get on with Lady Sutton.'

Tristan's eyes narrowed. 'What does Amanda have to do with this?'

'She's your guest at the wedding.'

Tristan shoved his hands in his pockets and relaxed back on his heels. She was jealous. Hell, he hadn't even come up with that one. He'd quite forgotten he'd agreed to partner Amanda at the wedding.

'She's no threat to you. She's just a family friend, and she isn't really my guest.'

Lily gave a derisive laugh. 'I'm not threatened.' She tilted her champagne flute towards the light and watched the bubbles fizz. 'But the local grapevine says she wants to be a lot *more* than just a family friend, and she does have the correct *lineage*.'

Tristan frowned. As if he cared about Amanda's lineage... 'Forget Amanda. She's irrelevant.'

'She'd no doubt be upset to hear you say that.'

Tristan frowned. This conversation was not going at all as he'd planned. He declined a glass of champagne as a passing waiter stopped, and determinedly turned his back on an Italian count he'd befriended at Harvard.

'I'd like to thank you for your help in solving my case,' she said politely.

'It was nothing.' Tristan waved away her gratitude.

'Still, I'd like to pay you for your services and—'

'*Pay* me!' Tristan thundered, halting her mid-sentence. 'Don't be absurd, Lily.'

She didn't seem pleased with his response, but no way was she paying him for something he'd wanted to do for her—had *needed* to do for her.

His narrowed eyes lingered on her face. 'Is this because I didn't bring you your tea this morning?'

'I beg your pardon?'

'Don't play games, Lily. You know what I'm talking about.'

She raked him with her gaze and he felt as if she'd actually touched him.

'Or are you upset because I didn't try to see you today?'

'Didn't you? I didn't notice.' She smiled, her wide kohl-rimmed eyes staring at him as if she'd like to slice him in half, her glossy peach-coloured lips clamped together tightly.

He wondered incongruously how the gloss tasted and felt an overpowering need to prise those lips apart and sweep his tongue inside the warm haven of her mouth. At least then they'd be communicating a little better than they were now.

'Look, I'm sorry. I would have but I thought you'd be—Damn, did I mark you?' His eyes had drifted down over her neck to where a slight shadow marred her golden skin.

'Er...no.' She automatically lifted her hand to the exact spot he had been talking about. 'I...scratched myself with the hairbrush.'

He didn't even try to curb the grin that spread across his face. *Hairbrush, my foot.*

'What's wrong?' he murmured softly, deciding it was time to cut to the chase.

She shrugged and glanced over his shoulder at the nearby guests. 'Wrong? What could be wrong?'

'I don't know. That's why I'm asking. But I'm not going to keep at it all night.'

That brought her eyes back to his. 'Is that supposed to be a threat?'

Why couldn't she just be happy he was willing to ask about

her feelings? He knew plenty of his friends who wouldn't have been. Hell, *he* would never have even considered having this type of conversation before Lily. He would have moved on long ago.

So what's different this time?

He couldn't answer his own question and so pushed it aside.

He ran a hand through his hair and shifted the weight on his feet. 'Lily, we had wild, uninhibited sex last night and now you can barely look at me. What's wrong?'

She smoothed at an invisible smudge on her cheek. 'I hardly think this is the place for that type of discussion.'

Tristan let out a frustrated breath. 'I couldn't agree more.' He grabbed hold of her elbow and all but frog-marched her across the room, smiling pleasantly at the familiar faces milling around but avoiding all eye contact.

He reached the side door and drew Lily out into the family's private corridor. She hadn't made a fuss, but then he'd been counting on the fact that she wouldn't.

He stopped beside a spindly hall table that was probably a thousand years old and turned, hands on hips, legs apart. 'Now talk.'

Lily folded her arms across her chest. 'Is this your usual approach after a night with a woman?'

'Don't push me, Lily.'

'Ah—your favourite expression comes out to say hello.'

Tristan's patience was wearing thin, and he knew she knew it. 'What. Is. Wrong?'

'What's wrong? You're behaving like an ape is what's wrong. We had sex. What do you want—a reference?'

'It wasn't just sex,' he denied.

'What was it, then?'

'Great sex.' He smiled—a slow, sensual smile that was meant to cajole her out of her mood. Unfortunately it backfired.

'Oh, well, pardon me. We had *great* sex. What more do you want? It's not like it was anything *special*, was it? I thought you'd be pleased to be able to get on with your life and…' Her voice trailed off and she clamped her lips closed, as if she didn't want to reveal too much of herself or her intentions.

'And what? Now you want to play the field? Get every other man's attention?' That had been his mother's area of expertise. 'You want to get it on with one of Oliver's cousins now that I've broken you in?'

Her shocked gasp reverberated off the vaulted ceiling and he knew his comment had been a low blow. But, dammit, he'd wanted to hear her deny any interest in other men. And now he wished she'd slap him. Anything was better than being stared down by this icy creature who just wanted to get away from him.

'I'm going back in.' She moved towards the door and his hand shot out to stop her.

Something wasn't right. She wasn't anything like his mother and he knew that.

'I'm sorry. That was uncalled for.' His gaze fastened on her face and she stared back at him, her eyes glittering with barely veiled pain.

Then the way she'd spat the word *special* at him, and *get on with your life* registered in the thinking part of his brain.

'You overheard me talking to Jordana this morning.' His tone was accusatory when he hadn't meant it to be, and her eyebrows hit her hairline.

'I wasn't going to embarrass you by mentioning it.'

'I'm not embarrassed.' Actually, he was still trying to recall exactly what he had said. He'd spent most of the day trying not to remember that particular conversation.

He tried to clear his head and think on his feet—something he was usually exceptionally good at, but which was eluding him tonight.

'You weren't meant to hear any of that.'

Lily shrugged as if it didn't matter. 'I'm sure you didn't say anything to Jordana that you wouldn't have said to me if I'd asked.'

Possibly. But hadn't he said he was sick of her case? And

that she wasn't special? And something about his future title? Had he really said she was after that?

Okay, he could understand why she had her back up. He probably would have too if their situations had been reversed.

He shoved his hair from his forehead and smiled at her. 'I know you're not after my title.'

She looked at him as someone might regard a mutant rodent. 'What a relief.'

'And after last night you must *know* I think you're special.'

'How am I special?' she asked immediately.

How was she special? What kind of a question was that?

Tristan tugged at his shirt collar, annoyed when she held her hand up.

'Don't bother answering that. I think I know.' Her voice was full of scorn, and that got *his* back up.

Why the hell did he feel guilty all of a sudden? They were both consenting adults, and she had asked *him* to make love to *her*!

'I didn't hear you complaining last night.'

'That's because I wasn't,' she agreed.

'Then what's the problem?' he asked aggressively.

'There *is* no problem. We had a good time and now it's over.'

'Just like that?'

'You want flowers?'

'Lily—'

She threw her hands up. 'Tristan, I can't do this.'

'Then how about we do this instead?' he murmured throatily, crowding her back against the hallway table, quickly reaching around her to snatch at a teetering vase that was probably two thousand years old.

He righted the vase, coiled his arm around Lily's waist and did what he'd wanted to do all day. Pulled her in close and sealed his lips to hers.

She resisted for maybe half a heartbeat, and then her mouth opened and his tongue swept inside. He groaned at the sheer heaven of her wildfire response and swept his hands down over the gauzy fabric of her dress. She gripped his shoulders and pressed her breasts into his chest. He wished he'd removed his jacket. And his shirt.

'Hmmm, nice gloss.' He licked his lips, tasting…cherries? And then nearly fell over the table himself when she let out a sharp cry and pushed him away from her.

'You *ever* kiss me against my will again and I'll slap you,' she said breathlessly.

'You wanted it,' he said definitely.

'No. *You* wanted it. I'm over it. And get that smug look off your face. Physically you're one heck of a package, but when it comes down to it you've got nothing I want.'

Tristan felt as if a bomb had just gone off in his head. His mind reeled, memories of his mother's words from over a decade ago dragging him under, but he shoved them away with steely determination, blanking the pain that threatened to tear him in half.

What was going on here? Was he actually about to beg? And for what? One more round in the ring? Not even his father had been that stupid. And Tristan could have any number of women. Didn't she know that?

He smiled—a true predator's smile. He'd nearly lost it over this woman and for what? Sex?

Forget it.

'Good to know,' he murmured evenly. 'Because unless you're willing to put out, *Honey Blossom*, you have nothing I want either.'

Lily's chin jerked up and she covered her mouth with the back of her hand and slowly wiped his kiss off before striding down the hallway. It was a good move. An admirable one. And he would have applauded her if she'd hung around.

Thank God he hadn't offered her anything more. Not that he'd been going to. He'd never offered a woman anything more than a good time between the sheets, or on some other serviceable surface, and Lily Wild was no exception.

He swore viciously. He hated her. God, how he hated her.

Making him remember his mother, engaging his emotions like she had. Like some courtesan deliberately setting out to trap him. To make a fool of him.

He glanced down at the antique vase and nearly picked it up and hurled it down the long corridor.

He was happy she was gone because his instincts about her had been right all along: she was nothing but trouble.

CHAPTER FIFTEEN

TROUBLE with a capital *T*, Tristan reminded himself the following morning as he stood beside Oliver in morning suit and top hat at the entrance to the Gothic cathedral, making small talk with yet another expensively dressed wedding guest.

It was a splendid day—except the sun had come out to grace Jordana's big day and brought half the paparazzi in the Western world along with it. No doubt the combined news of Lily's near-arrest and subsequent release and the many royal attendants at Jordana's wedding was causing them to swarm like coachroaches. The local constabulary was also out in force, to keep intruders at bay, as well as a top London security firm that looked as if it employed some of the men from Lily's premiere.

And if Tristan was feeling slightly seedy—well, that was just the Scotch he'd consumed last night, after a dinner that would surely go down as the worst ever. Having to sit next to Amanda Sutton and feign a civility he didn't feel while Lily made eyes at one of the Blackstone boys hadn't exactly put him in the best mood.

'Smile, you great idiot,' Oliver grumbled into his ear. 'It's my wedding day.'

Tristan cut him a dark look and then gracefully bowed over some old dowager's gloved hand.

'And *why* is it, exactly?' he drawled.

'What?'

He waited for Oliver to agree on the splendid weather they were having with the dowager's daughter.

'Your wedding day?'

Oliver looked flummoxed. 'Is that a trick question?'

'You said you'd never give up your freedom for anyone.'

'That was before I fell for your sister.'

'You could have just lived with her.'

Oliver shook his head. 'And have someone steal her away at the first opportunity? I don't think so. Anyway, I want the world to know that she's mine. That we belong together. She's my soul mate, and I can't imagine a life without her in it.'

Tristan fidgeted with the wedding rings in his pocket. 'If that's not already a Hallmark card you could probably sell it to them for a few quid. Carlo!' Tristan shook hands with the Italian count he'd stayed up drinking with last night. 'Good to see you up in time for the ceremony.'

'You didn't tell me there was alcohol in that Scotch last night, Garrett.'

'Hundred-year-old.'

'That's the last of the wedding guests.' The wedding planner stopped in front of them and gave the Count a scathing once-over. 'So,' she spoke to Oliver and Tristan, 'if you'd both like to make your way down to the altar?'

Oliver led the way, and when they finally reached the front of the church straightened Tristan's tie.

'Leave my bloody tie alone.'

Oliver grinned. 'You could just tell her and get it over with,' he whispered.

Tristan scowled. 'Tell who what?'

The harpist started up, and Oliver dashed a hand across his forehead. 'Stop being a coward, Garrett. It's obvious you're in love with her. Just *tell* her.'

Tristan swallowed. Hard. 'Am I supposed to know who you're talking about?'

Oliver threw him a dour look. 'Unfortunately ignoring it or denying it doesn't make it go away. Believe me, I did try.'

Tristan scowled.

'Now, shut up and do your job, would you?' Oliver growled. 'And for God's sake smile—or your sister is likely to make us do this all over again.'

A look of utter joy swept over Oliver's face as he did the non-traditional thing of turning to watch his bride walk down the aisle, and Tristan swallowed heavily as he too turned, his vision immediately filled with Lily walking behind Jordana in a flowing coffee silk and tulle creation that curved around her sublime figure like whipped cream. All the other women decked out in their wedding finery, including Jordana in her delicate couture gown, couldn't hold a torch to his Lily. She was so refined, so poised, and yet so vibrantly alive—and then he knew.

Oliver was right. He loved her. Maybe he'd always loved her. The words slotted into his head like the final piece in a puzzle. Actually, the second to last piece of a puzzle. The final piece was how she felt about *him*…and by the way she avoided eye contact with him as she moved closer he could see that wasn't looking good.

Lily gazed around at the grand ballroom of the manor house Jordana had chosen for her wedding reception. It was filled with circular tables, each with an enormous central flower arrangement and ringed with white cloth-covered chairs tied with bows at the back.

Jordana and Oliver's wedding day had been picture-perfect and she'd never seen her friend happier. Jordana's beautiful face was still aglow as she chatted and smiled contentedly with her wedding guests.

'I wanted to thank you for being such a good friend to my daughter, Miss Wild.' The eleventh Duke of Greythorn surprised her as he stopped beside Lily's chair.

'Actually, Your Grace, it is I who feels blessed to have Jordana's friendship.' Lily smiled, completely thrown by the

Duke's open warmth when previously, she knew, he hadn't approved of her at all.

'Tristan has informed me of all that you have done for Jordana over the years, and I know that if your parents were alive today they would be very proud of the person you have become.'

Lily felt tears prick behind her eyes, and if she'd been standing she would have dropped into a curtsey in front of this stately gentleman. He seemed to sense her overpowering emotions and patted her hand, telling her to enjoy her evening, and Lily watched slightly dumbstruck as he returned to his seat at the head of the table.

'Ladies and gentlemen.' The MC spoke over the top of the band members tuning their instruments and drew her attention away from the Duke. 'If I could please ask Earl and Countess Blackstone and their attendants Lord Tristan Garrett and Miss Lily Wild to take to the floor for the bridal waltz?'

The bridal waltz? Already?

Lily glanced around the room and noticed that Tristan had stopped conversing at a table in the opposite corner and was staring at her intently.

No way. She couldn't dance with him. She smiled serenely as she quickly threaded a path through the cluster of guests milling around on her pre-planned escape to the toilets.

She had managed to avoid being alone with Tristan the whole day, and had already decided that there was no way she could dance with him tonight without giving away just how broken-hearted she felt.

The band struck up a quintessential love song and Lily fairly flew out of the room—and right into Tristan's arms.

'Going somewhere?' he mocked.

Lily tried to steady her runaway heartbeat. 'The bathroom.'

'During the bridal waltz? I don't think so.'

'You can't dictate to me any more, remember?'

'No, but it's your last official obligation for the day, and I didn't take you for a shirker.'

Lily huffed out a breath and noticed the interested glances from the guests around them. 'I'll do it because it's expected,' she stated under her breath. 'Not because you challenged me.'

Tristan smiled. 'That's my girl.'

Lily was about to correct him and say that she wasn't his girl, but they were on the dance floor and he had already swept her into his arms.

She held herself so stiffly she felt like a mechanised doll, but there was nothing she could do about that. She couldn't relax, couldn't look at him. Then she remembered an old childhood trick she'd used to employ when she was in an uncomfortable situation. Counting. Once, she remembered, she'd counted so high she'd made it to seven hundred and thirty-five!

'You look exquisite today.' Tristan's eyes glittered down into hers and Lily quickly planted her gaze at a spot over his shoulder. One, two, three…

'But then you look exquisite all the time.'

Nine, ten…

He swirled her suddenly, and she frowned as she had to grip him tighter to stop herself from falling. He was wearing a new cologne tonight and the hint of spice was doing horrible things to her equilibrium. Nineteen, twenty…

'How's Hamish?'

Lily looked at him. She knew why he was asking that. She had found out from Jordana in a fit of giggles last night that her 'surprise' was to be set up with any of Oliver's three single cousins. Which was what Tristan had been so angrily referring to when they'd talked prior to dinner last night.

She hadn't known about Jordana's cunning plan then, and she knew Tristan's ego had been bruised when Jordana had fooled him into believing that Lily had welcomed her attempts at matchmaking. Which she hadn't. And she had apologised profusely to each of the men when she'd told them that actually she wasn't available.

They'd been completely charming, and she'd wished things were different so she might have been in a better position to invite their interest. But of course she wasn't. Her feelings for Tristan were too real and too raw for her to even attempt friendship with another man at this point.

Clearly Tristan's ego was still affected, if the way he was studying her was any indication.

'Fine, I expect,' she answered.

Tristan scowled and brought her hand in tightly against his chest. His other hand was spread wide against that sensitive spot in the small of her back. He was holding her so closely now Lily could hear the brush of her tulle skirt against his trousers.

Lily swallowed and concentrated on holding in the quiver that zipped up her spine, completely forgetting what number she was up to. *Damn.* One, two…

'Are you counting?' Tristan's deep voice was incredulous.

'Would you stop talking?' she whispered furiously, trying hard to ignore the growing tension in his big body.

Then he stopped dancing altogether, and Lily became acutely aware of the murmur of voices and the soft sway of Jordana's silk gown as she moved in time with the music. Lily stood in the circle of Tristan's arms, glancing around nervously at the interested faces of the wedding guests circling the dance floor.

She was just about to ask him what he was doing when he made a low sound in the back of his throat. 'Oh, to hell with it,' he muttered, deftly hoisting her and her close-fitted tulle skirts into his arms. 'Excuse us,' he threw at a surprised Oliver and Jordana as he strode past.

'What are you doing?' Lily squeaked, smiling tremulously as if nothing untoward was going on when it definitely was.

'Keep still,' he ordered, and Lily, not wishing to make any more of a scene, ducked her head into his neck just as she had done at the airport a little over a week ago, to hide her face from the amused glances of the wedding guests who were parting like the Red Sea to let Tristan through.

'Oh, I hate to imagine what everyone is going to think!' she fumed, scowling at the smiling waiter who had *kindly* held open the door to a smaller, private dining room and who was now in the process of closing it behind them.

She glared at Tristan, her heart beating a mile a minute, as he let her down, and stalked to the other side of the room, feeling marginally calmer with a two-metre-long mahogany dining table between them.

Tristan stood with his hands in his pockets and stared at her. 'They'll think I'm in love, I expect. Either that...' He paused as if to gauge her reaction. 'Or they'll think I've lost my mind.'

'Well, we both know the former isn't the truth,' she snapped. 'Don't play games with me, Tristan. I don't like them.'

Tristan blew out a breath. 'Lily, I need to talk to you, and this seemed the only way to achieve that objective.' He circled the table towards her, and stopped when he realised she was moving as well—but in the opposite direction. 'Would you stop that? I'm not going to bite you.'

Lily stared at him. He was so rakishly appealing with his ruffled hair and formal wedding attire it made her heart feel as if it was enclosed in a giant fist. She felt her old survival instincts rise up and did her best to blank out the pain of being so close to him and yet so far away.

'I'm getting a little tired of you thinking you can pick me up and carry me wherever you want. Next time it happens I won't be so concerned about creating a scene,' she warned with haughty disdain.

'Would you have come if I'd asked?'

His voice was soft, almost like a caress, and it confused her senses. Made her body soften. Lily did her best to clamp down on the rioting emotions running through her and focused on his question.

She lifted her chin and tried to stop her lips from trembling. Of course she wouldn't have come with him. She had nothing to say to him that wouldn't involve making a complete fool of herself.

'Say what you have to say so we can get out of here. I

don't have much time left,' she added, thankful that her voice sounded steadier than she felt.

'Time left for what?'

Lily noted Tristan's sharp tone and decided now was not the time to tell him she was booked on the red-eye back to New York this very evening. After enduring the rehearsal dinner and feeling so tense a slight breeze might have snapped her in half she had changed her travel plans so she could head back to London and fly home to New York early.

Being around Tristan and watching him smoulder with Lady Sutton last night had nearly done her in. She loved him too much to imagine him with another woman, so seeing him with one who could offer him everything she couldn't was just unendurable. Better that she start her life again without him as soon as possible. Facing her fears head-on...or perhaps just running away. She didn't care which at this point. Her only criteria was that when she finally broke down she did so in private.

Lily steeled herself to look at him and lifted her gaze once more to his. He stood across the table from her, his expression as fierce as an angry warlord facing down a known enemy. She had no idea why. Had something happened earlier that she didn't know about and for which she was about to get the blame again?

'Are you going to answer my question?' he asked, almost too politely.

'Are you going to answer mine?' she parried.

Tristan exhaled and ran an agitated hand through his hair. He looked tired and strung out—very unlike his usually composed self.

'Lily this doesn't have to end.'

Lily, stared at him, not sure what he was referring to.

'*We* don't have to end,' he clarified, a strange, shadowed look settling on his face.

Lily wet her dry mouth. All she could think about was how last night he had confirmed that he really didn't want her. That she had just been an itch he had wanted to scratch. 'Last night you said…'

'Please forget what I said last night. I was hurt and angry.'

'Hurt?'

Tristan gripped the back of the upholstered dining chair in front of him. This conversation was not going at all the way he had hoped. Lily was supposed to have picked up on his lame declaration of love and thrown herself into his arms. Instead she was spitting at him and looking much the same way she had when she'd felt she had to defend her honour after they had made love that first time.

Okay, so maybe he wasn't going about this very well. But he'd never told a woman he loved her before. Had never *wanted* to love a woman before. Opening up about his emotions wasn't exactly his strong suit after years of holding them at bay.

He cleared his throat, more nervous now than he had been during his first courtroom appearance—which, come to think of it, he hadn't been nervous about at all…'Lily, I'd like to say something to you and if you still want to leave after that then I won't try and stop you.'

Lily stared at him, seemingly transfixed, as he walked slowly around the table and pulled out one of the dining chairs for her to sit down in.

She slid into it, almost with relief, and Tristan paced a short way away and then stopped, turning to face her.

'I told you the other night that my mother left my father, but what I haven't told you is that on the day she left, when I was fifteen, I overheard my parents arguing. During the argument my mother told my father she hated him and that he had nothing she wanted—that I also had nothing she wanted and that she was taking Jordana with her and not me.'

'Oh, Tristan.'

He held up his hand gently and shook his head. 'I'm not telling you this so you'll feel sorry for me. It has no doubt coloured my past relationships, as your parents have coloured yours, but I need you to understand something. My mother was not an easy woman to love but God knows I tried. There was a big age gap between myself and Jordana and for a while I was my mother's saviour. Her little hero. Then Jordana arrived, my father started working more, and I became relegated to the sidelines. I never understood why, and slowly, over the years, I learned to protect myself by switching my feelings off. I became angry with my mother and blamed myself. Two nights ago you inadvertently helped me see that what I hadn't understood was that my parents just had an unhappy marriage and I was one of the victims of that.'

'Parents often don't see the impact they have on their children when they aren't happy within themselves.' Lily offered softly.

'No.' Tristan shook his head. 'And it certainly put me off wanting to risk my heart with another person, but…' He looked down at Lily's small hand enfolded in his, not even having realised that he had reached out to her. 'Lily, the other night I accused you of using your past as a shield, and I've only just come to realise that I do the same thing. I've put up barriers to my emotions my whole life because my mother's love was so unpredictable and my parents' relationship was so unstable and I don't want to do that any more. Actually, that's not completely true.' He looked up sheepishly. 'If I could still do that I probably would. But if I do I'll lose you, and after you walked away last night I realised that's more painful than everything else put together.'

Lily swallowed and looked down at their enclosed hands, then slowly back up to reconnect with his eyes. 'Why?'

Tristan leaned forward and kissed her. A kiss filled with all the love and tenderness he had been afraid to show her until now. He pulled back and waited for her eyes to flutter open. 'Because I love you, Lily. I think I always have.'

Lily shook her head, her expression dazed. 'You love me?'

'With all my heart. And the more I say it, the more I want to say it.'

'But you never approved of me...'

'Partly true. I disliked your lifestyle because I was always worried that Jordana would go the way my mother had, but really what I resented about you the most was how protective I felt towards you. Whenever I heard you were at one of your stepfather's parties, and I was in the country, I always came and got you out. I even did it once when Jordana wasn't with you. Remember?'

'I assumed you thought she *was* with me.'

'No. I knew she was home safe—and that's just where I wanted you to be. But it wasn't until Jo's eighteenth that my feelings for you changed. As soon as I saw you in that silver mini-dress I knew I couldn't deny that my feelings for you were more than just protective. I wanted you so much that night it hurt. But you were too young, and I was too closed to my emotions, and then when I came across that private party it was easy to blame you. It gave me an excuse to turn my back on the way you made me feel. But you changed me that night. I haven't been able to look at a woman since, be with a woman, without imagining she was you. Crazy, I know...'

'Not so crazy.' Lily reached up and almost reverently cupped his face. 'I fell so deeply in love with you that night I've compared every other man I've ever met to you and found him lacking.'

'Lily, does that mean what I think it means?'

Lily smiled and blinked back the tears blurring her vision. 'That I love you? Totally. Completely. How could you not know?'

Tristan felt such a deep surge of joy well up inside him he thought it would burst out. He grabbed Lily off the chair and hauled her onto his lap, crushed her mouth beneath his.

When he finally let her up for air he felt a sense of rightness with the world, but he could see by the way she gnawed her top lip that she still had questions.

'What is it?'

'I was just remembering yesterday morning, when you came

out of the bathroom. You looked…you looked unhappy…and then you told Jordana—'

'Oh, Lily,' Tristan said on a groan. 'Please forget that. I woke up that morning with such a sense of well-being it scared the hell out of me. Honestly, I just wanted to get away from you. I've never woken up with a woman before and—'

'Never?'

He shook his head. 'Never. And then Jordana cornered me and guessed how I felt before I did and it drove me deeper into denial. I didn't want to let you in, Lily, but of course you were already there, and I was fighting a losing battle. It wasn't until Oliver told me how he felt about Jordana and the reasons he was marrying her that I finally realised I felt the same way about you. And I didn't want to fight it—you—any more. I'd do anything for you, Lily, and after we're married we'll—'

'Married!'

'Of course married. Where did you think this was headed, sweetheart? A picnic in the park?'

'I…I didn't think that far ahead. I'm still reeling from the fact that you love me.'

'I know neither of us has had the best role models when it comes to marriage—'

'Well, my father never actually asked my mother to marry him,' Lily said.

Tristan nodded and cupped her face between his hands. 'I'm not your father, Lily. I'll never cheat on you or leave you. And I don't believe a marriage has to be full of conflict if a couple are equally committed and willing to work through any issues together.'

Lily's smile was tremulous. 'You really love me?'

'Haven't I just said that?'

'It just seems like a dream.'

'It's not. At least I hope it's not.'

Lily sighed and let Tristan gather her close, revelling in the feel of his hands moulding to her torso and fitting her against him. She could hardly believe this was happening, and knew Jordana would be ecstatic when she found out.

Then a thought struck, and she pulled back a little to look up into his beautiful face. 'You know I knew nothing about Jordana setting me up with Oliver's cousins last night?'

Tristan smiled. 'I know. I figured that out some time between the first and second bottle of Scotch I consumed last night.'

'Oh.' Lily laughed.

'It's not funny.' He grinned back at her. 'You were the reason I saw the bottom of both of those bottles. But I have a feeling that my sister has been playing a little reverse matchmaking between us.'

'I did wonder about that myself...'

'And it worked. I nearly locked you in a tower last night after she said you'd told her you were just cutting loose with me.'

'I *did* say that.'

'What?' he asked, stunned.

'I didn't want her to know how deeply I had fallen for you and after overhearing how you felt. I...I have my pride, you know.'

'I know you do.'

'And, anyway, you don't have a tower.'

'I'd have built one for just that purpose,' he growled, his hands exploring the fitted bodice of her gown with increasing fervour.

'I love you,' Lily sighed.

'I never knew those three little words could sound so delicious.'

'Oh, I've just remembered. I'm supposed to be flying to New York tonight. I'll have to cancel the flight.'

'Damned straight. But when *do* you have to return to New York? For work?'

'I don't have any films lined up until next year. I was planning to take some time off.'

'Perfect.'

'Although...'

'Although?'

'I'm thinking of taking the role of my mother in that play I was telling you about.'

Tristan kissed her. 'I think that's a wonderful idea. You'll slay them. As you do me. Now, let's go upstairs.'

'Upstairs?'

'I organised a room.'

'But the Abbey is only two miles away.'

'That's two miles too far if I'm going to be able to make love to you with any level of skill and control.'

'I'm quite partial to what we've done so far,' Lily whispered, feathering the silky hair at his nape between her fingers.

'And I'm quite partial to you, my darling Honey Blossom Lily Wild.'

He bent to kiss her again but Lily dodged him. 'We have your sister's wedding to finish first.'

'Believe me, after the way we exited the dance floor nobody is expecting to see us back any time soon.'

'But I need to catch the bridal bouquet,' Lily protested as Tristan gathered her up in his arms and strode for the door.

'Why do you need a bouquet when you've got your groom right here?'

'I hadn't thought of that,' she admitted provocatively. 'Good thing you're here.'

Tristan stopped and caught her chin between his thumb and forefinger, raising her eyes to his. 'I'll always be here for you,' he said, capturing her lips in a sweet, searing kiss.

Lily's mouth trembled with emotion as she stared into Tristan's loving green gaze, happier than she had ever been in her whole life. 'And I you.'

* * * * *

THE END OF
HER INNOCENCE

BY
SARA CRAVEN

Sara Craven was born in South Devon and grew up in a house full of books. She worked as a local journalist, covering everything from flower shows to murders, and started writing for Mills & Boon in 1975. When not writing, she enjoys films, music, theatre, cooking, and eating in good restaurants. She now lives near her family in Warwickshire. Sara has appeared as a contestant on the former Channel Four game show *Fifteen to One*, and in 1997 was the UK television *Mastermind* champion. In 2005 she was a member of the Romantic Novelists' team on *University Challenge—the Professionals*.

Sara Craven was born in South Devon and grew up in a house full of books. She worked as a local journalist, covering everything from flower shows to murder trials, before writing for Mills & Boon in 1975 when not writing. She enjoys films, music, theatre, cooking, and eating in good restaurants. She now lives near the sea in Warwickshire. Sara has appeared as a contestant on the former *Mastermind* Round game show *Brain of Britain* and in 1997 was the UK Champion in *Mastermind*. In 1997 she was a member of the Romantic Novelists' Association's former *Chairman*. *She Packs a Punch.*

CHAPTER ONE

'BUT, Chloe, I need you with us. I'm counting on you.' Mrs Armstrong opened limpid blue eyes to their widest extent. 'I thought you knew that.'

She paused. 'Besides, just think of it—an entire summer in the South of France. And we'll be away quite a lot, so you'd have the villa all to yourself. Now, isn't that tempting?'

'Yes, it is,' Chloe Benson returned equably. 'But, as I said when I handed in my notice, madam, I have my own plans.'

And staying in domestic service, no matter how gold-plated and lucrative, is not among them, she added silently. Nice try, Dilys baby, but no thanks.

'Well, I'm very disappointed.' Mrs Armstrong's tone took on the faint peevishness which was her nearest approach to animation. 'And I don't know what my husband will say.'

He'll say, 'Bad luck, old thing,' then go back to the *Financial Times*, just as he always does, Chloe thought, biting back a smile.

'If it's a question of money.' Mrs Armstrong allowed her perfect brow to wrinkle. 'If you've had a better offer, I'm sure we could come to some arrangement.'

On the contrary, Chloe wanted to tell her, it's love rather than money that's luring me away.

She allowed herself a happy moment to think about Ian. To summon up the image of his tall, broad-shouldered frame,

his curling brown hair and smiling blue eyes. To imagine
the moment when she'd go into his arms and say, 'I've come
home, darling, and this time it's for good. Just name the day
and I'll be there.'

She shook her head. 'It's nothing like that, madam. I've
simply decided to take a different career direction.'

'But what a waste, when you're so good at what you do.'

What talent did you really require for saying, 'Yes, madam,
very good madam?' Chloe wondered with faint exasperation.
For organising the smooth running of a house with every
modern convenience known to the mind of man and then
some. For making sure the other members of staff did their
jobs efficiently.

Whatever might be happening in the City, billionaire Hugo
Armstrong wanted an untroubled existence at his country
home, Colestone Manor. He was bored by day-to-day domestic detail, requiring any problems to be dealt with quickly
and unobtrusively, the bills paid, and his guests offered the
luxurious environment of a top hotel.

Quite simply, he asked for perfection, with the minimum
effort on his part, and, during her tenure as housekeeper,
Chloe had ensured that he got it.

She knew she was young for the job and she would have a
lot to prove, but she was bright, energetic and a good organ-
iser used to hard work, as her previous references attested.

Her responsibilities were manifold, her hours long, but
her astonishing salary more than compensated for these and
other inconveniences.

She was not, of course, expected to have any life of her
own. Christmas and Easter were busy times at the Manor. She
had not even been able to attend Uncle Hal and Aunt Libby's
thirtieth wedding anniversary, because the Armstrongs had
arranged a large house-party that weekend, and couldn't spare
her. Her salary that month had been augmented by a large

bonus, but it hardly made up for missing out on such a special occasion with people she loved, the only real family she'd ever had, and she still had feelings of guilt about it.

But she'd always known that the job was twenty-four-seven while it lasted. And now her notice was nearly up, and it was only going to last another week.

Losing her might cause her employers some temporary annoyance, she reflected as she went back to her quarters, but no-one was indispensable, and the Belgravia agency would supply a replacement for her with the minimum of fuss, so she was hardly leaving them in the lurch.

The computer in the housekeeper's office was regularly updated with details of the shops that delivered the Manor's supplies, and the tradesmen who provided any services required, plus the family's food preferences, fads and fancies, as well as a complete rundown on all meals served to guests over the past six months, and the bedrooms they'd occupied where appropriate.

Her successor, she thought with satisfaction, should enjoy a seamless takeover.

She would miss her flat, she admitted as she closed its door behind her and looked around. Though small, it was self-contained, and luxuriously equipped with its own wet room, an expensive fitted galley kitchen, and a queen-sized bed dominating the bedroom.

It would seem odd sleeping in the modest room at Axford Grange again, with Aunt Libby filling a hot-water bottle for her whether she needed it or not, and popping in to say goodnight, but it would not be for long.

Maybe Ian would want her to move in with him before they were married, she thought pleasurably. And if he did, she would agree without the slightest hesitation. It was more than time his patient wooing was rewarded. In fact, she couldn't understand why she'd held back for so long. At twenty-five and still a virgin, she was beginning to feel as if she was part of an endangered species.

And yet she'd remained celibate entirely through her own choice. Her creamy skin, tip-tilted hazel eyes with their long lashes and warmly curving mouth had attracted plenty of male attention since her teens.

She'd been sixteen when Ian arrived at the Grange on placement from his veterinary college and, almost from the first, she'd been sure that they were meant for each other.

As soon as he was qualified, he'd come back to work in her uncle's busy practice, and he was now a full partner.

Soon he'll be my partner too, she thought and smiled to herself.

He'd proposed for the first time just after she'd left university, but she'd demurred, knowing she wanted to test her newly fledged wings. She'd planned to work as a magazine journalist but jobs in the industry proved elusive, and as a temporary measure she'd joined an agency offering domestic help. Most of her friends at college had worked in bars or waited on restaurant tables to supplement their money, but Chloe, with Aunt Libby's training behind her, opted for cleaning jobs instead, working in the early mornings and earning a reputation for being reliable, fast and thorough.

She'd just laughed when she was nicknamed Chloe the Char, retorting 'honest work for honest pay'. Her view on that had never changed.

Ian had not been at all happy when she told him she'd been offered the job at Colestone Manor.

'It's one hell of a distance from here,' he'd protested. 'I thought you were going to find something locally. That we were going to have some real time together at last.'

'And so we shall,' she said. 'But it's also a chance to make some real money.'

'I'm not exactly earning peanuts,' he returned, his mouth tightening. 'You won't be living in penury.'

'I know.' She kissed him. 'But have you any idea what even the smallest wedding costs these days? And Uncle Hal and Aunt Libby have done so much for me all my life. This is one expense I can spare them. Besides, the time will soon pass. You'll see.'

Only it hadn't, and Chloe wondered sometimes whether she'd have taken the job if she'd realised how all-consuming it was, with the Armstrongs quite reasonably expecting her to be at their beck and call all day and every day.

Communication with Ian and the family over the past year had been largely through hurried notes and phone calls. Not a satisfactory state of affairs by any means.

But all that was behind her now, she thought, and she could concentrate on the future and turning herself into the ideal niece and the perfect fiancée.

Because of her savings, of course, she didn't even need to find another job—not immediately. So, she could take her time. Look around. Find the right thing, and stick to it for a couple of years until they decided to start a family.

It was all going to work out perfectly, she told herself and sighed with contentment.

She was waiting for the coffee percolator to finish brewing, when she heard a knock, and Tanya, the nanny to the Armstrong twins put her head round the door.

'The rumour mill is working overtime,' she announced. 'Tell me it's wrong for once, and you're not leaving after all.'

'Oh, but I am.' Chloe smiled at her and took down a second beaker.

'Tragedy.' Tanya slumped into a chair, stretching out long legs, her pretty freckled face disconsolate. 'Where can I go for sanity when the brats are driving me mad?'

'What have you done with them at the moment? Tied them to chairs in the nursery?'

'Dilys is taking them to a tea party—mummies only,' Tanya said grimly. 'I wish her luck.'

'My sympathies are with the hostess,' Chloe returned, pouring the coffee.

'Well, spare a thought for me. I'll be the one left holding the baby—literally—in the South of France while Dilys and Hugo do the Grand Tour from villa to villa and yacht to yacht,' Tanya said moodily. 'The only thing holding me together was the prospect of you being there too. I was sure she'd persuade you. Get you to withdraw your notice.'

'She certainly tried,' Chloe said cheerfully, handing her a beaker. 'But no dice. I'm off to get a life.'

'You have a new job lined up?'

'Not as such.' Chloe hesitated. 'Actually, I'm going to be married.'

Tanya's eyes went to her bare left hand. 'To that vet you mentioned back home? I didn't know you were even engaged.'

'Well, it's strictly unofficial as yet. I wasn't ready before when he asked me, but, now, settling down seems like a really great thing to do, so,' she added, smiling, 'I'm going to do it.'

'Won't village life seem tame after all this glitz and glamour?'

Chloe shook her head. 'I've never bought into it, any more than you have. I know my priorities and this job was always just a means to an end.

'Apart from getting my hair cut once a month,' she went on, running a hand through her mop of dark curls. 'And having the odd cinema and pizza jaunt with you when we could get time off together, I've hardly spent a thing. So I have a lot of money sitting in the bank right now.'

Her smile widened. 'Enough to pay for a wedding, certainly, and also contribute to the updating of Ian's cottage, which it sorely needs. Together, we can make it wonderful.'

Tanya's brows lifted. 'Does Ian share this view?'

Chloe sighed humorously. 'He seems to think all a kitchen requires is a stove, a sink and a second-hand fridge. Also that a rusting bath is a valuable antique. I intend to educate him.'

'Well, good luck to that.' Tanya raised her beaker in a faintly ironic toast. 'But maybe he's already put in a new kitchen in honour of your return. Did you think of that?'

'He doesn't yet know I'm coming back. I want to surprise him.'

'Christmas!' Tanya eyed her quizzically. 'You must be very sure of him.'

'I'm sure of us both,' Chloe told her serenely. 'And I can't wait to get back to Willowford.' She sighed again. 'I've missed it so much.'

'It must be a hell of a place to coax you away from the Riviera,' Tanya commented. 'What's so special about it?'

'Well, it's not exactly picture-postcard stuff,' Chloe said, frowning. 'There are no thatched roofs, and the church is Victorian. Although the Hall is considered rather splendid— Jacobean with later additions.'

'And does it have a squire who twirls his moustaches and chases the village maidens?'

Chloe's smile held faint constraint. 'I don't think that's Sir Gregory's style,' she said, after a pause. 'Even if his arthritis allowed it.'

'Is he married?'

Chloe shook her head. 'A widower.'

'Children?'

'Two sons.'

'The heir and the spare,' said Tanya. 'Very conventional.'

Chloe bit her lip. 'Not really, because the spare doesn't

feature much any more. There was a gigantic rift a few years ago, and he became *persona non grata*.'

'Aha.' Tanya's eyes gleamed. 'This is more like it. What happened?'

Chloe looked away. 'He had an affair with his older brother's wife,' she said at last. 'Broke up the marriage. All very sordid and nasty. So his father threw him out.'

'What happened to the wife?'

'She left too.'

'So are they together? She and—what do they call him?—I can't go on saying "the spare".'

'Darius,' Chloe said. 'Darius Maynard. And I don't think anyone knows where he is or what happened to him. Or even cares, for that matter.'

Tanya drew a deep breath. 'Well the place is clearly a seething mass of steaming passion and illicit desire. I can see why you want to get in on the action. And the heir needs another wife, presumably.' She gave a wicked wink. 'Maybe you could do better than a country vet.'

'No way.' Chloe drained her beaker. 'To be honest, I think quite a few people found Andrew Maynard a bit of a stuffed shirt and didn't altogether blame Penny, who was incredibly beautiful, for looking around. But Darius already had a bad name locally, so no-one ever thought he'd be the one to get a second glance.'

Tanya's eyes gleamed. 'What sort of bad name?'

'Expelled from school. Drinking, gambling, mixing with the local wild bunch. Parties that people only whispered about behind their hands.' Chloe shrugged. 'Plus rumours that he was involved in other even worse things—illegal dog fighting, for instance.' She added bleakly, 'No-one was sorry to see him go, believe me.'

'Well, for all that, he sounds more interesting than his brother.' Tanya finished her coffee and stood up. 'I'd better get back. I thought while the monsters were missing, I could fumigate the toy cupboards.'

Left alone, Chloe washed out the beakers and put them in the drying rack.

For the life of her, she could not fathom why she'd told Tanya all that stuff about the Maynard family. It was seven years since it had happened, she thought, and should have been relegated long ago to some mental dump bin.

She suddenly had an image of a man's face, tanned and arrogant, nose and cheekbones strongly, almost harshly, sculpted, the mouth wide and sensual. From beneath a swathe of dirty-blond hair, compelling green eyes had stared at the world with disdain, as if daring it to judge him.

Yet it had done so, and, starting with his father, had condemned him as guilty. The adulterer who'd betrayed his brother and been sentenced to exile as a result. Although that could have been no real hardship for Darius Maynard, she thought. He'd always been restless and edgy. Willowford was far too small and tame a world for him and always had been.

But it suits me just fine, she told herself, biting her lip. It's a decent little place with good people. Somewhere to put down roots and raise the next generation. It gave me a loving home when I was a small baby, and now it's given me Ian. It's security.

Sir Gregory had been part of that, she thought. A large, rather forbidding man, but rock-solid like his house. A pillar of his community, as the saying was. And Andrew Maynard was much the same. An outdoor man with a passion for climbing, more conventionally handsome than his younger brother, courteous and faintly aloof. Part of a continuing line or so it had seemed.

Except, 'Thank heaven there are no children to be hurt,' Aunt Libby had said quietly when the scandal broke.

But Darius had always been different—the joker in the pack. A throwback to some other, wilder time with his dangerous mocking smile, and cool smoky drawl.

My God—little Chloe grown up at last. Who'd have thought it?

She was suddenly aware she was gripping the edge of the sink so hard that her fingers were hurting, and released it hastily with a little gasp.

Memories were risky things, rather like pushing a stick to the bottom of a tranquil pool and watching the mud and debris rise. Far better, she thought, to let the water remain still and unsullied in case it never truly cleared again.

Oh, get a grip, she told herself impatiently as she returned to the sitting room. *Put your microscope away.*

It had all happened long ago, and should remain in the past where it belonged. If not forgotten, then ignored, as if Sir Gregory had only ever had one son. And as if that son had never married the Honourable Penelope Hatton and brought her back to Willowford Hall to tempt and be disastrously tempted in her turn.

I thought she was the most beautiful thing I'd ever seen, thought Chloe. *We all did. I think I even envied her.*

But now everything's changed. I'm the one looking forward to a happy future with the man I love. And, if she knew, she might well be the one envying me.

It had been raining first thing when she set off from Colestone, but now the skies seemed to be clearing and a watery sun was showing its face.

A good omen, Chloe thought happily, switching the car radio to a music station, and humming along as she drove.

Rather to her surprise, she'd found herself genuinely sorry to leave the Manor. After all, she mused, it had been the focus of her attention for the past year. Besides, however indolent and self-absorbed they might be, the Armstrongs had been generous employers in the only way they knew, and she'd liked the other staff.

In the bag beside her on the passenger seat was the pretty carriage clock they'd bought her as a farewell present, and she'd been moved almost to tears as she thanked them and promised it pride of place on her future mantelpiece.

'As for you,' she'd muttered as she hugged Tanya. 'I'm going to be needing a bridesmaid.'

'Happy to oblige,' Tanya whispered back. 'Unless I get arrested for twin-strangling in the meantime.'

Her successor had arrived—a widow in her forties with a brisk air. She had dismissed Chloe's computer system, saying that she had her own methods, at the same time running a suspicious finger along the office windowsill in search of non-existent dust.

Life at the Manor, Chloe thought wryly as she wished her luck, could become quite interesting quite soon.

She stopped at a roadside pub for a lunch of ham sandwiches and coffee to fuel her for the final two hours of her journey, choosing a table outside in a sheltered corner of the garden where bees were busy among the honeysuckle.

With the excitement of all the coming reunions bubbling away inside her, she almost had to force herself to eat.

As she poured her second cup of coffee, she reached into her bag for her mobile phone.

She'd called Aunt Libby again the previous evening to tell her what time she hoped to arrive, and while her aunt had seemed her usual warm self, Chloe had detected another faint nuance beneath the welcoming words.

'Is something wrong?' she'd asked at last. Libby Jackson had hesitated.

'I was wondering if you'd spoken to Ian yet—informed him you were coming home, this time for good.'

'But I told you, Aunt Libby, I want to surprise him.'

'Yes, darling, so you said.' Another pause. 'But I can't help thinking that a complete change of your whole life-plan like this, which involves him so closely, really needs some prior warning.'

'Not unless he's developed some serious heart condition and you think the shock could kill him.' Chloe was amused. 'Is that it?'

'God forbid,' said her aunt. 'When last seen, he looked as strong as a horse. But I keep thinking of these dreadful surprise parties people keep giving, which I'm sure are far more fun for the organisers than the recipients. Just a thought, my dear.'

And maybe it was a good one, Chloe decided, clicking on Ian's number. But it went straight to voicemail, indicating that he was working. So she left a message then rang the cottage, and announced herself on the answer-phone too.

Belt and braces, Aunt Libby, she thought. So now he should be ready and waiting.

She smiled to herself as she replaced the phone, imagining the smile in his eyes when he saw her, the warmth of his arms around her, and the touch of his lips on hers.

He was so worth waiting for, she thought gratefully. And now she was back, she would not leave again.

She had five miles still to go when the petrol warning light suddenly appeared on the dashboard, when only fifteen minutes before it had been registering half-full.

Chloe wrinkled her nose, wondering which was the true reading. 'Memo to self,' she murmured. 'Take the car to Tom Sawley's garage and get the gauge seen to. Particularly before the MOT becomes due again.'

Fortunately, she was approaching a turning for the main road, where there was a small filling station only a few hundred yards away.

All three pumps were busy when she arrived, so she joined the shortest queue, and got out of the car stretching.

And then she saw it, parked over by the wall, its number plate as familiar to her as that of her own car.

Ian's jeep, she thought joyously. What was more, the bonnet was up, and there he was bending over the engine with his back to her, his long legs encased in blue denim, as he made some adjustment.

She was sure he would sense her presence and turn, but he was leaning too far over, intent on what he was doing.

As soon as she was within touching distance, she reached for him, her mouth curving mischievously as she ran her fingers over the taut male buttocks and slid one hand between his thighs.

He yelped and sprang upright, cursing as he hit his head on the bonnet.

And as he did so, Chloe backed away gasping, praying for the ground to open up beneath her.

But it remained heartlessly intact, so that she was still there, open-mouthed with horror when the man swung round, and looked at her, his blond hair tousled, and the green eyes blazing.

'What the bloody hell do you think you're playing at?' asked Darius Maynard, his voice a snarl of pure anger. 'Or have you just gone raving mad?'

CHAPTER TWO

CHLOE took another step backwards, aware that she was burning from the soles of her feet up to her hairline, and probably beyond.

Oh, God, let me wake up, she prayed frantically, and find this is only a nightmare.

When she could speak, she said hoarsely, 'You—*you!* What are you doing with Ian's jeep?'

'Correction,' he said brusquely. 'My jeep for the past eight weeks. Cartwright was trading it in for a newer model and I bought it.'

'You've been back here for two months?'

'For over six, actually.' He added curtly, 'If it's any concern of yours, Miss Benson.'

Her flush deepened, if that was possible. 'I—I didn't realise.'

What on earth was going on? she wondered. Why had he returned when his banishment was supposed to have been permanent? How could that kind of breach possibly have been healed? Sir Gregory surely wasn't the type to welcome back the prodigal son. And how did Andrew, the betrayed husband, feel about it?

Above all, why had no-one mentioned it? How was it Ian hadn't said, 'By the way, I've sold my jeep, and to Darius Maynard of all people.'

'Why would you know?' He hunched an indifferent shoulder. 'You haven't been around much to catch up on the local sensations.'

'I've been working.'

'Most people do,' he said. 'Or are you claiming particular credit?'

I am not going to do this, Chloe told herself, swallowing back the impetuous retort that had risen to her lips. I am not going to stand here bandying jibes with Darius Maynard.

Because he's perfectly correct. However I may feel about it, his return is absolutely none of my business and I must remember that. I will remember it.

'Not at all.' She glanced at her watch. 'And now I must be going.' She took a deep breath. 'I—apologise for what just happened. It was a genuine mistake.'

'It must have been,' he drawled. 'After all, we were never exactly on goosing terms, were we, Miss Benson? I wasn't aware you had that kind of relationship with Cartwright either.'

'Clearly, you also have some catching up to do.' She turned away. 'Goodbye, Mr Maynard.'

She got back in her car, started the engine and swung the vehicle out of the forecourt towards the Willowford Road.

I'm shaking like a leaf, she thought, which is totally ridiculous. Yes, I've just made a complete fool of myself, but if it had been anyone else, they'd probably have helped me to laugh off the embarrassment somehow, not made it worse.

Of all the people in the world I never wanted to see again, he must be in pole position. Yet here he is, turning up like the proverbial bad penny. I wish I could ignore him, but we both have to live in the same small community, so that's impossible.

On the other hand, she thought, his return might be purely temporary. He'd frequently been absent in the old days, and might not be planning to stay for any length of time now. That was what she would hope for, anyway.

Besides, she added firmly, she would be too busy planning her wedding and her life with Ian to pay any heed to the Hall, and the vagaries of its occupants.

She'd travelled about a mile when the petrol light showed it meant business by letting the car slide slowly but very definitely to a halt.

Swearing under her breath, Chloe steered it to the verge. She'd had one thing on her mind at the filling station—escape—and this, of course, was what it had led to. Something else she could lay firmly at Darius Maynard's damned door, she thought, fuming.

She could use her mobile, she supposed. Send out an SOS to Uncle Hal or Ian to come to her rescue, but that, apart from leaving her looking like an idiot twice in one day, wasn't exactly the upbeat, triumphant return to Willowford that she had planned.

Better, she thought, grimacing, to start hiking, and as she reached for the door handle, she saw in her mirror the jeep come round the corner, drive past her, then pull in a few yards ahead.

She felt a silent scream rise in her throat, as Darius Maynard got out and walked back to her.

No, no, *no*! she wailed inwardly. This couldn't be happening. It wasn't possible.

'Having problems?'

'Absolutely not,' she said. 'Just—collecting my thoughts.'

'Pity you didn't collect some petrol while you were about it,' he commented caustically. 'I presume that was your purpose in the filling station, rather than renewing our acquaintance in that unique manner. And that's why you're stuck here?'

'Whatever,' Chloe returned curtly, loathing him. 'But I can cope.'

'Presumably by drilling for oil in the adjoining field. However, God forbid I should leave a damsel in distress.'

'Especially when you cause most of it.' She made her voice poisonously sweet, and he winced elaborately.

'Giving a dog a bad name, Miss Benson? Inappropriate behaviour, I'd have thought, for someone with her eye on a vet.'

She bit her lip. 'It happens that Ian Cartwright and I are engaged.'

'Good God,' he said. 'Does he know that?'

'What the hell do you mean?' Chloe demanded furiously. 'We're engaged and we'll be married by the end of the summer.'

'You know best,' he said softly. 'But I do hope you're not mistaking a girlhood crush for the real thing, Miss Benson. You're no longer a susceptible teenager, you know.'

She said in a small choked voice, 'How dare you? How bloody dare you? Just get out of here and leave me in peace.'

'Not without lending a kindly hand to a neighbour,' Damian retorted, apparently unperturbed. 'The jeep is diesel as I'm sure you remember, but I do have a petrol can in the back, and a brisk walk back to the filling station in the sunshine should do wonders for your temper.'

He paused. 'So, do you want it, or would you prefer to wait for the next chivalrous passer-by, yes or no?'

She would have actually preferred to see him wearing his rotten can, jammed down hard, but she bit her lip and nodded. 'Thank you.'

'Boy, that must have hurt.' His grin mocked her, before he turned and strode back to the jeep, lean-hipped and lithe.

He hadn't changed, she thought with sudden bewilderment, watching him go. The past seven years didn't seem to have touched him at all. Yet how was that possible?

No conscience, she thought bitterly. No regret for the havoc he'd caused. The ruined lives he'd left behind him.

She picked up her jacket from the passenger seat, and let herself out of the car. As she unfastened the boot, Darius came back with the can. He glanced down at the array of luggage and whistled.

'My God, Willowford's own Homecoming Queen. You really do mean to stay, don't you?'

'Yes.' She placed her jacket carefully across the top-most case, smoothing its folds as she did so. Hiding, she realised with annoyance, the fact that her hands were shaking. 'I have every reason to do so.'

'But I don't.' His mouth was smiling but his eyes were hard as glass. 'Is that the hidden message you're trying to convey?'

'As you said, it's none of my concern.' She held out her hand for the can. 'I'll make sure this is returned to you.'

'By courier, no doubt.' He shrugged. 'Forget it. I have others. And now, I fear, I must tear myself away.' He walked towards the jeep, then turned.

'I wish you a joyful reunion with your family and friends, Miss Benson,' he said softly. 'But as for that peace you mentioned—I wouldn't count on it, because you're not the peaceful kind. Not in your heart. You just haven't realised it yet.'

He swung himself into the jeep and drove off, leaving her staring after him, her heart pounding uncomfortably.

'You've lost weight,' said Aunt Libby.

'That is so not true.' Chloe hugged her again. 'I'm the same to the ounce as I was a year ago. I swear it.'

She looked round the big comfortable kitchen with its Aga, big pine table and tall Welsh dresser holding her aunt's prized collection of blue-and-white china and sighed rapturously. 'Gosh, it's wonderful to be home.'

'No-one forced you to go away,' said Aunt Libby, lifting the kettle from the Aga and filling the teapot. Her tone was teasing, but her swift glance was serious.

Chloe shrugged. 'They made me an offer I couldn't refuse. You know that. Besides it's been an education, seeing how the other half live.'

'The village will seem very dull after Millionaires Row.'

'On the contrary, I know for sure where I belong.' Chloe paused. 'Has Ian called? I took your advice and rang him to say I was arriving.'

'I think he was out at Farsleigh today. It's a bad reception area.' Her aunt passed her a plate of raisin bread.

'Heaven,' said Chloe, as she took a slice, smiling to conceal her disappointment over Ian. 'Is this the Jackson equivalent of the fatted calf—to welcome home the prodigal?' And paused again, taking a deep breath. 'So, how is everything and—everyone?' She tried to sound casual. 'Any major changes anywhere?'

'Nothing much.' Mrs Jackson poured the tea. 'I gather Sir Gregory is making progress at last, poor man.' She sighed. 'What a tragedy that was. I'm not a superstitious woman, but it's almost as if there's been some dreadful curse on the Maynard family.'

Chloe stared at her, the flippant retort that there was and that she'd seen it alive and well an hour ago dying on her lips.

'What do you mean?'

Mrs Jackson looked surprised. 'Well, I was thinking of Andrew, of course, being killed in that dreadful accident.'

Chloe's cup clattered back into its saucer. 'Andrew Maynard—dead?' She stared at her aunt. 'Never!'

'Why, yes, dear. Surely you saw it in the papers? And I told you about it in one of my letters.'

Had she? Chloe wondered guiltily, knowing that, once she'd made sure that everyone at Axford Grange was well and happy, she hadn't always read on to the end.

'I—I must have missed a page somewhere. What happened?'

'He was in the Cairngorms climbing alone as he often did. Apparently, there was a rock fall, and he was swept away.' She shuddered. 'Horrible.'

'And Sir Gregory?'

Aunt Libby shook her head. 'A stroke, brought on by the news.'

Chloe picked up her cup. Swallowed some tea. Schooled her voice to normality. 'I thought I glimpsed Darius Maynard when I stopped for petrol. Is that why he's come back? Because he's now the heir?'

'I think that it was concern for his father rather than the inheritance that brought him.' Aunt Libby spoke with gentle reproof and Chloe flushed.

'Of course. I'm sorry. It's just that I've—never liked him.'

'Something for which your uncle and I were always profoundly grateful,' her aunt said with a touch of grimness. 'He was always far too attractive for his own good.' She sighed again. 'But he's certainly provided Sir Gregory with the very best of care, hiring a charming girl as his live-in nurse who seems to have inspired the poor man and literally brought him back from the grave.

'And Mr Crosby, the agent, reckons Darius is really putting his back into running the estate these days, so perhaps he's become a reformed character during his absence.'

And maybe pigs might fly, thought Chloe. She took another piece of raisin bread. 'And—Mrs Maynard. Penny. Is he still with her?'

'No-one knows or dare ask. She's certainly not at the Hall. And she didn't attend Andrew's funeral, or the memorial service.' Mrs Jackson refilled her niece's cup. 'Apparently Mrs Thursgood at the post office asked Darius straight out if he was married—well, she would!—and he just laughed, and said, "God, no". So we're none the wiser.'

'But it's hardly a surprise,' Chloe said evenly. 'He's never been the marrying kind.'

'On the other hand, he's never been the next baronet before either,' Aunt Libby pointed out, cutting into a handsome Victoria sponge. 'That may change things.'

'Perhaps so.' Chloe shrugged. 'Maybe he's considering the charming nurse up at the Hall.'

'Lindsay?' Her aunt sounded almost startled. 'Oh, I don't think she'd do for him at all.'

'But, then, who would?' Chloe helped herself to a piece of sponge with its strawberry jam and cream filling. 'If I go on like this,' she added wryly, 'I'll be the size of a house by the time of the wedding.'

Aunt Libby gave her a swift glance, then looked back at her plate. 'Nonsense,' she said firmly. 'If anything, you could do with a few pounds. Real men don't want skeletons to cuddle.'

The wisdom according to Uncle Hal, no doubt, Chloe thought with an inward smile.

They were such darlings. Living proof of how well marriage could work, given the chance. And if their childlessness had been a sadness, they'd kept it well-hidden, opening their home and their hearts to her instead, when her mother, Aunt Libby's younger sister, had died suddenly of a thrombosis only two days after giving birth.

Her father, an engineer in the oil industry had been on his way back from Saudi Arabia to see his wife and child when the tragedy happened. Devastated by his loss, and with two years of his contract still to run, he knew that taking his newborn daughter back with him was impossible. Apart from the environmental problems, he'd been an only son and had no experience with infants. He'd been almost at his wits' end when his grieving sister-in-law had stepped in, making her momentous offer, which he'd thankfully accepted.

The original plan had been that Chloe should go to him as soon as he found a more appropriate job, but another contract succeeded the first, and from the conversations the Jacksons had with him when he was in the UK on leave, they knew that he'd become an ex-pat in spirit as well as fact. That he liked his life just the way it was. And contributing to his daughter's support was as far as he was prepared to go.

Eventually they heard that he'd met an American girl and was going to remarry, and resigned themselves once more to Chloe's loss. Only it didn't happen.

Her father's new bride-to-be, Mary Theresa, had reacted badly to the idea of a female stepchild when it had been put to her, and Chloe remained in Willowford.

She'd eventually been invited to Florida to see her father and meet her stepmother, together with the twin boys born a year after the marriage, but the visit was not a success, and had not been repeated. Now he was little more than a name on a Christmas card. Her birthday was clearly a date with associations he preferred to forget, and although this was bound to sadden her, she decided she could not altogether blame him.

But at some point she would also have to decide whether he, or Uncle Hal who'd loved her like his own, should give her away at her wedding. And that could be tricky.

When tea was finished she loaded the china and cutlery into the dishwasher and switched it on, then checked her mobile phone for a message or a text from Ian, but there was nothing.

She sighed inwardly. 'Do you need a hand with supper, or shall I take my things up to my room now?' she asked her aunt, replacing the phone in her bag.

'Yes, go and unpack, dear.' There was an awkward note in Mrs Jackson's voice. 'We've been decorating upstairs, doing some renovations too, so you'll find it all rather different. I hope you don't mind.'

'On the contrary, I'm intrigued.' Chloe spoke lightly, but when she opened her bedroom door, her reaction was stunned.

It was completely unrecognisable from the cosy, slightly worn haven that she'd loved, she thought numbly.

The rose-coloured carpet she'd begged for in her early teens had vanished, replaced by stripped, sanded and varnished boards. The pretty sprigged wallpaper had given away to plain walls in a rich, deep cream, and the curtains she'd made herself to go with the carpet had disappeared too. The new drapes were in a vivid blue, matching the tailored spread fitting the single brass bed.

The familiar shabby furniture had gone, but the small cast-iron fireplace was still there, filled with a display of blue teasels. And a fitted cream wardrobe and a mirrored dressing chest now occupied the alcoves on either side of the chimney breast, which Uncle Hal had once shelved to hold her books, toys and ornaments.

It was smart, shiny and new, and it looked terrific, but it was now very much a guest room, she realised with a swift pang. There was nothing left of her at all.

And the bathroom across the passage was an equal shock. The big cast-iron bath and wide basin had made way for a modern white suite, glittering with chrome accessories, and a glass cubicle with a power shower had been installed in the remaining space, while the walls and floor were tiled in turquoise and white.

But what's brought all this on? Have they had a lottery win I don't know about? Chloe wondered as she went back to the room that no longer belonged to her. Although the window seat was still there, and the view over open fields where cows grazed quietly hadn't changed.

She paused, her mouth twisting. Oh, for heaven's sake, she thought with sudden impatience. You're a grown woman, not a child to be hankering for a pink carpet, a collection of pottery owls and a complete set of the *Famous Five* books.

Things change, and you're about to move on yourself, so stop whingeing and get a grip.

She unpacked swiftly and neatly, stowed her cases under the bed, then returned downstairs.

Aunt Libby turned from the Aga with a look of faint apprehension as she entered the kitchen.

'What happened? Did some TV makeover team come knocking at the door? It all looks amazing.' Chloe knew her smile was a little too wide and too bright, but her aunt seemed reassured.

'Well, no, darling. Your uncle and I have a different reason for smartening the place up.' She paused. 'You see, we've decided to downsize.'

'Downsize?' Chloe's smile was wiped away, and replaced by shock. 'You mean you're—going to sell the Grange?' A thought struck her. 'Oh, heavens, has something happened to the practice? Is it the recession?'

'No, no, on the contrary.' Mrs Jackson's reassurance was swift. 'It's busier than ever, and that's the problem. It's always been a twenty-four-hour service, and your uncle isn't getting any younger.

'It's been a wonderful life, of course, and he's never wanted anything different, but now he's seriously considering retirement. Giving himself time to do the things he's never been able to fully enjoy before. His fishing, for instance. And he might even take up golf again. And we both used to love quite serious walking.

'So, they've been interviewing for a new assistant, and one

of Ian's friends from college might be interested in becoming a partner.'

'This isn't just a dream for the future, is it?' Chloe said slowly. 'This is a real plan for now.'

'Well, nothing will happen for a while, and wherever we go, there'll always be a place for you, Chloe. Never doubt that. But, at the same time, we know you have your own life to lead and we're so proud and so happy for you.'

'But you're not intending to leave the area, surely?' Chloe felt as if the flagged floor was shifting under her feet.

'Almost certainly,' her aunt said briskly.

'But I thought you loved Willowford.'

'It's a fine place,' Mrs Jackson nodded. 'And it's been good to us, but I don't think your uncle and I ever felt we'd end our days here. We've had a survey and valuation done on the Grange, and it seems we can afford to pick and choose where we'll go next.' She smiled. 'It's quite an adventure.'

'Yes,' Chloe agreed quietly. 'Indeed it is.'

And I—I have my own adventure to embark on too, so I shouldn't begrudge Uncle and Auntie a thing.

'We've started de-cluttering, as they call it, already,' Aunt Libby went on. 'You gather so much stuff over the years that you don't need, so the charity shops for miles around have reaped the benefit.

'Oh, not your things, darling,' she added quickly. 'We boxed and labelled it all for you, and put the cartons up in the attic, ready for whenever you want them.'

There'd be room at the cottage for them, thought Chloe. Although she'd get rid of the toys, except for the teddy bear her father had bought on his way home from Saudi to see his wife and new daughter. And the books which she'd keep for her own children—when they came along.

She waited for the usual glow of anticipation that occurred whenever she contemplated her future with Ian, but, for once, it seemed curiously muted. On the other hand, her entire homecoming hadn't been as expected either. It had been thrown off course by that dire humiliation at the filling station and had never really recovered.

I'll be better when I hear from Ian, she told herself, and at that same moment the telephone rang in the hall.

'And that's almost certainly for you,' said Aunt Libby, turning back to the meat she was browning for a cottage pie.

'So what's happened to the dream job?' Ian asked, once the 'it's wonderful to talk to you' preliminaries had been dealt with. 'Did you get fired?'

'No, of course not.' Chloe was taken aback. 'On the contrary. They wanted me to go with them for the summer to run their villa in the South of France.'

'And you turned that down for Willowford? Amazing.'

No, Chloe wanted to say. *I turned it down for you.*

Aloud, she said, 'I felt it was time to come home, back to real life again.' She paused. 'So, what time shall I see you tonight?'

He sighed. 'Can't manage tonight, Clo. There's a pony club committee meeting and I'm chairing it because Mrs Hammond's away. You must have known for ages that you'd be back today. I wish you'd told me sooner.'

'So do I.' She felt deflated, and oddly close to tears. 'But I wanted to surprise you.'

'Well you've done that all right.' He paused. 'Look, why don't I book a table at the Willowford Arms for tomorrow evening? Catch up with everything over dinner?'

Or why don't you suggest we see each other for a drink when your meeting is over? Or rush over here now?

She put a smile in her voice. 'Sounds great.'

'Then I'll pick you up just before eight,' he said briskly.

'Got to dash. I'm expecting a call from the Crawfords. Their whippet is about to litter and they're a bit concerned.'

It's a twenty-four-hour service, Chloe told herself as she put the phone down. Aunt Libby reminded you of that just now. And you've always known it—lived with it for the greater part of your life. Planned to stick with it. So you can't jib now.

A vet is like being a doctor, only the patients can't tell you their symptoms, and a successful practice is built on trust and availability. Haven't you heard Uncle Hal say so a hundred times over spoiled meals and cancelled outings?

It's not the end of the world. You've just endured one of those days, that's all, but everything starts again tomorrow.

Just keep thinking of that, and it will all work out just fine.

CHAPTER THREE

CHLOE lay back in the bath, appreciatively absorbing the scent of the rose geranium oil rising from the warm water.

In less than two hours, she'd be with Ian, and the time between would be spent pampering herself as never before.

I want to be irresistible, she thought, smiling inwardly.

All the same, she wasn't finding it as easy to slip back into the swim of things as she'd expected, although her uncle's affectionate greeting the previous evening had been balm to the soul, and he and Aunt Libby had tranquilly accepted that Ian was needed elsewhere, so she'd be eating cottage pie with them.

'That whippet's a beauty but she could be tricky. Let's hope this litter is the first and last,' had been Mr Jackson's only comment.

'So what are you doing with yourself today?' he'd asked that morning as he stood up from the breakfast table, stuffing his folded newspaper into his jacket pocket.

'Just pottering, I suppose.' Chloe had smiled at him.

'Well you could always potter over to Lizbeth Crane's, if you felt inclined,' her uncle said briskly. 'She's damaged her wrist gardening and Jack's in Brussels, so their retriever will need walking.'

'Of course I'll go.' Chloe didn't think twice. 'A wander

across the fields with a friendly dog like Flare is just what I need. I'll call round as soon as I've been to the post office.'

Which in itself had been an experience, she thought.

'So you're back.' Mrs Thursgood had greeted her with a faint sniff. 'Thought you'd deserted us for good. Come back for that young vet, I dare say. We all thought round here that the banns would have been called a year back or more. You don't want to leave it too long, missy,' she added with a look of faint disparagement. 'You're not getting any younger, and men go off the boil as quick as they go on it.'

Chloe, acutely aware that every word was being savoured by the queue behind her, paid for her stamps with murder in her heart and escaped.

But there had been more to come. She had to run the gauntlet of the shoppers in the main street, and by the time she reached the Cranes' house, she felt if one more person said, 'Well, Chloe, you're quite a stranger,' she would howl at the sky.

But Mrs Crane's delighted welcome, accompanied as it was by coffee and home-made biscuits, plus Flare's grin and gently offered paw had compensated for a great deal.

Except…

It had been a marvellous walk, the sun warm on her back, and Flare, plumy tail waving, bounding along ahead of her. After a mild disagreement over the retriever's wish to complete the pleasure of the morning by rolling joyously in a large cowpat, they turned for home. They'd just emerged from a field onto the lane leading back to the village and Chloe was fastening the gate behind her, when she heard the sound of a horse's hooves.

She glanced round and saw a handsome bay gelding trotting towards them, and paused, her throat tightening when she saw who was riding him.

'Good morning.' Darius brought the horse to a stand, and

bent forward to pat his glossy neck. 'Enjoying a constitutional, Miss Benson? I thought you'd be getting your exercise elsewhere on this lovely day—in some convenient haystack with your intended, perhaps.'

Her skin warmed. 'Do you have to make unpleasant remarks?' she asked coldly.

'On the contrary, the activity I'm referring to is entirely pleasurable.' He grinned down at her. 'Or perhaps you don't find it so. What a terrible shame, not to mention waste,' he added, his gaze sliding appreciatively over the thrust of her breasts under her white shirt, down to her slender waist and the curve of her hips.

Aware that her flush was deepening, Chloe bent hurriedly to clip on Flare's leash.

'Just as a matter of interest,' he went on. 'Why are you walking Lizbeth Crane's dog?'

'I'm being a good neighbour,' she said shortly. 'A concept you may find unfamiliar.'

'Not at all, as I hope to demonstrate over the coming months.' He paused. 'However, if true love has worked some miracle and you're really in Good Samaritan mode, you might consider extending your range as far as the Hall.'

As Chloe's lips parted to deliver a stinging refusal, he held up a hand.

'Hear me out, please. I don't get the chance to take Orion here out as much as I should, largely because any spare time I have goes to my brother's Samson, who's eating his head off in between throwing serious moodies.

'I seem to recall you were a damned good rider in the old days, so, if you'd consider exercising Orion for me sometimes, I'd be immensely grateful to you.'

She gave him a startled look. Gratitude wasn't something she'd ever have attributed to him. Or the paying of compliments. Not that it made any real difference. *I seem to recall*...

'I'm sorry,' she said. 'But it's quite impossible.'

'May I ask why?'

'I have a wedding to organise,' she said curtly. 'In case you've forgotten. I shall be far too busy.'

He sat, one hand resting on his hip, his gaze meditative as he watched her. 'I hadn't forgotten. But is it really going to take all day of every day? How many hundreds of people are you planning to invite, for God's sake?'

'That's none of your business,' she returned. 'Anyway, Arthur must still be at the Hall, so why can't he ride Orion?'

'Unfortunately, his arthritis won't let him, but it would break his heart if I pensioned him off and got a younger groom.'

He added flatly, 'And, for obvious reasons, my father finds even minor changes distressing.'

Chloe bit her lip. 'Yes—yes, of course.' She paused. 'I was—very sorry to hear about Andrew. I hadn't realised...' She took a breath. 'It was terribly sad.'

His face hardened. 'Not just sad but bloody stupid and totally unnecessary.'

She gasped. 'You don't feel, perhaps, that's too harsh a judgment? Whatever may have happened, he was still your brother.'

'Harsh, perhaps,' Darius returned coolly. 'Yet entirely accurate. However, this is not the time to debate Andrew's motives for risking his life by pushing himself to ridiculous and dangerous limits.

'And my proposition over Orion still stands,' he added. 'I'd like you to think it over, instead of just dismissing it out of hand because I'm doing the asking. You don't even have to give me a personal reply. Just ring the Hall at any time, and Arthur will have him tacked up and ready for you.'

He smiled faintly. 'And Orion would be grateful too, don't forget.'

He touched the horse with his heels, and they moved off.

Chloe stared after them, her mind a welter of mixed emotions. It was still impossible, of course—what he'd asked—but Orion was an absolute beauty, and the thought of cantering him along those flat stretches by the river in the Willow valley was a genuine temptation.

But one she had to resist.

She'd told herself the same thing at intervals during the day, and she was still saying it now as she stepped out of the bath and dried herself, and applied some of the body lotion from the satin-lined gift basket of Hermes' *Caleche* that the Armstrongs had given her for Christmas.

She repeated it as she put on her prettiest lace briefs and sprayed her arms and breasts lightly with matching scent. As she applied her make-up and combed her hair into glossy waves around her face. And as she finally slipped on the knee-skimming cream georgette dress with the deep-V neckline, which discreetly signalled that she was wearing no bra.

Too obvious? she worried in front of the mirror. Or simply a means to an end? A message to Ian that at last she was his for the taking.

Absurd to feel even remotely jittery about something that was so natural and would be so right, she thought sliding her feet into low-heeled sandals that echoed the colour of the lapis lazuli drops in her ears. Yet for some reason, she did.

Ian was in the sitting room talking to her aunt and uncle when she arrived downstairs. When he turned in response to her quiet, 'Good evening,' and saw her standing in the doorway, his jaw dropped.

'God, Clo, you look amazing—like someone from a magazine cover.'

'You look pretty good yourself.' And it wasn't just his looks, she thought as she went to him smiling, appraising his black-and-white houndstooth tweed jacket, worn with dark trousers and the ruby silk tie which set off his crisp white shirt. He'd dressed to kill too, for this important night in their lives.

It's going to be all right, she thought. It's going to be wonderful.

She lifted her face, offering him her lips, but he reddened slightly and deposited a kiss on her cheek instead.

'Have a wonderful time,' Aunt Libby whispered with a hug, as Ian paused to have a final word with Uncle Hal on their way out. 'I won't wait up.'

Chloe detected a hint of apprehension in her smile and hugged her back. 'Don't worry. I'm a big girl now. I know what I'm doing.'

When Chloe was growing up, the Willowford Arms had been just a village pub offering good beer, a dartboard and a skittle alley.

Over the years, under successive landlords, however, it had changed completely. The saloon bar still offered tradition, but the lounge had morphed into a reception area and smart cocktail bar for the restaurant, now housed in a striking conservatory extension.

There were no great surprises on the menu, but the freshness of the ingredients and excellent cooking had earned the pub favourable mentions in the county magazine and various food guides and, even early in the week as this was, there were few empty tables to be seen.

The staff were mainly locals, and they all seemed genuinely pleased to see Chloe, if a little surprised. Ian, she noted with some surprise of her own, was treated as a regular.

'That pork *afelia* you liked last week is on the specials board tonight,' their waitress told him as she showed them to their table, where Chloe was thrilled to find champagne on ice waiting along with the menus.

'Now there's a bit of forward planning,' she teased as their glasses were filled. 'What a terrific thought.'

'Well, I felt something special was called for to celebrate the return of the native.' Ian touched his glass to hers. 'It's great to see you, Clo. It's been a hell of a long time.'

'I know.' She smiled into his eyes. 'But now, I promise you, I'm home for good.'

She paused. 'Unlike, I've discovered, my aunt and uncle, busily transforming the Grange for the market and a major move. Rather a shock to the system, I have to say.'

'It was a surprise to me too,' he admitted. 'But—things change. People move on. It's the way of the world, and Hal's put his heart and soul into the practice for a long time, so he deserves to enjoy his retirement.'

She toyed with the idea of some jokey comment on the lines of, *however it means I'm going to be homeless. Any suggestions?* but decided it was too early in the evening, confining herself to a neutral, 'I'm happy for them too.'

Besides, the lead should definitely come from him, she thought as she sipped her champagne.

She'd played the scene so often in her imagination—hearing him murmur, 'It's so wonderful to have you back with me, darling. Stay for ever,' as he produced the little velvet jeweller's box—that she felt as if she'd somehow missed a cue.

'I think I might try this pork *afelia* you're so keen on,' she said as she scanned the menu. 'With the vegetable terrine to start with.'

'It's a good choice,' he said. 'I had it when I brought Lloyd Hampton, our new partner-to-be here. Wanted to convince him that he wasn't altogether moving away from civilisation as he knows it.'

'It's clearly done the trick.'

'I hope so. He's a really good bloke, and his wife's a doll.'

He's married then? was also going to sound like a sharp elbow in the ribs, thought Chloe.

'I shall look forward to meeting her,' was her chosen alternative.

'You're bound to,' he said. 'I'm pretty sure that Lloyd is interested in buying the Grange. He and Viv have two children, and the third's on the way, so they need the space.'

'Well, yes. It sounds ideal,' said Chloe, resolutely ignoring the pang of disappointment in the far corner of her mind which had visualised a very different future for her old home when she and Ian would also need more space than the cottage. Hopefully for the same reason.

When they took their seats at the corner, candlelit table waiting for them, Ian drank another half glass of champagne, then announced he was switching to mineral water.

'Because you're driving?' Chloe, settling for a glass of house red, gave him a rueful look. 'What a shame, because it's a lovely evening, and we could easily have walked.' *And the cottage is even nearer than the Grange when it's time for home...*

'Past all those twitching curtains?' He pulled a face. 'I'd really rather not. A vehicle at least gives an illusion of privacy.'

'Talking of which,' she said. 'I gather you sold your last jeep to Darius Maynard.'

'I heard he was in the market for something more serviceable in addition to that flashy sports car he's so fond of. I'd decided to trade up, so it seemed like serendipity.'

She said slowly, 'Yes, I suppose so. Although it seems odd—having him back here just as if nothing had happened.'

He shrugged. 'It must have been with his father's agreement, Clo, so it's their family business, not ours.'

'Yes, yes, of course.' She played with a fork. 'I understand Sir Gregory's getting over his stroke.'

'Indeed he is. Coming on by leaps and bounds, according to the latest reports.'

'I'm glad. I always liked him, although he could be intimidating.' She paused. 'I used to go up the Hall when I was in my teens and read to Lady Maynard when she was so ill.'

'How did that happen?'

'I won a school poetry competition that she judged. I enjoyed being with her. She was the sweetest person. Darius was with her a lot too and I always felt that he was secretly her favourite.' She paused. 'I was always glad she didn't know how he turned out. What he did to—Andrew.' She bit her lip. 'Betrayal's such a terrible thing.'

'It is,' Ian said quietly. 'But we don't actually know the circumstances. Maybe they couldn't help themselves.'

Upon which the first course arrived, and the conversation turned inevitably to the food.

And Ian was quite right about the pork, Chloe decided after she'd tasted one of the tender cubes of fillet, flavoured with garlic and coriander, cooked in wine, and served with savoury brown rice and *mangetouts*.

For dessert, she chose an opulent dark-chocolate mousse, well-laced with brandy, while Ian opted for cheese and biscuits.

'You should have picked another pud, so we could share like we used to,' she told him in mock reproach.

He gave a constrained smile. 'Out of practice, I guess.'

For what seemed like the umpteenth time that evening, he took his mobile phone from his pocket and checked it.

And what a very annoying habit that is, thought Chloe as she ate her last spoonful of mousse.

Aloud, she said mildly, 'Isn't Uncle Hal taking your calls this evening?'

'Well, yes.' Ian replaced the phone in his jacket. 'But I'm waiting for news of the Crawfords' Kirsty. She's a really good little bitch—won all kinds of shows already, and this may be her only litter, so it needs to go well.'

Chloe's brows lifted. 'But I thought it had already happened last night.'

'False alarm,' he said. 'Main event still expected at any moment, and they want me to stand by in case of emergency.' He signalled to the waitress. 'Would you like filter coffee or espresso?'

She took a deep breath, summoning up courage she hadn't thought she'd need. 'Why don't we make our minds up about that back at the cottage? It's been a gorgeous meal, but a bit public for a proper reunion, don't you think?' She reached across the table, and touched his hand with hers. 'I really think we need to spend some time alone together—and talk.'

'Yes, of course we should, and I want that too,' Ian said quickly. 'But not tonight, Clo.' He gave an awkward laugh. 'For one thing, the cottage is in a bit of a mess. For another—there's been barely minimum contact between us for a whole year now. I've hardly heard from you, let alone seen you. Being on opposite sides of the country didn't help, either, and both of us being so busy. And now you turning up out of the blue like this is frankly the last thing I was expecting.'

He added quickly, 'It isn't that it's not wonderful to see you, or that I don't want you—please believe that. Just that maybe we should take it easy for a while—get to know each other again—before, well, anything...'

His voice tailed off uncomfortably and in the silence that followed, Chloe could hear her heart beating a sudden tattoo—a call to arms. Because the situation was going terribly, disastrously wrong.

Men go off the boil as quick as they go on it... Mrs Thursgood's words rang ominously in her ears. But that couldn't be happening—not to them...

She removed her hand, and sat back in her chair. Summoned a smile that would somehow manage to be calm and amused at the same time. And give no hint of her inner turmoil of shocked disbelief.

'Actually, you may well be right in wanting not to rush things.' She made herself speak almost casually. 'Being wise for both of us, no less. And, anyway, taking our time could be much nicer. Even exciting.'

She paused. 'Besides, you're clearly up to your ears in work and the new plans for the practice. And I—I have to start looking for another job.

'As for coffee,' she added brightly. 'I think I'd prefer decaf. And when the bill comes, in line with our fresh start, I insist we go Dutch.'

And she stuck to her guns in spite of his obvious reluctance.

Now all I want to do is get out of here, she thought, reaching for her bag, and the blue-and-gold fringed shawl she'd brought instead of a jacket.

But the Fates hadn't finished with her yet.

As she walked back into the bar, the first person she saw was Darius Maynard at a table by the window, talking with apparent intimacy to a girl she'd never seen before, slim and very attractive in a sleeveless red dress, with blonde hair drawn back from her face into a smooth chignon at the nape of her neck

And it seemed Darius had spotted her in return, she thought, her heart sinking as he rose to his feet, smiling faintly.

'What a delightful surprise. Lindsay and I have been to the cinema in East Ledwick and we just popped in for a nightcap. Would you care to join us?'

'It's a kind thought, but I think I'll pass, if you don't mind.' She had no wish to allow any hint of the edgy state of her relationship to become apparent to those shrewd green eyes, currently assessing the deep slash of her neckline. Or expose it to the scrutiny of some strange blonde either. 'Stuff to do tomorrow and all that.'

'But the night is still young,' he said softly. 'So, what about you, Cartwright? Surely you can talk your lady round?'

'On the contrary,' Ian returned, a little frostily. 'Once Chloe's made up her mind, it usually stays that way. And I also have a busy day ahead of me. But thanks again, anyway.'

'I see that leopards don't change their spots,' Chloe commented as they walked to the jeep. 'Who's his latest fancy?'

'Her name's Lindsay Watson,' Ian said shortly. 'And she's his father's resident nurse.'

Aunt Libby's charming girl, thought Chloe and gave a faint whistle. 'Under the same roof, even,' she said lightly. 'How very convenient.'

'Not necessarily.' Ian started the engine. 'He's not irresistible, you know.'

When they reached the Grange, Chloe turned towards him. 'I won't invite you in, but does the fresh start merit a goodnight kiss?' she asked, her voice teasing. 'Or do we just shake hands?'

'Of course I want to kiss you,' he said with sudden roughness. 'Any man would. Hell, even Maynard was looking at you as if he could eat you.'

He pulled her into his arms, his mouth heavy and demanding where she'd expected tenderness—even diffidence. This was the moment she'd been dreaming of—longing for—yet she was struggling to respond, the thrust of his tongue between her parted lips feeling almost—alien.

As his hand pushed aside the edge of her dress to close on her bare breast, she tore her mouth free and sat up abruptly, bracing her hands against his chest in negation.

'Ian—no, please...' she protested hoarsely.

'What's the matter?' He reached for her again. 'Isn't this what you want—what tonight was all about?'

Not like this—never like this...

'But it has to be what we both want. You must see that.' She spoke more calmly, moving back from him, straightening her dress with finality. 'And you—to be honest, I just don't know any more.'

Because suddenly you're a stranger and I don't like it. Can't figure how to deal with it.

There was a silence, then he sighed. 'God, I'm sorry, Clo. You must think I'm insane. I suppose it's being without you for so long. So, can we simply forget tonight and start again?'

His face was looking strained, almost guilty, but perhaps it was a trick of the dim light.

She said quietly, 'That's a good thought.'

He nodded. 'I'll call you tomorrow.'

'Fine.' She paused. 'Then—goodnight.'

As she walked up the path to the door, she heard the jeep start up and drive away and realised her legs were trembling.

'You're back early.' There was music coming from the sitting room where Uncle Hal was relaxing, his paper open at the crossword. 'Have a good time?'

'As always,' she returned cheerfully, lowering herself into the chair opposite. 'What are you listening to?'

'Mozart, of course. A selection of favourite arias, and this is mine starting now.' He turned up the sound a little. 'The Countess lamenting her lost happiness from *Figaro*. *"Dove sono I bei momenti"*.'

'Oh, yes, I remember,' she said slowly. 'When you took Aunt Libby and me to Glyndebourne for her birthday. It was wonderful.' And quoted, '"Where are the beautiful moments of pleasure and delight? Where have they flown, those vows made by a deceitful tongue?"'

He nodded. 'A supreme moment of artistry.'

Then the poignant music and the soaring melancholy of the exquisite soprano voice captured them and held them in silence.

The aria was still in Chloe's head, plangent and heart-wrenching, as she went up to her room.

Maybe not the ideal thing to have listened to in the circumstances, she acknowledged wryly as she got ready for bed.

Yet nothing had really been lost, she thought. They'd just got off to a rocky start, that was all. And somewhere soon, with Ian, she would find that those 'moments of pleasure and delight' hadn't disappeared at all, but were still waiting for her.

It will all be fine, she told herself, turning on her side and closing her eyes. I know it.

CHAPTER FOUR

'I MET Sir Gregory's charming nurse last night,' Chloe remarked, watching her aunt extract a tray of scones from the Aga. 'She was in the Willowford Arms having a drink.'

Aunt Libby shot her a swift glance as she transferred her baking to a cooling rack. 'And you thought—what?'

Chloe shrugged. 'That she seemed intent on charming her patient's son and heir.'

'You mean she was with Darius?' Her aunt's brows lifted.

'Well, they're both single, so why not? Another blonde, like Penny, of course. He runs true to form.' Chloe espied a crumb escaping from the rack and ate it.

'I never noticed he had any particular preference,' her aunt said drily. 'However, Lindsay Watson's a lovely girl as well as being extremely capable with a lot of sense.' She added slowly. 'Darius could do far worse.'

'And often has.' Chloe tried to encourage the edge of another scone to make its bid for freedom and had her hand slapped away.

'Those are for the WI tea, madam. If you're hungry there's plenty of fruit in the bowl.'

'Yes, Auntie dear.' Chloe examined a fleck on her nail. 'But how do you think Sir Gregory would feel about it— Darius and his nurse I mean?'

'Thankful, probably,' Mrs Jackson returned briskly. 'It's

high time that young man married and had a family. It's his duty and exactly what the Hall needs, so it could well be the best thing all round. Besides, it would be good for his father to have grandchildren. Give him a new interest in life. Nurse Swann who helps with some of the night duties says he gets bored, which in turn makes him impatient—and that isn't helping his recovery.'

'No,' Chloe said slowly. 'I can understand that.'

She was less sure about her inner vision of Sir Gregory's stern stateliness under siege from a pack of blond infants.

While the image of Darius the married man was something else again.

Suddenly restive, she reached over to the fruit bowl, took an apple and bit into it. 'I thought I might drive over to East Ledwick later,' she went on casually. 'Call in at that agency that used to find me work when I was on vacation.'

Her aunt turned from the sink, staring at her. 'You said the other night that you were going to have a complete break for a while. Pursue other interests.'

Chloe shrugged. 'That was the idea, but now I've started to wonder if I'll find the other interests quite as interesting as I thought. The fact is I'm simply not used to being idle, and taking Lizbeth's dog for a daily walk, however enjoyable, just isn't going to do it for me.' She smiled at her aunt. 'After all, you don't want me getting bored and impatient too.'

'God forbid,' said Aunt Libby devoutly. 'But on the other hand, there's surely no immediate need to go rushing off in all directions? If you want occupation, you could give me a hand with the Grange project. I've decided to start on the dining room next.' She shook her head. 'I've never liked that wallpaper, it's far too dark.'

'On the other hand,' Chloe suggested. 'Might it not be better to leave a few things for Lloyd and his wife to decide for themselves?'

'Lloyd and his wife?' Mrs Jackson dried her hands. 'What do you mean?'

Chloe dropped her apple core into the waste caddy. 'Ian was saying something about them possibly buying the Grange.'

'Was he really?' Her aunt snorted. 'Well that would entirely depend on their offer. Your uncle and I are looking to maximise an asset here, not oblige Ian and his friends.'

Chloe gasped. 'Aunt Libby—you sound almost sharp.'

'Do I?' The older woman hesitated, smiling ruefully. 'Maybe your return has pointed up just how big an upheaval this move is going to be, and I'm having belated qualms.'

'Then don't,' Chloe ordained severely. 'I think it will be wonderful for you both, and, to prove it, I'd be happy to lend a hand with the decorating.'

Even if it isn't in the way I expected, she added silently, and suppressed a sigh.

She deliberately took Flare on a different route that morning, having no wish to encounter Darius again and have to endure any edged remarks he might make about the previous evening.

On the way back, she called into Sawley's Garage to arrange for her petrol gauge to be fixed.

'Heard you were back,' Tom Sawley commented affably. 'And a sight for sore eyes and no mistake, my dear.' He opened the big ledger that was his version of a computer, ran a finger down the crowded page and nodded.

'Tomorrow afternoon suit you? If I can't fix that gauge, I reckon I can find a new one out the back.'

Chloe hid a smile. Here was something that hadn't changed, she thought, Tom's legendary ability to supply any kind of spare part for any kind of make and model of vehicle. If someone brought in a Model T Ford needing a new running board, he'd probably nod and say, 'Got the very thing out the back.'

It must be like Aladdin's cave out there, she thought as the bell above the office door tinkled to announce a new arrival. Giving a casual glance over her shoulder, she saw Lindsay Watson had come in, neat in a navy skirt and white blouse. Beside her, Flare got to her feet with a little whimper of welcome.

Chloe put a restraining hand on her head. 'Sit, good girl.' She smiled at Lindsay. 'Hi, there. We were almost introduced last night. I'm Chloe Benson.'

The other flushed slightly. 'Yes, so Mr Maynard said.' Her voice was low and pleasant but held a note of constraint. 'I'm Sir Gregory's nurse, as I expect you also know.'

'Well, yes.' Chloe found the response curiously distancing, maybe deliberately so. Clearly the famous charm was not universally applied.

She turned back to Mr Sawley. 'Thanks, Tom, tomorrow it is. I'll drop the car off around two-ish.'

Heading for the door, she had to keep a tight hold on Flare who was eagerly pulling at her leash, trying to get to the newcomer, her tail wagging furiously.

'I'm sorry about this,' she said rather breathlessly. 'I hope you don't mind dogs.'

'I haven't had much to do with them,' Lindsay Watson said, stepping back.

Now that, Chloe thought indignantly, really was a snub. Practising for the day when she became the new Lady Maynard, no doubt, but totally misjudging her performance.

Pity you never met your predecessor, she addressed Miss Watson silently as she left. Because she was the warmest, kindest woman.

'While you,' she told Flare, who was still looking back and whining at the closed office door, 'are no judge of character.'

She felt an odd disappointment. She'd enjoyed the time she'd spent with Tanya, and having someone of her own age in Willowford to shop and socialise with occasionally would have been pleasant too. Yet it was clearly not to be.

Maybe Lindsay Watson was simply protecting her territory, Chloe thought, trying to be charitable, when, with Flare safely restored to her owner, she walked back to the Grange.

Perhaps she'd resented the threat of last night's *tête-à-tête* with Darius being interrupted by other company, especially when it included another female.

Well, you're way off track there, lady, she muttered under her breath. I made it clear that it wasn't my idea. I'm not poaching on those preserves, even in my worst nightmare. If you can get him, you're surely welcome to him.

And I won't tell Aunt Libby that her idol has feet of clay.

The home-made cakes at the Tea Rooms were in a category all their own, Chloe told herself as she tried to finish the last few crumbs of her chosen coffee and walnut confection without actually scraping the pattern off the plate, with 'spoiled for choice' and 'to die for' being the phrases that came most readily to mind.

It was market day in East Ledwick and she and Aunt Libby had spent over two hours trawling the fabric stalls seeking curtain material for the newly decorated dining room.

But when Mrs Jackson decided that the design she'd seen at the first stall was the best of the bunch, Chloe had sagged visibly.

Her aunt had patted her shoulder. 'Duty nobly done, dearest. Go and revive yourself with tea and major calories, and I'll meet you by the War Memorial at four o'clock.'

Chloe had obeyed with a thankful heart.

Mrs Jackson was a perfectionist, so it had been a tough week, with layers of old paper to be removed, the plaster beneath restored to a smooth finish, and the paintwork scrubbed down with sugar soap. All of which had taken a mind-boggling amount of time.

But the finished effect of warm sand-coloured walls combined with the brilliant white of the ceiling and cornices made Chloe's conviction that her pores would be permanently clogged with dust seem unimportant. It was a job well done, she realised with satisfaction.

And the new curtains, which the Jacksons would eventually take with them to their new home, were going to look magnificent too.

Work had proved a boon in other ways too, she thought as she drank the rest of her tea. It had given her the chance for some reflection, her relationship with Ian heading the list of potential topics.

She had somehow to overcome her disappointment with the way things had initially turned out between them. And, realistically, she had to shoulder much of the blame for it too.

She'd been hell-bent on earning big money in the short term, even though Ian had made it clear he didn't share her views.

And he was right, she'd told herself soberly. My real focus should have been on the two of us. He saw that. Why the hell couldn't I?

Instead I let the job absorb me so much that Willowford began to seem like a dream world. That I almost forgot there were real people living here who also needed my attention—and my presence.

I should have fought infinitely harder for my time off, concentrated more on maintaining my contact with my home rather than banking the Armstrongs' bonuses for indulging their never-ending demands.

If there was a problem, they threw money at it, and I let them. Stupid, stupid, stupid. Greedy too.

But now she had the chance to make amends. She'd seen Ian twice in the past week, each time for a quiet drink, deliberately ensuring that the atmosphere was more companionable than approaching any form of intimacy.

He hadn't yet asked her back to the cottage, but she wasn't pushing for it either.

Slow and steady, she thought. That's what wins the race.

She reached for the bill, picked up her bag and headed for the cash desk. As she reached it, the street door opened and Lindsay Watson came in. She stood for a moment, her eyes restlessly scanning the busy room, then she saw Chloe and her face seemed to freeze.

What is her problem? Chloe asked herself, exasperated, as she put a tip in the saucer provided, and the rest of the change in her purse.

She forced herself to smile politely. 'Good afternoon, Miss Watson. Looking for someone?'

'Oh—no,' the other girl returned quickly. 'I just wanted some tea.' She glanced round again. 'I didn't realise it would be so crowded.'

'It usually is—especially on market day. But my table's still free over in the corner.'

'Thank you, but perhaps I won't bother. I'm in rather a hurry.' Her attempt at a smile appeared an even greater struggle than Chloe's had been. 'Well—goodbye.'

She whisked out, and by the time Chloe reached the street, she was nowhere to be seen.

I hope she's a damned good nurse, Chloe muttered under her breath, because in other respects, she's seriously weird.

She was too early for her rendezvous with her aunt, and had no shopping of her own, so she decided to spend the time usefully by calling in at the employment agency.

The manager, however, was polite but brisk. 'We have no vacancies in your particular field at the moment, Miss

Benson. People locally are tending to cut back on their higher paid domestic staff because of the economic situation.'

She paused. 'It's a pity you gave up your last position without checking the situation first, and I have to say it might be easier for you to find permanent work in London.'

Which was just what she didn't want to hear, Chloe thought as she emerged, dispirited, into the sunshine.

'Back on the job market, Miss Benson? I'm astonished.'

An all-too-familiar mocking drawl stopped her dead in her tracks. She took a deep breath and turned to see Darius Maynard coming out of the neighbouring ironmongery wearing the close-fitting denim jeans and matching shirt which seemed to have become his uniform these days.

She lifted her chin and met his gaze. 'I fail to see why. Some of us have to toil for our crusts, Mr Maynard,' she retorted. 'We don't all have an income for life dropped into our laps.'

His brows lifted. 'I thought matrimony was about to supply that for you.'

'Then you were wrong,' she told him curtly. 'It doesn't work like that any more.'

'Excuse me if I don't offer my sympathy, sweetheart,' he said. 'Because, believe it or not, I too earn my keep, and have done so for some considerable time.'

'By gambling, I suppose,' Chloe said scornfully. 'As in the old days.' And shut her mind, shuddering inwardly, to the memory of those rumours about illegal dog fights.

'In various ways,' he returned, apparently unperturbed. 'For a while, I worked as a stockman in Australia. I've also helped to train racehorses in Kentucky, and latterly I've been running a vineyard in the Dordogne. All perfectly respectable occupations even by your unflinching standards,' he added, the green eyes a challenge. 'Would you like a copy of my CV?'

He paused, and gave a sharp sigh of irritation. 'Or alternatively shall we stop bitching at each other in this ludicrous way and remember that we used to call each other by our given names? That at one time we were something like friends?'

She felt an odd stillness descend, as if the grumble of the passing traffic and the noise from the market had suddenly faded to a great distance. As if she was entangled in some web which would not allow her to move. To walk away as she wished to do. As she knew she must.

Instead of standing there, as if she was frozen to the spot, looking back at him...

Somewhere a vehicle backfired with a noise like a pistol shot, and with that the world returned. Including her power of speech.

'Were we?' she demanded tautly. 'I really don't remember.'

He stared at her, his eyes narrowing, then shrugged. He said expressionlessly, 'As you wish.' He paused again. 'I note you haven't been up to the stables as I suggested. Am I to take it that your dislike of me is so fixed that you even refuse to exercise my horse?'

She said, 'I've been busy, helping my aunt. Why don't you ask your girlfriend—the one you were with the other night?'

He said flatly, 'Because she's at the Hall to look after my father.'

'Not this afternoon. A little while ago she was looking for you at the Tea Rooms.'

'Was she?' He looked past her, frowning a little. 'Anyway, I don't think she rides,' he added abruptly. 'Or certainly not well enough to handle Orion.'

'And I do?'

He sighed. 'You know it, Chloe. Don't play games. And I'll make a deal with you. Warn me in advance when you're

coming and I'll make sure I'm at the other end of the estate.
How about that?'

He looked at her rigid expression and his mouth tightened.
'Will you at least think about it?'

'Yes,' she said, staring at the pavement. 'I—I'll think about
it.'

But would she? Chloe wondered as she walked back towards the War Memorial. She'd thought about a great deal
over the past days as she'd scraped, peeled, filled and painted,
but Darius Maynard and the situation at the Hall had not been
on her chosen list of subjects. On the contrary, she'd been
careful to exclude both of them.

They did not concern her or the life she had planned for
herself. They never had. So she shouldn't consider even the
most marginal of involvement.

That, she told herself, would be a serious error of judgement.

The box marked 'Clothing' was stacked on top of the others
in the attic. Instantly accessible, Chloe thought wryly as she
lifted it down. As if it was waiting for me.

The weight alone told her what it contained—her jodhpurs,
boots and hard hat, along with a shirt and a couple of elderly
sweaters. None of it worn for years. Yet still retained for no
good reason.

In fact she'd hoped against hope that the whole lot might
also have been consigned to a charity shop or jumble sale by
now as part of the de-clutter, but no such luck.

No sign of moths in anything either—not on Aunt Libby's
watch.

She unfolded the jodhpurs and studied them critically.
They probably won't fit me, she thought. Not after this length
of time. After all, I'm hardly some slip of a girl any more.

And I've no intention of splurging on new kit—so, the

problem, which has no actual right to be a problem anyway, could be solved.

But the jodhpurs still hugged her slim hips and long legs as if they loved them. No valid excuse there then, she thought, biting her lip.

The blue shirt, however, strained across the increased fullness of her breasts, and she stared at her reflection with suddenly shadowed eyes, tracing the mother-of-pearl buttons with a fingertip.

This, she told herself, I should definitely not have kept.

Using both hands, she dragged open the front with one swift, almost violent gesture, tearing the buttons from the fabric and rendering the shirt completely unwearable, then dropped it into the waste basket.

And that, she whispered to herself, is the end of that.

'You took your time,' said Arthur. 'Been expecting you all week.'

He led Orion, tacked up and with his ears pricked in anticipation, out of his box and into the yard.

'And Mr Darius said to let you know he was over to Warne Cross this morning to look at the new plantation.' He sent Chloe a sideways look. 'Thinking of riding over there, was you?'

'No.' Chloe swung herself up into the saddle and waited while Arthur adjusted her stirrups. 'I thought I'd hack him round the park for a while, then take him up onto the hill.'

'He'll carry you right wherever you go and that's a fact.' Arthur ran an affectionate hand over the gelding's neck. 'Mr Darius got him in France. Had him shipped over. Great lad, aren't you? Plenty of spirit, but good-hearted with it.'

He sniffed. 'Unlike that other contrary devil in there,' he added, jerking his head towards the stable. 'God knows why Mr Andrew ever bought 'un. Could've broken his neck on him any day of the week. Didn't need to go climbing no mountain.'

'But Andrew was a good rider.' Chloe soothed Orion who had begun to sidle a little, impatient to be off.

'Fair,' Arthur said grudgingly. 'Not a patch on his brother. Took too many damned risks. Told him so, many a time, but made no damned difference.'

He paused. 'But I'm glad to see you round here again, Chloe gal. Good seat you always had and nice steady hands. You and this boy will get on fine, I reckon.'

'Or he'll come home without me,' Chloe sent him a grin, then turned Orion towards the archway.

But that was never going to happen. Orion attempted to take a few serious liberties in their early acquaintance, but soon realised the girl on his back would not allow such behaviour and decided to settle for mutual enjoyment instead.

And when they reached the long, straight stretch on top of the hill and Chloe gave him his head at last, she could have shouted her exhilaration to the skies as Orion flew along.

She cantered him slowly home, the pair of them in total amity. She'd been out for considerably longer than she'd planned and, as she walked him back under the archway, she expected to find Arthur waiting for them and began to frame an apology, but the yard was empty.

Not that it mattered, she thought. In the old days, she'd have done her own unsaddling and seen to her horse's comfort as a matter of course. She could do the same now.

As she got Orion settled and refilled his water bucket, she could hear restless movements from the box opposite and found a pair of glittering dark eyes in a handsome black head with a white blaze watching her with suspicion.

So this was Samson, she thought, feeling a stir of interest and excitement. Big with powerful shoulders and quarters, he certainly lived up to his name.

Chloe spoke to him softly, saying his name and he backed away, nostrils flaring.

She went a little closer. 'Beauty,' she crooned. 'Gorgeous boy. What's the matter, then?'

'Not a great deal. He's simply wondering how to get you near enough to take a piece out of your arm,' Darius said from the doorway. 'I don't advise you give him the opportunity.'

It was Chloe's turn to step backwards. She said with faint breathlessness, 'I thought you were at Warne Cross.'

'I have been,' he said tersely. 'But I realised I couldn't hang around there all day, even to oblige you. As it was, I was asking Crosby so many stupid questions, he must have thought I was losing my mind.'

He came in. Stood, blocking her path to the door. 'Arthur having his lunch?'

'I suppose he must be.' She turned hurriedly to pick up the saddle from the door of Orion's box. 'I—I'll just take this over to the tack room.'

'Leave it,' he said. 'I'll do it later.'

'It's no trouble—really.'

He said with faint amusement, 'Or at least it's the kind of trouble you can handle. Isn't that what you actually mean? But you have no need to worry, sweetheart. After all, you're sacrosanct. Promised to another in the shape of our worthy junior vet.'

'And that's supposed to be some safeguard?' The words were out before she could stop them. 'Your brother didn't find it so.'

'No,' he said very quietly. 'He didn't.' He paused. 'Perhaps you shouldn't have reminded me of that salient fact—and particularly not here. And not now.'

There was another of those odd intense silences. Chloe had the odd impression that she could hear the rush of blood through her veins. The whisper of the breath she was holding.

'I'm sorry.' Her voice was small, husky. 'I had no right to say that. No reason either.'

'No?' Darius asked. He took a step nearer. 'Can you put your hand on your heart and swear that?'

She swallowed. 'I've apologised. That should be enough.'

'Enough?' he repeated. 'That's a paltry kind of word, Chloe, when you consider some of the memories we share.'

She lifted her chin, her heart going like a trip hammer. 'I only remember a girl, little more than a child, who once nearly made a fool of herself and was only saved from a lifetime of regret because you remembered just in time that you wanted another man's woman far more.

'You were a disaster that didn't happen, Darius. That's all. So let's not pretend anything else.' She took a breath. 'And if you come any closer, I warn you I'm going to scream until Arthur and everyone else in the household hears me and comes running.'

For a moment, he was very still, then he moved ostentatiously to one side, leaning against the door of an empty box.

As she walked past him, staring rigidly in front of her, he said quietly, 'One day, darling, you're going to realise you're the one who's pretending. And when you do, I shall be waiting.' He paused. 'See you around.'

And to Chloe, trying desperately not to run to her car, his words were a threat, not a promise.

CHAPTER FIVE

'NEVER again.' Chloe hit the steering wheel with clenched fists, her words grating through gritted teeth. 'Never again.'

She'd headed for one of her favourite spots, driving pretty much on autopilot. But having arrived there and parked on the short grass, she found the car suddenly seemed confining, claustrophobic. She flung open her door and almost scrambled out, standing for a moment, drawing deep breaths of the warm, still air to calm herself.

Ahead of her, the ground sloped away down to where the Willow, glinting in the sunlight, pursued its leisurely course down the valley. She walked slowly down the narrow track towards the water until she came to a large flat boulder a few yards from the bank, and climbed up onto its smooth surface, resting her chin on her drawn-up knees.

How many times, she wondered, had she cycled out here over the years, to swim in the deep calm pool under the trees a few yards downstream, then sunbathe stretched out on this same rock?

But maybe she'd chosen the wrong refuge today, she thought, gazing unseeingly at the view. After all, this was also where she'd always come to think, not escape from her thoughts.

Besides, it held altogether too many memories, reminding her that once she'd been tempted into a dangerous, impossible dream that had no place in the kind of life she'd envisaged for herself. A dream from which, thankfully, she'd been swiftly and brutally awoken.

And the intervening years had only reinforced that awakening, teaching her to concentrate on a future that would provide stability as well as true happiness. The things, she told herself, that she'd grown up with, and which were what really mattered in life. So in a way, the past had taught her a valuable lesson.

Yet ever since she'd come back, she'd had the disturbing sensation that everything was changing, and that, in some strange way, the ground was being cut away from under her feet.

If I'd known that Darius was here, I'd never have come back, Chloe thought, closing her eyes. Or, at least, not to stay. I thought the past was safely buried, so how could I have guessed?

Well maybe by reading Aunt Libby's letters properly and asking the right follow-up questions, she thought, biting her lip with swift savagery. Only I didn't and now I have to live with the consequences—but perhaps not permanently.

She wondered restively just how committed Ian was to Willowford. If it wasn't too late to persuade him that they should also embark on a new start together somewhere completely different. But, naturally, he would want to know why, and what explanation could she possibly offer that would make some kind of sense without involving any potential damaging admissions?

Those vows made by a deceitful tongue...

The Countess Almaviva's words once more wound their sad way through her mind and her throat tightened.

Except, of course, there had been no vows of any kind.

In fact, nothing happened with Darius, she assured herself with a kind of desperation. Nothing. Not then. Not now.

But it could have done so easily. So terribly, even fatally easily. And I can never let myself forget that. Not for a single, solitary moment.

So why on earth did I go within a mile of the Hall today? Why did I believe he'd keep his distance and let myself succumb to the temptation to ride his beautiful horse? Didn't the events of seven years ago teach me anything? And, if so, why didn't I see what was coming?

However, she thought, pushing a hand through her dishevelled hair, Darius's behaviour does suggest a reason for Lindsay Watson's hostility. Something may have been said or merely implied which has caused her to see me as some kind of rival.

And I can't even take her on one side and say, 'Look, frankly, you've got hold of the wrong end of the stick. If you want the glamorous Mr Maynard, have him and good luck to you, because you'll need it.'

Especially, she reminded herself quickly, when no-one seems to know if Penny is completely out of the picture, or simply waiting in the wings, and found she was suddenly shivering in spite of the warmth of the day.

She slipped down from the rock and walked back to the car.

She didn't want to be alone, she thought as she started the engine. She wanted to adjust her focus back to the things that mattered, therefore she needed to see Ian, to sit with him and talk quietly like they used to. Like they should still be doing, because surely, by now, it was time they began to formulate some plans, even if they weren't the ones she'd had in mind when she returned?

Maybe we could both work abroad, she thought suddenly. I could suggest that to him—make it sound like an adventure. Establish completely new roots before we start a family.

But for that I need to see him face to face. Convince him it's not just some crazy whim.

It occurred to her that he usually went back to the cottage for his lunch break if he wasn't too busy. Maybe instead of continuing to wait patiently for an invitation which seemed a very long time in coming, she should simply pay him a surprise visit.

I'd have done it a year ago without thinking twice, she thought. So why not now? *Carpe diem*, as the saying is. Seize the day.

But there was no sign of Ian's jeep on the patch of waste ground by his fence where he normally parked. And the door and windows were all firmly closed.

Chloe gave a small defeated sigh. She'd already turned the car to head back towards the Grange when some impulse made her switch off the engine and get out. While she was here, she thought, she might as well take another look at her future home, even if it was to be only temporary, and, at the same time, see for herself the kind of chaos Ian seemed content, if apologetic, to live in.

It couldn't go on, of course, she told herself with mocksternness. She would have to take the situation in hand at some point, especially if he went along with her idea of a move and agreed to put the place on the market.

The kitchen and dining room were at the front of the house, with the sitting room, and Ian's office at the back, overlooking the small garden.

Bracing herself, Chloe decided to face the kitchen first, always supposing its windows were clean enough to look through, she added silently, wrinkling her nose.

But the panes were surprisingly grime-free, offering an uninterrupted view of the room beyond. Eyes widening, Chloe saw a row of herbs in pots on the windowsill, a new Belfast sink, crockery neatly set out on a small dresser, a gleaming white cooker and a square pine table with a bowl of fruit at its centre. And the room wasn't just tidy, she thought. It looked clean too. And herbs? She'd thought scrambled eggs represented the height of Ian's culinary ambitions.

The dining room told the same story, with an oak table, six chairs and a matching sideboard all neatly set out. None of them new, admittedly, and certainly not antique, either, but all gleaming with polish. And on the table this time two pottery candle-holders and a vase of flowers.

Chloe stepped back, frowning in bewilderment. What on earth had Ian been talking about? she asked herself. Because if this was a mess, then the Grange must be a pigsty. None of it made any sense.

She walked slowly round to the back of the house. The sitting room boasted a cream leather sofa and a matching recliner, neither of which she'd seen before, and the office with its desk, computer and filing cabinet was a picture of order.

So what had happened to all the cheerful squalor she'd been expecting?

She could only think he'd been overcome by guilt and hired a team of industrial cleaners to sort him out. But they would only do the basics. It must be Ian's own efforts that had made the cottage look so homelike and cosy.

I told Tanya I wanted to surprise him, she thought wryly. He must have been thinking on the same lines, and he's certainly succeeded. I'm the most surprised female in Willowford. And when I'm asked to pay my official visit, I'll jump for joy and praise him lavishly.

It was how she'd always visualised the cottage. Just how she'd wanted it to be, apart, possibly, from the cream leather seating, but perhaps that was a man thing. Yet she'd played no part in its transformation.

And while it was undoubtedly carping and churlish to feel disappointed over this, somehow she couldn't help herself.

I just wish he'd told me what he was planning, she thought restively. She wondered what improvements and modernisation had been carried out upstairs, but she'd need a ladder to find out, and anyway she was almost relieved not to know.

The house seemed to be beckoning to her—inviting her to enter and share its welcoming charm—but it was securely locked, and there was no way in, she thought, rattling at the handle of the back door in sudden frustration.

Her future home—and she was excluded. As if she was merely an outsider condemned to remain on the other side of a few panes of glass, looking in.

And, while she knew she was totally overreacting, she could not prevent this disturbing thought accompanying her all the way back to the Grange.

Where another unwelcome surprise awaited her.

'An invitation,' said Aunt Libby. 'Dinner at the Hall, no less. It used to be a regular occurrence, of course, when Lady Maynard was alive,' she went on. 'But rather fell into abeyance afterwards. I suppose these occasions really need a hostess, and Andrew's wife never gave the impression she was keen on indulging the locals. The Birthday Ball was as far as she was prepared to go, and that turned out to be the last, of course.'

'Yes.' Chloe bit her lip as she looked down at the note in Darius's imperious and unmistakable black handwriting.

And now, she thought, the Hall has a hostess again…

She took a swift, uneven breath. 'What excuse can we possibly give?'

'Don't be silly, dear,' her aunt returned briskly. 'This is the equivalent of a royal summons. I gather from Mrs Vernon, who brought the note round herself, that Sir Gregory is now well enough to see visitors, which is really good news, although he won't actually be joining us for the meal.'

'Well, I can't go,' Chloe insisted stubbornly. 'Ian and I have plans for next Wednesday.'

'Then you'll have to change them,' Mrs Jackson said firmly. 'Ian's also being invited, and as the Hall is a client of the practice, he certainly won't refuse. He can't afford to. And nor can we. Something you have to learn when you're in business in a small community.'

She shook her head at Chloe's mutinous expression. 'For heaven's sake, my girl, it's only a couple of hours or so out of your life, and Mrs Denver is still a superlative cook. What on earth is your problem?'

One, Chloe thought bleakly, that I cannot possibly share.

She shrugged. 'Perhaps I'm not very interested in the re-habilitation of Darius Maynard. I imagine this is what it's all about.'

He'd told her himself he intended to become a good neighbour, so maybe she should have seen this coming.

I'm being manipulated again, she thought, bitterly. And I don't like it.

So it was almost a comfort to know that Lindsay Watson would probably like it even less.

'Well, it's only to be expected, as he's the heir apparent. And if his father can accept the situation, who are we to quibble?' Aunt Libby paused.

'Besides, he was very young when it all happened, and we all do foolish things that we regret when we're young.'

Twenty-five, thought Chloe. He was twenty-five. Just as I am now.

She said expressionlessly, 'I suppose so.'

But I don't intend to regret anything. Not again. Never again...

Ian took her to East Ledwick that evening, to a small bistro that had recently opened to considerable acclaim.

'One of these evenings, you'll have to cook for me yourself,' she said, scanning the menu appreciatively.

'Have a heart, Clo. You know my limitations,' Ian said as he summoned the wine waiter and ordered a bottle of Rioja.

All evidence to the contrary, thought Chloe.

Aloud, she said lightly, 'I'm no longer sure you have any—something I find very intriguing.'

She paused. 'So, how do you think our renewed acquaintance is progressing?'

He flushed a little. 'What do you mean?'

Once again, it was hardly the response she'd hoped for, but Chloe persevered.

'I was thinking that maybe it was time we began to consider the future again. To talk about what we both want from life.'

He fiddled with his cutlery. 'I guess we should. Sooner or later.'

He was not, she thought, making it easier for her.

She said, 'Would it help if I told you I was wrong to take that job? To spend so much time away from here?'

'You had your reasons, Clo. You wanted to earn big money fast. No-one can blame you for that.'

'But it's as if I've come back to a different world,' she said. 'One that I don't understand.'

'Well, nothing stands still. Circumstances change. People change.' He smiled awkwardly. 'You're probably not the same person who went away either.'

'But that's what I came back to be,' she said slowly. 'I thought you knew that.'

He was about to answer when he looked past her towards the doorway, his gaze sharpening.

He said, 'It seems as if this is the venue of the moment,' and got to his feet.

Chloe did not need to turn her head to know who had just

come in. The butterflies suddenly cartwheeling in her stomach told her all that was necessary.

Oh, God, this can't be happening to me. Not a second time.

'What a very pleasant surprise,' Darius said lightly as he and Lindsay came to stand beside their table. She was wearing black tonight, a shade that set off her blond hair and pale skin, making her look oddly ethereal. He was totally casual in chinos with a dark red, open-necked shirt, and a light cashmere jacket slung over one shoulder, yet, at the same time, managed in some mysterious way to make every other man in the room look ordinary. 'Why don't we join forces—with you as my guests naturally?'

Chloe could think of all kinds of reasons and was sure that his companion could double the number, but as her lips parted in startled negation, she was instantly checked by Ian's stiffly uttered, 'Thank you, we'd be delighted.'

Aunt Libby's wise words about business and small communities nudged at her brain, as she rose silently to accompany them to a larger table, but surely there were limits?

Although they had apparently ceased to apply, she thought when, inevitably, she found herself placed directly opposite Darius.

She concentrated her attention ferociously on the menu, trying not to listen as he moved effortlessly into charming host mode, offering his enthusiastic approval of Ian's choice of wine when it appeared at the table.

I could always invent a headache and ask to be taken home, she thought, *but he'd know I was lying, and that I was actually running away again. And that would be even worse than having to sit here with my feet tucked under my chair to avoid even the slightest accidental contact with him.*

Indifference is what I should aim for, with a slight frosting of annoyance at this unwarranted intrusion on my tête-à-

tête. Especially as Ian and I seemed to be getting somewhere at last.

She smothered a sigh and asked for smoked salmon and a fillet steak, medium rare, conventional and easy.

'Is this your first visit here?' Ian was asking.

Darius shook his head. 'I came to the opening. The owner's a friend of mine—Jack Prendergast.' He looked across at Chloe, who no longer had a menu to shelter behind. 'Maybe you remember him from the last Birthday Ball? Large guy with red hair, rarely without a smile.'

She drank some water. 'I really don't recall much about that evening at all.' She spoke coolly, and saw the green eyes spark with swift amusement.

'What a shame,' he said softly. 'I'm sure he hasn't forgotten you. Clearly I'll have to make the next ball rather more memorable.'

She stared at him, instant embarrassment yielding as quickly to shock. 'You mean you're planning to revive it?' Her voice sounded hoarse. 'But why?'

'Because it seems a good—a neighbourly thing to do.' He gave her a faint smile. 'And it might also lay a few ghosts to rest. My father would like that.'

But how can that possibly happen, she thought, when everyone present will know that twenty-four hours later you ran away with your brother's wife?

'I wasn't around for the last one,' Ian said. 'Why is it called the Birthday Ball?'

'In memory of my great-great grandmother Lavinia,' Darius returned. 'She was a celebrated nineteenth-century beauty, fancied by the Prince of Wales, among others, and her doting husband, to whom she was entirely faithful, decided to mark her birthday at the end of July with a gala dance at the Hall each year.

'People came to it from all over the country,' he added.

'And subsequent generations continued the tradition, although they didn't cast their net for guests quite as wide. By my mother's time, it was pretty much confined to local people. But it was always a great night.'

How can you say that? Chloe demanded silently. When you know what you did—how you ruined people's lives? How can you live with yourself?

She said quietly, 'Won't Sir Gregory find it rather—taxing?'

'On the contrary, he's all for it.' It was Lindsay who replied. 'He gets very bored, and the arrangements for the ball will hopefully give him a new interest.'

Well, you're his nurse, thought Chloe, so you of all people should know. Or are you more concerned with being the belle of the ball and opening the dancing in Darius's arms? Have you already moved being Lady Maynard?

She said expressionlessly, 'Amen to that,' and drank some of her wine.

The arrival of the first course made things marginally easier, because the food could be discussed in place of trickier subjects.

Chloe made herself eat every scrap of her smoked salmon, while Darius cheerfully demolished a fair chunk of coarse pâté, but Lindsay treated her goat's cheese tartlet as if arsenic might be one of the ingredients and Ian seemed equally hesitant over his potted shrimps.

Listen, she addressed the pair of them silently, you may be no happier about the way this evening is going than I am, but why let it show? Let him play whatever game this is, and pretend that it doesn't matter to you. Or simply treat it as a rehearsal for dinner at the Hall.

'So,' Ian said, as their plates were being cleared. 'How's Samson these days? Still bent on self-destruction?' He turned to Chloe. 'I had to attend to his damaged hock when he tried to kick his way out of his box a few months ago. We had to sedate him to get near him.'

Darius shrugged a shoulder. 'He's the same evil-tempered swine that he ever was. But his malevolence is directed more towards the rest of the world these days. He scares Arthur stiff.'

He paused. 'However, he's seriously fast and he jumps like an angel, so I'm considering letting him put all that ferocious energy to some good use by sending him over to stud in Ireland.' He gave a swift grin. 'A few good-looking mares may give him a better outlook on life.'

'My sympathies are with the mares,' said Chloe tartly, and his smile widened.

'I wouldn't expect anything different,' he told her softly, and she sat back in her chair wishing she hadn't spoken.

A little later, it occurred to her, as she ate a steak so tender she could probably have cut it with her fork, that Ian and she could quite easily be married and on their honeymoon by the date of the Birthday Ball, which would solve a multitude of problems. It was something to aim for anyway.

And when the meal from hell was over and they were finally alone, she would convince Ian that she was entirely his. Go into his arms with tenderness and passion, and give him everything he'd ever wanted from her.

She thought of him kissing her, his mouth warm as it brushed her eyes, her cheeks, her parted eager lips. Of his teeth tugging gently at the lobe of her ear, as his fingertips stroked her throat, moving downwards with slow, exquisite deliberation.

Of him touching her at last, his hands gentle on her breasts, lingering on her thighs, making her body arc towards him in unspoken longing.

And his voice, husky with desire: 'Oh, God, my sweet, my angel, do you know what you're doing to me?'

For a moment, she felt her body flare with the fierce heat of arousal, her face burn in the voluptuous anticipation of pleasure.

She felt her entire being quiver into a sigh, then looked up and saw Darius watching her across the table, his eyes like emeralds in the candlelight, his gaze intent—rapt. Saw the faint, sensuous curve of his mouth, and the almost idle play of his fingers on the stem of his wineglass.

She realised with horror exactly whose caresses she was remembering. Whose lovemaking she had once invited with such total candour.

And, worst of all, knew that he knew it too. That he had read her every thought. Shared each memory. Recognised every secret need.

Leaving her, she thought, defenceless.

For a moment, the space between them seemed to crackle as if charged with electricity.

Chloe's hand moved in hasty, instinctive negation and caught the edge of her own glass, spilling its contents in a ruby flood across the white tablecloth.

'Oh, God, I'm so sorry. I can't believe I've been so clumsy. What a total mess. Shouldn't we put salt on it—or white wine?'

She was on her feet, babbling apologies to everyone, including the waiter who mounted an efficient and smiling rescue operation, removing all the empty plates, replacing the cloth with a clean one, and bringing fresh cutlery and glasses along with the dessert menus.

When Ian tried to pour some more wine for her, she refused. 'I think I've had more than enough, don't you? We don't want them adding in the laundry bill.' Smiling, making a joke of it, but with determination. Wanting to make the silent man on the other side of the table believe it was only alcohol which had set her aglow. And that anything else was entirely in his imagination.

Emphasising this by asking ruefully for black coffee instead of pudding. Then, by moving fractionally closer to Ian and touching his sleeve with a teasing fingertip. By taking a few grapes, a sliver of celery and some fragments of Stilton from his plate. Intimate gestures, she thought, which should designate precisely who was at the centre of her world. And restore her own equilibrium at the same time.

While Darius lounged in his chair, apparently too enthralled by the colour of the cognac he'd ordered to actually drink it, and his companion, eyes fixed on her plate, ate her way doggedly through a *crème brûlée*.

When Ian looked at his watch and spoke apologetically about having an early start in the morning, there was no demur from anyone. Darius simply nodded and signalled for the bill.

Outside on the pavement, there were the usual awkward moments of leave-taking, coupled with over-hearty expressions of gratitude from Ian.

Lindsay was the first to turn away, walking rapidly up the street to where Darius's car was parked.

He smiled at them as he prepared to follow her. 'Well,' he said softly. 'That was most enjoyable. I shall look forward once again to welcoming you to the Hall next week.'

On the surface, it was the polite—the conventional—thing to say.

But Chloe knew differently. She recognised the veiled threat beneath the formal courtesy, and she stood, trembling inside, as she watched him go.

And as she sat without speaking beside the equally silent

Ian on the homeward journey, one desperate question echoed and re-echoed in her brain. *What am I going to do? Dear God, what am I going to do?*

CHAPTER SIX

CHLOE found sleep elusive that night.

She had made no attempt to resume her interrupted conversation with Ian when they arrived back at the Grange. She'd felt obliged to offer him more coffee, but was thankful when he declined the suggestion, and after a swift, almost clumsy, peck on the lips, drove off, saying he'd call her.

Her aunt and uncle were intent on a game of Scrabble when she put her head round the sitting room door and wished them goodnight, so she was able to escape to her room without Aunt Libby's eagle eye spotting there was anything amiss.

But she couldn't hide from herself, or the turmoil raging inside her. She turned restlessly in the bed, seeking a cool place on the pillow, even the sheet seeming to press her down.

Eventually, she pushed it aside and got up, pulling on her cotton robe before making her way over to the window seat. There was no breeze coming through the open window, and the moon looked huge and heavy above the fields, a great golden orb preparing to drop out of the sky.

Chloe leaned back against the wall, closing her eyes.

She'd thought it was all over and done with long ago. That she'd relegated the past to some forgotten corner of her mind. Conquered her demons and laid them to rest.

Now it seemed she had to confront them again—one last time.

But it has to stop here, she told herself. I can't allow some ludicrous, meaningless memory to interfere with the life I've chosen for myself—everything I've planned for and worked towards for the last seven years.

I won't allow it.

I deal with it here and now, and then I let it go. For ever.

And if there's pain, I deal with that too.

It had been the same hot, still weather then, she remembered. But oppressive, too, as if an approaching storm was being signalled. And that wasn't simply a dramatic veneer imposed in retrospect by her imagination.

'Off to the Willow Pond again?' Aunt Libby had asked that afternoon so many years ago now, glancing up at the sky. 'In that case, take your waterproof. The weather's going to change.'

'Oh, I'll be back long before that happens,' Chloe had assured her breezily, tucking a towel and some sun lotion into her haversack and slipping her arms through its straps.

If she was honest, she'd been feeling at a bit of a loose end. School was over, and only the results of her public examinations remained, about which she'd been modestly confident. Her best friends Jude and Sandie had both been abroad with their parents on celebratory vacations, and long weeks had stretched ahead of her before the start of the university year.

Worse still, Ian was away assisting on an experimental inoculation programme for cattle in Shropshire, and his regular phone calls were no compensation at all.

At the same time, her woebegone expression had cut very little ice with Aunt Libby, who was kind but frank.

'Yes, he's a thoroughly decent boy, and your uncle and I think the world of him. He's going to make a fine vet and probably a good husband when the time comes, but it's far too soon for either of you to be thinking seriously about anyone.

'Enjoy your salad days, my dear, and fall in and out of love half a dozen times. That's what being young is for. But you also have your degree course to concentrate on, and a career to consider. Don't get sidetracked, however appealing it may seem at the moment.' She paused. 'And don't lead Ian up any garden paths either. He deserves better.'

And what she meant by that was anyone's guess!

It was all right for Aunt Libby, Chloe thought rebelliously later as she cycled through the lanes. She'd probably forgotten what it was like to be turned breathless by the sound of someone's voice, or feel your heart skip a beat when he walked into the room. That is, of course, if she'd ever known. She and Uncle Hal were sweet together, but...

Anyway, she ought to be glad that I've already met the man I want, she told herself. That there's no fear of me plunging off the rails at college, or anywhere else.

In addition to that, she decided with sudden mischief, Aunt Libby should be gratified that her niece had suddenly discovered a strong domestic streak and was taking a real, if unexpected, interest in housework. In learning the unfashionable arts of cooking, cleaning, washing and ironing, and for their own sake too, rather than just with an eye to the future.

Not very liberated, perhaps, but deeply satisfying in its own way. And what was so wrong in preferring order to chaos?

She found the Willow Pond deserted, as it often was midweek. Quickly she stripped to her pale pink bikini and slid down into the cool water, enjoying the sensation of its freshness against her heated skin. She swam to the other side of the pool and back, using a slow and dreamy breaststroke which seemed to lend itself to the general languor of the day.

She hauled herself out and went and sat on the rock where she'd left her towel, wringing the water from her waving mass of dark hair, and combing the damp strands with her fingers as she lifted her face to the sun.

'My God—little Chloe grown up at last. Who'd have thought it?'

The amused masculine drawl made her jump and she turned her head with a start, shading her eyes, her heart thudding as she realised who was standing a few yards away.

She said rather breathlessly, 'Darius—Mr Maynard, I mean. What are you doing here?'

'The same as you. Or that was the plan. And Darius will do just fine.' He walked forward and stood regarding her, hands on hips, the mobile mouth quirking. 'Thinking of changing your own name to Lorelei, my pet?'

She flushed under his scrutiny, suddenly aware just how skimpy her bikini really was and wishing she'd chosen to wear her former school's regulation one-piece swimsuit instead.

Or cycled to the swimming baths in East Ledwick.

She reached hurriedly for her discarded cotton cut-offs and elderly striped shirt, with a silent sigh for the dry underwear in her haversack. 'I—I'll get dressed and out of your way.'

'Please don't,' he said. 'Unless, of course, you want me to feel terminally guilty about driving you off. Surely, there's plenty of room for both of us.' He paused. 'Besides, I thought we were old friends.'

Which was, presumably, some kind of absurd joke, Chloe thought uncertainly. Because she and Darius Maynard were nothing of the kind. He knew her mainly from her reading sessions with his late mother, and on Lady Maynard's instructions had seen her to the main door when they were over, chatting lightly to cover her own tongue-tied silence as she walked beside him.

After that, she'd encountered him a few times when she'd been up at the Hall to exercise one of the old ponies that he and his brother had ridden as boys, and while he'd been perfectly pleasant, she'd always felt uneasy around him, and glad to get away.

But for the past two years she'd hardly seen him at all.

'Working abroad,' Mrs Thursgood had said with a sniff. 'Paid to keep away and out of mischief more like.'

Aunt Libby had uttered a mild remonstration, but Chloe could tell her heart wasn't really in it, and had wondered about the nature of the mischief.

Now, she was no longer a shy schoolgirl, mute in the face of his male sophistication, therefore there was no earthly reason for her to be shaken even marginally by this unexpected meeting.

So why did her mouth feel dry, and how could she account for this strange hollowness in the pit of her stomach? Her new-found poise must be more fragile than she thought, she realised without pleasure.

She said, 'I—I thought you were working away.'

'I have been. I came back yesterday. Thought I'd revisit some people and places. Renew old acquaintances.' His smile teased like the stroke of a hand on her skin. 'And with great good fortune, I find I'm beginning with you.'

He began to unbutton his shirt, and Chloe looked down at her towel, tracing its pattern with a fascinated finger.

She ought to leave, she thought. Make some excuse and—go. He was undoubtedly what Jude's grandmother had once described, eyes dancing from her own young days, as 'NSIT, my dears: Not Safe In Taxis,' reducing them both to gales of laughter. Only now it didn't seem so funny.

And she recalled Sandie, who'd seen him when the local hunt met near her village, had pronounced him 'utterly gorgeous'.

A splash told her that Darius was safely occupied in the pool providing her with the ideal opportunity to make a quick exit. Except that haste of any kind did not recommend itself in this kind of baking heat.

Nor did she wish him to know that he caused her even the slightest alarm, she thought, biting her lip. Especially when there was no reason for it. No reason at all.

She found herself reaching for her sun lotion and smoothing it gently over her arms, shoulders and the first swell of her breasts above the cups of her bikini, before proceeding down to her midriff and the slender length of her legs.

By the time he returned, lithe in black trunks, raking his wet hair back from his face, she was replacing the cap on the bottle.

She said with an assumption of composure, 'Was that good?'

He shook his head. 'Good doesn't come near it. And it may be our last chance for a while. There's thunder in the air. Can't you feel it?'

As he picked up his towel and began to blot the water from his tanned skin, it occurred to Chloe that she was aware of a number of sensations she would have much preferred to ascribe to atmospheric pressure.

At the same time, she realised that, while it was still hot, there was now a dull look to the sky, and the sun was a brazen globe behind a thin veil of cloud.

When he'd finished drying himself, Darius shook out the towel, spread it on the grass and stretched out on it a decorous few feet away from her.

'It's been quite a while, so how's the world treating you, Miss Chloe Benson?' He plucked a grass stalk and began to chew the end of it, watching her reflectively. 'School out for the summer?'

She shook her head. 'Out for ever. I've been offered a place to read English at London University, if my grades are good enough.'

He sat up. 'Truly? My God, that's terrific.' He grinned at her. 'Your family must be thrilled. Really proud too.'

She returned his smile shyly. 'They seem to be. And I'm quite pleased myself.'

'So what do you plan to do with your eventual degree. Teach?'

She shook her head. 'Journalism, I hope, at least to begin with.' She flushed a little. 'I've always wanted to write, and one day, when I know a little more about life, I might even manage a novel.'

'This calls for a celebration.' Darius got to his feet and strode up the track to where his Land Rover was parked. When he returned, Chloe saw to her astonishment that he was carrying a bottle of champagne and a paper cup.

'No crystal flute, I'm afraid, and it won't be as cold as it should be, but—what the hell?'

She gasped. 'Do you always have champagne in your car?'

'No,' he said, removing the foil. 'This was a farewell present.'

An instinct she'd not been aware she possessed told her that it was from a woman.

She watched with unwilling fascination as he extracted the cork with only the faintest 'pop' then poured the fizzing wine into the cup without spilling a drop.

She said, 'I thought it was supposed to explode out of the bottle and drench everyone around.'

'Only if you've won a Grand Prix.' He handed her the cup, and sat down on the edge of her rock. 'Here's to your first bestseller,' he said, and drank from the bottle.

Chloe hesitated. 'It's kind of you,' she began. 'But I really don't think I should.'

His brows lifted. 'Why not? You've reached an age where all kinds of delights are legally permissible—and this is one of them. It's not drugged, and there's not enough in that cup to render you drunk in charge of a bicycle, so there's no need to be nervous.'

'I'm not,' she denied swiftly.

'Perhaps scared stiff would be more applicable,' he said, his mouth twisting. 'But you're perfectly safe, because I know that if I upset you in any way, I'll have your formidable Aunt Libby to deal with, and she's even scarier.'

She was betrayed into a reluctant giggle.

'That's better,' Darius approved. 'You can't refuse to drink a toast to your own success.'

She lifted the cup to her lips and drank, feeling the bubbles burst against her throat.

'You talk as if it's a foregone conclusion.'

'Maybe because I believe it is,' he said. 'Though I think I'd have put my money on you becoming an actress rather than a writer.'

She took another swallow. 'Why do you say that?'

'I remember how you used to read to my mother,' he said slowly. 'The way you interpreted the words—got inside the characters. You made the books live—gave her real enjoyment.' His smile was reflective. 'She was very fond of you.'

Chloe looked down. 'It's kind of you to say so,' she returned awkwardly. 'I—I liked her too.' She hesitated. 'Actually, I was rather stage-struck for a brief time. But perhaps the readings got me focused on the way stories were constructed and made me realise I'd rather create my own words than interpret what other people had written. If that makes any sense.'

He nodded. 'I gather you still come up to the Hall sometimes to help with the ponies.'

'Yes, but that won't be for much longer.' She couldn't avoid the wistful note in her voice. 'Arthur says Mr Maynard intends to sell them. Yet they're so lovely, and still really strong and healthy. I—I thought he'd have kept them for his own children.'

Darius refilled her paper cup. 'Clearly he has other plans for when that happy time arrives. And Moonrise Lady is going too.'

'Mrs Maynard's mare?' She stared at him. 'But why?'

'Too nervous.'

'She's nothing of the kind.' Chloe's protest was instinctive. 'She has a wonderful temperament.'

'I was talking about the rider,' he said. 'Not the horse. It seems that Penny's not much of a country girl at heart, and much prefers four wheels to four legs.'

'Oh,' she said. 'Well—that's a shame, when Mr Maynard is so keen. My uncle was saying he'll be asked to be Joint Master of the Hunt next season.'

'I've heard that too. Following in a grand old tradition like his father and grandfather before him,' he added, lifting one smooth brown shoulder in a casual shrug.

'Don't you believe in tradition?' It must be the champagne, she thought. She would never have dared question him like this under normal circumstances.

'Fortunately I don't have to,' he said shortly. 'That's Andrew's job. But, for the record, I believe in progress. In doing what needs to be done.'

A sudden flash lit up the sky and he looked up, frowning. 'Which at the moment is to get dressed and out of here,' he added as thunder rumbled ominously in the distance. He emptied the rest of the champagne onto the grass. 'I'll go down by the water, and you use that clump of trees. That should preserve the decencies well enough. But be quick.'

Her hesitation was only momentary. She was just zipping her trousers when, with another crack of lightning, the rain began to fall in thick, heavy drops.

As she made for the track, Darius joined her. 'Get in the Land Rover,' he told her. 'I'll put your bike in the back.'

'But I couldn't ask you…'

'You didn't.' He handed her the keys. 'Now run before you're drenched.'

It was raining in earnest now so it seemed wiser to do as she was told.

She scrambled into the passenger seat, and waited, her heart thumping, while Darius retrieved her cycle and loaded it on board, along with the empty champagne bottle.

'Well, we can't say we weren't warned,' he commented as he started the engine, the rain thudding on the roof. 'But it's a pity our celebration had to end so suddenly. The glories of the English summer.' He glanced at her. 'Not too wet?'

'I'm fine.' She sat up straight, hands folded in her lap. 'It's—very kind of you.'

'What did you imagine?' His swift grin slanted. 'That I'd allow a future Booker prize-winner to risk pneumonia?'

Chloe flushed, and because she couldn't think of a single sensible reply, kept quiet.

When he drew up in front of the Grange he said, 'Here you are, home and dry. And I won't accept the kind invitation to come in for a cup of tea, which I'm sure is trembling on your lips,' he added, as he lifted out her bicycle. 'So let's just say that I'll see you around.'

He paused, then said softly, 'And when your first novel is bought by a publisher, I promise I'll open more champagne and douse you with it—every last inch from your head down to your toes.'

He blew her a kiss, got back in the Land Rover and drove away, leaving her staring after him, lips parted, oblivious to the rain.

Aunt Libby was waiting in the hall. 'My dear child, I knew the weather would turn. You must be soaked to the skin. I'll run you a hot bath.'

'I'm hardly even damp,' Chloe returned. She hesitated. 'Actually, I had a lift home.'

'Well that was good of somebody.' Aunt Libby led the way into the kitchen and busied herself filling the teapot. 'Who was it?'

Chloe tried to sound ultracasual. 'It was Darius Maynard, of all people.'

'Darius?' Aunt Libby placed the lid slowly on the teapot. 'I thought he was supposed to be working on a stud farm in Ireland. Where did you run into him?'

'He came back yesterday,' said Chloe. 'And I met him down at the Willow Pond. He'd gone there for a swim. Like me.'

'I see,' said her aunt in a tone that suggested the revelation was not altogether welcome. She poured tea into two beakers and handed one to her niece. 'I imagine he's back for the Birthday Ball. The invitations are being sent out this week, so I suppose it was inevitable.'

Chloe stared at her. 'You make it sound as if he should have stayed away.'

'Maybe he should, at that.' Mrs Jackson sighed sharply. 'It always seems that whenever Darius is around, there's invariably trouble and some of it, according to the talk in the village, has been serious. Not all his absences, especially the most recent one, have been entirely voluntary.'

Her aunt shook her head, her expression brooding. 'But perhaps it isn't entirely his fault. For one thing, he's so entirely different from his father and older brother, and, for another, being the second son with no actual role to play in the running of the estate can't be a happy situation for him. Maybe it encourages him to be wild. To see how far he can push the boundaries even if it means breaking the law.'

'The law?' Chloe repeated. 'I don't understand.'

'There's no reason why you should,' Aunt Libby said with finality. 'Just keep out of his way, my dear.' She added with faint grimness. 'And being far too attractive for his own good doesn't help either.'

'Well, he doesn't appeal to me,' Chloe said firmly, taking a sip of scalding tea, and hoping it would disguise any lingering hint of wine on her breath.

And just who am I trying to convince here? she asked herself. Aunt Libby—or myself?

Not that it matters. The Maynards belong in a totally different social sphere to the rest of the village, so our paths are unlikely to cross again.

A view confirmed in a few days when the village grapevine spread the word that Darius had left the Hall again, this time for London.

'Always restless, that one,' was Mrs Thursgood's opinion. 'Not happy in the same place for more than a week. Never was. Never will be. Was it a book of six or twelve stamps you were wanting?'

But at least Chloe felt able to relax a little without imagining she might bump into him around the next corner.

And his absence encouraged her to respond to a suggestion from the Hall, conveyed by her uncle over lunch, that as the ponies would be leaving early the following day, she might like to say goodbye to them.

'Well, yes.' She sighed. 'Although I can't believe that Mr Maynard has really sold them, when they've both got years left still. Or that Moonrise Lady is going too.'

'Well at least they're departing for new homes where they'll be loved and wanted, so it makes a kind of sense. And the ponies have been bought together.' Uncle Hal dropped a gentle hand on her shoulder as he rose from the table. 'I'll be passing the Hall presently if you want a lift, but you'll have to walk back.'

Chloe changed quickly, tucking a short-sleeved blue shirt into her jodhpurs. Her uncle dropped her off at the Hall's gates, and she was on her way up the winding drive when a car's horn tooted behind her.

Her heart gave a swift lurch, and she turned apprehensively to see Penny Maynard waving at her from her Alfa Romeo.

'Hop in,' she called. 'It's far too hot to walk.'

As always, she looked devastating, wearing a white skirt topped by a cyclamen-pink blouse, her ash-blonde hair cut into a sleek shoulder-length bob, and her violet eyes fringed by expertly darkened lashes.

She'd always been reed-slender, but now it seemed to Chloe that she was actually thin, and there was an increased definition to her cheekbones and a tautness to her mouth that had not been there before. That made her beautiful face look almost haggard.

'I'm sorry you're losing your playmates,' she remarked as the car sped off. 'After all, you're the one who's really bothered with them. But Andrew has finally accepted that horses are another interest we will never share, so I won't really be shedding any tears.'

There was an odd note in her voice that Chloe could not interpret, and, anyway, this was Sir Gregory's daughter-in-law she was talking to, so she confined her reply to a neutral, 'I suppose not.'

'Prenuptial agreements seem always to be about money,' the older girl went on flatly. 'I think their scope should be broadened, so that everyone knows exactly where they stand. No post-wedding shocks. Don't you agree?'

'I don't know,' Chloe returned with faint bewilderment. 'But you couldn't possibly include everything.' She paused awkwardly. 'Besides, isn't learning about each other all part of the fun of being married?'

'"The fun of being married",' Penny repeated almost musingly. 'Yes, you're quite right. That's what it's all about, of course.' She gave a short laugh. '"Oh, wise young judge".'

She stopped the car at the arch leading into the stable yard to allow Chloe to alight. 'Listen,' she said. 'I want you to know I'm really glad that you cared about the ponies and Moonrise Lady and made a fuss of them, and I'm sorry it couldn't be me. It would at least have been one way of justifying my existence.'

She drove off fast, her tyres scattering gravel, and Chloe watched her departure, astonished and embarrassed at the same time.

What on earth, she wondered, had all that been about?

Penny Maynard was at least six years her senior, and, until now, like most local people, Chloe had admired her at a distance. Certainly, they'd never exchanged more than the minimal formalities if they happened to encounter each other at occasions like the annual village concert or the flower show. And they'd never—ever—been on female chatting terms.

How could we be? Chloe asked herself. When I'm just a schoolgirl and she's a married woman? When she probably knows me only vaguely as the vet's niece? It makes no sense.

In the stable, Arthur Norris, the groom, was tacking up Moonrise Lady. He greeted Chloe with his usual unsmiling nod.

'Ponies are in the first paddock,' he said. 'I've put a few jumps up in the far one, not too high, so you can school this one over them, make sure she minds her manners. Girl she's going to isn't all that experienced.'

'But she's certainly lucky.' Chloe ran a gentle hand down the mare's neck, hearing her whicker softly in response. Penny Maynard, she thought, didn't know what she'd missed.

She extracted a plastic container of apple and carrot pieces from her shoulder bag, and went down to the paddock. The ponies met her at the fence, jostling each other for the pick of the treats, butting her arm and shoulder with eager affection.

She fed them and stroked their noses, whispering that they

should be staying here where they belonged, waiting to take Andrew's children on their backs, but that she'd remember them always. Always.

Then Arthur came down from the yard with Moonrise Lady, and she mounted, blinking back her tears, and rode the little mare into the other paddock.

The jumps were simple ones, and Chloe took her through them with easy grace, then turned, watching Arthur raise the rail a couple of notches on the final one, but keeping it still well within the Lady's capacity.

She rode back to the start, and put the mare at the first low hurdle. Moonrise Lady jumped it perfectly again, continuing to sail effortlessly over the others.

But as they approached the last, Chloe saw out of the corner of her eye a movement over by the paddock gate, and realised they'd been joined by someone else. Momentarily distracted, she allowed herself a quick glance to confirm the identity of the newcomer.

With a gasp, she tried to regain her concentration, but the rhythm of the mare's stride was broken. She took off at an awkward angle, stumbled on landing and sent Chloe flying over her head to hit the grass with a force that left her panting and breathless at the feet of Darius Maynard.

CHAPTER SEVEN

'WELL, I've seen more elegant descents.' Darius squatted beside her. 'Do you think you've broken anything or are you just winded?'

Chloe sat up wincing. 'Just—winded.' *And furious with myself for being such an idiot.*

'Also a little dishevelled,' he said softly.

Following his gaze, Chloe glanced down and saw to her horror that some of the little pearl buttons on her shirt had come undone during her fall, revealing even more of her firm young breasts in their lace-trimmed cups than her bikini bra had done.

'I have no objection, naturally,' Darius added, a quiver of amusement in his voice. 'But you might give poor old Arthur a heart attack.'

So to that fury, she could also add humiliation, she thought as she struggled to refasten her shirt with fingers made clumsy by haste and embarrassment. And in front of him, of all people.

It was a welcome relief when Moonrise Lady came wandering over to drop a soft and questing muzzle on her shoulder and she could bury her flushed face in the mare's neck.

'I'm sorry, darling,' she muttered. 'It was all my fault.'

'She already knows that,' Darius said crisply. He got to his feet, dusting bits of grass from his elegant charcoal pants.

He held out a hand. 'Up you come, my girl, and up you get—back on the Lady; restore her confidence in you by taking her over that last jump again. Properly this time.'

Chloe obeyed mutinously. Not that she had much choice with his hand clasped firmly round hers, pulling her upright.

She wasn't used to being thrown. She felt jolted all over and tomorrow she'd be bruised, and what she really wanted was to burst into tears and go home.

And to say that she'd made a mistake because his unexpected arrival had startled her was no excuse at all.

She lifted herself stiffly into the saddle, took a deep, calming breath then set off as instructed. This time there were no mistakes as Moonrise Lady soared safely and sweetly over the rail and came down as if she was treading on velvet.

As she brought the mare to a halt and made to dismount, Darius reached up, lifting her out of the saddle and depositing her gently on her own two feet, wobbly legs notwithstanding.

'Thank you.' She tried to say it normally but, with his strong hands still grasping her waist, it emerged as a squeak. She stepped back and removed her hat, shaking her hair loose. 'I—I'll see to the Lady.'

'Arthur will do that. I've been instructed to take you up to the house.'

She hesitated, glancing down quickly at the grass stains on her jodhpurs. 'I'm expected at home.'

'My sister-in-law has rung the Grange,' he said. 'Told them you're staying for some tea. Although there won't be much sympathy.' He produced a handkerchief and wiped her cheek, showing her the smear of earth he'd removed. 'And clean you up a little at the same time.'

Colour stormed into her face as she realised what she probably looked like. But she accepted, too, that there was little point in further protest. That she was doomed to appear a grubby urchin beside Penny Maynard's effortless chic.

She hadn't set foot in the house since Lady Maynard's death, but it didn't seem to have changed at all. The hall with its flagged floor, and the family portraits in massive frames on its panelled walls gave its usual cool and shady impression after the blaze of the sun, the only patch of colour provided by a massive silver bowl filled with roses on a long side table.

In the drawing room, Penny was standing by one of the mullioned windows staring fixedly at the garden beyond. As Darius conducted Chloe into the room, she turned, her gaze sharpening.

'Good God, what happened to you?'

'I fell off,' Chloe admitted in a tone of false brightness.

'Off one of my husband's gentle, noble creatures?' Penny's tone was mocking. 'I can hardly believe it.' She walked forward. 'You look as if you've been rolled on and trampled. I'll take you up to my room. Make you look more presentable.' She glanced at Darius. 'Tell Mrs Vernon to give us about twenty minutes before she brings tea, will you?'

As she followed Penny up the stairs, Chloe felt the past few years slip away, turning her back into the nervous fourteen-year-old being conducted to Lady Maynard.

But whereas that bedroom had been massive and stately, filled with valuable antique furniture, Penny's room was in total contrast.

It was all pale colours, and sleek modern lines, down to the low, wide divan bed.

'Andrew offered me free rein with the décor,' Penny tossed carelessly over her shoulder. 'So I took him at his word.'

'It's beautiful,' said Chloe. Beautiful, she thought, but also totally out of place in an old house like this. Nor could she visualise Andrew Maynard's tall, broad-shouldered frame being at ease in all this feminine magnificence. But no doubt he felt his glamorous wife was worth it.

The bathroom was another surprise in ivory and gold, and

more like a beauty salon than a place to wash and clean one's teeth. Or the Hall of Mirrors at Versailles, she thought with a shudder as she caught sight of herself in all her mud-stained glory in one of them. Only her shirt seemed to have escaped relatively unscathed.

'Have a shower if you want,' her hostess invited casually. 'There are loads of towels. And I'll find you something cleaner to wear. I imagine we're about the same size.'

'I don't want to put you to any trouble,' said Chloe, but it was a token protest. Her eyes were already glistening at the sight of the engraved glass cubicle with its power shower.

'You're not.' The denial was instant, but the accompanying smile seemed a little forced. 'Come down when you're ready.'

The cascade of hot water felt like balm on her aching body. When she returned to the bedroom, her jodhpurs had been removed and a pair of jeans with a designer label were waiting for her in their place, together with a short-sleeved white silk blouse, and a hair dryer.

The jeans fitted her like a second skin, and Penny was taller too, so Chloe had to turn up the legs a fraction. But the blouse was a little too large, so at least there was no chance of any more accidents with buttons, she decided, her face warming at the unwelcome memory.

Once dressed again, she sat down rather shyly at the dressing table with its array of scent bottles and cosmetic jars, praying she wouldn't break anything or move a pot of cream out of its designated place, and began to attend to her hair.

At the same time, she found her eyes straying round the room, remembering the enormous four-poster bed in Lady Maynard's bedroom, and the elegant *chaise longue* by the window where the Hall's former mistress had spent so many of her latter days, and wondering what she would have made of all this determined modernity. Or whether Penny would have been gently but firmly dissuaded from its more extreme aspects.

Because Lady Maynard had believed in tradition. Sometimes, when the reading was over and she'd felt well enough, she had talked to Chloe, reminiscing about her girlhood, spent travelling with her parents to various diplomatic posts all over the world, making the past live again with an almost wistful note in her voice.

She'd spoken too of the history of the Hall she'd been compiling over the years, admitting with regretful finality that it would never be finished.

'That will be someone else's task,' she'd said.

I wonder what happened to it? thought Chloe as she switched off the dryer and stood up.

When she got down to the hall, Mrs Vernon was just wheeling the tea trolley into the drawing room.

'Perfect timing,' Darius said, tossing aside the copy of *Horse and Hound* he was reading and getting to his feet as Chloe followed the housekeeper into the room. The green eyes skimmed her, sharpening in undisguised appreciation as they observed how the borrowed jeans moulded her slim hips and the length of her slender legs, before returning almost quizzically to the concealment of the white blouse.

No prizes for guessing what he was thinking, Chloe thought indignantly as the dull colour stole back into her face again. Head high, she stalked over to a chair as far from the sofa he'd been occupying as it was possible to get without actually leaving the room.

I don't want him to look at me like that, she thought passionately. I don't like the way it makes me feel. And I wish he'd stayed up in London, or never come back at all, because I don't like him. Full stop.

Penny was an attentive hostess, offering cucumber sandwiches, scones with jam and cream, and a Madeira cake that managed to be even lighter than Aunt Libby's.

How can she possibly stay so thin with Mrs Denver serving up feasts like this several times a day? Chloe wondered.

Penny chatted too, a rapid flow of words that scarcely demanded an answer, or an intervention from anyone else, telling Chloe how lucky she was to be going to university in London, and what a fun city it could be, talking of theatres, concert halls, galleries and nightclubs.

Or how to be a student on a private income, Chloe thought drily. But she was glad she did not have to sustain the other half of the conversation in any meaningful way. On the surface, it appeared to be a conventional afternoon occasion, but there was a tension in the room that was almost tangible.

And it had to be centred on Darius, she thought, acutely aware of him lounging on the other side of the room, his silk tie loosened, his shirt unbuttoned at the neck as he listened to every word, a half-smile playing round his lips. She remembered what Aunt Libby had said about him. Someone who pushed even the law to its limits.

She found herself wondering exactly what he had done, and why he'd been sent away.

But that was forbidden territory, and she was glad to be able to get up, murmuring that she must be going, thanking Penny for her delicious tea, but swiftly declining her offer of a lift, on the grounds that the walk back to the Grange would do her good.

'Stop me stiffening up too much,' she added.

'But you must take this with you. Your family's invitation to the Birthday Ball.' Her hostess handed her a square white envelope, addressed, Chloe saw, not just to her aunt and uncle, but, for the first time ever, to herself as well.

She held it awkwardly, feeling a bit like Cinderella. 'Thank you. I—I must pop back to the stables before I leave—pick up my bag.' She forced a smile. 'So thanks again—and goodbye.'

Hurrying as best she could, she'd reached the archway into the yard when Darius caught up with her.

She said tautly, staring straight ahead of her, 'You really don't need to see me off the premises. I know my way.'

'I'm sure you do.' He followed her into the stable, leaning against the door as he watched her tuck the invitation into her bag. Apart from the sounds of Moonrise Lady happily chomping on some hay in her stall and the cooing of a pigeon in the rafters, it was very quiet. Even, she realised, isolated, with Arthur nowhere to be seen.

He went on, 'But I also have something to give you.'

He took a small bottle of tablets from his pocket, grinning as her eyes widened. 'And it's not some weird drug to render you helpless and at my mercy, either. It's just arnica for the bruises. I'm sure your uncle has plenty, but consider it a precaution.'

Darius Maynard, Chloe thought bitterly as she accepted the bottle with a muttered word of thanks, and pushed it into her bag, king of the disarming gesture.

He added, 'And I'll drive you home.'

'No!' The refusal was too quick and too sharp, and she saw his brows lift mockingly.

'Chloe, my sweet,' he said softly. 'What must I do to prove that you can trust me?'

'Nothing,' she said raggedly. 'I simply don't want it to be necessary.' She swallowed. 'I know it's all a big joke to you, but it's one I don't happen to share.' She spread her hands almost helplessly. 'So, why can't you just understand that—and leave me alone?'

'Because this is not a joke,' he said with sudden harshness. 'Which is something that you in turn are failing to understand.'

He stepped forward, and his hands grasped her shoulders, pulling her towards him.

The breath caught in her throat. She lifted her hands, placing them flat against his chest in a hurried attempt to keep him away from her. Because she had to do something—*something*—to stop him. Before it was too late...

Then he bent his head and his lips took hers with a quiet and almost frightening precision, exploring its soft contours as if her mouth was some unknown territory he was learning by heart, and she knew, as if he had spoken the words aloud, that it was already too late. And perhaps always had been.

One hand moved down and grasped her hip, urging her body into an even more intimate proximity with his. His other hand also abandoned her shoulder to gently stroke the vulnerable line of her throat, and the delicate whorls of her ear before moving to the nape of her neck to let his fingers twine in the soft, dark fall of her hair.

Her own fingers were curling into fists, as they clutched the crisp front of his snowy shirt, holding him as if she was drowning, or her shaking legs would suddenly hold her upright no longer.

His lips coaxed hers apart to allow him to penetrate her mouth's inner sweetness and she felt the satin glide of his tongue teasing hers, playing with its tip in the kind of sensuous demand she'd never experienced before, and she felt the shock of it whisper through her body, startling her innocence with the promise of her own sexuality. Making it impossible for her to deny him the response he sought. Or even wish to...

His kiss deepened instantly, passionately, sending sharp tendrils of sensation quivering along her nerve endings. Her hands slid up to his shoulders, then fastened round his neck, the brush of his hair like silk against her fingers.

And the little voice in her head protesting that this was all wrong, that it was dangerous—it was madness and she should stop it now—*now*—faded to a whisper and then to silence.

They stood, mouths and bodies locked together. For the first time, Chloe felt her clothing as a barrier. She was aware that her breasts seemed to be blooming—swelling against the confines of her bra, pressing against the hard muscularity of his chest, and she wanted to be rid of it. Rid of everything.

As if in answer to some unspoken plea, Darius slid his hand from her hip to her waist, then upwards to cup one soft mound in his palm, while the ball of his thumb moved gently against the delicate rosy peak in deliberate, provocative arousal. She gasped against his mouth, a small choked sound that was almost a moan, as she felt the sudden rush of scalding heat between her thighs.

She heard him groan something that might have been her name, then his caressing hand stilled. He took his lips very slowly from hers and began to kiss her temples, her closed eyes, the line of her cheekbones, and, with great care, the corners of her mouth, just brushing her skin as softly as the wing of a butterfly.

She raised leaden lids and looked up at him, seeing a glitter in the green eyes that scared and excited her at the same time.

When he spoke, his voice was husky, almost slurred. He said, 'No—not here, my sweet one. Not—like this.'

He drew her close and held her for a long moment, his arms almost fierce, his face buried in her hair. Then he straightened, putting her away from him, looking down at her with faint ruefulness.

He said quietly, 'And now I really am going to take you home.'

There were tears on her face as she sat staring unseeingly into the darkness and Chloe wiped them away with her knuckles in a gesture that was almost childish. But every haunting memory of that time, seven years before, was conspiring to remind her that she had indeed been hardly more than a child just emerging into womanhood.

And I indulged myself with a child's dreams, she thought bitterly. Ignored the warnings from people who'd known him so much longer and so much better than I had and who, therefore, had no illusions about him. Told myself they were simply prejudiced, making unfair comparisons with Andrew, who never put a foot wrong.

Darius asked me to trust him, and for a while I did, although I had no cause—no reason to do so. Because I was young and stupid, I let his touch, his kisses tempt me to forget what I really wanted from life. Even to fool myself, for a brief time, that he might be the one—the other half of myself.

And, oh, God, he made it so easy for me. So terribly, heart-breakingly easy.

She shivered suddenly, wrapping her arms round her body.

I mustn't use emotive words like that, she told herself. My heart did not break. It didn't even develop a hairline crack, because Darius was just a diversion. Fate's way of teaching me to distinguish the substance from the shadow. A painful but necessary lesson.

And I won't make the same mistake again.

But she soon found that time hadn't totally done its healing work, and the pain still existed, twisting inside her as she remembered driving back to the Grange with him, her body hot and aching, her hands clasped in her lap to hide the fact that they were trembling.

When she asked him in a small, hoarse voice to drop her at the end of the lane, he made no protest, but she saw his mouth tighten wryly.

As she fumbled her seat belt he leaned across and released

it for her, running a finger gently down the curve of her cheek. He said, 'I'll be in touch,' and drove off.

'So, tea at the Hall,' said Aunt Libby. 'Did you have a nice time?'

Chloe met her enquiring gaze with as much composure as she could manage. 'Yes, Mrs Maynard was very kind. I must wash and iron the clothes she lent me and return them.' She handed over the big square envelope. 'And she sent you this.'

Her aunt's brows rose as she extracted the card and read it. 'You've also been invited, I see. I imagine you won't want to go.'

'Why not?'

'Because I recall you shuddering away from the idea not that long ago, describing the Ball as a bunch of old fogeys dancing the St Bernard's waltz,' Aunt Libby returned calmly.

Chloe flushed. 'Well, yes, I probably did—then.'

'But something's happened to change your mind?' Mrs Jackson's eyes were shrewd.

'It's probably my only opportunity to go.' She forced a smile. 'See if I was right about it. Once I'm at university, I'm going to have to find vacation work, so I won't be around so much.'

'No,' Aunt Libby said thoughtfully. 'There is that.' She was silent for a moment, then gave a brief sigh. 'Then I'll accept for the three of us. You'll need a dress, of course.'

'There's a hire place in East Ledwick,' Chloe said quickly. 'Or I can try the charity shops. It needn't cost much.'

'Clearly you have it all worked out.' Her aunt's tone was dry. 'We'll drive over later this week. See what's available.'

It was not a prolonged search. The woman who ran the dress hire ran a brisk eye over Chloe and nodded in approval. 'Lovely slim figure and slightly high-waisted too. I think I have the perfect thing.'

She disappeared to the back of the shop and returned with a swathe of filmy fabric in white, shot with the glimmer of silver, draped over her arm.

'I'm told this has been inspired by the new *Pride and Prejudice* film due out in the autumn,' she announced. 'Whatever, I think it's delightful.'

And when Chloe looked at herself in the mirror, she could only agree. It was a slender column of a dress, short-sleeved, the ankle-length skirt falling straight from a low-cut bodice which permitted an enticing but demure glimpse of the first swell of her breasts.

'Elizabeth Bennet to the life.' The manageress smiled at her, then turned to Aunt Libby. 'Is there a Mr Darcy waiting to dance with her?'

'Absolutely not.' Mrs Jackson spoke with a certain crispness. 'As such men only exist in the pages of books. But the dress is certainly charming, and I doubt whether anything else will have the same appeal, so we'll take it.'

A shoe shop in the High Street provided the final touch of an inexpensive pair of silver ballerina pumps, and Chloe accomplished the journey home in a mood of quiet elation, barely noticing that Aunt Libby was equally silent.

They were almost at the Grange when her aunt said abruptly, 'Next time Ian calls, why don't you ask him if he can get back for the weekend of the dance? I'm sure if we explain the circumstances, Mrs Maynard will give us an extra invitation.'

Chloe looked at her, startled. 'But it wouldn't be any use. The programme is an ongoing thing. He doesn't have weekends off.'

'Well there would be no harm in trying.' Aunt Libby shot her a swift glance. 'That's if you want him to go with you, of course.'

'Well, naturally I do.' Chloe recognised the defensive note in her voice. 'In fact, I'll ring him this evening.'

However, 'Not a cat's chance, I'm afraid,' Ian told her glumly. 'The team's one short as it is. Craig's off with shingles.'

'It can't be helped.' Chloe tried to sound consoling. 'It was just an idea.'

But as she hung up, she caught a glimpse of herself in the mirror above the hall table and knew, with shame, that her eyes were much too bright for real disappointment.

Over breakfast the next day, she said casually, 'I'd better iron Mrs Maynard's clothes and return them. I'd almost forgotten.'

'I hadn't,' said her aunt, composedly buttering a slice of toast. 'I laundered them, and got your uncle to drop them off at the Hall a couple of days ago.'

'Oh.' Chloe stared down at her plate, hiding her chagrin. 'I didn't mean you to go to all that trouble.'

'Nothing of the kind,' said Aunt Libby. 'It was my pleasure.'

And there, seething, Chloe had to allow the matter to rest.

But now, looking back down the years, she realised that her aunt had only been trying to be wise for her. To steer her gently away from the first real danger of her young life.

She could see it, she thought. Why couldn't I?

Except, of course, that it was already too late, she admitted, shivering. Because the damage was done, leaving her to face its bitter consequences and, somehow, learn to endure them.

CHAPTER EIGHT

By the night at the ball, Chloe had been so nervous she almost wished she'd developed shingles herself.

But the dress had looked even better than it had in the shop, and she'd caught back her newly washed tumble of dark curls, securing them away from her face with two pretty silver combs.

'You look lovely, my dear,' Uncle Hal greeted her as she came downstairs. 'Isn't she a picture, Libby? The belle of the ball in person.'

Her aunt, elegant in a plain black dress topped by a hip-length sequinned jacket, smiled affectionately and nodded, and if she still had concerns, she kept them well hidden.

The ballroom at the Hall was at the rear of the house, and was approached through a large conservatory where Sir Gregory waited to receive his guests, with Andrew Maynard beside him, the formality of evening clothes emphasising the rigidity of his demeanour, and making him look more like a soldier on parade than a man at the start of a pleasant social occasion.

But his tension appeared to be shared. Penny stood next to him, ravishing in a deep fuchsia-pink sheath, but her face under her immaculately piled-up hair was taut, and her smile seemed as if it had been painted on.

While of Darius, there was no sign.

As Chloe paused in front of Penny to say a shy, 'Good evening,' the older girl gave a slight nod, then turned calling 'Laurence.'

A tall, fair young man detached himself from a nearby group and came towards them.

'Yes, Mrs Maynard?'

'This is Chloe Benson, our local vet's daughter,' Penny drawled. 'It's her first Birthday Ball, so make sure she meets a few people of her own age, please.'

Laurence did not appear overjoyed to have been appointed resident babysitter, and Chloe, smarting at Penny's casual attitude, shared his reservations in full. It was far from being the introduction to the ball that she'd hoped for. Which proved only how silly it was possible to be, she thought as she followed him reluctantly.

And her misgivings seemed entirely justified as one of the girls in the group they were approaching looked at her dress and said in a stage whisper, 'I thought this was a dance, not a fancy dress parade,' setting off a faint ripple of amusement.

'Meet Chloe Benson,' Laurence announced. 'Apparently she's a local.'

'Really?' One of the other girls raised her eyebrows. 'I don't remember you at St Faiths?' She was referring to the expensive girls' day school on the other side of East Ledwick, and Chloe shook her head.

'I went to Freemont High School.'

'Oh,' said the other. 'Oh, I see. Well, I suppose that would explain it.'

'Did you think tonight was fancy dress?' The original speaker was back on the attack, looking her over.

Flushing, Chloe lifted her chin. 'No,' she returned. 'I'm simply wearing a dress I fancied.' And allowed her own appraising glance to suggest that scarlet taffeta was not the wisest choice for someone at least a stone overweight.

'And why wouldn't you?' A brown-haired girl with mischievous hazel eyes came forward. 'I'm Fran Harper,' she said. 'And, for the record, I think you look fabulous. Classic.' She paused. 'There's some great punch on offer in the dining room. Let's find you some and get acquainted.'

As they walked away together, she added in an undertone, 'Don't let Judy or Mandy get to you. They both fancy Laurence for some unknown reason, and you represent instant threat.'

'Not really,' Chloe told her ruefully. 'We were simply foisted on each other by Mrs Maynard. She probably thought she was being kind.'

'Good God,' said Fran. 'She's never struck me as the charitable sort. A lady with axes of her own to grind, I'd have said.'

She ladled punch into two small glass cups, and handed one to Chloe.

'To kindness, however unlikely it may be,' she announced, and drank.

Chloe sipped with rather more caution, feeling the warmth curl in her throat as she tried to glance round the room without making it too obvious that she was looking for someone.

But it was patently evident that Darius was still not around and she found herself stifling a pang of disappointment.

Ludicrous, she told herself firmly, and high time that she came to her senses and started to enjoy the evening simply for what it was rather than letting herself indulge in dangerous imaginings.

Besides, her view of the room was soon restricted as others came to join them, and she found herself in the middle of a cheerful group of people her own age or slightly older, most of whom had already embarked on their university careers, and appeared genuinely interested in her own plans.

Before too long, they'd all adjourned to the ballroom, and Chloe was immediately out on the floor, dancing firstly with

Fran's brother Bas, in his second year at Cambridge, followed by a whole series of other boys.

She was laughingly protesting that she needed a rest when she felt an odd tingle of awareness shiver down her spine and, looking over the shoulder of a stocky brown-haired boy with freckles, saw Darius on the other side of the floor partnering a tall grey-haired woman in emerald-green.

Her heart leapt so fiercely, she was ashamed. Nor was she proud, either, to be thankful that she too was dancing and not occupying one of the chairs at the side of the room in solitary splendour, dumped there by Laurence and co. Just in case he happened to notice.

But she must never forget either that, if circumstances had allowed, she'd have been here tonight with Ian, and happy to be so. That was the most important thing. So how could she possibly be even glancing in any other direction—and especially one so patently impossible?

I need to stop all this, she told herself with a kind of desperation. I need to stop it right now, before I make an utter fool of myself. And she gave Craig with the freckles the kind of smile that made his pleasant face light up in response.

But good intentions notwithstanding, she could probably have given a photo-fit description of every woman Darius had danced with throughout the evening. As for herself, there was no indication that he was even aware of her presence.

It was almost a relief when a halt was called for supper. This, served in the dining room, was on traditional lines, with large joints of ham and beef for carving, platters of salmon mayonnaise, coronation chicken, lobster patties, mushroom and asparagus tartlets, a huge array of salads, cheeses and baskets of crusty bread. Also on offer were bowls of rich chocolate mousse, tall frosted glasses of syllabub, and great dishes piled with strawberries accompanied by clotted cream.

Chloe wished that she wasn't feeling so tense, and could have done the spread rather more justice.

And on the heels of supper, came the birthday toast, proposed with due formality by Sir Gregory, flanked by both his sons, with Penny Maynard standing, slender as a willow wand but with all the rigidity of a steel rod at her husband's side, her faint smile looking as if it had been painted on.

'In asking you to pay this tribute to my great-grandmother Lavinia,' he announced, his deep voice booming over the crowded room, 'I would also like to include all the other wives since who have done such honour to the Maynard name as chatelaines here. Not forgetting my daughter-in-law Penelope,' he added, turning towards her. 'Who, I have no doubt, will bring her own charm and distinction to this role.'

He raised his champagne glass. 'My lord, ladies and gentlemen, I give you—the Maynard ladies.'

'The Maynard ladies,' was echoed smilingly round the room. Chloe, about to sip, found for some reason that her eyes were drawn to Penny Maynard who had blushed to the colour of a peony as Sir Gregory spoke. But as Chloe watched, the hectic flush faded, leaving her pale as a ghost apart from the artificial pink curve of her mouth and the vivid, over-bright eyes.

My God, Chloe thought in horror. She's going to faint.

There was little she could do from the back of the room, but she took an instinctive step forward just the same in time to see Penny turn and walk slowly and steadily away, leaving the three men standing together, like an awkwardly posed study in black-and-white.

The moment of crisis, if that was what it had been, seemed to have passed, but it left Chloe feeling curiously uneasy, just the same.

She was almost glad when the dancing resumed again, even though the knowledge that her aunt and uncle had no intention of staying on into the small hours made her feel far more like Cinderella than Elizabeth Bennet. She would just enjoy whatever time she had left, she told herself.

She was recovering her breath and drinking some lime and soda when she saw Laurence, of all people, making his way towards her with an ingratiating smile.

'Come on, princess,' he said softly as he reached her. 'I think it's time we got it together, don't you?'

'Afraid not, old boy.' The speaker, a tall red-haired young man appeared from nowhere. 'She's promised to me.

'And I have a definite feeling,' he went on, steering Chloe expertly towards the French windows which had been opened onto the terrace. 'That we should sit this one out.'

Chloe tried to pull away in swift alarm. 'I really don't think so.'

'Trust me, sweetheart.' Clasping her firmly, he whirled her down to the far end of the terrace in some kind of old-fashioned waltz that had nothing to do with the music being played. 'They don't call me Honest Jack Prendergast for nothing.'

'I wasn't aware they called you anything at all,' Chloe snapped, still trying to free herself.

'Well why don't you check with a mutual friend?' he said soothingly, and swung her round as a dark figure emerged from the shadows. 'Here she is, mate, delivered as per request, feathers a little ruffled, but I'm sure you can deal with that.' He gave a broad grin. 'Bless you my children.' And he strode back up the terrace leaving Chloe looking up at Darius.

'Sorry about the cloak and dagger stuff,' he said lightly. 'But every time I tried to get over to you, I was intercepted for one reason or another. An elliptical approach seemed better, so I enlisted Jack's assistance and took a different route.'

'I can't imagine why,' said Chloe, unsure whether she was

breathless from the waltz or the shocked clamour of her own heartbeat.

'And you say you're going to be a writer?' he queried softly. 'You'll have to use your imagination better than that, Miss Benson.' His hands went round her waist, drawing her slowly and inexorably towards him so that they melded into the shadows.

And even though a small warning voice in her head was telling her to release herself from his grasp and run back to where there were lights and people and safety, in reality her lips were already parting, longing for his kiss.

His mouth was warm and almost frighteningly gentle as it took hers but his lightest touch was enough to send every sense, each nerve ending in her untutored body into quivering, aching response. Chloe pressed herself against him, her arms twining round his neck as she gave herself up to the sweet delirium of the moment.

She felt his clasp tighten around her to the point of ruthlessness, as his kiss deepened, and his tongue invaded her mouth in frankly sensual demand and clung to him with all the passion of her newly awakened flesh.

When Darius raised his head, his breathing was ragged. 'God, sweetheart.' His voice was unsteady. 'Have you any idea what you're doing to me?'

'Yes.' The word was scarcely more than a breath. How could she not know, she thought, when every waking and sleeping moment since their last meeting had burned with the memory of him? Of their last encounter...

No—not here. Not like this...

His words, heavy with a desire that was now overwhelming her with the need for surcease. The necessity to know—everything.

Her fingertips wonderingly explored the planes and contours of his face, stroking the high cheekbones and the hard line of his jaw. She took his hand and kissed it, then pressed it to the delicate mound of her breast and its taut, excited nipple, hearing him groan softly as he began to caress her, his fingers pushing aside the concealing fabric of her dress.

But in that same moment, they heard the sudden sound of voices and laughter from the other end of the terrace, and knew they had company.

'We can't stay here,' Darius said, his tone oddly harsh. 'I have to be alone with you. Will you go with me?'

She nodded, the movement little more than a nervous jerk of the head as she realised exactly what her consent entailed. What she was deliberately inviting.

He took her hand, steering her quickly round the corner of the terrace and down some stone steps onto the wide gravelled path that traversed the house until they came to a side door.

Inside was a flagged passage and, at its end, a flight of wooden stairs leading up to a swing door and beyond it a dimly lit, thickly carpeted corridor that she had never seen on any of her previous visits, although instinct told her what their ultimate destination would be.

Halfway along, Darius paused and opened another door, ushering her inside. It was his bedroom, as she'd known it would be, even if the lamp left alight on the night table had not revealed as much.

But a first glance told her that it was far from the kind of room she'd have expected. For one thing, it wasn't very large and the furnishings, including the three-quarter-size bed under its plain green quilt, were fairly sparse, consisting of a single wardrobe in some dark wood, a matching chest of drawers with a mirror, and a small armchair.

There were no pictures on the plain walls or ornaments on any of the surfaces, and if it hadn't been for the hairbrushes and small group of toiletries on the dressing chest, the discarded jeans and shirt tossed over the chair, the small pile of books on the night table and the neat pile of luggage in one corner, she'd have believed it was simply a spare room, furnished as an afterthought and only used when the house was full.

A temporary place, she thought, suddenly bewildered, for someone who was just passing through, but surely not for a son of the house?

Then Darius, his dinner jacket and black tie discarded, took her in his arms and all thought surrendered helplessly to sensation as he lifted her and carried her to the bed, kicking off his shoes and dark silk socks before joining her.

For a while, they lay wrapped in each other's arms, kissing slowly and languorously, then Darius began to touch her, his hands moving without haste, exploring the slender lines of her body through the thin layers of material that still hid her, before unfastening the small row of buttons at the back of the bodice and slipping it off her shoulders so that his fingers and his lips could enjoy her bared breasts, stroking and suckling them with sensuous tenderness.

Chloe, eyes closed, let her head fall back on the pillow, a faint moan escaping her throat as she experienced the heavenly torment of this new delight, her nipples hardening to sensitised peaks under the subtle play of his tongue.

'Oh, God, my sweet.' His voice was husky, and she discovered the erotic charge of tasting her scent on his mouth as it returned to hers, while his sure hand released the remaining buttons, so that he could slide down her dress and remove it with infinite care, leaving her with her tiny white lace briefs as her only covering.

She gave a little murmur compounded of pleasure and shyness, her unpractised hands trying desperately to deal with the studs on his dress shirt so that she could feel his naked skin against her own. And Darius helped her, almost negligently

stripping the crisp linen away from his body and dropping it
to the floor beside the bed, then drawing her against him so
that his smooth tanned chest grazed her rounded softness.

She lifted herself, pressing against him in her need to be
closer yet, some instinct she'd not known she possessed until
that moment telling her there was only one path to the fulfilment of her desire. That he had to be part of her, one flesh
with her.

He whispered her name against her mouth, then kissed her
with ascending passion and yearning, his hands sliding the
length of her spine and pushing away the few inches of lace
in order to caress the silken swell of her buttocks. A heartbeat
later and the lace was gone, leaving her naked in his arms

Darius lifted himself onto an elbow and looked down at
her, his eyes shadowed as he gazed at the flushed ivory of
her body, the deep rose of her aroused nipples, the concavity
of her belly, and the soft dark smudge at the joining of her
thighs.

He said in a voice she hardly recognised, 'Do you know
how lovely you are? How totally adorable? My glorious, radiant girl.'

His hand swooped over the curve of her hip, then trailed
downwards with deliberate purpose combined with a tantalising lack of haste.

Chloe gasped helplessly, as her body responded with a
scalding rush of betraying heat to this new and devastating
promise and the certainty of where it must lead.

Her own fingers gripped the broad muscular strength of
his shoulders, then feathered down over his ribcage and taut
abdomen to the waistband of his pants, fumbling with the
fastening and tugging down the zip, feeling the hot, steel-
like hardness of him through the silk shorts beneath.

Darius freed himself swiftly from the enveloping fabric
and kicked it away, sending his shorts after it, then pulling

her to him, letting her feel the ramrod urgency of him between her bare thighs.

She made some small incoherent sound and opened herself to him. His mouth took hers and she felt the silken play of his tongue mirroring the first heart-stopping glide of his fingertips as they moved on her with a lingering and exquisite finesse she'd never dreamed could exist.

But no dream had ever taken her this far, overwhelming her in mind, body and soul, making her ache, burn and melt. Turning her innocence in a few brief moments to a distant and unregretted memory.

And if in some dazed corner of her mind, she realised this was because she was in the hands of a master in the art of seduction, she did not attempt to resist because she also knew that she could not, even if she wanted to.

He found her woman's tiny sensitive mound among the heated satin folds of flesh and stroked it softly and sweetly, arousing it to a throbbing peak of anticipation. Yet, all the same, when his exploration of her deepened to a first gentle penetration, she could not help flinching a little as it occurred to her what the reality of a full physical consummation would mean.

Darius stopped instantly. 'I'm hurting you?'

She found a voice from somewhere. 'No. At least… It's just that I've never…'

Her voice tailed away in embarrassment, and she waited for him to take her in his arms and offer reassurance. Tell her that he would make her transition into womanhood beautiful for her.

Instead, there was an odd silence.

Then, as she was trying to pluck up the courage to look at him, he said very quietly, 'Of course. How could I possibly not realise? Hell, how blind and selfish is it possible to be?'

She did stare at him then, her eyes widening endlessly in

bewilderment and a kind of fear as she heard the detached weariness in his voice.

She said, faltering again, 'Is something wrong?'

'Just about everything, I'd say.' He was moving to the edge of the bed, reaching for his clothes, presenting her with the implacable view of his naked back. 'But principally—that I haven't the least right in the world to make this kind of demand of you. And thank God you made me see it before too much harm was done.'

'I don't understand.' Her voice shook. 'I thought you wanted me.'

'Who wouldn't, my sweet?' His drawl made the words no easier to hear. 'As I said earlier you are—very lovely—and frantically desirable. But that is no justification for stealing your virginity in what would probably be a pretty one-sided transaction.'

'Then why did you bring me here?'

He told her why in a brief explicit crudity that brought the colour storming into her face, and impelled her to cover herself with her hands. Not that he was even glancing in her direction.

'I suggest you also get dressed,' he went on. 'I'd leave you in privacy, but you're going to need help with those damned buttons.'

Through the tightness in her throat, she said, 'I managed at home, thank you.'

'Then I'll go. It would naturally be better if we don't arrive downstairs together.' His tone was brisk, almost impersonal. 'If you turn right out of here, then left at the end of the corridor, you'll come out in the Long Gallery. You'll remember your way from there.' He went to the door, carrying his jacket and tie, then turned. In the lamplight, his face was a stranger's—bleak, even haggard.

He said, 'This should never have started, and I can only

ask you to forgive me, and believe me when I tell you that parting now is totally for the best. One day, I hope you'll understand.'

No, Chloe thought, as the door closed softly behind him. I never will.

Not as long as I live.

For the moment, she felt numb, but soon there would be the pain of humiliation and the sheer agony of regret, and she could only pray she'd be safely back at Axford Grange before they kicked in.

Her hands were trembling so much that getting back into her dress was a nightmare, but even the struggle with the buttons was infinitely better than having to submit to his touch again.

Now all she had to do was live with the knowledge that she'd naively offered everything of herself that she had to give to Darius Maynard and been rejected, presumably because her confession of total inexperience had suddenly made her less appealing.

But surely he must have known I'd never been with a man before? she thought, forcing herself to use his brush to restore her hair to some kind of order. Or had he listed me as one of the local tarts? The thought made her shudder.

Her bag was down in the ballroom, so she had no lipstick to return some colour to her white face. One of her combs was missing too, and she had to search for it in the bed, but at last she was fit to be seen again.

As she descended the staircase, Penny Maynard appeared. 'Oh, there you are at last. Your aunt and uncle have been looking for you. I think they're ready to leave.'

'Thank you. I'm sorry I kept them waiting.' Chloe forced a smile. 'I think I had too much punch earlier, so I needed a few quiet moments.'

Penny shrugged. 'It happens,' she said. 'It was one of

Darius's concoctions and they're always lethal. You've probably had a lucky escape.'

'Yes.' Chloe kept her smile, although it felt as if it had been nailed to her mouth. 'I think I probably have.'

And she walked quietly away to find the people who loved her and go home with them, so she could break her heart in secrecy and peace.

CHAPTER NINE

CHLOE stirred awkwardly on the window seat. She was cold and cramped, but that did not explain or justify the tears running down her face. Remembering the events of seven years before had hardly been an exorcism of her personal demons, after all, but more the deliberate opening of an old and still-vicious wound.

She had cried for what remained of the night of the Birthday Ball too, deep racking sobs that threatened to tear her apart. Earlier, she'd explained her disappearance at the dance to her aunt and uncle by saying that she'd felt unwell after supper, and thought she'd eaten something which had disagreed with her.

'You look like a little ghost.' Aunt Libby had viewed her, frowning anxiously. 'Don't think about getting up tomorrow. Sleep as long as you want.'

And, in the end, when there were no tears left, she'd done exactly that. She'd eventually woken around midday, had a bath and dressed in jeans and a tee shirt, but the face that looked back at her from the mirror as she brushed her hair was still wan with deep shadows under the eyes.

Sooner or later, she would have to face Darius again, probably in public, she told herself, and right now she didn't see how that could ever be possible.

She had to practise a few cheerful expressions before she went downstairs.

When she went into the kitchen Uncle Hal had returned for lunch, and he and Aunt Libby were standing by the window, their faces grave, having a low-voiced conversation which ceased abruptly when Chloe entered.

She checked. 'I'm sorry. Is this something private?'

'No. Oh, no.' Aunt Libby's distress was evident. 'It's common knowledge by now, I don't doubt, in every sordid detail. Mrs Thursgood will have seen to that.'

Chloe felt a sudden inexplicable chill. 'Why, what's happened?' *Oh, God did someone see me leaving his bedroom? Has something been said?*

'There's serious trouble at the Hall,' Uncle Hal said abruptly. 'Mrs Maynard—Penny—has left Andrew and run off with his worthless brother. It seems they were found together in his bedroom at some unearthly hour this morning in what's known as "compromising circumstances."' He pronounced the words with distaste. 'It's anyone's guess how long it's been going on.

'There was a terrible scene apparently,' he went on. 'Shouting, hysterics, and even blows exchanged. In the end Sir Gregory told Darius to go and never come back. And he has gone, taking her with him. Cleared out, the pair of them, lock, stock and barrel. And no-one knows where they've gone.'

There was a peculiar roaring in Chloe's ears, and she felt as if she was looking at her aunt and uncle down a long tunnel.

She thought, I must not—I cannot—faint…

Aunt Libby was speaking. 'Mind you, it was pretty obvious last night that all wasn't well. I don't think she and Andrew even had a duty dance together. But all marriages go through rough times, at one time or another.' She sighed.

'Such a good-looking couple, too. It seems so sad. And so awful for Sir Gregory, who values his privacy, to have his family's dirty linen washed in public like this.'

She shook her head. 'I suppose there'll be a divorce.'

'Inevitable, I'd say,' her husband agreed.

Chloe swallowed. 'How—how did you get to know all this?' she asked, astonished that her voice could sound so normal.

'Mrs Thursgood's niece Tracey was helping with the clearing up after the dance,' said her uncle. 'As soon as the row began, they were all out in the hall listening, and, of course, they heard everything. Especially Sir Gregory bellowing at Darius that he didn't have a single shred of decency in his entire body and that if he didn't get out, he'd throw him out with his own hands. And shortly afterwards, Darius and Penny came down with their cases, got into his car and drove away. Well, he's always been the rotten apple in the Maynard barrel with his womanising and other antics. And I dare say a lot of people will be saying "good riddance".'

To bad rubbish. Wasn't that how the quotation ended? Chloe asked herself. And how could she argue with it when Darius, knowing full well that he was committed to someone else, however illicitly, had deliberately set out to seduce her?

But why? she asked herself, feeling genuinely sick to her stomach as she thought of him entwined with Penny on the same bed where he'd been making love to her only a few hours previously. How many women could he possibly want at a time?

She supposed she should be thankful that what passed for his conscience had spared her when she told him she was a virgin. Maybe there was a lingering shred of decency in him after all.

My glorious, radiant girl. The remembered words made her shiver, her throat muscles tightening convulsively. Everything he'd said and done meant nothing. It had all been simply a means to an indecent end. The gratification of a spare hour. If not her, then someone else. But someone with experience, not an innocent idiot. That was what had stopped him, she told herself.

'It's time we ate.' Aunt Libby was bustling around, placing a bowl of salad on the table and cutting slices of a bacon-and-egg pie.

And Chloe had to eat. Had to sit at the table and listen to all the continued conjecture and force down the food, one small mouthful at a time.

'I think Penny Maynard must have taken leave of her senses,' said Aunt Libby. 'How could she not be happy with a decent man like Andrew? And what kind of life is she expecting with that—fly-by-night?'

But she wasn't happy, thought Chloe. Not ever. How could anyone not see that? She was always tense—on edge. So brittle you expected her to snap.

Uncle Hal shrugged. 'Maybe it was just a fling and she never intended it to be found out, only they got careless.' He shook his head. 'Whatever, they're stuck with each other now.'

But were they? Chloe wondered now, uncurling herself from the window seat and standing up. Why wasn't Penny there at the Hall with Darius? Was it all over between them, or had Sir Gregory's forgiveness only extended to his own flesh and blood, permitting no more than the return of the prodigal?

And what does it matter anyway? she asked herself silently as she dried her face, wiped her eyes, blew her nose and got back into bed. It was all a long time ago, and we are different people with different lives now. I know what my future will be and who I'll spend it with. Probably Darius does too, she added, thumping the pillow, and if Lindsay Watson turns out to be his choice, at least his father should approve.

It took her a while to fall asleep, and when she finally did so, she found herself tormented with the kind of dreams that hadn't troubled her for a long time. Dreams that she was imprisoned by silken cords, unable to resist, while a man's hands and mouth explored her body with voluptuous sensuality.

And when she woke, her skin was slick with sweat and her entire self was one shivering ache of yearning.

While the words *my glorious, radiant girl* were, for reasons she did not dare examine too closely, still churning somewhere in her brain.

And Memory Lane, she told herself grimly, is now permanently out of bounds.

'So they're having another of their Birthday Balls,' said Mrs Thursgood, with a sniff. 'Asking for trouble, I'd say. Who's going to be running off with someone they shouldn't from this one, I wonder?'

Chloe, her face wooden, placed her letter on the scales. 'Postage to France, please,' she said.

'France is it?' Mrs Thursgood adjusted her glasses and peered at the electronic reading. 'Getting a job over there, are you?'

'No,' said Chloe. 'I have a friend who's working on the Riviera.'

If it's any of your business, you nosy old bat, she added silently. But I'd rather be interrogated about Tanya than talk about the Birthday Ball.

But Mrs Thursgood was not to be deterred. 'Darius Maynard's been away in London for a good while. It's a wonder his father can spare him. But he's always here and there, that one. Probably keeps a lady friend up there out of the way.'

Chloe, conscious of a growing and interested queue behind her, bit her lip until she tasted blood and forced herself to concentrate on Tanya.

The postcard received from her two days before had said, *Ignore the blue skies. The mistral has been blowing for all week and the kids are hyper.* Les parents *have pushed off to Italy with friends, and I'm stuck at the above address going quietly insane. Help.*

Trouble is I've no real help to give, Chloe thought, as she attached the stamps and waited to receive her change. In fact it had been a hell of a struggle to try to sound cheerful and positive in return, when there was so much that she could not or would not mention, such as tomorrow night's dinner party at the Hall. At which, of course, Darius might or might not be present.

It's been one long whirl here, she'd written at last. *I've been riding, dog-walking and generally getting back into the local swing. My uncle is retiring quite soon, and I've been helping redecorate the house before they sell it.* She'd paused, chewing the end of her pen, then added, *When my feet eventually touch the ground, Ian and I plan to sit down quietly and sort out a date for the wedding.*

But would they? They dated a couple of times a week, but their relationship was still worryingly static, without even the anticipated invitation to the cottage anywhere on the horizon. And if as Ian had indicated, they needed to restart their relationship, it was a pretty muted affair, plodding along rather than sweeping her off her feet as she'd secretly hoped, and so badly needed to happen.

She wished she could confide in Tanya, but found herself jibbing at expressing her concerns in black-and-white, as if by doing so she would somehow set them in stone. Make them seem more serious than they really were.

After all, she reminded herself, marriage was for life and Ian was merely being sensible for both of them. Making sure they were sure.

But one of these days, Chloe told herself, when he wasn't

on call, or attending a meeting, or playing squash, she would seize the initiative and drive over there, taking the ingredients of a steak and wine dinner for two in a carrier bag.

'I hear the Grange is going on the market soon.' Mrs Thursgood intruded on her thoughts once again. 'So you'll be moving on too, I dare say.'

'I have plenty of time to make my own plans,' Chloe returned coolly, putting her coins in her purse and heading for the door.

Safely outside, she drew a deep breath. An errand at the post office often resembled an encounter with a grinding machine, she thought broodingly, and how nice it would be when she could brandish her engagement ring in front of her inquisitor and say, 'I'm going nowhere.'

Not a noble ambition, she admitted silently, but Mrs Thursgood effortlessly brought out the worst in her.

She returned slowly to her car. She'd planned to drive up to the Hall, as she'd done each day following Darius's departure ten days earlier and two increasingly irascible messages from Arthur, in order to exercise Orion. But the postmistress's comments on the reasons for his trip had managed to get under her guard in some unexpected and infuriating way.

It shouldn't have happened, she thought bitterly. Not when she'd been telling herself over and over again that his continuing absence was a relief. A case of 'out of sight, out of mind'.

But being forced to consider what he might indeed be doing while out of sight had aroused a sharp pang deep inside her, of which her damaged lip was only an outer sign.

It's none of my concern what he does, she told herself forcefully. He's a law unto himself and always has been. And if anyone should feel injured by his behaviour, it's certainly not me.

In the past few days, while she was out with Flare or

shopping in East Ledwick, she'd caught several glimpses of Lindsay Watson walking slowly along, her head bent, shoulders slumped and clearly deep in thought. And to judge by her body language, her thoughts were not particularly happy ones.

Chloe could imagine why. According to the village grapevine, Sir Gregory's condition was improving every day, which meant that he would soon not need a full-time nurse and Lindsay would be looking for another job.

Which meant that if she'd been entertaining hopes of securing Darius as a husband, her time could be running out, a situation not improved by his continuing absence in London. And maybe she too had her suspicions about what drew him there.

Maybe I should feel sympathy for her, thought Chloe. But somehow I can't. And anyway, I have my own problems.

When she arrived at the stable yard, she was surprised to see Samson out of his box, saddled and bridled but tied up securely. He clearly resented the restriction, moving restively, his head jerking and eyes rolling. Every glowing inch of him a magnificent challenge, thought Chloe, her heart missing a beat.

'Am I riding him today?' She couldn't keep the eagerness out of her voice, and Arthur snorted.

'Not on your life, gal. Mr Darius warned me before he went away that you weren't to be allowed anywhere near the nasty devil.'

'Oh,' said Chloe. 'Did he really?'

'Yes, missy, and he meant it, so you can take that look off your face. And Samson's going tomorrow, off to stud in Ireland, which I won't be sorry for.' He nodded severely. 'Tim Hankin, the gamekeeper's eldest boy has been coming over each afternoon to exercise the blighter, but he'll be early today as he has to rejoin his regiment. Off to Afghanistan again, seemingly.'

Chloe frowned. 'Tim? I don't think I know him.'

'Good lad,' said Arthur. 'But wild when he was a youngster. Mr Darius, being a pal of his, had to drag him out of all kinds of trouble, some worse than others.'

Chloe lifted her chin. She said coolly, 'It sounds to me like six of one and half a dozen of the other.'

'Does it?' said Arthur grimly. 'Then maybe you don't know as much about Mr Darius as you think, my girl. Now I'll finish tacking up Orion for you.'

Chloe leaned against the wall, watching Samson as he fidgeted, ears pricked, clearly bored and becoming irritable. In the stable she could hear Arthur's chiding voice telling Orion to stand still.

Seriously fast, she thought with longing, and jumps like an angel. Darius said so himself in the restaurant that night. But off to Ireland, so I may never get another chance.

And how dare he tell Arthur to warn me off, as if I was some stupid little novice who can't be trusted with a difficult horse? I'll show him—I'll show both of them that I can really ride. But I won't go too far—just down to the first paddock and back in order to make my point.

She began to walk towards Samson, who acknowledged her approach by curling back his lip to show his teeth.

She said softly, 'Come on, beautiful. Show me how nice you can be.'

But *nice* did not seem to be a word that Samson understood. As she approached, he began to stamp, swishing his tail, his nostrils flaring ominously. Chloe halted, trying to quell her sudden apprehension.

Dangerous, she thought. Dangerous and unpredictable. Both attributes which had attracted her once before and almost led her to disaster.

She took a deep breath. If you get the better of Samson, she thought, then maybe you can also conquer this ludicrous obsession with Darius, and put it behind you where it belongs, once and for all.

It's something you have to prove to yourself, for heaven's sake, if you're to have any hope for the future.

As she got closer, Samson began to sidle around, trying to jerk loose from his tethering ring probably in order to lunge at her.

Murmuring nonsense in a low, soothing voice, wondering which of them she was trying to calm most, herself or the horse, Chloe warily adjusted the girth and the stirrups.

And then, as if by magic, all the angry restless movements were suddenly stilled and his head even drooped a little.

Well, what do you know? thought Chloe. Maybe all he ever needed was a woman's touch.

Very gingerly, she untied him and, without having lost a hand, swung herself up into the saddle.

For a moment, everything was quiet, but it was only the lull before the storm as Samson's powerful muscles bunched and, with a squeal of pure rage, he wheeled round then reared up, in an attempt to throw her off his back and into oblivion.

His hooves clattered down and he went into a series of fierce bucks, forcing her to cling on desperately, winding a hand in his mane in addition to the reins.

Every atom of concentration in her body was fixed on staying in the saddle, because she knew that if she was thrown, she would be kicked and trampled. That the least she could expect was serious injury.

She was half blind with fright, almost deafened by the noise of his drumming, relentless hooves, overwhelmed by her helplessness in the face of such fury, and yet, somewhere in her consciousness, there seemed to be men's voices shouting.

Someone was there, a stranger, tall and broad-shouldered, seizing the bridle as Arthur arrived on the other side, both of them clinging there, fighting Samson to a breathless, swearing halt, while another pair of strong arms reached up and dragged Chloe without gentleness out of the saddle, hauling her back across the yard and out of the range of those viciously kicking back legs.

Sobbing drily, wordlessly with relief, she looked up into Darius's white face. Saw the emerald blaze of his eyes, felt herself scorched by an anger that left Samson as a mere beginner, and knew that any thought of safety was an illusion.

He said between his teeth, 'Hell, woman, are you suicidal or just bloody insane?'

She tried to speak, to explain, but no sound would come from the tightness of her throat. His arms were iron, caging her, making her listen as his voice went on, soft and menacing, never repeating himself, as his words seemed to flay the skin from her bones.

At last she began to cry, the scalding tears pouring silently and remorselessly down her pale face, and his grasp slackened.

He said with great weariness, 'Oh, God,' and looked across to where Samson stood, defeated and sullen, between his two warders.

He said, 'Tim, Miss Benson's car's just outside. Drive her back to Axford Grange, will you, and I'll see you for a farewell drink at the Butchers Arms in an hour.'

She began to say that she could drive herself, trying to snatch back some atom of dignity from the situation, but the look he sent her stopped her in her tracks.

Tim Hankin's hand under her elbow was firm, but there was kindness in it too, and she went with him without further protest.

They were outside the Hall grounds and on the road to the village when he eventually spoke, his tone gentle.

'You don't want to take what Darius said too much to heart, Miss Benson. Yes, you did a silly thing, but his bark's always been worse than his bite, as I have cause to know.'

Chloe was blotting her face with a handful of tissues from the glove compartment. She said chokingly, 'No-one's ever spoken to me like that before. As if they—hated me.'

'Well,' he said. 'Fear takes people in different ways. And he was much rougher on me, I promise you, because I deserved it more.'

She said, sniffing, 'I can't believe that.'

'Then you'd be wrong.' He pulled the car onto the verge, and switched off the engine. 'It's not something I'm proud of, but maybe you need to hear it.'

He paused. 'It was a long time ago.' His voice was quiet and serious. 'We'd always been mates from young kids, Darius and me. But he'd been away—school then university—and I was bored, being expected to follow in Dad's footsteps as a gamekeeper and not sure it was what I wanted, so I got in with a bad crowd.

'Darius found out somehow—he always could—and discovered what they were up to. I'd not wanted to get involved because it was against the law and vile too, but I didn't know how to break free. I knew the kind of men they were and what they'd do to me if I tried.'

Chloe gasped. 'Was it—dog fighting?'

'Yes.' Tim Hankin spoke heavily. 'Darius knew that the police were tracking the gang organising it and there was going to be a raid. He also knew what it would do to Mum and Dad if I was caught with them, and he came to find me. Got me out some way, God knows how, and we headed for home, miles across country dodging the police who were everywhere. He was taking one hell of a risk for me.

'When we'd gone far enough to be safe, he went for me. Called me every name under the sun and a few more even I hadn't heard of. Then he hit me. Knocked me down, and I didn't even try to defend myself because I knew I'd asked for it and more.

'Then we sat down and talked, and the next day he drove me to the nearest recruiting office and I joined up, got into a regiment where I could work with horses.'

She said, 'There were—rumours—afterwards, about Darius. That he was the one going to dog fights.'

'I know that, and I'm sorry for it. But he never cared much about local gossip or what people thought of him.'

He gave her a sober look. 'However, I could have ended up in jail, Miss Benson, and you could be laid in that yard with your neck broken, and how could he ever have lived with that? Think about it.'

He restarted the car. 'And now I'll get you home.'

CHAPTER TEN

'PAPERWORK?' Chloe repeated. 'You have to catch up on paperwork? Oh, Ian, surely not.'

'Look.' His voice down the phone sounded harassed. 'I'll still be coming to the wretched dinner party. I just won't be able to pick you up first. But there's no real problem, surely, when you can go with your aunt and uncle?'

'No,' Chloe agreed with an effort. 'Of course not.'

But that's not the point, she longed to shout at him. I wanted to arrive with you, as one half of a couple, so I wouldn't have to face Darius tonight on my own. I was relying on you to be with me from the start.

And I can't even tell you why without admitting the lethally stupid thing I did trying to ride Samson. Maybe Darius was right and I did take leave of my senses. But I can't bear anyone else to know, especially Aunt Libby and Uncle Hal.

They hadn't been at home when she'd returned the day before. A scribbled note left on the kitchen table explained they'd gone into East Ledwick to talk to an estate agent, and her lunch—a pan of home-made vegetable soup keeping warm on the range, fresh bread and some good cheese—was waiting.

She only managed a few spoonfuls of soup, her churning stomach resisting any thought of solid food.

She was still shaking with reaction to the abominable risk

she'd taken and the consequent scene in the stable yard. Nor could she stop crying. It didn't matter how many times she tried to tell herself that Darius had no right to speak to her like that, she still knew in her heart that the fault was hers and she deserved every damning word.

Her immediate thought was to invent some illness in order to avoid the following night's dinner party, and only the conviction that Darius would know she was faking it kept her on track. The prospect of having to endure more of his icy scorn when they did eventually meet was more than she could bear.

Her battle with Samson had left her physically as well as mentally bruised, so when she had cleared lunch away, she went upstairs and indulged in a long, hot bath.

But if the warm water eased her body, it also freed her mind, and she found herself thinking back over everything Tim Hankin had said, especially with regard to the illegal dog-fighting ring and the role Darius had played in it, contrary to all reports.

She had to be glad that he hadn't been involved in anything so disgusting, but while he might have been misjudged over that, there was still plenty to set to his account, she told herself resolutely. He hadn't suddenly turned into the Archangel Gabriel. And there was certainly no need for her to make excuses for him.

She found some arnica tablets in the bathroom cabinet, and remembered too how Darius had once offered her the same remedy.

For a moment she stood, staring into space, the small bottle clutched in her hand. Then she took a deep breath and said aloud, 'I will not think about him. I will not.'

But it was obvious that she needed something to take her mind off the past few hours and hard work was usually the best diversion, she thought as she recalled Aunt Libby saying that the borders in the front garden needed weeding.

Accordingly, she put on old jeans and a tee shirt and went out to tackle them.

'Kerb appeal,' she muttered as she dealt with a persistent dandelion. 'And I hope the punters appreciate it.'

Her aunt and uncle were certainly appreciative of her efforts, especially as three valuations of the Grange had been scheduled for the start of the following week. But, over supper, they also began to enquire, albeit tactfully and gently, about her own plans, and she could tell them nothing.

It's time Ian and I stopped shilly-shallying, she told herself when she was in her room, having offered gardening fatigue as an excuse for an early night and an escape from further questions. If I'd had my wedding to plan, I'd have had no time to waste on exercising other people's horses, and saved myself a load of grief.

Against the odds, she slept soundly, and woke determined to be positive.

'I'm getting my hair done in honour of tonight's dinner party,' Aunt Libby announced over breakfast. 'Shall I ask Denise if she can fit you in too?'

Chloe shook her head. 'I'll give myself a shampoo, thanks, and just leave it loose.' She paused, smiling. 'The way Ian likes it.'

Her aunt gave her a swift glance then looked back at her plate. 'Just as you wish, my dear,' she said equably. 'I presume he'll be driving you to the Hall tonight.'

'Indeed he will,' said Chloe.

Only now he wouldn't, so there was embarrassment to add to the disappointment of his phone call, she realised as she busied herself preparing a ham salad for lunch.

Her uncle was later than usual and came in apologising. 'I've been up at the Hall,' he said. 'In case a shot of something was needed to get that damned horse of Andrew Maynard's into the box for transit. But Darius had summoned a couple of grooms over from that stud farm of his in Ireland, and they got the job done.'

'Oh.' Chloe set down his plate with more than usual care, aware her heartbeat had quickened nervously. 'I—heard Samson was going.' She tried to keep her tone casual, wondering if anything had been said about her visit the day before, and steeling herself for another dressing down, but Uncle Hal was serving himself from a dish of new potatoes with apparent unconcern, so she seemed to have been spared.

Yet that made the prospect of the evening ahead no more enticing, although she felt that she could be reasonably satisfied with her appearance at least. She was wearing a favourite dress in a close-fitting silky fabric that enhanced every slender curve, knee-length, long-sleeved and scoop-necked in a dramatic shade of deep red. Her lips and nails had been painted to match, and she had the antique garnet-and-pearl drops that had been part of her twenty-first birthday present, in her ears.

Fighting colours, she thought ironically, as she viewed herself in the mirror. Nothing even slightly penitential, although she had reluctantly decided that some word of regret for her escapade the previous day be appropriate if a suitable opportunity occurred, at the same time, crossing her fingers that it wouldn't. And she knew that she should also be thankful that her stupidity hadn't been mentioned.

Only she didn't feel even remotely grateful. Just terribly apprehensive.

Although she told herself a dozen times that she was overreacting, it was a feeling that somehow, in spite of her best efforts, refused to go away.

Chloe had hoped that Ian would deal quickly with the VAT returns or whatever was holding him up, and be at the Hall, waiting for her.

But one glance round the drawing room soon disabused her of that notion, and her heart sank.

Oh, Ian where are you when I need you? she whispered under her breath.

Sir Gregory was seated in a high-backed armchair beside the fireplace. While he was undoubtedly resplendent in a dark green velvet smoking jacket, his face was sunken with one side of his mouth turned down a little. And he appeared, Chloe thought instantly, to have shrunk in some odd way.

Or perhaps he just seemed smaller in contrast to the tall young man in the charcoal suit and pale grey brocade waistcoat, standing beside him and resting a casual arm on the back of his father's chair.

And who was now walking forward, smiling. 'Mrs Jackson. It's a pleasure to see you again. And Mr Jackson.' They all shook hands, then Darius let his glance drift past them to the girl standing in silence behind them.

'Chloe,' he said, inclining his head with cool politeness.

She returned a breathless, 'Good evening,' joined her aunt and uncle in their polite greetings to Sir Gregory, then turned away rather too hastily to speak to Dr Vaughan, the head of the neighbourhood GP practice and his wife. The vicar was there too with Mrs Squires, and so were Hugo Burton and Prunella Burton, the local MP and his wife, and by the time she'd greeted them all, and taken a glass of orange juice from the tray of drinks being brought round by a maid, she was beginning to feel rather more comfortable. But she would only be able to relax properly, she told herself, when Ian arrived.

Which he seemed in no hurry to do, and she could only hope he'd put in an appearance before dinner was actually announced.

When the drawing room door eventually opened, she turned hopefully, but it was to see Lindsay Watson walk into the room. She was wearing a dark navy dress with a white starched collar and cuffs. There was a small silver watch pinned to her breast pocket, and her blond hair was drawn back into a severe bun.

On the surface, she was every inch the calm, efficient nurse, but her eyes were very bright and her face unusually flushed.

But why wouldn't she be looking a little flustered? Chloe thought, taking a gulp of orange juice to ease the sudden dryness in her throat, if she's aiming to be the next Lady Maynard and everyone in the room knows it?

Lindsay went straight to Sir Gregory, bending over him solicitously, and he nodded, smiling with an obvious effort.

Uncle Hal came over to Chloe. 'Just what is Ian playing at?' he asked in a displeased undertone. 'I've tried to phone him, but I can't get a signal in here.'

'I'll go out on the terrace and text him,' Chloe said quickly. 'Perhaps he's been called out to an emergency.'

'Then why didn't he ring and say so?' Uncle Hal demanded with inexorable logic, and Chloe could not think of an answer.

She slipped out through the French windows and went over to the balustrade, but she'd barely begun her message when she heard the crunch of footsteps on gravel and saw Ian appear round the corner of the house on the path below her, his face moody and preoccupied.

She leaned over the balustrade. 'Ian—where on earth have you been? And what are you doing, anyway, coming in this way?'

He glanced up with a start. 'Oh—Chloe.' He gave an uneven laugh. 'I forgot this was a social occasion and parked round by the stables. Force of habit, I guess.'

She drew a deep breath. 'Well, at least you're here. I was beginning to worry.'

He shrugged almost defensively. 'I was busy. I just—lost track of time.'

'Yes,' she said. 'Yes, I understand.'

Except that I don't. I don't understand any of this, and I'm even more scared now than I was earlier, and I need you to take me in your arms and tell me that everything's going to be all right. I need to walk back into that room with my hand in yours and make a joke about you getting lost.

But I already know in my heart that's not going to happen. That somehow I'm on my own here.

And she thought of Darius's cold green glance reaching her across the room, and suppressed a shiver.

She lifted her chin. 'So,' she said. 'Let's go in and have dinner.'

As Aunt Libby had prophesied, the food was a dream, and even Chloe's persistent feeling of unease could put up no real resistance to its allure.

Ian was seated beside Lindsay Watson on the opposite side of the table and while they seemed to have little to say to each other, Chloe noticed with relief that he was chatting readily enough to Mrs Burton, his other neighbour. But he was also, she saw, enjoying more of the excellent wine being served than was wise.

Darius too appeared fully occupied at the far end of the table, entertaining Aunt Libby on one side and Mrs Vaughan on the other.

At the same time, Chloe was assailed at intervals during the long meal by a sharp tingle of awareness, warning her almost starkly that he was looking at her. In return, she tried hard to seem oblivious and did not allow herself as much as a glance in his direction.

Yet, all too often, she found herself remembering the brief snatch of conversation between Darius and Lindsay that she'd inadvertently overheard on the way into dinner.

'Why the uniform, Lindsay?' he'd asked. 'You're supposed to be off duty tonight, remember?'

'Because I thought it was more appropriate.' She did not look at him or smile. 'Under the circumstances.'

Clearly, he'd expected her to present herself as his future wife rather than his father's paid carer, thought Chloe, biting her lip.

When the meal was over, Sir Gregory rose slowly and with obvious difficulty and apologised for not joining the party in the drawing room for coffee.

'Dr Vaughan will tell you that I must ration my excitements for the foreseeable future,' he told them.

Chloe went upstairs with the rest of the women to comb her hair and renew her lipstick, but on her way down again she saw Darius standing at the foot of the stairs, and realised he was waiting for her.

She halted, disconcerted, before reluctantly continuing her descent, and his sardonic smile told her that her hesitation was not lost on him.

'My father is resting in his library,' he said. 'However, he would like to talk to you, if you can spare him a few minutes.'

'He wants to see me?' She could not hide her surprise.

'I've just said so.'

She stood for a moment, fiddling with the clasp of her evening bag. 'Is he also going to tell me off about Samson?'

'Good God, no.' His tone was short. 'You think I mentioned that to him? What the hell do you take me for?'

'I don't think I know any more.' She took a deep breath. 'But, while I have the chance, I need to say that I'm sorry for trying to ride him. I knew perfectly well that I shouldn't.'

'Yes,' Darius said. 'But I gather you're not wholly to blame. Because for you to hear that I'd said exactly that was like showing a red rag to a bull, according to Arthur, who's been kicking himself ever since for telling you.'

'So now I'm a bull.' She pretended to wince. 'But thank you too for not mentioning it to my uncle—or anyone else.'

He said quietly, 'The matter was dealt with in house. And I've never been a squealer, Chloe.'

'No.' She paused, then said in a rush, 'Tim told me what you did for him—about the dog-fighting.'

'Did he?' He shrugged. 'Well, it hardly matters. It was a very long time ago.'

'Yes,' she said. 'But people thought that you were involved in it, not Tim.'

'Yes,' he said. 'They did. But I managed to live with it.' He gave a faint smile. 'Or maybe I should say away from it.'

'What do you mean?'

He said flatly, 'That it helped convince me that Willowford was not for me, and my place was elsewhere.'

She said uncertainly, 'Yet you're back now.'

'For the time being.' His voice was curt again. 'And we're keeping my father waiting.'

In spite of the warmth of the evening, Sir Gregory was sitting with a rug over his knees beside a small fire. His eyes were closed, but one hand was beating a restless tattoo on the arm of his chair.

Darius said gently, 'Here's Chloe, Father.'

'Good,' Sir Gregory said after a pause. 'That's good. Please sit down, my dear.'

As Chloe took the seat opposite, she heard the library door shut and realised Darius had left them alone together.

There was a silence, then Sir Gregory said, 'My wife used to say you would be a beauty, my child, and she was quite right.'

Chloe flushed. 'She was always very kind to me.'

He said haltingly, 'She had great hopes for you. Believed you should be allowed to stretch your wings and fly.' He paused. 'She talked to you, I think, about her early life. The cities and foreign embassies that became her home?'

Chloe smiled. 'Yes,' she said gently. 'She did. She made it all sound wonderful—exotic, exciting.'

'She loved to travel. Perhaps even she did not realise how much it meant to her.' He lifted a handkerchief to the corners of his mouth. Went on slowly, 'When we first met and married, we planned to continue in the same way. To see the rest of the world together. Then my father died very suddenly, and we were obliged to come back here instead.

'And, of course, everything changed. A house like this— an estate—brings its responsibilities with it. We could not just leave it behind and go. Or so I believed. But then I was born and brought up here, and although I knew it was a backwater, it was *my* backwater, and I loved it.'

He sighed. 'Then the boys were born, and that seemed another reason to build our lives around the home we were making here.

'I thought Margaret shared my contentment, but in reality, she felt stifled by village life and its obligations. Being constantly under a spotlight. Eventually, Willowford began to seem like a prison to her.'

Chloe stirred uneasily. 'Sir Gregory, I don't think...'

He held up a hand. 'Please, my dear, I need to tell you these things. My wife would have wished me to. Because you made the break when you went to university and afterwards, just as she'd always hoped you would. You took flight away from this small world.

'Yet now, my son tells me, you have come back to be married and to settle here, so it is vital for you to be sure that this is really the life for you.

'That it's the only possible future you can see for yourself.'

He paused. 'I believe you once wanted to be a writer. Has that been forgotten about?'

She stared at him, her breathing quickening, sharply, inexplicably. 'No, not entirely,' she said jerkily. 'But I can always write after I'm married. I'll have more time then. And Willowford is the only real home I've ever had. I—I always meant to return.'

He leaned forward with an effort, his gaze boring into hers. 'And is it just as you remember, or has it changed? Are you even the same person that went away?'

'Yes,' she said huskily. 'I am. And I admit that things here are different in many ways. But that doesn't matter because I've come back to find the man I love, and be happy with him, just as I've always dreamed.'

There was a silence, then he said, 'Ah,' and leaned back against the cushions piled behind him. He turned his head slowly and gazed at the flames burning in the fireplace. 'Then may your dreams come true, my dear. And now I wish you goodnight.'

Chloe stood outside the library door, her arms wrapped defensively across her body, as she tried to make sense of what had just happened. She would have sworn that Sir Gregory was barely aware of her existence, and yet he'd talked as if he knew and was concerned about her.

As, apparently, Lady Maynard had once been. A woman whose own wings had been clipped by duty, but who had always longed for the larger world she'd left behind. Who'd found village life stifling and oppressive.

But I'm not like that, Chloe whispered to herself. I don't want to escape. Because I do belong here. I do!

'Chloe.' The thick carpet had muffled the sound of his approach, and she gasped, taking an instinctive step backwards.

'I know my way back to the drawing room.' She faced him, her heart pounding unevenly. 'You really didn't have to collect me.'

'I came to bring you a message,' Darius returned equably.

'Your boyfriend seemed a little the worse for wear after his double brandy, so your aunt and uncle decided to take him home. He can collect his car tomorrow.'

'They've already left?' Chloe shook her head, mortification over Ian's behaviour warring with other concerns. 'Then how am I supposed to get back to the Grange? Or am I allowed three guesses?' she added bitterly.

'I think you'd lose.' He sounded faintly amused. 'The Vaughans live in your direction. They say they'll be happy to drop you off.'

It was the last thing she'd expected to hear, and she managed a weak, 'Oh. Well—thank you,' in return.

It was time she returned to the drawing room and other people, but Darius was still there, not exactly blocking the way, but certainly too close for comfort.

She took a deep breath. 'Ian doesn't usually drink too much,' she declared. 'He—he's been under a lot of stress lately.'

'I can imagine,' Darius said silkily. 'Brought on by the prospect of his approaching nuptials no doubt.'

I led with my chin there, Chloe thought biting her lip savagely. Will I never learn?

'Who knows?' she said. 'You may be tempted to hit the bottle yourself when your own day comes.'

'Unlikely,' he said. 'I've no wish to bring a hangover to my wedding night.' He smiled at her, his gaze unhurriedly brushing aside the cling of her dress as if it didn't exist. 'On the contrary,' he went on musingly. 'My wife will receive my sober and undivided attention.'

'And that,' Chloe said stonily, 'is altogether too much information.' She stepped forward. 'Would you excuse me, please? I need to find the Vaughans. I can't miss out on another lift.'

'Of course not,' he said. 'But what are you going to do, Chloe, when you have no more places left to run to or people to rescue you? What will happen when you realise you've made the biggest mistake of your life?'

'I already did that,' she said with sudden hoarseness. 'Seven years ago when I was fool enough to listen to the things you said to me—to let you anywhere near me.'

'Rather an exaggeration, my sweet.' His tone was light, but his face seemed carved from stone in the dim light of the passage. 'Any damage caused was far from irreparable. And I was the bigger fool to let you off so lightly. It won't happen next time.'

'Next time?' Her attempt at a laugh sounded as if she was choking. 'Have you taken leave of your senses?'

'Not yet,' Darius said very quietly. 'But when I do, I'll take you with me.' His hand snaked out and caught her arm, pulling her towards him. His fingers slid under the shoulder of her dress, baring the pale skin beneath it for the burn of his mouth.

The stark male heat of him pressed against her was igniting her quivering body, racing through her bloodstream and melting her bones.

His lips moved downwards, pushing aside the fragile lace that cupped her breast, in order to quest its hardening nipple and suckle it with heart-stopping sensuality.

'No. Oh, God, no.' The words seemed to come from nowhere, torn from her aching throat. Her hands thrust at him in an attempt to distance herself before her self-betrayal became complete.

His fingers wound themselves in her hair, pulling back her head so that he could look down into her white, desperate face and tormented eyes.

He said harshly, 'Stay with me. Stay tonight. I'll make some excuse to the Vaughans.'

'No.' Chloe dragged her dress into place with shaking

hands. 'Never. And you have no right to ask. Because I hate you. You—you disgust me.'

'In other circumstances,' Darius said very softly, 'I would take you to bed right now and make you retract every word you've just uttered. As it is, my little hypocrite, I have to get back to my guests. However, I hope you have had a pleasant evening, and that you derive equal enjoyment from the sleepless night alone that's waiting for you.'

He bent his head and let his mouth brush hers gently but with an agonising slowness that was somehow worse than any kind of force.

He said, 'Until we meet again, Chloe.'

And left her.

CHAPTER ELEVEN

'I wasn't drunk,' Ian said irritably. 'But I admit I was probably over the limit. Although that was hardly my fault,' he added defensively. 'Perhaps our gracious host shouldn't have topped up my glass quite so often.'

Or maybe you should have simply put your hand over your glass to stop him, like all the other drivers, thought Chloe, but kept silent.

She said quietly, 'I'm not having a go—truly. I think I'm just disappointed that we didn't get to spend more time together.' She paused. 'I seem to see so little of you these days.'

'Well, with your uncle's retirement looming up, I guess that's inevitable.' Ian shrugged. 'I have a lot to learn in the way of office management, for one thing.'

And what are the other things? Chloe asked herself. It seemed wiser, however, not to pursue the topic, while Darius's mocking words about the possible cause of Ian's stress still twisted painfully in her mind.

But she would rather think about them than their incredible, shameful aftermath in his arms. And the implied threat in his parting remark which still made her shiver.

Once alone, she'd gone straight to the downstairs cloakroom, and splashed cold water on her wrists in an attempt to calm her tumultuous pulses, but there was little she could do about her flushed face and fevered eyes.

When she got back to the drawing room the party was breaking up, and her faint dishevelment seemed fortunately to go unnoticed in the flurry of goodbyes.

She'd expected to face some strong words about Ian's conduct from Uncle Hal when she got back to the Grange but, to her surprise, neither he nor Aunt Libby mentioned it, preferring apparently to discuss the delicious food and Sir Gregory's undoubted improvement in health.

She'd also anticipated that Ian would be eating his share of humble pie when she saw him next, but she was wrong about that too, she thought, sighing.

Pressure of work had reduced the already limited amount of time they spent together. They'd met for drinks a couple of times, had dinner in East Ledwick once, and been to the cinema to see a film during which Ian had gone to sleep.

All in all, it did not seem an appropriate time to raise the subject of their postponed engagement, although the situation could not be allowed to drag on indefinitely.

After all, she had come back to Willowford for him, she told herself, and now, more than ever, she needed the safeguard of his ring on her hand and the public declaration of commitment that would justify her return.

It should also be sufficient to keep Darius at bay both physically and mentally, she thought fiercely, recalling the shaming fantasies that had made her toss and turn all night long, just as he'd predicted.

Also, in less than ten days' time there would be the ordeal of the Birthday Ball to be endured with all its particular resonances that she would still give so much to forget.

I can't look back, she thought. I dare not. And I must never let him near me again.

I have to plan for the future and disregard everything else, including all the strange things Sir Gregory said to me the other night. Particularly those.

And wondered why they suddenly seemed so important.

'So that young nurse is leaving the Hall, I hear,' said Mrs Thursgood. 'Must mean that the old gentleman is properly on the mend.' She gave Chloe a bland smile. 'You won't be so sorry to see her go, I dare say.'

'I'm certainly glad Sir Gregory is well enough not to need anyone,' Chloe returned carefully, aware that her heart had skipped a beat at the news.

'And that's not all,' the other woman went on. 'That other one—Mr Andrew's widow—is coming back.' She nodded in satisfaction at Chloe's startled expression. 'She'll be here the day after tomorrow for the Ball, by all accounts. So, there's a turn up for the books, and no mistake. I never thought we'd set eyes on her again.'

She sniffed. 'But it's all forgive and forget, seemingly. And maybe we'll be having another wedding, if Mr Darius decides to do the right thing by her, that is.'

'Yes,' Chloe said, in a voice she didn't recognise. 'Perhaps so.'

She paid for what she'd bought as if she was on autopilot, and went out into the relentless sunshine, releasing the leash of a delighted Flare from the rail provided for the purpose.

Penny, she thought in stupefaction. Penny, no longer in disgrace, and returning to Willowford to be with her lover—the man for whom she'd once abandoned everything. To be reinstated—accepted as Sir Gregory's daughter-in-law all over again. It couldn't possibly be true—could it?

But if it was, if the incredible, the unthinkable, was really happening, then small wonder that Lindsay Watson had decided to cut her losses and go.

Yet, I can't, she thought numbly, staring down at the footpath with eyes that saw nothing, as she began to walk out of the village, heading for the fields the dog loved.

Because I have to stay here somehow and watch it take place. Live with the knowledge that she and Darius are together and happy. As they may have been all this time.

Oh, dear God, to be confronted by it all on a daily basis and have to pretend that it doesn't matter, because I have my own life. To make everyone believe that I don't care. To try to make myself believe it.

What am I going to do? How can I possibly bear it?

She stopped dead in the middle of the lane, shocked by what she was thinking. Horrified by the sheer enormity of the revelation that had come to her at last, and was now tearing her apart.

The realisation that the man she'd really fallen in love with seven years ago—the man she had never ceased to want in her secret heart, despite everything he'd done—was Darius Maynard.

That it had always been him and always would be.

That all her efforts to rip her memories of him, her longing for him out of her mind had been totally in vain. That they were what drew her like a magnet back to Willowford, in spite of the time and distance between them, because one day she'd known she would find him here.

I must be insane, she thought with a kind of desperation. Because this isn't happening to me. It can't be. I won't allow it. I came back to Ian, to make a home with him. That was the plan for my life—wasn't it?

Feeling safe, knowing that he was waiting for me. That I could trust him to make everything all right.

Telling myself over and over again that I loved him. That I cared for him in a way that was good—and real, knowing he was kind and reliable, and that I would never have to worry about being hurt again.

She took a deep, wrenching breath, recognising that she'd treated all these hopes as certainties, wrapping them round her like some kind of security blanket, and hiding there. Unable—unwilling—to face the truth about her inmost feelings.

But just how secret had they really been? she wondered, as she went over her interview with Sir Gregory once again. Was he aware of her brief, wretched involvement with Darius seven years ago, and had he been trying to warn her that she still had nothing to hope for and that she would have done better to stay away for good?

Judging by her undisguised disapproval of Darius, Aunt Libby too must have guessed, and done her best to deflect her vulnerable niece from inevitable heartbreak.

And had Penny also known, and maybe even encouraged Darius to pay attention to a moonstruck teenager in order to conceal what was really going on between herself and her brother-in-law?

Although, she certainly wouldn't have expected matters to escalate towards a full-scale seduction, unless, of course, sexual fidelity didn't weigh very heavily with either of them.

Perhaps to Darius, I'm simply unfinished business, Chloe thought, feeling sick. A way to amuse himself while waiting to be reunited with Penny.

But at least the whole pitiful situation seemed to have escaped Mrs Thursgood's far-reaching antennae, although that was little enough to be thankful for.

Flare barked sharply, pulling at her leash, eager to resume her walk, startling Chloe out of her unhappy reverie and back to the immediate present.

Oh, God, she thought guiltily, realising she was still standing like a statue in the middle of the lane, if a car had come round the corner at speed, it couldn't have avoided us, and Flare at least doesn't deserve it.

She moved hurriedly over to the verge and set off again, her mind teeming endlessly, wretchedly.

'What am I going to do?' she whispered under her breath. 'What *can* I do?'

She remembered she'd once thought of trying to persuade Ian to move away and start again elsewhere. Now there seemed even less chance of his agreement, and maybe, now she'd faced up to her real feelings, she should cut Ian out of the equation altogether.

I've led him up the garden path for quite long enough, she thought, steeling herself, even if I meant it all for the very best, and would have done all I could to make him happy.

But if I'd loved him as I should, I would never have kept him waiting all this time. I'd have wanted to give myself—be his in every way, married or not. How could I not see that?

I've got everything so very wrong, she told herself. Treated him so badly. But now I must start putting it all right—for my own sake as well as his.

Because my next priority will be to contact my agency in London for a long-term job abroad in Europe or even America. Cut myself off completely and pray that time and distance will do its work.

Whatever happens here, she thought bleakly, I can't be around to witness it. And the fact that my aunt and uncle are moving away too will help, because their news will be about another place and other people.

She recalled how Sir Gregory had asked her if she was the same person who had gone away all those years ago.

I said I was and I am, she thought bitterly, swallowing past the harsh tightness in her throat. Which is my own private tragedy. Because I was cut to ribbons through loving Darius when I first left—when I went away to university. It took me a year just to get my head together and start to do some work. I was amazed they didn't throw me out.

He said the other night that he'd let me off lightly, but it isn't true, because he nearly destroyed me.

Now, here I am, loving him still, and facing heartbreak all over again. And I haven't even the excuse of being a teenager any more.

Flare was tugging her towards a favourite gateway, and she lifted the iron latch, unclipped the leash and let the dog bound into the empty meadow beyond, while she followed more slowly. The grass sloped down to a narrow stream and Chloe sank down in the shade of the solitary copper beech which grew on its edge, leaning thankfully back against its trunk.

Flare splashed straight into the water, emerging damp, joyous and, after she'd shaken herself vigorously, ready for a game with the squeaky toy which she knew her silent companion had in the pocket of her jeans.

She's so much wiser than me, thought Chloe, caught between tears and laughter. She knows that life simply goes on.

And however I may feel now, one day there'll be another place far from here with a tree at my back and sunlight on water, and I'll be healed. Or that's what I have to believe. And then I may even be ready for a love and trust that will last for the rest of my life.

Her dress, classically strapless and full-skirted in jade-green taffeta, was hanging on the outside of the wardrobe. It was the last thing she'd seen before going to sleep the night before, and the first she glimpsed when she woke on the morning of the ball itself.

She sat up, hugging her knees, and warily contemplating its glowing magnificence through the shrouding plastic cover.

No Lizzie Bennet lookalike this time, and not what she'd intended to buy at all.

It had been extremely expensive for one thing, and wearing it would almost certainly be a one-off. A dramatic statement that could not be repeated.

But there would never be any need for that, she thought, because in twenty four hours it would all be over. And the new Chloe Benson would be preparing once more for flight to a new life, having first sloughed off the half-truths and pathetic self deceptions of the old one. So maybe it was worth it.

Of course, there were still hurdles to be negotiated, like the essential long talk with her aunt and uncle, even if she could not be entirely frank with them about her motives for leaving.

A change of heart, she told herself. That was what she would say. And it was at least an approximation of the truth.

But Ian would have to be told first, and in spite of the personal difficulties they'd experienced since her return, she was not going to find it easy. Because she'd seen him for a drink the previous evening, and it had been strangely like old times in so many ways, with Ian quietly relaxed and in a reminiscent mood, as well as holding her with real tenderness as they said goodnight.

It had made her see why she'd thought she could make it work, she admitted ruefully. Even if the need for him—the ache for his touch—had never actually come between her and sleep. Which, in itself, should have warned her.

It was only when he'd driven off that she realised they hadn't actually finalised what time he would pick her up for the ball.

Their last date, she thought, even though she had no real right to be going anywhere as his partner. Not any more. But she needed to dance, laugh and look like a girl without a care in the world. Someone with nothing but a lifetime of happiness in front of her.

The alternative, of course, was to invent some minor ailment—a stomach upset perhaps—and cry off. But she had not given that serious consideration.

Because she needed to know, she told herself. To see Darius and Penny together, the future baronet and his lady, and understand once and for all that she had nothing to hope for and it was time to draw a line and move on. After she had said a silent and final farewell.

She felt her throat muscles contract harshly, and closed her eyes, deliberately putting Darius out of her mind. She would deal with that situation when she had to, and not before.

She would think instead of other—minor—leave-takings. People and places she would miss. And, of course, saying goodbye to Flare.

Lizbeth Crane's wrist was better now, and her husband had returned from Brussels the previous day, so her dog-walking services were no longer required.

'You've been an absolute star.' Mrs Crane had hugged her exuberantly. 'I don't know what I'd have done without you.'

'I was happy to do it,' Chloe assured her. She paused. 'I suppose I'll see you at the ball.'

'We wouldn't miss it,' said Lizbeth and hesitated in turn. 'Although there are all kinds of strange rumours concerning it floating round the village.' She gave Chloe an odd look. 'And some of them, if they were true, could cause the most terrible damage. But I'm sure it's all a pack of lies, and there's nothing to worry about.'

She shook her head. 'John's always said that, in more enlightened times, Mrs Thursgood would have been ducked in the village pond.'

'Almost certainly,' Chloe said, forcing a smile, and wondering just how far the gossip about Darius and herself had spread in the past few days, and what had triggered it.

But at least it did not seem to have reached Ian, she reflected now as she made herself get out of bed and off to the bathroom for her shower. And she could only hope it never would. She did not want to add to the hurt she was bound to inflict anyway.

But, in that case, why was she maintaining the illusion they were still a couple? How unkind and unfair was that? She had stifled her pangs of conscience by telling herself it was dire necessity for her to go to the ball with an escort.

Now she had to face facts. I'm using him, she thought unhappily, as the hot water streamed over her. And that's entirely wrong. I should have the guts to tell him first that it's over between us, but that, although it's a lot to ask, I'd still value his company this evening, and let him make the choice.

The chances were, of course, that he'd refuse, and angrily too. But that was a risk she'd have to take, even if it meant reverting to Plan B and staying away from the ball altogether.

'Is Ian on duty at the centre this morning?' she asked her uncle, who was swallowing the last of his coffee en route to the door.

'No, he asked if he could have the time off for some reason, so I'm covering for him.'

'Probably wants a rest before tonight's frivolity,' Chloe said lightly. It would be much easier, she thought, to talk at the cottage, although, ironically, it would be her first as well as her last visit to the Mark II version of it. But at least the alterations there were all Ian's doing, and she had no vested interest in it.

Uncle Hal snorted. 'Just as long as he's not indulging in some Dutch courage as well, as he obviously did before that dinner party,' he said drily, and left.

And just as long as nothing about tonight resembles that

dinner party in any way, shape or form, Chloe thought, sliding bread into the toaster.

She was just finishing breakfast when Aunt Libby bustled in looking, harassed. 'The agents have just rung to say they want to bring some people round at eleven o'clock for a viewing. And everywhere's such a mess.'

The house was fine, Chloe knew, as it had been for the previous three viewings, but her aunt needed it to be immaculate.

She rose, putting her crockery in the dishwasher. 'Then let's get cracking,' she said briskly. 'Give the place the hard-sell treatment.'

'But you have an appointment at the Charm School in East Ledwick.'

'Yes, but not till half-past eleven. I can lend a hand here first.'

Although it meant she wouldn't have time to call on Ian on the way to the beauty salon as she'd planned, she thought. But the return trip would serve just as well. And maybe being manicured, pedicured and facialled first would provide her with a form of emotional body armour.

It was good to relax under the skilled hands of Bethany, the Charm School's owner, and by the time the face mask was being removed Chloe felt totally refreshed, and had rehearsed exactly what she needed to say to Ian.

Except that he wasn't there. The door of the cottage was locked, the curtains were half-drawn, and his car was gone.

I should have phoned first, Chloe told herself, as she went back to her own vehicle. Made sure he was around. Now I'll just have to catch him later.

The first thing she noticed when she arrived back at the Grange was a 'sold' sticker across the house agent's board in the garden.

'Wonderful news,' she called out as she entered the house. 'Is the champagne on ice?'

To her surprise, there was no reply. And when she walked into the kitchen, she found Aunt Libby sitting, staring into space, an untouched cup of coffee going cold on the table in front of her.

Oh, heavens, thought Chloe. It's suddenly hit her that it's done now, and there's no going back. And that leaving is going to be a bigger wrench than she bargained for.

She said gently, 'Listen, darling, it's all for the best, and I'm sure, in your heart, you know that. And you'll find another house you really love…'

But Mrs Jackson was shaking her head. 'It's got nothing to do with the house, Chloe. It's something—completely different.' She took a deep breath. 'Ian's been here. He arrived just after the other people had left.'

'Which explains why I missed him at the cottage.' Chloe refilled the kettle. 'I suppose he came to say what time he'd pick me up tonight.'

'No,' said her aunt. 'No, he didn't. Because he won't be going to the ball. He's off on a week's unpaid leave instead.' She was silent for a moment, then said in a sudden burst, 'Oh, Chloe, my dearest, he's gone away with Lindsay Watson—to be married.'

Chloe put the kettle down very carefully, her head whirling.

She said carefully, 'Ian—and Lindsay? I don't understand.'

'Oh, the gossip about them started not long after she arrived,' Mrs Jackson said bitterly. 'But I took no notice. They were both single, so I thought it was just—Willowford putting two and two together to make half a dozen.'

She paused. 'But the rumours seemed to persist. Only then you announced you were coming back, and you seemed so confident about your relationship that I decided to say nothing. That maybe you'd both had flings while you were apart, because that's how things are these days.'

'No,' Chloe said. 'I didn't.' *But not for Ian's sake, although I made myself believe that it was, but because I wanted someone else to the exclusion of all others.*

'I suspected that things weren't right between you,' Mrs Jackson went on. 'And wondered if I should say something, but I didn't want to interfere, not again, and now I wish that I had, although I had no real evidence. They were both very discreet.'

She reached across and extracted an envelope from beneath a pile of house agents' details.

'He brought you this letter,' she said, and put it on the table between them. She rose. 'I expect you'd rather read it alone.'

'Not at all.' Chloe shook her head. 'After all, I know what's in it.'

And I should have realised for myself from the start. All that business about getting to know each other all over again. The alterations to the cottage. Lindsay's hostility and the fact that Flare obviously knew her from somewhere. How could I not see it?

She remembered too Mrs Thursgood's warning about men going off the boil, and her comment on Lindsay's departure: 'You won't be sorry to see her go, I dare say.'

Everyone knew but me, she thought. And I was too busy thinking about myself to notice.

The envelope contained a single sheet of notepaper. 'Dear Chloe,' it ran. 'I know what you must think of me, and I can't possibly feel more of a louse than I already do. I should have told you from the outset that I'd met someone else, but it never seemed the right moment. My only excuse is that you were gone so long, and I was lonely.

'Trying not to upset you, I ended up hurting Lindsay instead, and matters came to a head just before the dinner party.

We had a terrible row and she told me to make up my mind once and for all or she was clearing out.

'She also said I shouldn't worry about you too much, because she'd bet good money that you had other fish to fry. Maybe you know what she means.

'Whatever, I wish you every happiness in the future. Ian.'

And good evening, friends, thought Chloe.

She passed the letter to Aunt Libby. 'There's nothing private. It's really just a confirmation of what he told you.'

'Oh, Chloe,' her aunt said when she'd read it. 'My dear, dear girl. I'm so very sorry.'

'Then you mustn't be.' Chloe retrieved the kettle and put it on the range. 'It's all for the best.' She paused. 'I suppose I had this image of Willowford in my mind as a haven, where everything would always be just the same, and I could step back into it whenever I wanted and find my place waiting for me.' She sighed. 'A kind of Garden of Eden in miniature.'

'With Mrs Thursgood as the snake,' Aunt Libby said grimly.

'How true,' Chloe agreed. 'But, of course, it was never like that. It was just wishful thinking on my part. And I was having my doubts about settling here permanently,' she added, choosing her words carefully. 'So maybe Ian's done me a favour.'

'I wish I could think so,' Aunt Libby said unhappily. 'You always seemed so certain that he was the one, and in many ways I was glad of it. Because I could feel justified about having intervened before, and tell myself I'd done the right thing.'

Chloe paused in spooning the coffee into the beakers. She said, 'I'm afraid you've lost me. When did you intervene, and why?'

Her aunt began to tidy the pile of papers, aligning them with acute precision. She said, 'He wrote, you see, wanting to contact you in London. And because I didn't answer his letter, he came back. He came here.'

Chloe was very still. She said huskily, 'Aunt Libby—are you—can you be talking about—Darius?'

Her aunt nodded jerkily. 'He said that he was going abroad almost immediately, but that he had to see you—to talk to you first. That there were things you had to know, that he needed to explain. He wanted your address, or just the name of your college. He—he almost begged.'

Chloe's throat was dry. 'And you said?'

'That he'd ruined enough lives already, and I wouldn't allow him to spoil yours,' Mrs Jackson said quietly. 'That I couldn't believe he had the gall to show his face in Willowford after what he'd done, and that he should go away and never return, because neither you nor anyone wanted to see him again.

'And I must have convinced him,' she added. 'Because he went.'

She paused. 'I don't know why I'm telling you—and at a time like this. I never intended to. And I suppose that's why I tried to be glad about Ian. Because I believed you'd be safe with him.'

'I did too,' said Chloe, and brought the coffee to the table. 'So we were both mistaken.' She bent and dropped a kiss on her aunt's greying hair. 'But you mustn't beat yourself up about Darius. You were absolutely right to send him away.' She took a deep breath. 'I—I shall always be grateful for that.'

And realised, her heart sinking, that it was only the first lie of many she would have to tell in the days to come in order to survive.

CHAPTER TWELVE

THE house seemed blessedly quiet as Chloe came downstairs.

In a way, Ian's departure, although something of a shock, had provided her with a perfect, indisputable excuse to miss the Birthday Ball, on the genuine grounds that she did not feel up to meeting people, and that she had a lot of thinking to do.

Except there was only one person she really wished to avoid. Two, she supposed wretchedly, if she counted Penny. As she knew she must.

Her need to think, of course, was nothing but the truth. She had plans to make, for one thing. And tomorrow the village's reaction to the news about Ian would break over her like a tidal wave. She therefore needed a story that would somehow show him in a reasonable light, while not presenting herself as a victim.

And she would be expected to comment on Penny's return too.

Lucky Mrs Thursgood, she thought. Two bombshells for the price of one.

However, it had taken serious perseverance to convince her aunt and uncle that she would be perfectly all right spending the evening alone. That she was planning to have a warm bath and an early night, and that they should go to the dance as arranged.

And even then they had fussed, asking worriedly if she was quite sure.

Uncle Hal, of course, had been incandescent about what he saw as Ian's betrayal, declaring he'd never been so deceived in anyone, and how glad he was that the partnership would soon be ending.

He had also received a note from Ian, left at the centre, announcing that he was taking a week's unpaid leave so that he and Lindsay could be married by special licence.

'I'd like to tell him to go on permanent leave,' he said grimly.

They were both so concerned for her, so convinced she was heroically concealing her grief over Ian's loss, and it was best they went on believing that. If she tried to tell them, or anyone else, that she'd been planning to end it anyway, her aunt and uncle would think she was trying desperately to salvage her pride. Other people would probably mutter, 'Sour grapes.'

And all of them would be wrong.

She poured herself a glass of wine and curled herself into a corner of the sofa, tucking the folds of her towelling dressing gown around her.

Yes, she was shaken by the day's events—not least by the voice in her head screaming endlessly, *Why—why—why?*

But the question, with its jagged, persistent pain which made her want to moan aloud, had nothing to do with Ian, but had been triggered by Aunt Libby's reluctant revelation that Darius had not simply walked away from her without a backward glance all those years ago.

On the contrary, that he'd even risked coming back to Willowfold, with all the possible repercussions his visit might lead to, in order to try and find her.

To explain…

But how? Chloe wondered wearily. How could one ever

explain the indefensible—the unforgivable? Or justify the destruction of his own brother's marriage and the misery that had been caused?

The ball tonight might be an attempt to paper over the gaping cracks in the Maynard dynasty, but how could it possibly succeed?

Lives had indeed been ruined, as Aunt Libby had said, but Chloe was determined that hers was not going to be one of them. That she was going to tread a different road.

Because Penny was still there in his life and had probably never been away. That was the sickening truth she somehow had to face.

'I will get over this,' she said aloud. And, more strongly, 'I will get over *him*.'

She took a drink of wine, as if toasting her own resolution, but the Sauvignon Blanc tasted oddly bitter in her throat. So she could not even rely on alcohol to numb the torment within her, she thought ruefully, putting down the glass.

Then sat bolt upright as she heard the rattle of a key in the front door. She stifled a groan. So, her aunt and uncle were back, presumably convinced she should not be left after all.

The door slammed and she heard footsteps coming hard and swift down the hall. One person. Not two. She sat up, her whole body stiffening with apprehension, her head turning towards the sitting room door as it was flung open and Darius walked in.

She said hoarsely, 'What the hell do you want?'

'I was told your so-called engagement was over and you were too heartbroken to leave the house,' he returned. He came to stand in front of her, elegant in his evening clothes, a crimson cummerbund emphasising his lean waist. His gaze swept her. 'I must say that the sackcloth and ashes are very becoming. Intriguing too,' he added softly looking at her bare feet. Chloe hastily covered them, glaring at him.

'Anyway, I decided I must come and see this phenomenon for myself,' he went on. 'Especially as I'm willing to bet good money that the disappearance of your errant swain isn't causing you even a moment's real regret, apart from a few twinges of damaged pride. So why pretend?'

'What do you know about it?' she demanded defensively, shaken equally by his sudden arrival and the awareness of her own vulnerability. The soft elderly towelling covering her was no longer a comfort but seemed to be grating against her bare skin like sandpaper.

'More than you think,' he said. 'Don't forget I've been a close observer of this curious little triangle since your return.'

'Not just an observer,' Chloe snapped back. 'You were dating Lindsay Watson yourself, after all.'

'No,' he said. 'I was not. Or not in the way you imagine. Ian had promised her months ago that he'd write to you, tell you it was over. Only he didn't, and suddenly there you were, back in town, talking about weddings. And he was still dithering. Lindsay was miserable and jealous and needed a friend.' He paused. 'Quite understandably, she wanted to make him jealous too, and as I was also involved elsewhere, I was useful.'

Involved elsewhere... The words cut into her like sharp knives. She moved restively. Changed direction.

'Just how did you manage to get in here?'

'Your Aunt Libby lent me her key.'

She gasped. 'I don't believe it. She would never do such a thing.'

He shrugged. 'All right, I lured her into the shrubbery and mugged her for it.'

She gestured impatiently. 'She really gave it to you? But why?'

'Maybe she feels she owes me,' he drawled. 'Or perhaps when I told her I was coming to collect you and whisk you to the ball like Cinderella, she decided belatedly to play Fairy Godmother. You must ask her sometime.'

'I have news for you,' said Chloe icily. 'You are not and never will be Prince Charming.'

'No hardship,' he said. 'I've always had him down as a total idiot, letting the girl he wanted run out on him because a clock struck twelve. He should have gone after her and dragged her back, rags, tatters and all.'

'Fascinating,' she said. 'Now perhaps you'd leave.'

'Not without you.' He glanced at his watch. 'So, put your dance dress on and we'll be going.'

'No,' she said fiercely. 'I won't—and we won't. I'm staying right here.'

'To perpetuate the myth of the betrayed fiancée?' He shook his head. 'That doesn't work and you know it. If you were so crazy about him, you wouldn't have gone off and left him alone for all those months. And you'd certainly have been back from time to time to stake your claim, as it were. Make him as happy as you knew how. My God, you wouldn't have been able to keep away.'

His voice slowed, became quieter. 'But that was never a problem for you, was it, Chloe? Keeping away. You must have had that poor guy climbing the walls. I wonder when it first occurred to him you weren't looking for a real man of your own, but the father you'd never known. That it wasn't intimacy or passion you were after but a safety net. While you—you couldn't see what was right under your nose. That if there'd ever been a right time with him, it had run out long ago.'

She scrambled to her feet. 'Shut up,' she said hoarsely. 'Shut up now. What the hell do you know about love or loyalty, anyway? You've never had a faithful bone in your body, so you have no right to talk to me like this. No right at all. Do you hear me?'

'And to hear is to obey?' He shook his head. 'Think again, my sweet.'

'You know nothing about it.' The words were running into each other. 'About us. Nothing. I loved Ian. I did. There was never anyone else...'

She stopped, staring at him, hearing the silence between them fill with her own ragged breathing, as she realised her denial was a nonsense born out of sheer desperation and that they both knew it.

Knew too that there was no longer anywhere for her to hide. From him or from herself.

And that she was terrified.

At last Darius said evenly, 'Shall we agree that is the last lie you will ever tell me? Now, go and change, or we'll miss the birthday toast.'

'Please—why are you making me do this?' Her voice was a pleading whisper. 'What can it matter to you whether I go or stay?'

'That,' he said, 'is something we might discuss later—when we have more time. Perhaps all the time in the world. As we should have had.'

The breath caught in her throat. She wanted to fly at him. To hit him with her fists and scream, But why didn't we? If I meant so much to you, then why did you go away with your sister-in-law? And how can you stand there—saying these things to me—reminding me of the past—when you know she's back here with you? When she's the one who's really waiting for you.

Except that she'd already gone too far down the path of self-betrayal. She could risk no more.

Instead, she lifted her chin, forcing herself to meet the intensity in his green gaze. To challenge it.

She said, 'Now who's telling lies?' Then turned, going out into the hall and up the stairs.

Darius followed.

She watched him take the key from her bedroom door and pocket it.

Cutting off what she'd hoped might be her last line of retreat.

He lifted the jade dress down from the wardrobe door and removed its protective cover.

There was a long pause, then he said softly, 'It's beautiful. And you will make it even lovelier. Put it on for me, my darling. Please.'

There was a note in his voice which, in spite of herself, turned her legs to water, and made her quiver inside.

Under her robe she was naked and they both knew it. He'd seen her without her clothes before, touched her, explored her with lingering intimacy, but that had been in some other lifetime.

My glorious, radiant girl...

Shyness paralysed her, and a sudden fear that in seven years her body might have changed. That she would not be as he remembered.

And besides, there was Penny, whom she could never allow herself to forget, no matter how deep the ache of longing to have him look at her, even touch her again. Penny, who was waiting at the ball, probably checking her wristwatch, wondering why he'd found it necessary to leave her, and how much longer she would be alone.

Penny, whom, very soon, I shall have to face, she thought.

She stared across at him mutely, her eyes enormous, begging him to understand why it had become so impossible for her to strip in front of him and heard him sigh. He put the dress carefully on the bed, then walked out of the room, closing the door behind him.

The dress had its own petticoat, so the underwear it required was minimal, just a pair of French knickers in cream satin, edged in heavy lace.

She stepped into the dress and drew it up over her body. Fastening the zip was a struggle, but she managed it in the end, because she didn't dare call him back to ask him for assistance.

Even now, she thought, and in spite of everything, I dare not trust myself.

She ranged her cosmetics on her dressing table, but decided her hands were shaking too much to do more than apply some of the clear coral lipstick that matched the polish on her toes and fingers.

It was not, she thought, a very brave face looking back at her from the mirror, but her pallor would be attributed to the fact that she'd just been jilted. No-one at the ball would expect her to be brimming with *joie de vivre*.

She hung small jade drops from her ears, collected the silver evening purse that matched her sandals, then, drawing a deep breath, she went to the door.

Darius was leaning against the wall opposite, but he straightened instantly as she appeared, his eyes raking her.

He had no right, she thought, her heartbeat quickening, to look at her with such open hunger. No right at all.

He said quietly, 'Dear God, Chloe, you take my breath away.' Then walked downstairs with her and out to the jeep in silence.

This Birthday Ball, Chloe soon realised, was a very different proposition from the last one. Last time it had seemed a pretty exclusive affair. Tonight, it appeared that everyone in the village had been invited, including Mrs Thursgood with her husband, a tall man with a heavy moustache, who was as quiet as his wife was talkative.

As Chloe walked into the ballroom, there was a sudden

hush. For a brief instant, she was sharply aware of the rustle of her taffeta skirts and the firmness of Darius's hand under her elbow, guiding her up the room, then the moment passed and everyone began chatting twice as hard.

She said in an undertone, not looking at him, 'Well, you've got me here. Perhaps you'll now permit me to join my aunt and uncle so you can enjoy the rest of your evening.'

'I'll come with you,' he said. 'After all, I have some keys to return.'

Without making a scene, there seemed little she could do. Biting her lip, she accompanied him to where the Jacksons were standing, talking to a blonde woman in pale blue.

As they approached, she turned, smiling, holding out her hand.

'Chloe,' she said. 'How lovely to see you again.'

Chloe heard her voice, small and husky, reply, 'Penny—Mrs Maynard. Good evening.'

And made herself touch the proffered fingers in a parody of goodwill.

The moment she'd dreaded had come, and it was worse than she could ever have imagined. Because the taut, thin figure she remembered was now beguilingly rounded, the proud swell of her abdomen under the gentle drape of her soft silk crepe dress proclaiming her pregnancy. The face had softened too, the happy curve of Penny's mouth suggesting that she smiled a lot these days and her eyes were shining.

She'd always been striking, but now she looked beautiful, thought Chloe with sudden anguish. Fulfilled.

Penny was turning to Darius, her glance tinged with laughing complicity. 'You're just in time, my pet. Your father's been getting restive. He wants to make the announcement.'

'Then I'd better go to him.' He paused. 'Are you feeling up to it? Because I know he wants you to come too.'

'Yes,' she said, her fingers resting briefly and protectively on her stomach. 'Of course.' Her smile swept the Jacksons, encompassing Chloe in its warmth. 'You'll excuse me for a few minutes? There'll be plenty of time to talk later while everyone's still recovering from the shock.'

Her glance rested on Chloe. 'And especially as we're going to be seeing a lot of each other in future, I hope.'

Chloe watched her go at Darius's side, her hand on his arm, then said in a low voice, 'Aunt Libby—how could you? Why did you let him do this to me? Bring me here?'

'Because I didn't really have much choice.' There was a note of tartness in the response. 'I think I've always underestimated that young man's determination to get his own way. Clearly we all have,' she added with a faint snort.

At the end of the room, Sir Gregory was being helped onto the small platform. He stood at the microphone with Darius standing on one side of him and Penny seated on the other, and Chloe could see the glances and hear the whispers, a ripple of anticipation sweeping through the room like a wind blowing across barley.

She thought, I don't want to be here. I don't want to listen to what's going to be said, and have to smile and applaud with the rest of them. I can't bear it.

But to make an exit now would attract too much attention, because the band leader was giving the signal for a short drum roll asking for silence.

Sir Gregory began slowly, leaning on his silver-topped cane. 'It is a great pleasure to see so many friends and neighbours here in this house tonight, for what will be the last ever Birthday Ball.'

He waited for the astonished murmurs to die away, then went on, 'My recent illness gave me a lot of time to reflect, on the past as well as the future. It made me see that my view of family continuity here at the Hall for the coming generations was not necessarily the right one.

'For one thing, there are increasingly difficult economic facts to be faced in maintaining a house of this size with its land.

'But, far more important, I also realised that my remaining son, now my heir, has built his own very different life elsewhere, and established business and personal commitments in Europe and other parts of the world. I cannot, in conscience, expect him to abandon any of these for another career, and other responsibilities that he never expected or desired.'

He paused. 'I have therefore decided to sell the Hall and the greater part of the estate to the Hatherstone Group to become part of their spa-hotel chain, and the deal will soon be finalised. They intend to recruit staff locally, so the sale will bring jobs to the area, and, I hope, be a whole new beginning for Willowford.'

This time, the gasp was audible.

'I have, however, retained the plantation at Warne Cross,' Sir Gregory went on. 'And will be living there in the former Keeper's Cottage, which has been refurbished and extended for me, with my good Mrs Vernon to look after me still and Mrs Denver to cook, so I expect to enjoy a very happy and stress-free existence for the time I have left. And I trust you will all come and see me from time to time.'

He added, 'Needless to say, I shall also look forward to seeing my grandchildren, when my son and the lady who is soon to be his wife bring them to visit.'

He looked slowly round the room. 'And now, I have little more to say but—goodbye and God bless you all. Oh—and on with the dance!'

'Well I'm damned,' said Uncle Hal as an excited hubbub broke out around them. 'It seems we're not the only ones downsizing, Libby, my dear.' He shook his head. 'But it certainly wasn't the announcement I expected to hear.'

'No.' His wife's tone was thoughtful, her eyes resting

shrewdly on her niece's pale face. 'But perhaps that's another deal still to be finalised.'

Chloe wasn't listening. She stood, staring ahead of her, unable to comprehend what she'd just heard. The Maynards, she thought incredulously, giving up the Hall after more than three centuries? No, it wasn't—it couldn't—be possible.

Yet that was what Sir Gregory had said, therefore it had to be believed.

So I don't have to worry about watching Darius presiding at the Hall with Penny beside him, she thought, because he has a life elsewhere, and other commitments. How ironic is that?

Or did Sir Gregory feel that installing Penny once again as lady of the manor, after all that had happened, would be just too much for the locals to accept, for all their loyalty to the Maynards?

She felt a sob rising in her throat and hastily turned it into a cough.

She said, 'It's very stuffy in here. I think I'll get some air.'

'That might be wise,' Aunt Libby said gently, and paused. 'I can see all this has come as something of a blow, darling. Did you really have no idea?'

She shook her head. 'None at all.' *Especially about Darius becoming a father...*

She forced a smile. 'But I'm sure it's all for the best.'

Because what it really means, she whispered silently, is that once I leave here, I'll never see him again. Or his wife. Or his coming baby. And 'out of sight equals out of mind'— isn't that what they say? I can only pray that it's true.

'That's right, my dear,' Uncle Hal said awkwardly. 'It's been a day of shocks altogether, but you're putting a brave face on them, and we're both proud of you. Very proud indeed. And you look a picture,' he added.

Chloe smiled again, shook her head, and made for the

French doors leading to the terrace, moving with swift determination as if she didn't see any of the people eager to detain her and talk over recent events.

And as if she hadn't noticed Darius gently helping Penny down from the platform and guiding her to the chairs at the side of the room.

With a small, bitter sigh, she went out into the darkness.

CHAPTER THIRTEEN

SHE stood for a moment, drawing deep breaths of the cool garden-scented air. Then, when she felt calmer, she walked down the steps leading down to the gardens, and descended them, carefully lifting her skirt above her ankles.

There was a stone bench just below the terrace, and she sank down onto it, listening to the wafts of music coming from the ballroom, and staring up at the starlit sky, wondering where her next view of it would come from. Not that it really mattered, she thought. All she asked was for it to be a very long way away from here. And with a lot of work to fill her days and make her too tired to stay awake at night. Or dream.

Her reverie was suddenly interrupted by the sound of footsteps on the flagstones above, and Darius's voice saying sharply, 'Chloe—where are you? I know you're out here.'

She froze incredulously, holding her breath. He'd followed her? But how was that possible—in these circumstances?

It's as if I'm being punished, she thought, goading herself into anger. But what have I done—except try and make a life for myself without him? And what blame is there in that, when he made me fall in love with him, then left me? When he's flaunting Penny in front of us all?

She waited on tenterhooks while long minutes passed, as aware of his silent presence a few yards away as if he had laid a hand on her bare shoulder. Trying hard not to shiver. Then—eventually—she heard him move away, his footsteps receding. Back to the ballroom, she thought bleakly, and to his duties as host, to his father, and to the woman carrying his child.

But she couldn't follow. Couldn't pretend any more, because she had to get away. She had money in the evening purse she was clutching like a lifeline, and there was a phone in the stables, so she could call the local taxi company and leave. Go home and pack. And tomorrow begin her next journey and find some sort of freedom.

All she had to do was cut across the gardens.

She took a deep breath then rose, shaking out her skirts, and started off across the lawn.

Only to hear his voice from behind her saying softly, triumphantly, 'At last.'

She realised in that instant that he'd gone nowhere, but simply remained where he was on the terrace, biding his time until she moved.

She tried to run but stumbled as the heel of her sandal sank into the soft turf. She wrenched herself free of it and carried on, limping clumsily and ridiculously on one bare foot.

He caught her easily within a few yards, her sandal dangling from his hand.

He said, 'When I called you Cinderella earlier, my sweet, it was meant as a joke.'

'Then perhaps I'm suffering a sense of humour failure.' She faced him defiantly, her heart hammering unevenly inside the boned confines of her bodice. 'But for me, midnight struck a long time ago, and I want to get out of here.'

'My own feelings entirely.' He sounded rueful. 'But I can't leave yet for obvious reasons, so why don't we wait a little longer and go together tomorrow?'

She was trembling almost violently. She said huskily,

'Because that isn't possible. It never was. So, please, *please* don't say things like that. Can't you show me a little mercy?'

'I already did that,' he said, slowly. 'Seven years ago when I gave you your freedom. When I began to make love to you and suddenly realised that if I took you, I would never let you go, and that you were much too young to be tied into the serious relationship that I longed for. You had your university course—your dreams of a career—your whole future waiting.'

He took a swift, harsh breath. 'I told myself that I couldn't rob you of your chance to discover who you were and what you wanted from life. That it would be cruel and unfair to ask you to give it up and come away with me, just as my mother had once warned me.

'She loved my father, but she knew how difficult it was to adjust to a life you weren't altogether ready for. And I knew I had to accept that and remove myself from temptation by going back to France the next day without you, even if it meant tearing out my heart.'

The lean face was taut, his mouth compressed.

'However, I had every intention of keeping in touch. I reasoned if I wrote to you from wherever—saw you regularly in London—that you might one day realise that what you really wanted was me. That all I had to do was wait.'

He added, 'But as we both know it didn't work out like that.'

There were tears, raw and thick in her throat. 'But you left me—for *her*.' The words she'd sworn she would never say out in the open at last.

'No,' he said steadily. 'I left *with* her. A very different situation, and forced on me when, by pure mischance, Andrew found us together in my bedroom.' He paused. 'All hell broke loose, of course. Andrew was like a crazy man, shouting accusations, calling us both every foul name he could think of, and the row brought my father down on us too.

'I knew Andrew was on the edge of violence, and my father was angrier than I'd ever seen him, and refused to listen to any kind of explanation.'

He sighed abruptly. 'I was already packed and ready to go, even before he ordered me out of the house for ever. But I felt I couldn't risk leaving Penny there alone. Therefore I took her with me to London.'

Her voice shook. 'How could you possibly explain all that—to anyone?'

'Quite easily now,' he said. He glanced around him. 'But not here. For this, we need privacy.'

Before she could stop him, he'd swept her up into his arms and carried her back across the grass to the gravel walk and round the corner of the house.

As they reached the side door and Chloe realised where she was being taken, she began to struggle.

Her voice was a gasp. 'No—I won't…'

Darius bent his head, stifling her protest swiftly and passionately with his mouth as he carried her into the house and up the stairs to his bedroom.

When, at last, he set her on her feet, she was breathless and her lips felt swollen, but she faced him stormily.

'How dare you bring me here—where you had sex with her? Where you'll no doubt spend tonight with her. Am I supposed to accept this—as if it didn't matter?'

'No,' Darius said. 'Because you're wrong on both counts. Penny and I are not and never have been lovers in this room or anywhere else. As for tonight, I imagine her husband will expect her in their bed as usual. She would have introduced him to you earlier but he was upstairs, checking on their little boy.'

There was a silence, then she said in a voice she hardly recognised as hers, 'Penny—married?'

'Very much so,' he said. 'To Jean Pierre, the friend who manages my vineyard in the Dordogne. They met a few years back when he came to London on a sales trip and were married a couple of months later.'

'But you were the one she wanted first.'

He shook his head. 'She came to me because she was desperate to leave Andrew. That was all.'

'But why—if it wasn't for you?'

Darius took her hand, leading her to the bed and sitting beside her. He said, his tone quiet, almost flat, 'Andrew and I were never particularly close, when we were children or later. He led a blameless life. I didn't. Also he was something of a loner and very conscious of being Dad's heir. He didn't seem to have many close friends, and, although he dated girls occasionally, there didn't appear to be anyone special.

'So his engagement to Penny came as something of a surprise—to me, at least. I'd no idea they were involved. But I was pleased for him. She was a stunner and fairly lively too, and I thought she might be just what he needed.

'I was away a good deal, but when I was at home I soon realised that all wasn't well between them. Andrew seemed more of an introvert than ever, and Penny was a shadow of what she'd been before the marriage. I tried once to talk to him—ask a few tactful questions—but he froze me off as usual.

'But when I came back for the Birthday Ball, I could see things had gone from bad to worse. This time I spoke to my father about it, but he glared at me and said that Andrew was a model husband, coping with a difficult and neurotic girl, and as my own private life was an open disgrace, I should kindly refrain from comment or interference.'

He took Chloe's hand, stroking her fingers gently, and the

breath caught in her throat as she responded to the promise of his skin against hers.

'What he didn't know, because I'd only just found out myself, was that my life had changed for ever, dating from the moment I went to the Willow Pond for a swim and found a dark-haired siren sitting on a rock, waiting for me to fall in love with her.'

She bent her head, letting her hair fall around her flushed face, the turmoil within her changing to a different kind of excitement.

'Because fall I did,' he went on. 'Between one breath and the next.' He gave an unsteady laugh. 'I'd never been so happy, knowing for the first time I had someone to work for—to plan a future beside. But I couldn't ignore what was going on around me, especially when Penny started seeking me out, telling me she needed to talk.

'I was pretty sure Andrew had noticed this too, so I was careful to keep my distance, which, in retrospect, was a mistake, because I failed to realise how near the edge she really was.

'The ball finished earlier than usual that year, and I was thankful, because I'd found having to go on being civil was almost impossible when I was feeling so raw over you. When I came up here, I could still smell your perfume on my pillow, remember how glorious you'd looked, and how your eyes had smiled into mine.'

He took a sharp breath. 'I told myself that I'd been a fool to let you go. That it wasn't too late to drive over to the Grange and say, "I will love you for the rest of my life. Come away with me now and we'll be married as soon as I can get a licence".'

'You wanted to tell me that?' Her voice shook. 'Oh, why didn't you?'

'For all the excellent reasons already stated,' Darius said

ruefully. 'Plus I was terrified you might say no. It seemed best to stick to my plan for a lengthy and patient wooing.'

He sighed. 'Just as well I didn't know exactly how long, or that when we met again you'd claim to love someone else. I fell asleep that night thinking about you, wanting you, and when someone touched my shoulder and said my name, I suppose I hoped it was you. That by some miracle you'd come back to me and our life together could begin.'

He paused. 'Instead, I found Penny standing by my bed in her dressing gown. She said, "When you leave tomorrow, you have to take me with you. I can't bear any more. My cousin Helen in Kensington will let me stay there until I sort myself out. I'm just going to take my clothes—not my car or anything else Andrew has given me. That wouldn't be right".'

'I thought at first she'd been drinking, and wondered how I could get her back to her own room when the house was still full of people clearing up after the ball. But I couldn't get out of bed either, because I always sleep naked, so I was stuck both ways.

'I tried to sound soothing—said I was sure it couldn't be as bad as all that, and suggested she got Andrew to take her away somewhere romantic on a second honeymoon.'

He grimaced. 'And with that the floodgates opened. She collapsed on the bed beside me, crying her eyes out. Told me it had never been a real marriage. That Andrew had made a few half-hearted attempts to have sex with her in the first couple of weeks, but they'd ended in failure, and they no longer even shared a room. She claimed he'd never loved her, and had married her only for an heir to the Maynard name, except he couldn't force himself to do what was necessary. And my father had begun dropping pointed hints.'

'Oh, God.' Chloe drew a shaken breath. 'How awful for her. For them both.'

'But she hadn't finished,' Darius said grimly. 'And this

was the worst of all. She said maybe Andrew wasn't the kind of man who should be married, or not to a woman anyway. Except that was something he wouldn't admit, even to himself.

'And while I was still reeling from that, the door opened and Andrew himself came in with my father close behind him, and found her on the bed with my arm round her.'

He shuddered. 'God, it was terrible. He was shouting he'd always suspected there was something going on. Accused us of meeting secretly in London. Said she was nothing but a dirty tart.'

Chloe gasped. 'But he couldn't have meant it.'

'Not unless he saw it as a convenient way of getting rid of a girl who'd become an embarrassment—a living reproach in his own home. And apart from the obvious denials there wasn't much we could say. Penny wasn't prepared to tax Andrew with his failings as a husband in front of his father, and I respected her for that.'

She said quietly, 'Poor Penny, knowing her life was in pieces and unable to do anything about it.' She hesitated. 'But should you be telling me all this? Won't she hate my knowing these things?'

'It was her own idea. She's always felt that, by asking my help, she cost me my family, my home and the girl I loved for seven whole years. She told me she needed to set the record straight.'

She said, 'Did she tell your father—about the marriage?'

'She didn't have to.' Darius sighed again. 'Andrew wrote to him before that last climbing trip, saying he'd realised the truth about himself a long time ago, but had never been able to accept it. Saw it as some kind of betrayal of his heritage. I think the rogue horses and dangerous sports were just symbols of the ongoing struggle his life became.'

He shook his head. 'It was the letter combined with the

shock of his death that probably triggered Dad's stroke. On the other hand, while he was recovering, it changed his perceptions of a great many things, as he made clear tonight. But, I believed it was much too late for me. Because, when I tried to contact you afterwards and explain, your aunt sent me away, saying you were totally disgusted and never wanted to see me or speak to me again.'

His mouth twisted. 'I'd been condemned without a word in my own defence and that hurt, so I left bitter and angry.'

He added softly, 'But I couldn't forget you, Chloe, no matter how hard I tried. Then I heard you were coming back, and I felt I'd been offered another chance.'

She began to smile. 'You weren't very nice to me when we met that first time.'

His mouth relaxed into a teasing grin. 'You thought I was someone else. And then you hit me with your supposed engagement. I knew Lindsay and Ian were an item and I thought you were simply using him as an excuse to keep me at bay.'

She said in a low voice, 'I think I was. I told myself I couldn't bear to be hurt again. So I tried to fight my feelings and lost every time. I only wanted to stay away tonight because I'd heard Penny was back. When I saw she was pregnant, I thought it must be your baby, and that you were going to marry her and the pain of that was so bad I had to run away.'

He said gently, 'My darling, there's only one girl in the world I've ever wanted to be my wife and the mother of my children.' He paused. 'I said earlier, I was prepared for a long and patient wooing, but my patience has almost run out.' He smoothed back her hair, cupping the curve of her face in his hand as he looked into her eyes. 'I want you so much, my sweet one. Are you still going to make me wait?'

Her whole body clenched in sweet, fierce yearning. She

moved into his arms, her hands gripping his shoulders through the layers of cloth, her lips already parting for his kiss.

His mouth was warm and urgent on hers, his hands trembling as he dealt with the long zip at the back of her dress, peeling the jade taffeta away from her body, and dropping it to the floor.

She clung to him, gasping as his crisp dress shirt grazed her bared breasts, her hands stroking his hair, offering him kiss for kiss in the rising tumult of their mutual desire, so long unsatisfied.

His hands caressed her body, moving over her skin in something like wonderment as if he still could not believe that she was here with him—about to be his at last.

His lips traversed the supple line of her throat, letting his tongue make a delicate foray into the inner whorls of her ear, his teeth nibbling delicately at its lobe, while his hands moved down to cup her breasts in his palms and tease each rosy nipple into aching arousal with his fingertips.

She murmured his name pleadingly, her own mouth tracing the strong line of his neck.

When he released her it was only to tug back the covers on the bed, and place her gently against the pillows. He began to strip off his own clothes, his eyes scanning restlessly down her body, still partly concealed by her silk-and-lace knickers.

He said quietly and huskily, 'Take them off.'

She obeyed, wriggling out of them slowly, languorously, smiling up at him as she watched his emerald gaze kindle. He was naked too, now, and she held out her arms to receive him.

They came together in a breathless, almost anguished silence. Chloe had only instinct and her own burning need to guide her as she held him, opened herself to him. As she found herself welcoming the swift lancing pain of his first penetration of her because it meant she belonged to him completely at last. To him and to no-one else—ever.

And as she lifted her hips to meet each long, heated thrust of total possession, locking her slim legs round his waist to draw him into her ever more deeply, wanting to please him—to satisfy him—to make him forget every other woman he'd ever held in his arms.

Only to discover how richly her generosity was to be rewarded, as the driving force of his lean body ignited new and undreamed of sensations in her inexperienced flesh.

Darius changed his position slightly, so that his hardness came into sensuous contact with her tiny hidden mound, deliberately and deliciously arousing its exquisite sensitivity. Taking her to some edge and beyond.

Chloe could feel the first ripples of pleasure in her innermost self. Recognised with bewilderment the moment when they began to build into a mindless spiral of delight. Tried for an instant to resist their mounting intensity, scared by her own response, only to find herself overtaken, overwhelmed by a harsh, scalding ecstasy that had her sobbing with incoherent joy into his mouth.

And heard his own almost agonised cry of rapture echo hers.

Afterwards he held her wrapped in his arms, his lips against her hair, whispering words she had never heard before. Never believed she would hear.

She lay, her head pillowed on his shoulder, and knew that all the safety and security she had ever wanted was here with her now, and always would be.

Eventually, he said lazily, 'At some point, we're going to have to dress and go downstairs. It's the last Birthday Ball, and I need to dance with you.'

'Oh.' Chloe stirred guiltily. 'What will people think?'

'The truth probably, but what do we care? We won't be here when the rumour mill starts.'

'We won't?'

He shook his head. 'I have to go back to France tomorrow. The vineyard needs my attention.' He paused. 'But it occurs to me that this may not be what you want, or not on a permanent basis. The deal with Hatherstone hasn't gone through yet, and I know how much Willowford has always meant to you. So if you want to live here—have the Hall, the title, the whole bit—it can still be done. The choice is entirely yours.'

'None of those things mean anything to me,' she said, adding simply, 'I never thought of them as mine, anyway.'

'Ah,' he said, and she heard the smile in his voice. 'So if I say to you, my adorable angel, "Come with me now, and we'll be married as soon as I can get a licence", what will you reply?'

'What I'd have said seven years ago if you'd asked me.' Chloe turned her head, pressing her lips to the pulse in his throat. 'That my life is yours, wherever it takes us, now and for ever.'

Darius said softly, 'I think you just rewrote the marriage service.' And began to kiss her again.

* * * * *

RUTHLESS RUSSIAN, LOST INNOCENCE

BY
CHANTELLE SHAW

Chantelle Shaw lives on the Kent coast, five minutes from the sea, and does much of her thinking about the characters in her books while walking on the beach. She's been an avid reader from an early age. Her schoolfriends used to hide their books when she visited—but Chantelle would retreat into her own world, and still writes stories in her head all the time. Chantelle has been blissfully married to her own tall, dark and very patient hero for over twenty years, and has six children. She began to read Mills & Boon® novels as a teenager, and throughout the years of being a stay-at-home mum to her brood found romantic fiction helped her to stay sane! She enjoys reading and writing about strong-willed, feisty women, and even stronger willed sexy heroes. Chantelle is at her happiest when writing. She is particularly inspired while cooking dinner, which unfortunately results in a lot of culinary disasters! She also loves gardening, walking, and eating chocolate (followed by more walking!). Catch up with Chantelle's latest news on her website: www.chantelleshaw.com

CHAPTER ONE

The Louvre Auditorium—Paris

IT HAPPENED in an instant. A fleeting glance across the crowded auditorium of the Louvre and *wham*, Ella felt as though she had been struck by a lightning bolt.

The man was standing some distance away, surrounded by a group of seriously chic Frenchwomen who were all vying for his attention. Her first impression in those few heart-stopping seconds when their eyes met was that he was tall, dark and devastatingly handsome—but when she tore her gaze from his piercing blue stare she instinctively added the word *dangerous* to the list.

Shaken by her reaction to a complete stranger, she stared down at her champagne glass, dismayed to find that her hands were trembling, and tried to concentrate on her conversation with a music journalist from the culture section of *Paris Match*.

'The audience were enraptured by you tonight, Mademoiselle Stafford. Your performance of Prokofiev's second violin concerto was truly outstanding.'

'Thank you.' Ella smiled faintly at the journalist, but she was still supremely conscious of the intense scrutiny of the man standing on the other side of the room, and it took all her willpower to resist turning her head. It was almost a relief when Marcus appeared at her side.

'You know everyone's saying a star has been born tonight?' he greeted her excitedly. 'You were bloody marvellous, Ella. I've just sneaked a preview of the review Stephen Hill is writing for *The Times*, and I quote—"Stafford's passion and technical bravura are out of this world. Her musical brilliance is dazzling, and her performance tonight cements her place as one of the world's top violinists." Not bad, eh?' Marcus could not hide his satisfaction. 'Come on—you need to circulate. There are at least half a dozen other journalists who want to interview you.'

'Actually, if you don't mind, I'd really like to go back to the hotel.'

Marcus's smile slipped when he realised that Ella was serious. 'But this is your big night,' he protested.

Ella bit her lip. 'I realise that the party is an ideal opportunity for more publicity, but I'm tired. The concert was draining.' Particularly when she'd spent the few hours before her solo performance ravaged by nerves, she thought ruefully. Music was her life, but the crippling stage fright she suffered every time she played in public was far from enjoyable, and sometimes she wondered if pursuing a career as a soloist was what she really wanted when it made her physically sick with fear.

'You attracted an A-list audience tonight, and you can't just disappear,' Marcus argued. 'I've seen at least two ministers from the French government, not to mention a Russian oligarch.' He glanced over Ella's shoulder and gave a low whistle. 'Don't look now, but Vadim Aleksandrov is heading this way.'

With a heavy sense of inevitability Ella turned her head a fraction, and felt her heart slam beneath her ribs when her eyes clashed once more with a startling blue gaze. The man was striding purposefully towards her, and she stared transfixed at the masculine beauty of his classically sculpted features and his jet-black hair swept back from his brow.

'Who is he?' she whispered to Marcus.

'A Russian billionaire—made his fortune in mobile phones and now owns a satellite television station, a British newspaper and a property empire that is said to include half of Chelsea—or Chelski, as some now call it,' Marcus added dryly. He broke off quickly, but Ella did not need the sight of Marcus's most ingratiating smile to tell her that the man was close behind her. She could feel his presence. The spicy scent of his cologne assailed her senses, and the tiny hairs on the back of her neck stood on end when he spoke in a deep, melodious voice that was as rich and sensuous as the notes of a cello.

'Forgive my intrusion, but I would like to offer my congratulations to Miss Stafford on her performance tonight.'

'Mr Aleksandrov.' Marcus's hand shot past Ella's nose as he greeted the Russian. 'I'm Marcus Benning, Ella's publicist. And this, of course —' he patted Ella's shoulder in a faintly possessive manner '—is Lady Eleanor Stafford.'

Ella blushed, and felt a surge of irritation with Marcus, who knew she disliked using her title but insisted that it was a good marketing tool. But as she turned to face the man, Marcus, the other guests, everything faded, and only Vadim Aleksandrov existed. Her eyes flew to his face and her blush deepened at the feral gleam in his gaze. A curious mix of fear and excitement shot through her, together with the ridiculous feeling that her life would never be the same again after this moment. She felt a strange reluctance to shake his hand, and shock ripped through her when he lifted her fingers to his mouth and pressed his lips to her knuckles.

'Eleanor.' His accented gravelly voice sent the same quiver of pleasure down her spine that she felt when she drew her bow across the strings of her violin. The feather-light brush of his mouth against her skin burned as if he had branded her, and with a little gasp she snatched her hand back, her heart beating frantically beneath her ribs.

'It's an honour to meet you, Mr Aleksandrov,' Marcus said eagerly. 'Am I right that your company holds the monopoly on mobile phone sales in Russia?'

'We certainly took advantage of the gap in the communications market in its early days of trading, but the company has grown and diversified widely since then,' Vadim Aleksandrov murmured dismissively. He continued to stare intently at Ella, and Marcus finally took the hint.

'Where are all the damn waiters? I could do with a refill,' he muttered, waving his empty champagne glass before he wandered off towards the bar.

For a split second Ella was tempted to race after him, but the enigmatic Russian's brilliant blue eyes seemed to exert a magnetic hold over her, and she was so overwhelmed by his potent masculinity that she found herself rooted to the spot.

'You played superbly tonight.'

'Thank you.' She struggled to formulate a polite response, her whole being conscious of the electrical attraction that arced between them. She had never experienced anything like it before, never been so acutely aware of a man, and it was frankly terrifying.

Vadim's sardonic smile warned her that he recognised her awareness of him. 'I have never heard another non-Russian play Prokofiev with the passionate intensity for which he—and many of my countrymen—are renowned,' he murmured, in a crushed-velvet voice that seemed to enfold Ella in its intimate caress.

Was that a roundabout way of telling her that *he* was passionate? The thought came unbidden into her head, and colour flared along her cheekbones as she acknowledged that he had no need to point out what was so blindingly obvious—even to her, with her severely limited sexual experience. Vadim Aleksandrov wore his virility like a badge, and she found the bold appreciation in his eyes as he trailed them over her body deeply unsettling.

'Are you enjoying the party?'

Ella glanced around the packed reception room, where several hundred guests were all talking at once. The hubbub of voices hurt her ears. 'It's very nice,' she murmured.

The glint of amusement in Vadim's eyes told her he knew she was lying. 'I understand you are giving another performance tomorrow evening, so I assume you are staying in Paris?'

'Yes. At the Intercontinental,' she added when his brows lifted quizzically.

'I'm at the George V, not far from you. I have a car waiting outside—can I offer you a lift back to your hotel? Maybe we could have a drink together?'

'Thank you, but I can't rush away from the party,' Ella mumbled, aware that a couple of minutes ago she had planned to do just that. But Vadim Aleksandrov's blatant sensuality disturbed her composure far too much for her to contemplate socialising with him. The hungry look in his eyes warned her that he would expect a drink in the bar to lead to an invitation up to her room—and she was very definitely not the sort of woman who indulged in one-night stands.

But supposing she *had* been the sort of woman who invited a sexy stranger to spend the night with her? For a second her imagination ran riot, and a series of shocking images flashed into her mind, of Vadim undressing her and touching her body before he drew her down onto the crisp white sheets of her hotel bed and made love to her.

What *was* she thinking? She could feel the heat radiating from her face and hastily dropped her eyes from Vadim's speculative gaze, terrified that he might somehow have read her thoughts.

'The party is in your honour. Of course I understand your eagerness to remain,' he drawled in a faintly mocking tone. 'I'll be in London next week. Perhaps we could have dinner one evening?'

Ella swiftly dismissed the crazy impulse to accept his invitation. 'I'm afraid I'll be busy.'

'Every evening?' His sensual smile caused her heart to skip a beat. 'He's a lucky man.'

She frowned. 'Who is?'

'The lover who commands your attention every night.'

'I don't have a lover—' She stopped abruptly, realising that she had unwittingly revealed more about her personal life than she'd wished. The gleam of satisfaction in his eyes triggered alarm bells and she sent up a silent prayer of thanks when she caught sight of Marcus making signs for her to join him at the bar. 'If you'll excuse me, I think my publicist has arranged for me to give an interview.' She hesitated, while innate good manners battled with the urge to put as much distance as possible between herself and the disturbing Russian, and then said hurriedly, 'Thank you for the invitation, but music takes up all my time and I'm not dating at the moment.'

Vadim had moved imperceptibly closer, so that she could feel the heat emanating from his body. She stiffened, her eyes widening in shock when he reached out and stroked his finger lightly down her cheek. 'Then I shall just have to try and persuade you to change your mind,' he promised softly, before he turned and walked away, leaving her staring helplessly after him.

London—a week later

The Garden Room at Amesbury House buzzed with the murmur of voices as guests filed in and took their seats. The members of the Royal London Orchestra were already in their places, and there was the usual rustle of sheet music and a ripple of conversation from the musicians as they prepared for the concert.

Ella lifted her violin out of its case and gave a tiny shiver of pleasure as she ran her fingers over the smooth, polished maple. The Stradivarius was exquisite, and incredibly valuable. Several collectors had offered her a fortune for the rare instrument—more than enough for her to be able to buy somewhere to live and still leave her with a sizeable nest egg should her career falter. But the violin had belonged to her mother; its sentimental value was incalculable and she would never part with it.

She flicked through the music sheets on the stand in front of her, mentally running through the symphony, although she had little need of the pages of notes when she had put in four hours of practice that afternoon. Lost in her own world, she was only vaguely conscious of the voices around her until someone spoke her name.

'You're miles away, aren't you?' her fellow first violinist, Jenny March, said impatiently. 'I *said*, it looks as though one of us has an admirer—although sadly I don't think it's me,' she added, the note of genuine regret in her voice finally causing Ella to look up.

'Who do you mean?' she murmured, casting a curious glance around the room.

The orchestra had performed at Amesbury House in London's west end on several occasions. The Garden Room held an audience of two hundred, and provided a more intimate atmosphere than larger venues, but Ella preferred the anonymity of the Royal Albert Hall or the Festival Hall. Her eyes skimmed along the front row of guests and juddered to a halt on the figure sitting a few feet away from her.

'Oh! What's *he* doing here?' she muttered, jerking her head away seconds too late to avoid the familiar glinting gaze of the man who had plagued her dreams every night for the past week.

'You know him?' Jenny's eyes widened, and she could not disguise the hint of envy in her voice. 'What a dark horse you are, Ella. He's seriously gorgeous. Who is he?'

'His name is Vadim Aleksandrov,' Ella said in a clipped tone, aware that Jenny would badger her for information all night. 'He's a Russian billionaire. I've met him once— briefly—but I don't *know* him.'

'Well, it's obvious he'd like to get to know you,' Jenny said musingly, intrigued by the twin spots of colour staining Ella's cheeks. Lady Eleanor Stafford was renowned for being cool and composed—so much so that she had earned the nickname of ice princess by a few of the other orchestra members—but at this moment Ella was looking distinctly flustered.

'I can't understand why he's here,' Ella muttered tensely. 'According to the gossip column in the magazine I read, he's supposed to be at the film festival in Cannes with a famous Italian actress.' The photo of him and his voluptuous companion had lodged in Ella's mind, and to her annoyance she had been unable to forget it, nor dismiss the shocking image in her head of a naked Vadim making love to his latest mistress. His private life did not interest her, she reminded herself sharply. Vadim Aleksandrov did not interest her, and she absolutely would not give in to the urge to turn her head and meet the piercing blue gaze she sensed was focused on her.

But her prickling awareness of him did not lessen, and she had to force herself to concentrate as the audience settled and the RLO's principal conductor, Gustav Germaine, lifted his baton. She adored Dvorak's *New World Symphony*, and she was annoyed with herself for being distracted by Vadim's presence. Taking a deep breath, she positioned her violin beneath her chin, and only then, as she drew her bow, did she relax and give all her attention to the music that flowed from wood and strings and seemed to surge up inside her, obliterating every other thought.

An hour and a half later the last notes of the symphony faded and the sound of the audience's tumultuous applause shattered Ella's dream-like state, catapulting her back to reality.

'Good grief! Gustav's almost smiling,' Jenny whispered as the members of the orchestra stood and bowed. 'That must mean he's satisfied with our performance for once. Too right—it sounded pretty well perfect to me.'

'I wasn't entirely happy with the way I played at the start of the fourth movement,' Ella muttered.

'But you're even more of a perfectionist than Gustav,' Jenny said, unconcerned. 'From the audience's response, they loved it—especially your Russian. He hasn't taken his eyes off you the whole evening.'

'He's not *my* Russian.' Ella did not want to be reminded of Vadim Aleksandrov, or learn that he had been watching her. She certainly did not want to glance over in his direction, but, like a puppet tugged by invisible strings, she turned her head a fraction, her eyes drawn inexorably to the dark-haired figure in the front row.

Jenny was right—he was gorgeous, she admitted reluctantly. Music dominated her life, and usually she took little notice of men, but Vadim was impossible to ignore. He was tall—three or four inches over six feet tall by her estimation—with impressively broad shoulders sheathed in a superbly tailored dinner jacket. His jet-black hair and olive-toned complexion hinted at a Mediterranean ancestry, which made his vivid blue eyes beneath heavy black brows even more startling. His hard-boned face was exquisitely sculpted, with razor-sharp cheekbones, a patrician nose and a square chin that warned of a determined nature, while his beautifully shaped mouth was innately sensual.

Oh, yes—seriously gorgeous, and her reaction to him was seriously unnerving, Ella acknowledged, feeling her heart slam beneath her ribs when those blue eyes trailed over her in a leisurely inspection and his lips curved into an amused smile that warned her he was well aware of the effect he had on her.

'So, where did you meet a sexy Russian billionaire?' Jenny muttered beneath the sound of the audience's applause. 'And if you're not interested in him I think it's only fair you introduce him to me. He's practically edible.'

Jenny was irrepressible, and despite herself Ella's lips twitched. 'I met him in Paris.'

Jenny's eyes widened. 'Paris—the city of romance. This gets better and better. Did you sleep with him?'

'*No!* Absolutely not.' Ella gave her friend a scandalised glance. 'Do you think I'd jump into bed with a man I'd only just met?'

'Not normally, no.' Ella's coolness with members of the opposite sex was well known. 'But perhaps if he looked at you the way he's looking at you now…' Jenny murmured shrewdly.

Ella knew she was going to regret her next question. 'How is he looking at me?' she asked, striving to sound uninterested—and failing.

'Like he's imagining undressing you, very slowly, and

stroking his hands over every inch of your body as he exposes you to his hungry gaze.'

'For heaven's sake, Jen! I don't know what kind of books you've been reading lately.'

Jenny watched Ella's face flood with colour and grinned. 'You asked—I'm just telling you what I reckon is in your Russian's mind.'

'*He's not my Russian.*' Ella took a deep breath, and by sheer effort of will did not glance over at Vadim—but she could not dismiss the memory of the searing attraction she had felt the first time she had met him. A force beyond her control demanded that she turn her head, and as her eyes clashed with his brilliant gaze she felt a fierce tug of sexual awareness in the pit of her stomach. To her horror she felt an exquisite tingling sensation in her breasts as her nipples hardened, and mortification swept through her when Vadim deliberately lowered his eyes to the stiff peaks straining beneath her clingy silk jersey dress. Scarlet-faced, she jerked her head away from him and by sheer effort of will forced her lips into a smile as she faced the audience and bowed once more.

Vadim felt a surge of satisfaction when he noted the betraying signs that Ella Stafford was not as immune to him as she would like him to believe. When they had met a week ago he had been blown away by her delicate beauty, and intrigued by her coolness. He wanted her badly—perhaps more than he had ever wanted a woman, he brooded as his eyes skimmed over her slender body, following the slight curve of her hips, the indent of her tiny waist and the delicate swell of her breasts beneath her black cocktail dress.

Her hair was swept up into an elegant chignon, and for a

moment he indulged in the pleasurable fantasy of removing the pins so that the pale blonde silk fell around her shoulders. To his shock, he felt himself harden. He hadn't been this turned-on since he was a testosterone-fuelled youth, he acknowledged self-derisively, and he inhaled sharply, his nostrils flaring slightly as he imposed ruthless self-control over his hormones.

The members of the orchestra were now filing out of the Garden Room. He was aware that Ella had determinedly not looked in his direction, but as she stepped forward she shot him a lightning glance, and colour flared along her cheek-bones when he dipped his head in acknowledgement.

Her reaction pleased him. He had known when they had met in Paris and he had seen the flare of startled awareness in her eyes that the attraction was mutual. Sexual alchemy was a potent force that held them both in its grip, but for some reason she had refused his invitation to dinner in a cool tone that had been at variance with her dilated pupils and the tremulous softness of her mouth.

He dismissed the rumour circulating among certain individuals of her social group that she was frigid. No one could play an instrument with such fire and passion and have ice running through her veins. But her resistance was certainly a novelty. He had never before encountered a problem persuading any woman into his bed, Vadim mused cynically, aware that his billionaire status accounted for much of his attraction.

But Ella was different from the models and socialites he usually dated. She was a member of the British aristocracy; beautiful, intelligent and a gifted musician. The sexual attraction between them was indisputable, and as Vadim turned his head to watch her slender figure walk out of the Garden Room he felt a surge of determination to make her his mistress.

The evening at Amesbury House was a fundraising event organised by the patron of a children's charity, and after the performance by the RLO a selection of cheeses and fine wines were served in the Egyptian Room. Ella smiled and chatted with the guests, but she was conscious of the familiar empty feeling inside her that always followed a performance. She had put her heart and soul into playing, but now she felt emotionally drained, and the hubbub of voices exacerbated her niggling headache.

She had not seen Vadim since she had caught his amused stare on her way out of the Garden Room, and she assumed that he had left immediately after the performance. It was a relief to know she would not have to contend with his disturbing presence for the rest of the evening, she thought as she stepped through the door leading to the orangery—a glass-roofed conservatory that ran the length of the house, and which was blessedly cool and quiet after the stuffy atmosphere of the Egyptian Room. It was beautiful here among the leafy citrus trees, but she longed to be back at Kingfisher House, beside the River Thames, her home for the past few years. She glanced at her watch, wondering how soon she could slip away from the party, and gave a startled gasp when a figure stepped out of the shadows.

'I thought you'd gone.' Shock lent a sharp edge to her voice, and Vadim Aleksandrov's dark brows rose quizzically.

'I am flattered that you noticed my absence, Lady Eleanor.'

His deep, accented voice was so innately sexy that she could not restrain the little shiver of reaction that ran through her. The only light in the orangery came from the silver moonbeams slanting through the glass, and she hoped he could not see the flush of colour that surged into her cheeks.

'Please don't call me that,' she said tautly. 'I never use my title.'

'You would prefer for me to call you Ella, as your friends do?' In the pearly grey half-light Vadim's smile revealed a set of perfect white teeth which reminded Ella of a predatory wolf. 'I am delighted that you regard me as a friend,' he drawled. 'It marks a major step forward in our relationship.'

She froze, infuriated by his mocking tone, and aware of an underlying serious note in his voice that warned her to be on her guard. 'We don't have a relationship to move forward, backward, or anywhere else,' she snapped.

'An unsatisfactory situation that can easily be remedied. I have two tickets for *Madame Butterfly* at the Royal Opera House for Thursday evening. Would you care to join me? We could have dinner after the performance.'

'I'm flying to Cologne to play at the Opernhaus on Wednesday,' Ella told him truthfully, assuring herself that the faint twinge of regret she felt was only because Puccini's famous opera was one of her favourites.

Vadim shrugged, drawing her attention to the formidable width of his shoulders, and she felt a curious tugging sensation low in her stomach. 'I'll rearrange the tickets for another night.'

His supreme self-confidence was that of a man who was used to getting his own way, and his arrogant smile made Ella's hackles rise. Clearly he expected women to fall at his feet, and no doubt there were plenty who would leap at the chance to spend an evening with him—and then probably leap into his bed with the same eagerness—but she wasn't one of them. She had tried to rebuff him politely, but obviously blunter tactics were needed. 'Which part of *no* don't you understand?' she queried icily.

Far from seeming offended, he widened his smile and strolled towards her, his piercing blue gaze trapping her as helplessly as a rabbit confronted by car headlights. She was of average height, and her heels gave her the advantage of another three inches, but he still towered over her, the muscular strength of his chest a formidable barrier which barred her escape from the orangery. He had invaded her thoughts day and night for the past week, and now, as she inhaled the exotic tang of his cologne, her senses swam and she could not deny her agonising awareness of him.

'This part,' Vadim said softly, sliding his hand beneath her chin and lowering his head before she had time to comprehend his intention—or react to it.

CHAPTER TWO

'*No!*' ELLA'S outraged gasp was muffled beneath the firm pressure of Vadim's mouth on hers, and shock rendered her immobile. His lips were warm and beguiling as he kissed her with an expertise that caused her heart to slam against her ribs. He moved his hand from her chin to her nape, while his other hand settled on her hip and urged her closer. He did not exert force, and she could easily resist—*should* resist, her brain pointed out—but her body seemed to have a will of its own, and it craved even closer contact with the most mesmeric man she had ever met.

His tongue traced the shape of her mouth, playing havoc with her equilibrium, but when he probed gently between her lips, demanding access, she stiffened and her pride belatedly stirred. She knew what kind of man he was. After meeting him in Paris she had been sufficiently intrigued to find out more about him, and had discovered that he had a reputation as a playboy whose wealth and undeniable charisma attracted women to his bed in droves. His relationships never lasted long before he moved on to his next conquest, and she would not be one of them, Ella vowed fiercely.

She did not want a love affair, and she was certain that love was not on Vadim's agenda. He wanted to have sex with her.

She might be inexperienced, but she was not completely naïve, and from the moment their eyes had met in Paris she had recognised the hungry desire in his gaze. He wanted her, but she was determined he would not have her. She'd never had a problem freezing out other men who had shown an interest in her, and the fact that she was finding it hard to remain cool with Vadim was all the more reason to stick to her resolve.

She knew about men like him, she brooded bitterly. Her father had repeatedly broken her mother's heart with his affairs. Even when Judith Stafford had lain dying the Earl had been cavorting with his mistress on the French Riviera, and had barely made it back to England in time for his wife's funeral.

But as Vadim continued his unhurried exploration of her lips she was aware of a curious melting sensation that seeped into her bones, undermining her determination to resist him, so that she could not prevent herself from sagging against him. His arm snaked around her waist, pulling her closer still, so that she could feel the solid hardness of his thigh muscles. In a frantic attempt to push him away she laid her hands flat against his chest, and was instantly entranced by the warmth of his body through his fine silk shirt.

Now he increased the pressure of his mouth, forcing her lips apart, and with a bold flick of his tongue he delved into her moist warmth, taking the kiss to another level and demonstrating a degree of eroticism that was beyond anything Ella had ever imagined. She felt strangely light-headed as her blood drummed through her veins, every nerve-ending in her body acutely sensitive, so that the faint rasp of his cheek against her tender flesh sent a quiver of reaction the length of her spine. Just as music transported her to another world, Vadim's kiss took her to a place she had never been before, where sensation ruled and all that mattered was that he should continue to move his mouth on hers in the slow, delicious tasting that caused a curious throbbing ache in the pit of her stomach.

She had no idea how long the kiss lasted. It could have been minutes, hours. While she was in his arms she lost all sense of time, and when at last he lifted his head and withdrew his hand from her waist she swayed slightly, the dazed expression in her eyes gradually changing to one of appalled self-disgust.

'How dare you?' she whispered through numbed lips, the realisation that she had capitulated utterly to his mastery sending shame cascading through her, so that her face flooded with hot colour.

He gave her an amused smile. 'How can you ask that after responding to me with such passion?' He ran his finger lightly over her flushed cheek, and then traced the swollen contours of her lips, his eyes darkening when he caught the faint catch of her breath. 'The word among some of your male friends is that you are frigid. But what do they know?' he murmured, his gravelly accent sounding deeper and more sensual than ever. 'They're just young bucks who are piqued that you have not chosen one of them to be your boyfriend. But you should not have boys, Ella. You need a man who appreciates your sensual nature.'

'Are you suggesting I need *you*?' she choked, seizing anger as a weapon to fight the insidious warmth that his sexy voice and provocative statement evoked inside her. The sultry gleam in his eyes was too much to bear. 'Your ego is…*monumental*. And I don't care what anyone thinks of me,' she added tightly.

She was aware of the speculation among the brothers of some of her friends that her refusal to date them must mean she was either frigid or gay. The true explanation was that she simply wasn't interested, but Vadim's suggestion that she had been holding out for a highly sexed, overconfident man like him—a man like her father—was laughable. She had made it clear that she wanted nothing to do with him, and it was his problem if his ego couldn't accept her refusal to have dinner with him.

She had given out a mixed message tonight, though, she conceded grimly, shuddering at the memory of how she had responded to him with shameful enthusiasm. She should have pulled away from him the moment he had touched her, but instead she had melted in his arms. Mortification swept through her, together with a growing sense of panic as Vadim traced his finger down her throat and continued lower, coming to rest on the faint swell of her breasts, visible above the neckline of her dress. Her breath hitched in her throat, and she was terrified that he must be able to see her heart jerking unevenly beneath her ribs. Every instinct screamed at her to slap his hand away, but to her shame a little part of her longed for him to move his fingers the few necessary inches to curve around her breast.

Her eyes flew to his face, and the feral gleam she saw beneath his heavy lids warned her he had read her mind. 'The game of cat and mouse has been amusing,' he said in his sinfully sexy accent, 'but now I grow bored with it. Perhaps you are shocked by the intensity of the sexual chemistry between us, Ella, but you cannot deny it exists. When we kissed, you felt it here.' He placed his hand directly over her heart, his fingers brushing against her breast. 'Just as I did. Passion pounds in your veins as it does in mine, and the only logical conclusion is for us to become lovers.'

She could not possibly be tempted, Ella told herself frantically. She was incensed by Vadim's arrogant assumption that she was his for the taking, that he could simply pluck her like a ripe peach, and yet she could not block out the little voice in her head which was urging her to agree, to succumb to the passion that, as he had rightly guessed, was pounding in her veins, making her feel hot and flustered.

Common sense fought the wild recklessness that had gripped her and won. She would not be Vadim Aleksandrov's *plaything*. She recalled a newspaper article about his recent split from glamour model Kelly Adams, in which Kelly had accused him of cruelly dumping her by text message. The accompanying photo had shown the stunning redhead sobbing heartbrokenly outside the hotel where Vadim had taken up residence since his arrival in the capital. 'Vadim Aleksandrov has a lump of granite instead of a heart,' Kelly had told the tabloids, and the image of the model's tear-streaked face had reminded Ella of her mother's anguished expression when Lionel Stafford had rejected her for one of his many mistresses.

'When you say lovers, what exactly do you have in mind?' she queried coolly. 'I know from press reports that you travel widely for your company, and I am frequently on tour with the RLO, so I'm not sure how we could maintain a meaningful relationship.'

He frowned, clearly taken aback by her words. 'To be honest, I had not thought that far ahead,' he drawled. 'I am suggesting that we explore the sexual attraction that exists between us, but talk of a relationship is a little premature, don't you think?'

Vadim Aleksandrov and the late Earl Stafford had a lot in common, Ella brooded, not least their cavalier attitude towards women. 'I might have known that a man like you would only be interested in physical satisfaction,' she said bitterly, forcing herself to sound coldly dismissive to disguise her intense awareness of him.

Vadim's eyes narrowed at her haughty tone. 'A man like me?' he queried softly. The expression on Ella's face was dismissive, scornful, and anger flared inside him. Did she think he was beneath her because he had started out in life with nothing, while she had been born into the wealthy, privileged lifestyle of the British upper class?

He was used to women who played games, and he had cynically assumed that Ella had been cool with him because it amused her. Now he wondered if her refusal to date him was because she deemed him a lowly immigrant from the Eastern bloc who had made a fast buck, not worthy of her. He assured himself he did not give a damn about her opinion of him, but to his annoyance his pride stung. 'What kind of a man do you think I am?' he demanded harshly.

As Ella stared at his hard-boned face her mind flew back across the years and she was back at Stafford Hall, huddled at the top of the stairs, peering through the banisters to the hall below, where her mother was sobbing as she pleaded with a cold, arrogantly handsome man.

'*You're going to* her *again, aren't you? Did you think I was unaware of your latest mistress when the whole of London knows you spend your nights with your tart instead of with me? For pity's sake, Lionel…*'

Judith Stafford lifted her hands beseechingly towards her husband, but there was no pity in the Earl's eyes, just cold indifference which turned to anger when his wife clutched the lapels of his jacket.

'*Why on earth would I want to spend any more time than I have to with you? You're a neurotic, pathetic mess.*' *Lip curling with distaste, Lionel Stafford pushed the weeping woman away from him with such force that she stumbled and fell to her knees.* '*Pull yourself together, Judith, and be thankful I go elsewhere for my pleasures when you consistently deny me my rights in the marriage bed.*'

'I'm not well, Lionel. You know my heart condition means I have to be careful…'

'Well, I'm bored with your illness.' The Earl flung open the door and gave one last withering glance at his wife, still kneeling on the cold marble floor. 'Don't wait up,' he said mockingly. 'I don't know when I'll be back.'

Ella remembered the anger that had surged through her as her father had slammed the door behind him, and the pity and the feeling of utter helplessness as she'd watched her mother slowly drag herself to her feet and make her way wearily to the stairs. At twelve years old she had been unable to voice her hatred of her father, and less than a year later, after her mother had died of heart failure, she had been packed off to boarding school and left in the charge of a nanny during the holidays, while the Earl disappeared abroad. Her resentment had continued to fester inside her. Lionel Stafford had died before Ella had had the opportunity to tell him how much she hated him, but now, as she stared at Vadim's arrogant face, her bitterness came tumbling out.

'I think you are the kind of man who selfishly takes what you want and gives nothing in return. You have a reputation as a playboy, but you have no respect for women.' She lifted her head and glared at him, determined not to be fazed by the mocking gaze that so infuriated her. But there was no amusement in those piercing blue eyes, just a feral gleam that made her feel hot and shivery at the same time, and she had the uncomfortable feeling that he could see inside her head.

Anger surged up inside her, making her tremble with its intensity. How dared he make the casual suggestion that they should become lovers? And how dared he kiss her with such shocking hunger that he had forced her to respond to him against her will? She could not drag her gaze from his mouth, couldn't forget the sensual pleasure of his lips sliding over hers, but no way did she want him to kiss her again—of course she didn't, she assured herself fiercely.

'I'd rather die than have you touch me again.' As soon as the words were out she knew she'd sounded childish and overdramatic, and her blush deepened when he gave her an amused glance.

'If I thought you really meant it I would walk away and never trouble you again,' he said softly. 'But we both know it isn't true. You desire me as much as I want you, and have done since the moment we met in Paris. The attraction between us was instant, like wildfire, but you don't have the guts to be honest about it.'

Incensed, she stared at him, shaking with rage, and yet deep down she was aware of a need to goad him, to make him do…what? 'How can you possibly think you know my mind better than I do?' she gritted.

'I know you want me to kiss you again.' His voice was suddenly rough, the amusement in his eyes replaced by scorching heat. 'Let's try a little experiment, shall we?' His arm shot out and he jerked her against him, ignoring her struggles to escape with insulting ease as he lowered his mouth to hers.

There was no gentleness this time, just raw, primitive passion as he took without mercy, forcing her lips apart with a bold flick of his tongue before he thrust deep into her moist warmth and explored her with ruthless efficiency. Fighting him was impossible when his arms were clamped like a vice around her body. But she did not have to respond to him, her brain pointed out. She could simply remain passive until he'd finished with her. But, to her shame, her willpower was non-existent, and the delicious pressure of his mouth proved an irresistible temptation.

It was ridiculous that at twenty-four she did not know how to kiss a man properly, Ella mused. But her music consumed her so utterly that she had never felt more than mild curiosity about the opposite sex, and on the rare occasions she had agreed to go on a date she had found the obligatory fumbling kiss in the car, with the gear lever jammed into her ribs, totally uninspiring.

Being kissed by Vadim was a completely different experience. He was a master in the art of seduction, while she was dangerously out of her depth. The erotic sweep of his tongue destroyed her thought processes, and she gave up trying to deny him when it meant denying herself, initiating a tentative exploration of her own that elicited a low groan from him as he felt her complete capitulation.

She was flushed and breathless when he finally released her. 'You see—you survived,' he taunted softly.

Ella wished she could make some cutting retort, but her brain seemed to have stopped functioning. Her lips felt swollen when she traced them with her tongue, and she doubted she could have uttered a word.

Vadim's eyes darkened as he watched the darting foray of her pink tongue-tip, and he muttered something she assumed was Russian as he made to pull her back into his arms. But suddenly, shockingly, the orangery was flooded with a brilliant glare as someone pushed open the door and flicked the light switch.

'Oh…sorry.' Jenny did not bother to disguise her curiosity as she watched Ella flush scarlet and spring away from the gorgeous Russian hunk who had been eyeing her up all night. 'Ella, there's been a mix-up with the taxis. They've only sent one car, and Claire's cello will take up half the back seat. The driver says he'll come back for you after he's driven us home, as you live in the opposite direction. Do you mind waiting?'

'No, that's fine.' Ella forced a smile, despite the sudden feeling that her head was about to explode. The migraine she had sensed brewing earlier had kicked in with a vengeance, the pain escalating as quickly as it always did with her, so that she could barely concentrate on anything else. She refused to make a fuss about the travel arrangements, even though the prospect of waiting around for her lift home seemed unbearable when a dozen hammers were beating against her skull. She supposed she could ring another cab company, but moving her head even slightly was agony, and she was conscious of the unpleasant queasy sensation in her stomach that usually preceded a bout of sickness.

'Are you okay?' Jenny's voice sounded like a pneumatic drill to Ella's ultra-sensitive ears. 'You look a bit green.'

Somehow Ella managed another faint smile. 'A headache. It's nothing. You'd better go, or the taxi will leave without you.'

Jenny hesitated, frowning at Ella's sudden pallor. 'Are you sure?'

'I'll take Ella home.' Vadim's deep voice was firm and decisive, and at any other time she would have railed against his authority, but right now getting home as fast as possible was imperative, so she nodded her head very slightly, trying not to wince as stars flashed in front of her eyes.

'Thank you.' She sensed his surprise at her sudden meekness, but the pain was worse, blinding her, so that she stumbled after him, back through the Egyptian Room and out to the foyer, where she collected her violin from the security desk and then followed Vadim out onto the street. She'd hoped that a few gulps of fresh air would lessen the nauseous feeling, but if anything she felt worse, and after easing carefully into his low-slung sports car, and muttering instructions on how to reach her house, she closed her eyes and prayed she would not throw up over his leather upholstery.

If there was one thing Vadim couldn't stand it was a woman who sulked. He did not even know why he was bothering with Ella, he thought grimly, after his attempts at conversation were met with a barely monosyllabic response. He took his eye off the road for a second and threw her an impatient glance, his mouth tightening when he saw that she had turned her head away from him and was staring fixedly out of the window. He knew of half a dozen extremely attractive women he could phone who would be happy to provide a few hours of pleasant company and uncomplicated sex. So why was he hung up on this pale, underweight girl, who changed from hot to cold quicker than a mixer-tap, and was now subjecting him to the big freeze because he had proved that she was sexually attracted to him?

Her coolness intrigued him, he admitted, particularly now he had sampled the heated passion she kept hidden behind her ice-maiden façade. But his attempts to get Ella to have dinner with him, let alone persuade her into his bed, had so far come to nothing, and he was beginning to wonder if she was worth the effort. Maybe he should drop her home and put her out of his mind? His hectic work schedule meant that he hadn't had a lover for weeks. Celibacy did not agree with him, he acknowledged self-derisively. But Ella Stafford was too much like hard work.

'Stop the car,' she cried suddenly.

He frowned. 'According to the sat-nav we're still a mile from your address.'

'Just stop the car *now*. Please.'

The urgency in her voice puzzled him. Did she want him to leave her at the side of the road because she was afraid that if he drove her all the way home he might demand an invitation into her house? He swore violently in his native tongue and pulled up in a lay-by, his frown deepening when she immediately shot out of the car and raced towards the bushes a few feet back from the road.

'Ella…?'

'Don't follow me,' she yelled.

He swore again. God damn it, what did she think he was going to do to her? He swung back to the car and then paused at the unmistakable sound of retching coming from the bushes. A few minutes later she reappeared, whey-faced, her eyes like great hollows in her pinched face. She looked like death, and his impatience faded as some indefinable emotion tugged in his chest.

'What the hell is the matter with you?'

'Migraine.' Ella forced the word past her chattering teeth, took one look at Vadim's horrified expression and wanted to die of embarrassment. There was no hint of desire in his eyes now, she noted grimly, but that was hardly surprising when he had just heard her lose the contents of her stomach. 'I occasionally get them after a performance. Playing is incredibly draining, and it seems that a surfeit of emotions affects me physically.' She leaned weakly against the car, wondering if he would allow her to get back in, or whether he expected her to walk the remaining distance to her house for fear that she would be sick again. 'You're partly to blame,' she muttered, not daring to look at him and see the disgust he must surely feel. 'You unsettle me.'

He gave a rough laugh, but when he spoke the anger had gone from his voice. 'Honesty at last! If it's any consolation, you unsettle me too. But I'm not sure I like the idea that I make you physically ill.'

'You don't… I mean, it wasn't you…' Why on earth had she admitted that he unsettled her? Ella asked herself crossly.

She was naturally reserved—a trait that was frequently mistaken for aloofness—and she hated the nickname she'd earned of Ice Princess, but right now she would give anything to appear cool and collected. 'I find Dvorak's *New World Symphony* very emotional to play,' she muttered, colour flaring on her white face.

'I'm relieved to know that my kissing you did not make you sick.' There was amusement in Vadim's voice now and Ella glared at him, or tried to, but the pain across her temples was excruciating and she closed her eyes, wishing she were back home at Kingfisher House rather than standing by the side of the road with a man who infuriated her and fascinated her in equal measures.

'Do you have medication for your headache?'

She forced her eyes open to find him standing close beside her, and for some inexplicable reason she wanted to rest her pounding head against the broad strength of his chest. 'My prescription painkillers are at home. I usually carry some with me, but I forgot them tonight,' she muttered ruefully.

'Then I'd better get you home quickly.' Vadim helped her into the car and strode round to the driver's side, coiling his long frame behind the wheel. 'Here, let me do that.' He leaned across her and adjusted her seat belt, and despite the throbbing pain in her head Ella was acutely conscious of his closeness, her senses flaring as she breathed in the subtle scent of his cologne.

In the glow from the street-lamp his swarthy olive skin gleamed like silk, but the brilliance of his blue eyes was shielded by thick black lashes. His mouth was inches from hers, and she recalled the firm pressure of his lips easing hers apart, demanding a response she had been helpless to deny. She suddenly felt hot, when seconds ago she had been freezing cold, but she could not blame her erratic temperature swing on her migraine, she admitted dismally. For some reason this man affected her in a way no man had ever done—made her feel things she had confidently assumed would never trouble her.

When Vadim had told her that some of her male friends thought she was frigid, she hadn't been surprised. It had occurred to her that the reason for her complete lack of interest in the opposite sex might not only be due to the hatred she had felt for her father, and that she must simply have a low sex-drive. But the erotic dreams that had plagued her since this Russian had first kissed her hand in Paris had turned that notion on its head. He had awoken her sensuality—but far from wanting to explore the feelings he aroused in her—her instinct was to run and keep on running.

Vadim stared at her, and said in a half-amused, half-impatient voice, 'For pity's sake, don't look at me like that *now*, when you know damn well there's nothing I can do about it.'

'Like what?' she mumbled, dazed with pain and overwhelmed by his potent masculinity.

'Like you want me to kiss you again and keep on kissing you, until the slide of mouth on mouth is no longer enough for either of us and only the feel of hands caressing naked skin will satisfy the ache that consumes us both,' he said, in a low tone that simmered with sexual promise.

Face burning at the images he evoked, Ella jerked upright—and drew a sharp breath when a burning poker pierced her skull. 'I didn't… I don't…'

'Liar.'

She was so pale she looked as though she might pass out. Vadim controlled his frustration and fired the ignition, wondering how he could ever have bought into the image Ella projected of cool, reserved, independent woman. Instead she was a seething mass of emotions, intense, hot-blooded and surprisingly vulnerable, and she intrigued him more than any other woman had ever done. Walking away from her was not an option right now, he conceded grimly. He wanted her, and he knew damn well that she wanted him; he simply had to convince her of that fact.

But now was not the time, he acknowledged when he shot another glance at her wan face. She looked achingly fragile, and he was surprised by the level of his concern. He drove along the main road until the satellite navigation system instructed him to take a right turn into a side street which he suddenly realised was familiar, and his frown deepened when he swung onto the driveway of a large, beautiful mansion house.

'*This* is your house?' he queried harshly.

'I wish,' Ella muttered, too overwhelmed by the pain in her head to wonder why Vadim sounded puzzled. 'It belongs to my uncle. He owns an estate agency business, and when Kingfisher House came onto the market a few years ago he snapped it up as an investment. He rents the main part of the house out to tenants, and I live in the adjoining staff quarters and act as caretaker when the house is empty—as it has been for the past couple of months.' She climbed out of the car and glanced wistfully at the gracious old house that she had fallen in love with the minute she'd first seen it. 'Hopefully when Uncle Rex finds new tenants they'll allow me to continue living here.' The American businessman who had rented Kingfisher House the previous year had travelled extensively with his job, and had been happy for Ella to stay and keep an eye on the place, but new people might want to use the staff quarters, which would mean she would have to move out. The possibility of having to find somewhere else to live had been worrying her for weeks, but right now all she could think of was swallowing a couple of painkillers and crawling into bed, and so she started to walk carefully towards the front door on legs that felt decidedly wobbly.

Strong arms suddenly closed around her, and she gave a startled cry when Vadim swung her into his arms. 'Stop fighting and let me help you,' he said roughly. 'You're about to collapse.' Her eyes were shadowed with pain, and the shimmer of tears evoked another tug of compassion that surprised him when usually he had little patience for weakness. His childhood had been tough, and devoid of kindness, and two years doing his national service in the Russian army had been brutally harsh. He had learned early in life that survival was dependent on physical and mental strength, and he acknowledged the truth in the accusation by some of his ex-lovers that he was hard and unemotional.

He'd spent so long suppressing his feelings that it came as a shock to realise he had the capacity to feel pity; Vadim brooded as he strode up to the house. But for some reason the woman in his arms elicited an emotion in him that might almost be described as tenderness. His mouth tightened. The idea that he was drawn to Ella by anything more than sexual attraction was disturbing, and he swiftly rejected it. All he asked from the women who briefly shared his life was physical satisfaction—the slaking of mutual lust until desire faded and he grew bored and moved on to someone new. Ella was no different, he told himself grimly. He wanted her, and soon he would have her. But the beginning would spell the end, as it always did.

CHAPTER THREE

'YOU can put me down now,' Ella insisted, the moment Vadim had pushed open the front door and carried her across the entrance hall towards the sweeping staircase which led to the upper floors. 'My part of the house is on the ground floor, through that door. I'll manage fine, thank you,' she added tersely, when he did not set her down as she had hoped, but turned towards the door she had indicated.

He shouldered the door and strode into her sitting room, glancing around the spacious room which was dominated by an enormous grand piano. The room was at the back of the house, and through the French windows he could make out a sweeping lawn and beyond it the wide expanse of the River Thames, gleaming dully in the moonlight.

'You must have a wonderful view of the river.'

'Oh, yes, and of Hampton Court on the opposite bank. I love it here,' Ella confessed. 'I can't bear the thought that I may have to move out. It was very good of Uncle Rex to persuade his previous tenant to allow me stay here, but I might not be so lucky next time. The trouble is, there aren't many flats that I can afford with rooms big enough for the piano, or where I can practise my music for hours on end without disturbing the neighbours.'

'Why don't you sell the piano? My knowledge of musical instruments is limited, but I know Steinways are worth a fortune.'

'I'll never sell it,' Ella said fiercely. 'It was my mother's. She loved it, and it was one of the few possessions of hers I fought to keep when I had to sell Stafford Hall. That was the family pile,' she explained, when Vadim gave her a querying look. 'Stafford Hall was a gift to one of my ancestors from Henry VIII, and the house, along with a sizeable fortune, was passed down through the family for generations—until it reached my father.'

The undisguised bitterness in her voice stirred Vadim's curiosity. 'What happened? And where are your parents now?'

'They're both dead. My mother died when I was thirteen,' she revealed in a low tone, which hardened as she added, 'My father died five years ago—after he'd drunk and gambled away all the money. When it ran out he went though the house and sold off anything of value, but fortunately my mother had bequeathed her violin and piano to me in her will, and he wasn't able to touch them. After he died I had to sell the Hall to clear the mountain of debts he'd left, and that's when Uncle Rex allowed me to move in here.'

The Stafford fortune had not only been wasted on the late Earl's love of whisky and the roulette wheel but also on his love of women, Ella thought bitterly. Her father had been a notorious playboy, and from early childhood she had vowed never to be attracted to the type of man who treated women as a form of entertainment.

So why, she asked herself angrily, had she allowed Vadim Aleksandrov—a man who changed his mistresses more often than most men changed their socks—to kiss her tonight? And, even worse, why had she responded to him—perhaps given him the idea that she was willing to hop into bed with him?

The searing pain of her migraine was no excuse for her to have weakly let him carry her into the house. She was acutely conscious of the feel of his arms around her waist and beneath her knees. Held close against his chest, she could hear the steady beat of his heart beneath her ear. It made her feel safe somehow, secure, but that was an illusion, of course, because the last thing she would be with Vadim was *safe*. He was a man like her father, a handsome heartbreaker, and from the moment she had met him her instincts had warned her to steer clear of him.

'Put me down, please.' She moved restlessly in his arms, but he ignored her struggles and strode across the sitting room to the door which stood ajar to reveal her bedroom.

'Where are your painkillers?'

'In the bedside drawer.' He lowered her slowly onto the bed, but the movement caused her to draw a sharp breath as the pain in her head became unendurable. She moaned when he flicked on the lamp, and as soon as he'd found her medication he doused the light so that the only illumination in the room was from the moonlight glimmering through the open curtains.

'I'll get you some water.'

She heard him walk into the *en suite* bathroom, and he returned seconds later to hand her a glass of water. The safety lid on the painkillers was beyond her, and she was grateful when he opened it and tipped two tablets into her palm. They were strong, and she knew that in ten minutes, fifteen at most, she would sink into oblivion and escape from the pain that was making her feel so sick.

'Can you see yourself out?' she whispered as she sank back against the pillows.

'I will, once you're in bed.' Vadim's velvet-soft voice was

strangely soothing, and she closed her eyes, only to open them again with a jolt when she felt his hand on her ankle.

'What are you doing?'

'Taking your shoes off.' He sounded faintly amused. 'You can't get into bed wearing stiletto heels.'

How could the feel of his hands lightly brushing the soles of her feet as he removed her shoes be so intensely erotic? Ella wondered fretfully. Even in the throes of an agonising migraine she was desperately aware of him, and she could only pray he had not noticed the tremor that ran through her.

'Now your dress.'

'No way are you going to take my dress off.' She glared at him through pain-glazed eyes, daring him to touch her, but he ignored her and rolled her gently onto her side, so that he could slide her zip down her spine.

'You're telling me you can undress yourself?' He took her fulminating silence as a no, and, with a deftness she assumed he'd gained from regularly removing women's clothes, drew her dress over her shoulders and down to her waist. Arguing with him was impossible when her head was about to explode. More than anything she wanted to go to sleep and blot out the pain, and when he told her to lift her hips she obeyed, and allowed him to slide her dress down her legs. She didn't even care that he could see her functional black bra and knickers. Shivering with pain, she was past caring about anything, but when he drew the covers over her and stood up, good manners prompted her to speak.

'Thank you for bringing me home.'

Ella looked achingly fragile, and the fact that she hadn't fought him like a wildcat when he had removed her dress was an indication of the severity of her headache, Vadim mused wryly. 'Do your migraines usually last long?'

'I should be fine in the morning, hopefully,' Ella mumbled sleepily, her eyelids already feeling heavy as the painkillers began to work.

'Good. As for thanking me, you can do that when you have dinner with me next week.'

It took a few seconds for his words to sink in, and when she forced her eyes open he was already on his way out of the door. 'I told you, I'm going to Germany next week,' she called after him.

He glanced over his shoulder, and his sensual smile made her heart lurch. 'But you're back at the weekend. I checked with one of the other members of the orchestra. I'll be in touch.'

Ella didn't know whether to take that as a threat or a promise, but he had strolled out of her room and closed the door quietly behind him while she was still trying to think of another excuse. Irritating man, she thought angrily as she settled back on her pillow. But as she teetered on the edge of sleep she reminded herself that his ability to disturb her equilibrium also made him a dangerous man, and she was utterly determined not to have dinner with him.

Ella had completely recovered from her debilitating migraine by the time she flew to Cologne with the RLO. She had visited the city many times before, and instead of joining Jenny on a sightseeing trip she made up for her lost practice time by rehearsing for several hours before the concert. The programme of concertos by Bach and Beethoven was received with much acclaim; the orchestra received excellent reviews and arrived back at Gatwick on Saturday morning.

'I wouldn't mind being greeted with a bouquet of flowers,'

Jenny commented enviously as they walked through the arrivals gate and spotted a courier clutching a huge arrangement of red roses.

Ella watched the courier talking to one of the orchestra members up ahead, and she gave Jenny a puzzled glance when he walked purposefully in their direction.

'Eleanor Stafford? These are for you.'

Struggling to hold her violin and suitcase, as well as the bouquet that had been thrust into her arms, Ella was nonplussed. 'There must be a mistake…'

'Open the card. Here…' Jenny rescued the violin, and with fumbling fingers Ella ripped open the envelope and read the note inside.

Welcome home, Ella. Dinner tonight, 7 p.m. I'll pick you up from Kingfisher House.

It was signed 'Vadim', and the sight of the bold black scrawl filled Ella with a mixture of annoyance and jittery excitement that she swiftly quashed. 'He hasn't even left a phone number so that I can cancel,' she noted irritably.

Jenny gave her a look that told Ella she was seriously questioning her sanity. 'Why would you want to? He's incredibly good-looking, mega-rich and as sexy as sin,' she listed. 'And he's sent you two dozen red roses. What more do you want? This guy is clearly keen.'

'I don't want anything from him,' Ella snapped. 'And all he wants is to take me to bed.'

'So, what's wrong with that?' Jenny stopped dead on the way out of the airport terminal and stared at Ella. 'You've always said—right back from when we were pig-tailed first-years at boarding school—that you never wanted to get married.'

'I don't.' Ella frowned, wondering where the conversation was leading.

'But you're saying you don't want an affair either? What are you going to do—live like a nun for the rest of your life?'

'Yes—no—I don't know,' Ella muttered. They had been friends for over a decade, and Jenny knew her better than anyone, but she couldn't explain her violent reaction to Vadim when she didn't understand it herself. 'Are you advocating that I should become Vadim Aleksandrov's plaything?' she demanded tersely.

'I can think of worse fates,' Jenny said cheerfully. 'Seriously, Ella…' Her smile faded. 'I know you didn't get on with your dad, and that he treated your mum badly, but you can't cut yourself off from the world, from men and relationships, because your parents' marriage didn't work out.'

'I haven't.' Ella defended herself tersely, but she knew deep down that she was lying. Jenny didn't understand. How could she, when her parents had been married for thirty years and her father was a gentle, kindly man who patently adored his wife and four children. Ella had spent many happy school holidays with Jenny and her family, and would have gladly swapped the lonely grandeur of Stafford Hall for the Marches' cramped bungalow in Milton Keynes, which was full of love and laughter. Jenny had no idea what it had been like to witness her father destroy her mother with his mental and sometimes physical cruelty, but the emotional scars ran deep in Ella's mind, and she had promised herself she would never put herself in a position where a man had any kind of hold over her.

'When was the last time you went on a date?' Jenny demanded.

Ella shrugged. 'A couple of months ago, actually. I had dinner with the flautist Michail Danowski when the Polish orchestra visited.'

Jenny gave her a look of mingled pity and exasperation. 'He's gay, so he doesn't count.'

Ella was saved from answering when a taxi drew up, and they spent the next few minutes stowing violins and luggage in the boot. 'You can't put those in here; they'll get crushed,' Jenny said when Ella crammed Vadim's flowers on top of her case. The roses were beautiful, she conceded when the taxi finally pulled away, and she stared at the bouquet on her lap. The velvety petals were a rich ruby-red, filling the car with their sensual perfume.

Red roses were for lovers; the thought stole into her mind together with Jenny's taunt about spending the rest of her life as a nun. Of course she wasn't going to do that, she assured herself. It was just that music and her career, both with the RLO and as a soloist, took up all her time, and she couldn't fit in a relationship right now. Not that Vadim was offering a relationship—he had admitted as much when he had kissed her at Amesbury House. All he wanted was an affair, and she refused to be another notch on his overcrowded bedpost.

The sight of Kingfisher House and the weeping cherry trees that lined the drive, bathed in spring sunshine, lifted Ella's spirits, and she couldn't wait to throw open the French doors at the back of the house and walk down the lawn to the private jetty beside the majestic River Thames. But first there was the usual pile of mail to deal with, and a message on the answer-machine drained all the pleasure from her homecoming.

'Ella, Uncle Rex here. I've found a new tenant for Kingfisher House. He's interested in buying the place, but he wants to rent it for six months to see whether it's suitable for him. There's no rush for you to move out. He's happy for you to stay on in the caretaker flat until he decides what he's

going to do. I'll give you another call to arrange a time when you can meet him—hopefully some time this weekend.'

Ella's heart sank. She'd known that her uncle had been thinking of selling Kingfisher House, now that the high-end property market was improving after the downturn of the previous couple of years, but she'd put it out of her mind. Now it seemed likely that she would have to move within the next few months, and the problem of finding somewhere to live with rooms big enough to fit a concert grand piano would not make flat-hunting easy.

Life suddenly seemed full of uncertainty, and the prospect of seeing Vadim again added to her tension. She spent the rest of the day in a state of nervous apprehension, which grew worse as seven o'clock drew nearer. She was sure he had deliberately not included his phone number on his dinner invitation to prevent her from cancelling, but if he thought she was the type of woman who would meekly allow herself to be dominated by him, he'd better think again. No man was ever going to boss her around, she resolved fiercely, ignoring the twinge of her conscience that pointed out that it had been good of him to drive her home when she'd been in agony with a migraine. Colour flared on her cheeks when she recalled how he had removed her dress. But, far from taking advantage of her in her vulnerable state, Vadim had behaved like a gentleman and tucked her into bed.

Damn it, *why* couldn't he get the message that she wanted nothing to do with him? she brooded irritably as she arranged the mass of red roses in a vase. She didn't want him to send her flowers, but they were so beautiful that she couldn't bring herself to throw them in the bin. Most women would be delighted to receive roses from a gorgeous billionaire, she acknowledged ruefully, thinking of her conversation with

Jenny. But she was not most women, and although she had denied it to Jenny, she knew that the fear and hatred she'd felt for her father continued to influence the way she felt about all men.

As usual when she felt tense, music was her salvation. She was building a successful career as a violinist, but she still played the piano purely for pleasure, and she was soon lost in another world as she moved her fingers over the smooth ivory keys, finding a release for her pent-up emotions in her favourite pieces by Chopin and Tchaikovsky.

Vadim was met by the haunting melody of Beethoven's *Moonlight Sonata* as he climbed out of his car and strode up the drive of Kingfisher House. He paused to listen, and felt the hairs on the back of his neck stand on end. Ella possessed a truly remarkable gift, and her brilliance as a musician fascinated him as much as her delicate beauty stirred his desire. Loath to disturb her by knocking on the front door, he walked around to the back of the house, where the French windows were thrown wide open and the lilting notes drifted on the air.

She was totally absorbed, and did not look up as he lowered himself onto one of the patio chairs, leaned back and closed his eyes, shutting out everything but the music. He had never played an instrument in his life; luxuries such as music lessons had not been affordable during his childhood, growing up in what had at that time been the USSR. His father's job as a factory worker had barely brought in enough money to pay the rent on the tiny apartment they had shared with Vadim's grandmother, and life had been dominated by the struggle to buy enough to eat during the frequent food shortages. He knew little about the great composers, or of musical techniques, but for some reason music had the power to soothe his restless soul, to reach deep inside him and force a chink in the granite wall around his heart.

As the last lingering notes of the melody faded Ella flexed her fingers, suddenly aware that the room was no longer flooded with afternoon sunlight, but shadowed with the onset of dusk.

'You play like an angel.'

The familiar, toe-curlingly sexy accent caused her to jerk her head towards the French windows, and her heart thudded beneath her ribs as she jumped to her feet and stared at Vadim.

'How long have you been there?' Shock at his appearance sharpened her voice. Playing the piano was an intensely personal experience, a special link with her mother, and she had poured her soul into the music. She had been unaware that she had an audience, and she felt as though she had unwittingly exposed her private emotions to Vadim.

He shrugged and stepped into the room. 'Twenty minutes or so.' His brilliant blue gaze skimmed over her tee shirt and faded jeans, and moved up to her hair, falling in a curtain of pale gold silk around her shoulders. This was the Ella Stafford the world did not see. Over the past few years she had been expertly marketed as a violin virtuoso; much had been made of her aristocratic pedigree, and she was portrayed on the covers of her numerous CD albums as a sophisticated artiste. The woman staring at him across the grand piano looked younger than her public image, and her intense awareness of him that flared, undisguised, in her stormy grey eyes made her seem painfully vulnerable.

A kinder man would not take his pursuit of her any further, Vadim knew. Beneath her ice-cool image he sensed an emotional fragility that warned him not to get involved. He liked his affairs to be uncomplicated, and he ensured that the women he bedded always knew the score: mutually satisfy-

ing sex with no strings attached. Ella seemed curiously innocent, although in reality that was unlikely for a modern and
successful woman in her mid-twenties, he reminded himself.
Seeing her like this, in jeans that moulded her slender hips like
a second skin, her face bare of make-up and her hair falling
loose to halfway down her back, only intensified his desire
for her.

The sexual chemistry between them was white-hot, and
kindness was not an attribute he possessed—he had learned
that of himself many years ago, Vadim acknowledged grimly.
He was hard; undoubtedly he was selfish, and he took what
he wanted without compunction or compassion. He would
take Ella because he found her pale, elfin beauty irresistible,
but he would accept no responsibility for her emotions once
he had slaked his hunger to possess her body.

'I had no idea you could play the piano with the same skill
with which you play the violin.'

Ella shrugged. 'I don't play to performance standard. My
mother was an astounding pianist. She could have had a wonderful career; should have done, but—' She broke off abruptly,
feeling the familiar pain in her heart as she recalled her
mother's gentle smile and her unending patience when she
had tutored her daughter to play. Instead of enjoying the glittering career as a pianist that she had deserved, Judith Stafford
had fallen in love and sacrificed her ambitions for a husband
who had expected her to devote her life to being his social
hostess. In return the Earl had broken her heart with his brazen
infidelity. She would not make the same mistake as her
mother, Ella vowed. And she would certainly never fall in love
after she'd witnessed the devastation it caused.

Vadim flicked back the cuff of his jacket to glance at his
watch, and Ella felt a peculiar sensation in the pit of her

stomach when she glimpsed his olive-skinned wrist overlaid with dark hairs. He was so innately male, and so big, his broad shoulders sheathed in a black Armani jacket that he wore with the easy grace of a man who possessed supreme self-confidence.

She was conscious of his brief appraisal of her jeans, and blushed at his faintly sardonic smile. 'I assume you lost track of time. I'll phone the restaurant and tell them to hold our table while you get changed.'

She snatched a breath and said quietly, 'If you had given me a contact number, I would have phoned to explain that I'm unable to have dinner with you tonight—' she hesitated '—or any other night. This is a very busy time for me right now,' she added quickly, her blush deepening beneath his cool stare.

'But you do find time in your hectic schedule to eat, I take it?' he drawled. 'Although from what I saw of your body the other night, you clearly don't eat enough.'

'Well, I'm sorry if you found me a disappointment,' Ella snapped, infuriated by his reference to the embarrassing episode she would prefer to forget. If she hadn't been in such acute agony that night she wouldn't have allowed him to lay a finger on her, let alone undress her. As it was, Vadim had helped her out of her dress, but from the sound of it the sight of her bony figure and pathetically small breasts had not sent him wild with desire. A good thing too, she assured herself, suppressing a stupid wish that she possessed voluptuous curves like his glamorous ex-mistress Kelly Adams. She did not *want* Vadim to be interested in her, and perhaps now he'd discovered that she had the allure of a stick-insect he would leave her alone.

'I didn't say I found you disappointing,' he murmured, the sudden gleam in his eyes causing her heart to miss a beat as he strolled towards her. He was impossibly handsome, she recognised numbly, unable to tear her gaze from his sculpted features. The razor-sharp edges of his cheekbones and the hard planes of his face were cruelly beautiful, softened only slightly by the sensual curve of his mouth. He was almost unreal—like a marble figurine by one of the Old Masters, or one of those male models from the glossy magazines, who had been airbrushed to perfection. But Vadim was very real, a flesh-and-blood man who was standing unnervingly close to her, so that she could see the tiny lines that fanned around his piercing blue eyes.

'You know I am attracted to you. I have made no secret that I desire you,' he said, in such a bland tone that he might have been discussing the weather. But the expression in his eyes wasn't cool, it was scorching hot, and Ella caught her breath when he slipped his hand beneath her chin and lowered his head.

'But I'm not... I don't want...' She trailed off helplessly, transfixed by his mouth hovering tantalisingly close to hers.

'You don't want to date? Perhaps not other men,' he conceded arrogantly, 'but I'm different. I unsettle you,' he reminded her when she opened her mouth to argue, and then took advantage of her parted lips by covering them with his own and kissing her with a ruthless efficiency that blew her mind.

An instinct for self-protection warned Ella to resist, to freeze in Vadim's arms and jerk her head away so that he was denied access to her mouth. But another instinct, as old as womankind, caused molten heat to flood through her veins and evoked a shocking hunger inside her that was new and terrifying and yet utterly consuming. She wanted him to kiss her, taunted a voice in her head. For the past week she had been unable to forget the demanding pressure of his mouth on hers when he had kissed her at Amesbury House, and her dreams had been full of erotic images of what might have happened if they had not been disturbed. Now those dreams were reality, and his lips were once again working their sensual magic, coaxing her response until she opened her mouth for him and he thrust his tongue deep into her moist warmth.

No man had ever kissed her the way Vadim was doing. In the past she had dated a couple of musicians from the RLO, but her innate wariness made her seem cold and uninterested, and the relationships had quickly petered out. With Vadim it was different. He seemed to view her diffidence as a challenge, and had bulldozed through her defences to awaken her sensuality. For the first time in her life Ella felt the piercing intensity of sexual desire, and any idea of resisting its lure flew out of her mind as she sagged against the solid wall of his chest and felt his arms tighten around her.

He slid one hand into her hair and tugged, angling her head and deepening the kiss so that it became a sensual feast, hot, hungry and fiercely possessive, escalating her excitement so that the pressure of his lips and the bold thrusts of his tongue were not enough and she wanted more. His other hand roamed up and down her body and cupped her bottom, hauling her close so that she was made shockingly aware of his powerful arousal pressing against her pelvis. She should not be allowing him to do this, a warning voice whispered in her head. But he dominated her senses, and a little shiver of need ran through her when he slid his hand beneath the hem of her tee shirt and skimmed his palm over her flat stomach, the sensation of his fingertips stroking her bare flesh intensifying the hot, throbbing ache between her legs.

His hand continued its determined journey upwards. Any second now he would discover that she wasn't wearing a bra. His questing fingers brushed the underside of her breast and

Ella snatched a sharp breath, lost to everything but her longing for him to touch her where she had never permitted any man to touch her before, to curve his hand around the small, firm mound and caress the swollen nipple at its centre.

But, to her shock and scalding disappointment, he abruptly ended the kiss. 'We need to leave soon, or we'll lose the restaurant booking,' he murmured coolly as he dropped his hand and stepped away from her. 'You've got five minutes to get changed.'

Ella stared at him dazedly, her heart-rate gradually slowing as shame at her wanton response to him replaced the frantic drumbeat of desire. How could she have been so weak-willed and so stupid? she wondered bitterly. She had given Vadim completely the wrong idea about her, and now he no doubt believed he could buy her dinner in exchange for sex. For a wild moment she debated locking herself in her bedroom until he went away—but what if he refused to leave? He had already demonstrated his determination to get his own way, and she had a strong suspicion that in a battle of wills he would emerge the victor. Besides, she would be safer with him in a busy restaurant, she reasoned as she marched, stiff-backed, into her room and flung open her wardrobe. She thought it unlikely that he would make a public spectacle by kissing her in front of the other diners, and hopefully over a meal she would be able to convince him that she was serious about not wanting to have an affair with him. But as she stared at her face in the mirror, saw her swollen, reddened lips and her glazed eyes with their enlarged pupils, she acknowledged that the difficulty was going to be convincing herself.

CHAPTER FOUR

UP UNTIL eighteen months ago, Ella's working wardrobe had consisted of elegant but unexciting black dresses which she wore for performances. But when Marcus Benning had become her publicist and taken over the marketing side of her career he had insisted that she should go for a sexier image, and had persuaded her to buy daring designer outfits in a variety of coloured silks and satins. Naturally shy, she had struggled with her new look, especially when she'd found herself the focus of male attention, but now she was grateful for the make-over that had included lessons on how to apply make-up for her publicity photo-shoots. A light foundation, grey eyeshadow to highlight the colour of her eyes and black mascara to emphasise her lashes created a mask to hide behind, and the addition of bright red gloss on her lips completed the illusion of an elegant, coolly self-confident woman who was more than capable of rejecting unwanted advances from any man.

Unfortunately it *was* just an illusion, Ella acknowledged as she stepped into a red silk cocktail dress with spaghetti straps and a skirt that was shorter than she remembered it being when she'd tried it on in the shop. She felt brittle with nerves, and the pulse beating erratically at the base of her throat was a giveaway sign of her tension, but after sweeping her hair up into a chignon and spraying perfume on her wrists she could not put off returning to the sitting room and Vadim any longer.

He was standing by the fireplace, studying the many photographs of her mother, but turned as she entered the room. The flare of heat in his eyes as he subjected her to a leisurely inspection rattled her shaky composure. 'You look stunning, but I get the feeling you're making some sort of statement,' he murmured sardonically.

His perception was uncomfortably close to the mark, and Ella flushed. 'You'd prefer me to wear a sack?' she demanded tightly.

'You would look beautiful whatever you wore.' He paused for a heartbeat before adding outrageously, 'And exquisite wearing nothing at all.' He had closed the gap between them and was standing too close for comfort, the scent of his aftershave—a subtle blend of citrus and sandalwood—teasing her senses. 'However, I'd like to make one improvement.' He moved before she could guess his intention, placed his thumbpad over her lips and wiped off her lipstick. 'That's better. Your lips are infinitely more kissable when they're not covered in gunk.'

'You've got a damn nerve,' Ella breathed, trembling with anger. 'I'm afraid you'll have to go to dinner alone. I've suddenly lost my appetite.'

'That is a pity, because I'm ravenous.' His eyes glinted wickedly as he trailed them down from her elegant hairstyle to her red stiletto shoes. 'And I hate to eat on my own; it makes me irritable, which is bad for my digestion. Anyway, you have to have something for dinner, and there's nothing in your fridge apart from a yoghurt that's past its sell-by date— I noticed when I helped myself to a glass of water and pinched a couple of ice-cubes.' He took advantage of Ella's fulminating silence to drop a stinging kiss on her lips before he spun her round and, to her utter fury, tapped her lightly on her derriere. 'A word of warning, angel face: I can't abide women who sulk,' he murmured dulcetly. 'Shall we go?'

'You are the most arrogant, overbearing...' Cheeks the same shade of scarlet as her dress, Ella snatched up her stole and purse and swept through the door he'd opened for her, her steps faltering as she passed the vase of roses on the dresser. The last rays of evening sunshine slanting through the windows turned the petals blood-red, and their sensuous fragrance seemed to mock her, but good manners forced her to turn to him. 'Thank you for the roses,' she muttered stiltedly. 'They're beautiful.'

'My pleasure.'

How could he infuse two simple words with such a wealth of meaning? she wondered. Or was she badly overreacting? She guessed that most of the women he dated were skilled in the art of flirting, and happy to indulge in verbal foreplay. But she felt on edge, unsure of her ability to handle a man as self-assured as Vadim, and it didn't help that her lips were still tingling from that last unsatisfactorily brief kiss.

On the way to the restaurant she was relieved that he did not seem to want to talk, although his brooding silence did nothing to ease her tension, and she darted him a surprised glance when he activated the CD player and her latest recording of Mendelssohn violin concertos filled the car.

'I first heard you play a year ago,' he said quietly, 'and I was blown away by your incredible talent. Undoubtedly your career will go from strength to strength.'

Sales of the CD had been high—hundreds, if not thousands of people must have listened to her play—but as the haunting

notes of Mendelssohn's exquisite composition trembled between them in the close confines of the car Ella once again
felt as though she had revealed her deepest emotions to Vadim,
and it made her feel acutely vulnerable.

She was glad when they arrived in Mayfair. Simpson-
Brown was reputed to be one of the best restaurants in the
capital, and bookings were taken months in advance, but
when they walked into the elegant front bar Vadim was
greeted by the *maître-d'* like a long-lost brother and they
were immediately escorted to a table.

'Do you come here often?' Ella queried when they finally
took their seats, after Vadim had paused several times on their
journey across the restaurant to greet other diners who had
eagerly sought to gain his attention. The clichéd line sounded
horribly gauche, and she coloured and quickly stared down
at her menu, irritated with herself for acting like a teenager
on her first date. It didn't help that Vadim was so impossibly
gorgeous. She had been aware of the speculative glances
directed his way by several beautiful women as he had crossed
the restaurant. But his magnetism was due to more than the
perfection of his sculpted features and the inherent strength
of his lean, hard body. He possessed a raw, primitive quality
which, laced with unquestionable power and more than a hint
of danger, made him utterly irresistible to just about every
female between the ages of sixteen and sixty.

He shrugged. 'I dine here maybe two or three times a
month. I don't yet have a permanent base in London, so I've
been living at a hotel in Bloomsbury for the past six months.'
He paused fractionally and gave her an enigmatic glance
across the table. 'But that situation is about to change.'

'Will you be going back to Paris? I read somewhere that you
have a home there.' Even better, maybe he was planning to

return to his native Russia, she mused, wondering with a sharp stab of impatience why her stomach dipped at the thought.

'It's true I have an apartment on the Champs-Elysées, but I intend to settle in London for the foreseeable future to pursue various…' again he paused for a heartbeat '…interests.'

Undoubtedly he meant *business* interests, Ella assured herself frantically. But she could not control the quickening of her heart rate at the blatant sexual hunger in his gaze, nor drag her eyes from his sensual mouth that had wreaked havoc on her composure earlier. Get a grip, she ordered herself angrily. She was twenty-four years old, she had a successful career, and this was not the first time she'd been invited to dinner with a good-looking man—although it *was* the first time in her life she had been so intensely aware of a member of the opposite sex, she acknowledged ruefully.

The arrival of a waiter at their table to enquire whether they would like cocktails before they ate broke the tangible tension. 'I'll have a vodka martini.' Vadim glanced at Ella. 'We'll decide on red or white wine when we order dinner, but would you like an aperitif? Anton, here, can recommend several non-alcoholic cocktails if you prefer.'

Did he think she was so unsophisticated that she couldn't handle alcohol? Ella thought irritably. She gave him a cool smile and racked her brains for the name of a cocktail—any cocktail— that she'd heard of. 'I'd like a Singapore Sling, please.'

His dark brows lifted. 'Are you sure? The combination of gin and cherry brandy can be lethal on an empty stomach.'

In a minute he'd be ordering her a milkshake! 'I'll be fine, thank you,' she assured him coldly. The waiter left them, and she glanced around the packed restaurant, conscious that for the next hour or so she faced the unsettling prospect of talking exclusively to Vadim. Her nerves felt as taut as an overstretched elastic band as she cast around for something to say, and she was relieved when the waiter reappeared almost instantly with their drinks.

Vadim lifted his glass. 'To new friendships…and new experiences,' he drawled, amusement glinting in his eyes when Ella took a cautious sip of her drink and made a choking sound which she hastily turned into a cough. Once again he was struck by her air of innocence, but in his experience all women were game-players, and no doubt Ella had her own agenda for acting the ingénue. He relaxed back in his seat and studied the menu, but to his irritation he could not prevent his gaze from straying across the table to absorb the delicate beauty of her face, the fragile line of her collarbone and the gentle curve of her pale breasts above her red dress. She was very lovely, and she had invaded his thoughts far too often recently, he mused as the dull ache in his groin intensified to a hot, throbbing sensation that caused him to shift uncomfortably in his chair.

'As a Russian who appreciates good caviar, I can recommend the Royal Beluga to start,' he murmured. 'And for the main, grilled Dover sole with Béarnaise sauce, or the grilled *poussin* with thyme and lemongrass are both excellent.'

Ella gave up struggling to understand the exotic menu, which featured among other things veal with a wasabi sorbet, and calf's liver with truffle mash. She could at least recognise caviar, although she had never tasted it, and she loved Dover sole. 'The caviar sounds fine, and I'd like the sole to follow, please.'

'I'll have the same.' Vadim gave their order to the waiter. 'And a bottle of Chablis, thank you.'

The waiter walked away, and, needing something to do with her hands, Ella lifted her glass and took another sip of her innocuous-looking red cocktail. It was rather too sweet for her liking, and tasted similar to cough linctus, but the alcoholic punch didn't seem so strong now that she was used to it. Aware that Vadim was watching her, she gave him a cool smile and took another sip.

'So, how old were you when you discovered your musical talent?' he queried.

'My mother gave me my first violin when I was four, but I was picking out tunes on the piano from as soon as I could climb up onto the piano stool.' Ella smiled softly. 'My earliest memories are of hearing my mother play. She was a truly remarkable musician, and I feel very privileged to have inherited a little of her talent.'

'Do you have any brothers or sisters?'

'No.' Ella paused. 'Mama developed a serious heart condition soon after I was born, which meant that she couldn't have any more children. We were very close,' she revealed huskily. 'Music created a special bond between us.'

Vadim gave her an intent look. 'I believe you said you were a teenager when she died? It must have been hard to deal with such a tragedy when you were so young.'

After more than a decade Ella still wasn't sure she had come to terms with the death of the person she had loved most in the world, but the conversation was straying into an area of her life she never discussed with anyone, so she gave a non-committal shrug. 'It's in the past now. And at least I've been able to follow Mama's dream. She never had the opportunity to perform.' Ella's voice hardened. 'Especially once she married my father. But she always hoped I would have a successful career as a violinist. Before she died she set up a trust fund and left instructions for my musical education,' she explained to Vadim. 'Thanks to my mother I've studied under some of the best violin tutors in the world.'

'And do you enjoy performing? Was your mother's dream also your dream?' Vadim asked softly.

Ella frowned at him. 'Of course it was…is. What a strange question. Music is my life and I love playing.'

'That's not what I asked.' Vadim shrugged. 'It sounds a little as though your life has been dictated by your mother from beyond the grave. I merely wondered whether you had ever considered a different career, or whether you truly have a burning ambition to be a successful soloist.'

'My life is not dictated by my dead mother,' Ella denied furiously. 'She just wanted me to have the chances that she never had, and I'm glad I've been able to fulfil her dream.' A solo career *was* her dream too, she assured herself, trying to ignore the voice in her head which pointed out that, although she loved playing as part of an orchestra, she did not enjoy the mind-numbing stage fright she suffered as a soloist. As for ever considering a different career—it was true she had briefly considered studying law, after she had been inspired by a talk at school given by a human rights lawyer. But she had quickly dismissed the idea. Music was her life, and she felt honour bound to follow the path her mother had planned for her.

'Mama hoped I would have a successful career so that I would be financially independent and never have to be reliant on a man, as she was on my father,' she said quietly. 'Music has given me that independence, and I regard that as my mother's greatest legacy.'

It was the second time she had intimated that she had issues regarding her father, and although Vadim never took an interest in the personal lives of the women he dated, he couldn't deny he was curious to learn more about Ella.

'After your mother died, I assume your father brought you up? Did you have a close relationship with him?'

For a second Ella pictured her father's cold, thin-lipped face, and the expression of undisguised dislike in his eyes on the few occasions when they had met. He had known that she'd hated him, and with his warped sense of humour and cruel tongue had found it amusing to taunt and provoke her, aware that her fear of him prevented her from voicing her feelings about him.

She suddenly became aware that Vadim was waiting for her to reply. 'No.' The single word snapped like a gunshot, and, seeing his surprise, she added hastily, 'I was away at boarding school, and he preferred to live in his villa in the South of France rather than at Stafford Hall, so I didn't see him very often.'

She could tell that Vadim wanted to ask more, but to her relief the waiter reappeared at their table with the first course. The caviar was heaped in a crystal bowl, which was set in a larger bowl filled with crushed ice, and as Ella stared at the small, shiny, black fish eggs, her appetite vanished.

'Um…this looks delicious,' she mumbled when the waiter set a plate of small buckwheat pancakes in front of her.

Vadim hid his smile. 'Have you actually eaten caviar before?'

Honesty seemed the best policy. 'No,' she admitted ruefully. 'I've heard it's an acquired taste.'

'It's the food of the gods,' he assured her. 'The proper Russian way of eating it is straight off the spoon, accompanied by a shot of frozen vodka. But, seeing as you are a caviar virgin, I think we'd better forget the vodka so that you can experience the ultimate pleasure of the taste and texture in your mouth.'

Ella felt her face flood with colour, and she wondered if Vadim had guessed that her virginity did not only encompass eating caviar. She watched him scoop a few of the shiny black eggs onto a glass spoon, and her eyes widened when he leaned across the table and held the spoon inches from her lips.

'Close your eyes and open your mouth,' he ordered, his deep, accented voice as sensuous as crushed velvet. His brilliant blue eyes burned into hers, and the atmosphere between them was suddenly charged with electricity as the restaurant, the other diners and the hubbub of voices all faded and there was only Vadim.

Utterly transfixed, Ella obediently lowered her lashes and felt the cold edge of the spoon against her lips, followed by the curious texture of smooth, round berries on her tongue. The taste was indescribable: slightly fishy, slightly salty and overwhelmingly rich, she noted, as her taste buds were seduced by the intensity of flavour. Her eyes flew open and locked with Vadim's piercing gaze. He was watching her reaction intently, and the whole experience was so incredibly sensual that Ella could not restrain the little shiver that ran down her spine.

'What is your verdict?'

She swallowed the last morsel of caviar and touched her tongue to her lips to catch the lingering taste, the unconscious action causing heat to burn in Vadim's groin. 'Heavenly,' she murmured huskily.

He inhaled sharply and forced himself to sit back in his seat, shattering the sexual tension that had held them both in its grip. 'Then eat,' he invited. 'Top a blini with sour cream, add a little of the caviar, and enjoy.'

As Ella followed his instructions she was shocked to find that her hands were shaking. For a moment there she had been completely bewitched by Vadim, and in all honesty she knew she would have been powerless to stop him if he had walked around the table, pulled her into his arms and made love to her right there in the middle of the crowded restaurant. Panic surged up inside her and she suddenly longed for the evening to be over. Vadim was too much. He overwhelmed her and made her feel things she had never felt before. Her body felt taut, each of her nerve-endings acutely sensitive, and when she glanced down she was horrified to see that her nipples were jutting provocatively against her red silk dress.

She shot him a furtive glance, and swallowed when she discovered that he was watching her, his eyes gleaming beneath his hooded lids before he deliberately dropped his gaze to her breasts. 'Do you go back to Russia often?' she asked him, in a desperate attempt to break the sensual spell he had woven around her.

'I own a house on the outskirts of Moscow, but I only go back once or twice a year now that most of my business interests are in Europe.'

'What about your family? Do they still live in Russia?'

For a second something flared in Vadim's eyes—a look of such raw pain that Ella almost gasped out loud. But then his lashes swept down and hid his expression, and when he met her gaze across the table his face was a handsome, unreadable mask. 'I have no family,' he said bluntly. 'Both my father and my grandmother, who helped to bring me up, died many years ago.'

Still shaken by the look she had glimpsed in his eyes, Ella took a sip of her wine, feeling instinctively that the loss of his father and grandmother had not been responsible for the savage emotion that had flared in his brilliant blue depths.

'What about your mother?'

He shrugged. 'She left when I was seven or eight. My father was a dour man, who spent most of his time at work or busy with his duties as a communist party official. As far as

I know, my mother was much younger than him. I vaguely remember her smiling occasionally, which my father and grandmother never did, and I assume she wanted a better life than the one she had.'

'But she left you behind,' Ella murmured. She stared at Vadim's hard-boned face and felt something tug on her heart as she pictured him as a lonely little boy who had been abandoned by his mother. 'Was your grandmother kind?' What a ridiculous question, she berated herself impatiently, but for some reason his answer mattered. 'I mean…did she take good care of you?'

He gave a sardonic smile. 'My grandmother came from a remote village in Siberia, where winter temperatures regularly drop to minus thirty degrees centigrade, and she was as tough as the climate she grew up in. She was in her seventies when I was born, and I doubt she welcomed having to take on the role of parent in her old age. She certainly never seemed to find any pleasure in my presence, and despite her elderly years she had a heavy hand with the belt—until I learned to run fast enough to escape her, when she passed the duty of beating me over to my father,' he said, in a voice devoid of any emotion.

'That's horrible,' Ella said, paling. 'It sounds like you had a tough childhood.'

Vadim thought briefly of the relentless greyness of his early years, and gave another shrug. 'I survived. And compared with the two years I spent in the army my boyhood was a picnic.'

He said no more, but his silence was somehow more evocative than words. Ella recalled a newspaper article she had once read about the institutional violence and bullying that was regularly meted out to young recruits in the Russian army, and she guessed that Vadim had learned to be physically and mentally tough to cope. She tore her gaze from him and forced herself to eat her dinner. The Dover sole was delicious, but her appetite had disappeared. She could not forget the flash of pain in his eyes when she had first asked about his family, and she couldn't help feeling that there were secrets in his past he had not revealed.

'Have you ever tried to trace your mother? I mean, she might still be alive.'

Vadim ate the last of his fish and took a long sip of his wine. 'Very possibly, but I have no interest in her. Why would I?' he demanded coolly. 'She walked away when I needed her most, and I learned from the experience never to put my faith in another human being.'

He had clearly been more affected by his mother leaving than he admitted, perhaps even to himself, Ella brooded. She knew from experience that the emotional scars from an unhappy childhood still hurt long into adulthood, and now she had a better understanding of why he had earned a reputation as a womaniser who refused to commit to any of his lovers.

She and Vadim shared a common bond in that they had both been affected by their upbringing, she realised. Having witnessed the misery her mother had endured at the hands of her father, she was not looking for commitment, and certainly not for marriage. She valued her independence as much as Vadim did—but could she have a no-strings affair with him, as he had suggested, and emerge with her heart unscathed? Her instincts warned her that she would be playing with fire, but the feral gleam in his eyes stirred a feeling of wild recklessness within her and a longing to experience the hungry passion he promised.

She darted a glance across the table and discovered that he was watching her with a brooding intensity she found unnerving. In an effort to lighten the curiously tense atmosphere that had fallen between them she gave him a tentative smile.

Why did Ella's smile remind him of Irina? Vadim asked himself savagely. With her pale blonde hair and English rose colouring she bore no resemblance to his wife, who had been olive-skinned, like him, and had had thick, dark brown hair. But the two women shared the same smile. He closed his eyes briefly, as if he could somehow blot out the pain that surged through him. Irina's face swam before him, and her gentle, hopeful smile tore at his heart. She had been a quiet, shy young woman, as gentle as a doe with her soft brown eyes. She hadn't asked for much from life, he acknowledged grimly—just that he should love her. And he had, Vadim assured himself. He *had* loved Irina—but to his lasting regret he had not appreciated how much she had meant to him until he had held her limp, cold body in his arms.

Ella's smile faded when Vadim's hard expression did not lighten, and her stomach lurched with a mixture of embarrassment and disappointment when he continued to stare at her meditatively. She had the impression that although he was looking at her he did not see her, and she wondered where his thoughts had taken him.

To her relief the waiter arrived, to enquire whether they wanted dessert. Vadim suddenly jerked back to the present, his mouth curving into a sensual smile that made her heart race, and to her chagrin she could not prevent herself from smiling back at him. When he turned on the charm he was utterly irresistible, she thought ruefully. She knew it would be very easy to fall for him, but he was a far more complex man than his playboy persona revealed, and her instincts warned her to guard her emotions against him.

Vadim steered the conversation onto other topics for the

rest of the meal. He was an entertaining and intelligent companion, with a dry wit that frequently made Ella smile, and over the delectable bitter chocolate mousse she chose for dessert she found herself falling ever deeper under his spell. He could charm the birds from the trees, she thought ruefully. But the few scant facts he had revealed about himself over the course of the evening she could have discovered on the Internet, and she wondered if he ever permitted anyone to see the real Vadim Aleksandrov. He possessed an inherent dangerous quality that both repelled and intrigued her, but although she reminded herself that he was a heartless playboy, like her father had been, she sensed an unexpected vulnerability about him that made her wish she could learn more about the man behind the mask.

'So, what are your plans for your career?' he asked her over coffee. Although he had revealed little about himself, he had encouraged her to talk about her life as a musician, and her years studying at the Royal College of Music, and somehow he had drawn her into telling him personal confidences that she only ever shared with a few close friends.

After her cocktail and two glasses of wine Ella was feeling pleasantly relaxed, and filled with an uncharacteristic boldness which had led her to discover that flirting was fun—particularly with a man as wickedly sexy as Vadim.

'I'm giving a solo performance at the Palais Garnier in Paris next week, and after that I'll mainly be in London, to record the soundtrack for a film and work on my next solo album.'

His slow smile stole her breath, and the heat in his eyes caused a peculiar dragging sensation deep in her pelvis. 'It so happens that I will also be based mainly in London for the next couple of months, which presents us with an ideal opportunity to get to know one another better,' he said with undisguised satisfaction.

His vivid blue eyes lingered on her mouth, before trailing a leisurely path over her slim shoulders and down to her breasts, leaving Ella in no doubt as to how he hoped to get acquainted with her body. Her new-found confidence trickled away, and she said hurriedly, 'I'm going to be working incredibly hard, and I really won't have time for anything else…'

He leaned across the table and stopped her flow of words by placing his finger across her lips. Her eyes flew to his, her unguarded expression of fearful anticipation causing Vadim to once again question his motives. There was a sweetness and a curious naïveté about her that reminded him of Irina, and for a moment his conscience nagged that it would be unfair to instigate an affair when he was certain he would tire of her within a matter of weeks. He would not want to get her hopes up that she could ever be more to him than a fleeting sexual encounter. But her lips felt soft and moist against his skin, and the temptation to replace his finger with his mouth and kiss her into submission caused his body to harden. Fantasies about making love to her had dominated his thoughts from the moment he had met her, and the only solution, he decided grimly, was to sleep with her until he'd got her out of his system.

'You know what they say about all work and no play,' he drawled softly. 'We could have fun together, angel face.'

Maybe he was right, Ella debated silently while he settled the bill. An affair with Vadim would undoubtedly be fun while it lasted, and, contrary to her friend Jenny's belief, she did not want to live like a nun for the rest of her life. She might be inexperienced, her knowledge of sex gleaned from movies and popular women's magazines, but she knew enough to be confident that Vadim would be an inventive and uninhibited lover, who would arouse her to a fever-pitch of desire and appease the aching need he evoked.

The London streets were buzzing when they left the restaurant, the pavements crowded with people and the roads jammed with traffic, car headlights and street-lights illuminating the night sky. Vadim slid a protective arm around Ella's waist as she was jostled by a group of young men who had piled out of a bar. 'Do you want me to take you home, or would you like to go on to a club?'

His hard body was pressed against hers, making her acutely aware of the muscular strength of his thighs, and she could feel the heat that emanated from him and smell the intoxicating scent of his cologne mingled with another perfume that was innately male. Her common sense insisted that she should ask him to take her home, where she would bid him a polite goodnight and make it clear that she did not want to see him again. But for the first time in her life she felt like rebelling against the constraints of her life, which suddenly seemed to be one long round of practising and performing, leaving her little opportunity to socialise. She usually went to bed after the ten o'clock news—but she was twenty-four, for heaven's sake, she reminded herself impatiently, and it was time she lived a little.

'A club might be fun,' she murmured, and was rewarded with a sensual smile that sent a quiver of awareness down her spine.

'I'm a member of Annabel's in Berkeley Square. It's not far from here. Are you happy to walk?' As he spoke, Vadim curled his big hand around her smaller one, the faint abrasion of his skin against the softness of her palm so incredibly sensual that Ella simply nodded and fell into step beside him, her heart thudding in time with the tap of her stiletto heels on the pavement.

CHAPTER FIVE

ANNABEL'S nightclub was a popular haunt of the rich and famous, and Ella spotted numerous celebrities on the dance floor, but she noticed that guests and staff alike seemed slightly in awe of Vadim. Once again she was aware of his power and his magnetic attraction, which drew beautiful women to him in droves. He could take his pick from any of the number of models and socialites in the bar, many of whom brazenly tried to catch his attention. They were uniformly exquisite, with long, tanned limbs, perfect figures and flawless features, and Ella couldn't help comparing herself with them and wondering why on earth he was interested in her.

But Vadim seemed to only have eyes for her. She could not help but find his attention flattering, and as the night progressed and the champagne flowed she began to relax and enjoy herself. Dancing to the funky club classics was fun, and dancing with Vadim, held close against his chest while he moved his pelvis sinuously against hers, sent molten heat coursing through her veins.

'Enjoying yourself?' he drawled, his blue eyes gleaming as he glanced down at her flushed face. The music had slowed and they were drifting around the dance floor, hip to hip, while his hand strayed up and down her spine in a sensuous caress.

'Yes,' Ella admitted honestly. There seemed no point in denying it when she felt more alive and exhilarated than she could ever remember feeling.

'Good.' Vadim lowered his head slowly towards her, and she could not restrain a little shiver of excitement when he slanted his mouth over hers and initiated a slow, drugging kiss. His lips were firm, demanding her response, and she gave it helplessly, her whole body trembling when he slid his tongue into her mouth and explored her moist warmth with devastating efficiency until she sagged against him, so lost in this new world of sensory pleasure that the people around them on the dance floor faded, and there was no one but Vadim.

It was three a.m. when they finally left the club, and as they stepped outside the blast of fresh air made Ella's head spin.

'This isn't your car,' she mumbled, when a sleek black limousine pulled up next to them and its chauffeur sprang out to open the rear door.

'I never drive after I've had a couple of drinks. I arranged for my driver to take the Aston Martin back to my hotel and come back to collect us in the limo.' Vadim frowned as he watched Ella wobble precariously on her high heels. 'Are you okay?'

'Of course I'm okay. Why shouldn't I be?' She bent to climb into the car, misjudged the height of the door fame and winced as she hit her head. 'I've never felt better,' she assured him brightly. It was true; several glasses of champagne had replaced her usual reserve with brimming confidence, and she felt sexy and uninhibited and desperate for Vadim to kiss her again. She stared at him hopefully and instinctively traced her lips with the tip of her tongue, anticipation shivering through her when his eyes narrowed and gleamed with feral hunger.

But it was warm in the car, and the smooth motion of the engine had a soporific effect on her, so that her eyelids felt heavy and her head drooped onto Vadim's shoulder. She looked about sixteen, he brooded impatiently. Tendrils of hair had escaped her chignon, and he carefully released the clip on top of her head so that the silky mass tumbled around her shoulders.

The type of woman he usually dated would have spent the journey home stroking her hand over his thigh as a prelude to a night of mutually satisfying sex—not snuggling up to him like a sleepy kitten. There was something about Ella that tugged at his conscience, and not for the first time he wondered if he had made a mistake by pursuing her—especially since he had discovered that she carried a truckload of emotional baggage which seemed to be linked with her unhappy relationship with her father.

Emotions were complicated, which was why he did not deal in them. He had failed Irina and broken her heart, and he refused to ever be responsible for another woman's emotional security.

Ella frowned when the comfortable pillow beneath her neck moved, so that her head lolled unsupported. Someone gripped her shoulder and shook her, and an impatient voice sounded in her ear. 'Ella, wake up. We're back at Kingfisher House.'

Her heavy lids lifted and she stared into Vadim's startling blue eyes. His face was inches from hers, his mouth so tantalisingly close that she moistened her lips with the tip of her tongue in unconscious invitation.

Hot sexual excitement uncoiled in Vadim's gut, and for a few seconds he was tempted to ignore the nagging voice of his conscience, which warned that Ella seemed far more innocent than he had first thought. She was a consenting adult, and she wanted him, the voice in his head argued. Her grey eyes were smoky with desire, and her soft parted lips were just begging for him to possess them. But she'd had a couple of glasses of champagne on top of the wine and cocktails they had drunk with dinner, and he was sure she was not used to drinking alcohol. He had done many things in his past which he regretted, and he refused to add taking advantage of a naïve girl who reminded him too much of his dead wife to the list.

'Come on, I'll see you inside,' he said abruptly, when she scrambled inelegantly out of the car and stood beside him on the gravel drive, swaying slightly.

Ella gave a puzzled frown when Vadim took hold of her arm and marched her up to the house. A moment ago she had been sure that he was about to kiss her, and she had been surprised and disappointed when he had abruptly pulled back and leapt out of the car. Maybe he had been conscious of the presence of the chauffeur and wanted to be alone with her when he kissed her? She cast a sideways glance at his handsome face and a frisson of excitement tingled down her spine as she imagined him slanting his sensual mouth over hers. Would he stop at kissing, or was he intending to sweep her into his arms, carry her through to her bedroom and make love to her?

She fumbled in her bag for her key, opened the front door and turned back to face him, heart thudding painfully beneath her ribs. His sensual smile stole her breath, and she felt as taut as an overstrung bow as she waited for him to take her in his arms.

'Goodnight, Ella.'

Goodnight! She stared at him in confusion as he stepped back from her. When they had left the nightclub the hungry gleam in his eyes had convinced her that he wanted to take their relationship a step further. He intrigued her in a way no other man ever had, and on the journey back to Kingfisher House she had made the decision that she was ready to explore the sexual chemistry that simmered between them.

But Vadim was leaving! Perhaps he was waiting for a sign

from her that she would not reject him if he kissed her? He had turned away from her and was walking towards his waiting car. Taking a deep breath, she blurted out, 'Would you like to come in…for coffee?'

He paused and slowly turned back to face her, his intent stare causing hot colour to stain her cheeks. Seconds ticked past, stretching her nerves, but then he gave a shrug and strolled back up the drive. The moonlight slanted across his face, throwing his sculpted features into sharp relief. He was so incredibly handsome, and so intensely male, Ella thought as she inhaled the exotic scent of his cologne mingled with the subtle perfume of pheromones that inflamed her senses. He rejoined her on the doorstep, and the heat emanating from his muscular body caused a curious melting sensation deep in her pelvis. She had never been so sexually aware of a man in her life, and acting purely on instinct she swayed towards him, lifted her face to his.

He muttered something in Russian, but Ella was too distracted by her longing to feel his mouth on hers to wonder what the words meant. Her heart slammed against her ribs when he lowered his dark head and brushed his lips over hers in a delicate tasting that left her quivering for more. Lost to everything but his sensual sorcery, she opened her mouth for him to deepen the kiss, and felt a jolt of pleasure when he slid his tongue deep into her moist warmth and initiated an intimate exploration that escalated her excitement to fever-pitch.

She could not resist him, nor the dictates of her body, which was eager to experience this new world of sensory pleasure. With a soft sigh she slid her arms up to his shoulders so that her breasts were pressed against his chest. She was impatient for him to curve his arms around her waist and draw her closer still, but to her utter shock he suddenly ended the kiss and caught hold of her hands to prevent her from linking them around his neck.

'Thanks for the invitation,' he drawled, 'but I have to get back.'

Still trembling with sexual anticipation, Ella could not disguise her disappointment. 'But I thought…' She trailed to a halt and snatched her fingers out of his grasp, her cheeks burning when she realised that Vadim was not about to carry her into the house and seduce her. She had practically leapt on him, she thought sickly. She had instigated the kiss, and from his mocking smile he was clearly amused by her eagerness.

Something flared in his eyes when she jerked away from him.

'It's debatable who you're going to hate most tomorrow, angel face—yourself, or me,' he said gently. He turned and strode back to his car without a backward glance, and with a yelp of fury at her own stupidity Ella shot into the house and slammed the door behind her.

Ella opened her eyes to find bright sunshine streaming into her room, and when she glanced at the clock she was shocked to discover that it was almost midday. Her head felt woolly, but, like a theatre curtain slowly opening, the mist in her brain cleared and her memory returned with a vengeance. Last night she'd had dinner with Vadim and he had fed her caviar. Afterwards they had visited a club and danced until the early hours before he had brought her home, whereupon she had practically begged him to spend the night with her—and he had rejected her!

Utterly mortified, she rolled onto her stomach and dragged the pillow over her head. What had she been thinking? she asked herself furiously. But of course she *hadn't* been think-ing—not properly—and her actions had been fuelled by too much champagne. That must have been the case—because why else would she have decided that she could handle an affair with Vadim, when she knew he was a playboy and the sort of man she usually avoided like the plague?

She would never be able to face him again, she thought miserably, her face burning with shame when she recalled how she had leaned close to him when they had stood on the doorstep, made it clear that she wanted him to kiss her. Had he found her eagerness off-putting? Maybe he had been playing a game, which he'd won once she had shown her willingness to sleep with him? The idea made her feel sick, and she hauled herself out of bed and staggered into her small kitchen to discover that she had run out of milk and teabags.

Several glasses of water and a shower later she felt margin-ally better—physically, at least. But the recriminations and self-disgust continued, and, desperate to get out of the house, she pulled on jeans and a tee shirt, flung open the French doors and stepped outside. The garden was a blaze of colour, the emerald lawn bordered by flowers in a variety of brilliant shades, but it was the sight of Vadim—sitting at the garden table further along the terrace—that stopped her in her tracks.

'What…what are you doing here?' she croaked, so taken aback by his appearance that she could barely articulate the words. Her shock at seeing him, after she had hoped that they would never meet again, had turned her legs to jelly, and she dropped weakly onto a chair opposite him. It didn't help that he looked utterly gorgeous, in sun-bleached jeans and a black polo shirt open at the throat to reveal a glimpse of bronzed skin overlaid with dark chest hair. Unlike her, he was clearly not suffering any adverse effects from the champagne they had drunk at the club last night, she noted darkly. He looked completely relaxed as he leisurely perused the Sunday papers, while the delicious aroma of freshly brewed coffee rose from the jug in front of him.

'Good afternoon,' he drawled, glancing pointedly at his watch. 'I take it you slept well.'

'I don't understand why—or how—you're here,' Ella muttered, wishing he would remove his designer shades so that she could see the expression in his eyes. A high-pitched voice drew her attention down the garden, and her surreal feeling intensified when she watched her cousin's young daughter, Lily, run across the lawn.

'Ella! We came to see you, but you were asleep,' the little girl greeted her. 'Grandpa said we'd better not wake you up.'

'Yes, I had a bit of a lie-in this morning,' Ella said weakly, flushing when she caught Vadim's amused glance. She hugged Lily. 'Is Grandpa here?'

'He's there.' Lily pointed, and Ella looked round to see her uncle Rex, walking across the lawn towards them.

'There you are, Ella.' Rex Portman studied his niece's pale face and chuckled. 'Been partying, have you? Good for you. I've always said you spend too much time locked away with your violin. Girls of your age should be out having fun.' His eyes moved from Ella to Vadim and back again, 'I take it you've introduced yourself? I phoned a couple of times earlier, to let you know Vadim was taking over the tenancy of Kingfisher House today, but you must have been out for the count. I don't suppose you even heard the delivery van arrive, or the army of staff Vadim hired to carry his things into the house—did you?'

'I…' Ella made a strangled sound and decided she had obviously been transported into the world of Alice in Wonderland. She wouldn't be surprised if an oversized white rabbit suddenly appeared and they all had a tea party.

'Don't look so worried,' her uncle said jovially. 'I've explained to Vadim that you currently live in the caretaker flat, and he's happy for the situation to continue—at least for the next couple of months.'

'Yes indeed.' Vadim's gravelly Russian accent was deep and melodious compared to Uncle Rex's chirpy, good-humoured voice. 'I frequently travel abroad for business, and it suits me that the house will not be completely empty while I'm away.' His smile oozed charm, but for once Ella was immune to it and clenched her fists beneath the table. 'Until I decide whether or not to buy Kingfisher House I won't be employing any live-in staff, so you are welcome to remain in the staff accommodation,' he said smoothly. He paused, and then added softly, 'I understand you need to find a flat big enough to house a grand piano?'

'That piano's a liability, if you ask me,' Uncle Rex said before Ella could comment. 'Monstrous thing it is. You might have to think about selling it, Ella.'

She shook her head fiercely. 'Mama's piano is one of the few mementos I have of her. I'll never sell it.'

Her uncle grimaced. 'Well, thanks to Vadim's generosity, you won't have to for now.'

The words on Ella's tongue, which had been queuing up to tell Vadim in no uncertain terms what he could do with his offer for her to remain at Kingfisher House, juddered to a halt. Her eyes flew to his face, and she was certain that behind his concealing shades his eyes were glinting with satisfaction that he had her right where he wanted her. *Nothing* would induce her to sell her mother's piano, and even if she spent every spare moment searching for a flat it would be weeks before she found somewhere suitable, she acknowledged grimly.

'Grandpa, I want to see the water,' Lily piped up. She darted, quick as an eel, across the lawn, and Uncle Rex hurried after her.

'Hang on a minute. Don't you go too close to the river, young lady.'

Ella watched them go, and then turned angrily to Vadim. 'Is this your peculiar idea of a joke?' She snatched a breath and rushed on, without giving him a chance to reply. 'I can't believe you had the *gall* to engineer this.'

Dark brows rose quizzically. 'Engineer what, specifically?'

'You taking over the tenancy of Kingfisher House,' she said fiercely. 'Don't tell me it wasn't planned. I suppose you decided to rent the house after you found out that I live here.'

'Actually, there was no Machiavellian plot,' he said mildly. 'I've known Rex Portman for some time, and my company has bought several properties with development potential through his estate agency. When he heard I was looking for a base in the UK he showed me around Kingfisher House, and I immediately decided to rent it for six months.' Okay, that was stretching the truth, Vadim conceded silently, but he saw no reason to admit to Ella that he had originally decided to move into a house in Belgravia, but had changed his mind the night he had driven her home after the concert at Amesbury House.

Ella blushed as she recalled how he had rejected her the previous night. Of course he had not plotted to share the house with her, she told herself impatiently. But during their dinner date she had been so sure that he desired her, and when they had danced together at Annabel's she had felt the hard proof of his arousal nudge insistently against her pelvis. Had she read the signs wrongly? Or had Vadim for some reason had a change of heart on the drive back to Kingfisher House and decided that he no longer wanted to explore the sexual chemistry between them? His face was shuttered, giving no clue to his thoughts. He was an enigma, and once again she had the feeling that there were secrets in his past she knew nothing about.

He finally took off his sunglasses, and the amused gleam in his brilliant blue eyes fuelled her temper. 'You must see the situation is impossible,' she said bitterly. 'I can't live here with you.'

Vadim leaned back in his chair and studied her broodingly. 'We won't technically be living together,' he murmured laconically.

She glared at him, her pride still smarting. 'You're right— we won't,' she said sharply. 'The staff flat has its own separate entrance, and the door between the flat and the main house will be locked at all times.'

She knew from the way his eyes narrowed that she had angered him, but his voice was level when he spoke. 'What do you think I'm going to do—barge my way into your room and force myself on you? I have never taken a woman against her will in my life,' he assured her coldly. 'You have nothing to fear from me, Ella. But may I remind you that yesterday you made it clear that you hoped I would spend the night with you.'

Scarlet with embarrassment, Ella was forced to bite back her angry retort when Lily dashed back up the garden and threw herself onto her lap. 'Mummy's had a new baby,' the little girl announced.

'I know. His name's Tom, isn't it?' Ella ruffled her goddaughter's curls and thought briefly of her cousin Stephanie, who had given birth to her second child three days ago. 'Is he tiny?'

Lily nodded and held up her doll. 'I've got a new baby too. Her name's Tracy.' She paused, her attention drawn to the big, dark-haired man sitting opposite. 'What's your name?'

'Vadim,' he replied, his smile deepening when the little girl frowned.

'You sound funny.'

Ella shot him a lightning glance, but to her surprise Vadim appeared quite at ease talking to a young child.

'That's because I come from another country,' he explained, in the gravelly accent that brought Ella's skin out in goose bumps. 'I am from Russia.'

Lily's eyes were as round as saucers as she regarded Vadim for several seconds before nodding her approval. 'You can hold Tracy if you like.'

'Thank you.' Vadim stared down at the rag-doll Lily had placed on the table in front of him, and closed his eyes briefly as pain swept through him. It was incredible how after all this time the sight of a doll could open up the floodgate of memories. His mind flew back across the years and he saw another doll, another little girl.

'*You hold my dolly, Papa. Sacha's scared on the swing.*' He could hear Klara's sweet, childish voice, speaking in Russian, as clearly as if she had just uttered the words. '*Promise you'll take care of her, Papa?*'

'*Of course I will, devochka moya. I'll take care of both of you.*'

But he had broken his promise, Vadim thought grimly, pain slicing his insides like a knife in his gut. He hadn't taken care of his little daughter, nor her mother. He picked up Lily's beautifully dressed doll, with its bright golden curls, and thought of the raggedy doll with brown wool hair that Irina had so painstakingly mended each time the stitching had broken and more stuffing had spilled out.

'*When the business does better I'll buy Klara a new doll,*' he had told Irina as she'd squinted to thread her needle in their poorly lit apartment.

'*She likes this one.*' Irina had stared at him, her pretty face troubled. '*And she'd rather see her papa more often than have a new doll.*'

It was a pity he hadn't listened. The guilt would be with him for ever.

'Do you like Tracy?' Lily's voice wrenched him back to the present. 'I got her for my birthday.'

'She's a beautiful doll,' he assured her gravely. 'How old were you on your birthday, Lily?'

'Five.'

The knife sliced again, deeper; the pain no longer the dull ache that served as a constant reminder of the past but so agonisingly sharp that he inhaled swiftly. Klara had been just five years old. It was no time at all, he brooded dully. She should have had so much longer on this earth, but instead she had been buried by the tons of snow that had hurtled down the mountainside and all but wiped out Irina's home village.

Ten years had passed since that fateful day when his wife and little daughter had been killed by an avalanche, and he had learned to contain his grief. But Lily, with her cheeky smile and halo of curls, was an agonising reminder of all he had lost. And the limp rag-doll, which travelled with him wherever he went in the world, was a poignant link with the only two people he had ever loved.

CHAPTER SIX

'WELL, Vadim, I think we'd better give you some peace to settle into Kingfisher House,' Rex Portman gasped, panting and pink-faced from chasing his granddaughter around the garden. 'There's not much else to show you, apart from the summerhouse down by the river. If there's anything else you need to know, Ella will be able to help. She's lived here for—what is it now, Ella—four years? She was responsible for most of the interior decoration too. I'm sure you'll admit she's done a classy job.'

'The house is delightful,' Vadim murmured, replacing his sunglasses on his nose so that his expression was unreadable. The demons that haunted him were too private and personal to be shared, and he had never spoken of his past to anyone.

'Oh, I almost forgot. Photos of the new baby.' Rex extracted a packet of photographs from his pocket and handed them to Ella. 'Handsome little chap, isn't he? Steph says he looks a lot like me.'

Ella stared at the round red face and bald head of her cousin's newborn baby son, glanced at her uncle's sweat-beaded pate, and conceded that there was a strong resemblance.

'He's very sweet,' she said softly, surprised by the pang of maternal longing that gripped her.

Uncle Rex nodded. 'I expect you'll want to settle down and have a couple of kids of your own soon.'

She shook her head firmly. 'I doubt I'll ever have children. For one thing, I believe children should grow up with two parents who are committed to each other,' she explained, when her uncle gave her an incredulous look, 'and as I never want to get married I'm just going to have to enjoy being a godmother.' She gave Lily a hug, and was rewarded when the little girl squeezed her so hard that her ribs felt in danger of cracking. It wasn't that she did not like children, she mused. She adored Lily, and loved spending time with her, but music and her career put huge demands on her time and she had always thought it would be selfish to have a child when she spent five or six hours a day playing.

'Well, there's plenty of time for you to meet a chap and change your mind,' Uncle Rex assured her cheerfully, patently believing she needed reassurance that she wouldn't end up a childless spinster. But she wouldn't change her mind, she thought fiercely. She accepted that not all marriages were the route to hell—Rex and her mother's sister, Aunt Lorna, had been happily married for thirty years—but they were the exception rather than the norm. Many of her friends had divorced parents and split families, and she would never put herself or a child through all that misery.

But if she was certain she did not want to get married, what *did* she want? Ella brooded later that afternoon, asking herself the same question that Jenny had posed when Vadim had sent her the bouquet of red roses. Until now music had dominated her life and she hadn't given men or relationships much thought. But all that had changed when she had met Vadim in Paris. Since then he had invaded her mind far too often, and when he kissed her and touched her… She bit her lip and tried to dismiss the erotic fantasy of their naked bodies intimately entwined.

Suddenly her life, which had been plodding along quite nicely, was in turmoil, and she no longer knew what she wanted. She could not remain at Kingfisher House when Vadim would be an unnervingly close neighbour, but she had no choice until she found another flat, she debated with herself. There was only one way to deal with the confused thoughts in her head, and that was to lose herself in music. Her violin was a faithful friend, and a sense of calm settled over her when she settled her chin on the chin-rest and drew her bow across the strings.

For the next hour or two there was no danger that she would disturb the new tenant of Kingfisher House. Shortly after Uncle Rex and Lily had left Vadim had announced that he was going to a nearby pub for lunch. She had turned down his invitation to join him, citing the need to get on with some household chores. She would spend an hour running through the piece by Debussy that she hoped to include on her next album, and after that she would no longer be able to put off visiting the supermarket to restock her fridge.

'Do you realise you've been playing virtually without a break for three hours?' Vadim's deep voice came from the French doors, which Ella had left open. 'Maybe longer,' he added. He had arrived back at the house after lunch to hear the strains of Elgar drifting across the garden, and instead of a reading an important financial report, as he had planned, he'd spent the afternoon listening to Ella play. 'It's time to come and eat,' he told her, when she lowered her violin and frowned at him.

'Eat?' she said vaguely. 'What's the time?'

'Almost seven.'

'Damn!' Ella came back to reality with a thump. The super-market shut at four on Sundays, her fridge was a barren wilderness, and the growl from her stomach reminded her that she hadn't eaten all day. A delicious smell was drifting in from the terrace. She sniffed appreciatively and Vadim's lips twitched.

'I ordered dinner. Do you like Thai food?'

Hunger battled with the decision she'd made earlier that, for the few weeks until she found another flat, she and Vadim would lead completely separate lives. Hunger won. 'I love it.'

'Good.' His brief smile broke the stern lines of his face, but she noticed that it did not reach his eyes. He seemed remote, almost sombre tonight, and for a moment she sensed an inner loneliness about him that tugged on her heart. It was gone before she could define what she had seen. His mask slipped back into place and his smile widened seductively, causing her heart to flip in her chest. 'Come through when you're ready,' he invited, and disappeared back to his part of the house.

There was no reason why she should not eat with him dressed as she was, Ella acknowledged, glancing down at her jeans. But the sultry June evening provided a perfect excuse to change into the delicate silvery-grey silk dress she'd bought recently, after Jenny had persuaded her that it brought out the colour of her eyes. It took mere seconds to darken her lashes with mascara and apply a pale pink gloss to her lips, and she left her hair loose, sprayed Chanel to her pulse-points and swiftly appraised her reflection in the mirror, dismayed to find that the eyes staring back at her were as dark as woodsmoke, and her cheeks were flushed with the rosy glow of unbidden excitement.

It was just dinner, she reminded herself when she slipped out of the French doors and walked a few steps along the terrace to the second set of doors leading into the main house. Tonight she would be on her guard against Vadim's seductive charm. She paused in the doorway, her eyes drawn to the table set for two, the tall candles in elegant silver holders casting soft light over the centrepiece of white roses. It was intimate, romantic… Ella swiftly dismissed the idea. Vadim was not interested in romance. She had thought that he wanted to sleep with her, but now she wasn't sure about that—any more than she was sure about what she wanted, she admitted to herself ruefully. But when he walked towards her, looking devastatingly sexy in close-fitting black trousers and a fine white silk shirt through which she could see the shadow of dark body hair, her heart set up a slow, thudding beat, and she could almost touch the searing sexual electricity that quivered in the air between them.

'You look beautiful,' he greeted her quietly. Three simple words, but the slight roughness of his voice turned the compliment into a sensual caress that made the tiny hairs on her skin stand on end, and the gleam beneath his heavy lids evoked a slow-burning fire deep in her pelvis.

'Thank you.' Did that breathless, *sexy* voice really belong to her? When he drew out a chair she sat down thankfully, and took her time unfolding her napkin while she fought for composure.

'Would you like champagne?' Vadim lifted a bottle of Krug from the ice bucket, but Ella shook her head and quickly filled her glass with water from the jug on the table.

'Water will be fine, thanks,' she murmured, blushing at his mocking smile that told her he understood her determination to keep a clear head this evening. He trapped her gaze and she found it impossible to look away, the tension between them almost tangible until suddenly, shockingly, a figure walked into the room and the sensual spell was broken.

'Ah—dinner,' Vadim announced, walking around the table to take his place opposite her. 'Tak-Sin is one of the best Thai chefs in London. I hope you're hungry,' he added, when the man pushed a trolley laden with a variety of dishes over to the table.

'When you said you'd ordered dinner, I assumed it would be delivered in plastic cartons,' Ella murmured wryly, her taste buds stirring as Tak-Sin placed a bowl of clear, fragrant soup in front of her. She smiled at the chef, who promptly reeled off the names of the dishes he was placing on the table.

'Gai phadd prek, goong preaw wann…'

'He doesn't speak much English,' Vadim explained, when she looked at him helplessly. 'The first dish is chicken with green peppers, and that one is prawns with sweet and sour vegetables. This is some sort of beef dish—I think…'

'Well, it looks and smells gorgeous, so I guess the names don't matter,' Ella said as she picked up her spoon and tasted the soup. The food was nectar to her empty stomach, and she spent the next ten minutes sampling each of the dishes with such concentration that Vadim smiled.

'I'm glad to see you enjoy your food. Most of the women I know seem to survive by nibbling on lettuce leaves and the occasional breadstick.'

'I guess I'm lucky that I can eat what I like and never gain weight,' Ella said with a shrug. 'But the downside is that I'll probably always be scrawny and flat-chested.'

'I would describe you as slender, rather than scrawny.' Vadim paused and trailed his eyes over her slim shoulders and the delicate upper slopes of her breasts revealed above the neckline of her dress. 'And although your breasts are small they suit your tiny frame. I think it's a pity that so many young women have breast implants and end up looking as though they've stuffed a couple of footballs under their clothes. I definitely prefer the natural look,' he added softly, his eyes gleaming wickedly when Ella blushed.

Trying not to dwell on the hordes of women he had dated in the past, and desperate to steer the conversation away from the size of her breasts, she seized on the first thing that came into her head. 'I believe your company is the biggest mobile phone company in Russia, and now has a major stake in the European market? How did you start out selling phones?'

'I actually started out selling Russian dolls. Yes, really.' Vadim laughed when Ella looked at him disbelievingly. 'Matryoshka dolls—you've probably seen them; they're made of wood, usually about seven in a set, and they fit one inside another from the smallest to the biggest. When I left the army the political situation in Russia was changing, and in the early days of post-communism it was possible for the first time to set up a private business.' He paused to take a sip of champagne before continuing. 'I was working as a porter at a hotel; the wages were not good, and I was desperate to escape the life of poverty and drudgery that had been my father's miserable existence.'

Vadim's face hardened. 'I would have done anything—and, trust me, there was a thriving black market operated by criminal gangs who lured young, dissatisfied men into their fold with the promise of easy money. But I was lucky.' He shrugged. 'At the hotel I met a German businessman who owned a chain of toy shops across Europe. One day he asked me about the traditional Russian dolls he had seen, and voiced an interest in stocking them in his shops. By that evening I had sourced a supply of dolls and negotiated a deal with Herr Albrecht to act as his supplier. That was the beginning of my career. Within a couple of years I had made enough money to be able to invest in other ventures. The gap in the mobile phone industry was waiting to be filled, and I seized the opportunity.'

'You make it sound easy,' Ella murmured, utterly transfixed by the story of Vadim's route to success. 'But I'm sure it can't have been. You must have made personal sacrifices.' She hesitated, and then said quietly, 'I sometimes feel that when I was growing up I sacrificed many of the things that other young people take for granted. Music demanded so much of my time that I rarely socialised with kids of my own age, and now my career is so consuming that I have virtually no time for friends or...' she hesitated fractionally '...relationships.' She gave him a faint smile. 'I wonder if one day we'll look back and wonder if the dreams we chased so hard were worth the heartache?'

There was a depth to Ella that he had never found in any other woman, Vadim mused darkly. Her insight was uncomfortably close to the mark, but she had no idea that he had sacrificed the happiness and ultimately the lives of his wife and child on the altar of his ambition.

Had the single-minded determination he'd given to chasing his dreams been worth it? He now had wealth beyond anything he had ever imagined when he'd made that first deal with Herr Albrecht all those years ago. But sometimes, in the dark hour before dawn, when he surfaced from the regular nightmare that had haunted him for the past ten years and heard the echo of Klara's terrified screams for him to save her, he knew he would gladly give up everything he owned to hold his daughter in his arms once again.

Tak-Sin had prepared an exotic fruit salad for dessert, and Ella helped herself to slices of mango and passion fruit, relishing the sweet, fresh flavours on her tongue. Vadim shook his head when she offered him the fruit bowl, and instead drained his champagne glass and refilled it. He had lapsed into silence—a brooding silence she felt reluctant to break. She sensed that his thoughts were far away, and she wondered what memories from his past had caused him to look so grim.

The weather seemed to be reflecting his mood. While they had been eating the evening sunshine had been replaced by ominous-looking clouds, and now the air was still and heavy, the atmosphere charged with electricity that made the tiny hairs on Ella's arms stand on end. Through the French doors she saw the sky was black, and she caught her breath when lightning seared the heavens and briefly filled the room with brilliant white light. She flinched when a low growl of thunder sounded from across the river.

'I hate storms,' she admitted shakily as Vadim returned from wherever his thoughts had taken him and focused his piercing blue gaze on her. 'When I was a child, one of the gardeners at Stafford Hall was struck and killed by lightning.'

He frowned. 'You saw it happen?'

'Oh, no—fortunately; but it was all the other staff talked about for weeks afterwards. They said his violent death would mean another ghost would haunt the Hall.'

'Did you have many staff?' Vadim asked curiously. 'I've seen photographs of Stafford Hall and it looks a vast place.'

Ella nodded, thinking of the great grey-walled house with the stone gargoyles over the front door that had given her nightmares as a little girl. 'It is—seventeen bedrooms, numerous reception rooms and a chapel in the grounds where it was rumoured that a priest was murdered on the orders of the King, hundreds of years ago. When my father first inherited the Hall from my grandfather we had a small army of cooks, butlers and maids, but as the money ran out he sacked the staff until there was only the housekeeper, Mrs Rogers, left. She was about a hundred,' Ella added ruefully, 'but she helped to care for my mother, and as my father wanted as little to do with Mama as possible, he allowed dear Betty to stay.'

Thunder rumbled again, louder this time, so that it seemed to reverberate around the room. 'Did you believe the house was haunted?' Vadim murmured, sensing Ella's tension as the storm approached.

She hesitated, and then gave a reluctant nod. 'I was a very imaginative child, and because my mother was often unwell I spent a lot of time on my own. I convinced myself that the stories I'd heard about the headless baron and the Grey Lady, who was said to have been stabbed to death by her cruel husband, were true. The room at the top of the tower where she was supposed to have met her death was thought to be the most haunted room in the house. It was always cold, and none of the staff would go up there.' She paused again, and then revealed in a low tone, 'My father used to lock me in that room as punishment for any misdemeanour I committed. And, as I only had to walk into the same room as him to incur his annoyance, I was punished pretty often when he was home.'

Vadim felt a violent surge of dislike for Ella's father. 'Did he know you were scared?'

'Oh, yes,' Ella said grimly. 'I would be hysterical with fear when he dragged me up there—that's why he enjoyed doing it. Refined cruelty was his forte.'

It was obvious that Ella had feared her father as much as she had feared the ghosts she had believed roamed her child-hood home, and some indefinable emotion tugged on Vadim's heart as he imagined her as a terrified little girl. 'Did he ever punish you physically?' he asked harshly.

Ella gave a start as a thunderclap shook the room, and she glanced nervously out at the black starless sky that seemed to smother the garden beneath a heavy cloak. 'No,' she said slowly. 'He never hit me, but sometimes my mother would have bruises… She always said she'd fallen, or banged into the door… But I knew it had been *him*. Fortunately he never stayed at the Hall for long. He only came back from his house in France when he was short of money and needed to sell off another family heirloom, and it was a huge relief when he went away again.'

'But if your father treated your mother so badly, why did she remain married to him?'

It was a question Ella has asked herself countless times, and she had never come to terms with the only answer she'd ever been able to come up with. 'I suppose she loved him,' she said at last. 'She once told me that she had fallen in love with him the moment they met, and I think that whatever he did, however many times he broke her heart with his infidelity and his indifference, she never stopped loving him.' She shook her head. 'My mother was such a sweet, gentle person. I don't understand why my father didn't love her the way she loved him,' she cried angrily.

'Maybe he couldn't,' Vadim said quietly. He stared unseeingly across the dark garden while the familiar demon, guilt, stirred from its slumber. Irina had been gentle, and her sweet, shy smile had been the first thing he had noticed about her each time he'd walked into the grocery store where she had worked. He *had* loved her, he assured himself, but the painful truth was that he hadn't loved her enough. He had known he was the centre of her world, but, much as it shamed him to admit it, she hadn't been his.

His business, the pursuit of wealth and success, had been his mistress. He had not been unfaithful to his wife, as Ella's father had been to her mother, but could he really say he had been a better husband than Earl Stafford when he had not spent enough time with Irina and Klara?

'The reason he didn't love her was because he was selfish and only cared about his own interests,' Ella said bitterly.

Her words echoed in Vadim's head and his guilt choked him.

Ella shivered. 'I never want to be like my mother and fall in love with someone so desperately that I lose my pride and self-worth. Loving my father didn't make Mama happy, and ultimately I believe it destroyed her. No man is worth that,' she stated fiercely.

As she spoke, lightning zig-zagged across the sky and the crash of accompanying thunder was so loud that she screamed and dropped the glass of water she had just picked up. It smashed on impact with the tiled floor, but as she jumped out of her chair and bent to collect the shards Vadim strode around the table and pulled her to her feet. The room was plunged into darkness as the wall-lamps went out; the candles continued to flicker bravely for a few seconds before a gust of wind whipped through the open doors and snuffed out the flames.

'It must be a power cut. Wait there while I find a torch.'

He was back within seconds, shining the torchlight in front of him as he took Ella's hand and guided her over the broken glass. 'I'll clear it up later, when the power's restored.'

The storm was directly overhead now, and thunder boomed like pagan drums while the darkness was rent apart periodically by flashes of lightning. Vadim could feel the tremors running through Ella as he led her over to the French doors and turned her so that she was looking out over the garden. 'The power of the elements is awesome, but you are safe from the storm here with me,' he murmured, sliding his arms around her waist and drawing her close, so that her back was pressed up against his chest.

From the storm outside, perhaps, Ella thought shakily. But her instincts screamed that she was not safe from Vadim—or herself. The storm raging inside her was equally violent as the tumult in the skies above, and the pressure of Vadim's hard thighs pushing against her bottom evoked a burning heat in her pelvis. She could feel the erratic beat of his heart, and it seemed to pulse through her own veins as the drumbeat of desire thudding through her built to a crescendo.

He was a man like her father, warned a voice in her head, a heartless playboy who used women and discarded them when he had tired of them. But she could no longer deny the sexual chemistry that had simmered between them since the night they had met in Paris and was now at combustion point.

There was no danger she would fall in love with him, she assured herself, desire shivering through her when he pushed her hair aside and trailed his lips up her neck to the sensitive spot beneath her ear. She would never repeat the mistake her mother had made. The hard ridge of his arousal nudging insistently between the cleft of her buttocks was irrefutable proof of his hunger for her, and at this moment, as the storm crashed and trembled around them, her whole being quivered with the need for him to assuage the longing inside her that was as old and insistent as mankind.

CHAPTER SEVEN

HE NEEDED a woman tonight. Correction—he needed *this* woman, Vadim acknowledged as he turned Ella to face him and stared at the tremulous softness of her lips. He did not want to dwell on the past, and he had learned that the future was never assured. For him, the here and now was all that mattered, and at this moment the urge to make love to Ella burned like a fever in his blood. He slid his hand beneath her hair, the feel of the soft silky strands against his skin causing a sharp stab of desire in his gut, and with a muttered oath he cupped her nape and brought his mouth down on hers.

A lightning flare lit up the room and threw the sharp angles and planes of Vadim's face into stark relief. He seemed so remote and forbidding that for a second Ella felt a surge of fear, but the first brush of his mouth and the bold thrust of his tongue between her lips obliterated any lingering doubts that this was where she wanted to be. Desire licked through her veins like wildfire, heating her blood and making every nerve-ending so exquisitely sensitive that she moaned when he cupped her breast in his palm and stroked his thumbpad over the taut nipple straining beneath her silk dress.

He deepened the kiss, taking it to another level that was flagrantly erotic, and she melted against him and wound her arms around his neck, her eyes flying open when she felt the floor suddenly disappear from beneath her feet.

'Guide me,' he commanded roughly as he scooped her into his arms, collected the torch from the table and handed it to her.

'Where are we going?' she asked shakily.

'Bed.'

His desire for Ella had spiralled out of control, Vadim acknowledged grimly. Last night he had listened to the voice of his conscience, but tonight he could not resist her. Perhaps it was the pagan power of the storm, or perhaps it was her revelations about how her father had terrified her as a child that had induced this primal feeling to protect her and claim her as his woman. All he knew was that tonight he was driven by an instinct as old as mankind to make love to her.

The hungry gleam in Vadim's eyes caused Ella's heart to skitter in her chest. 'If you object, now is the time to say so,' he warned her as he strode out of the room and across the hall to the stairs.

Her brain told her she should demand that he set her on her feet, bid him goodnight and return to her part of the house—but her body ached with a need that decimated her thought processes and robbed her of words. Talking about her childhood had reminded her of how much she had hated her father, but she was no longer a child, and she was shocked to realise how much she had allowed her feelings about Earl Stafford to affect her adult life. He was the reason she was terrified of falling in love, the reason she had always frozen off any man who had shown an interest in her, and why she was still a virgin. But she was damned if she would allow her hatred of her father to dictate her actions any more, she thought fiercely. She was an independent woman who was capable of making her own choices, and tonight she chose to have her first sexual experience with Vadim.

But despite her brave avowal her heart thudded unevenly as he climbed the stairs. The torchlight flickered over the pale walls of the upper landing and the artwork she had chosen. She knew every inch of Kingfisher House and had decorated every room—including the master bedroom, with its huge bed covered in a navy satin bedspread that matched the colour of the carpet and complemented the ivory silk wallpaper.

The doors leading to the balcony were open, the sounds of the storm outside clearly audible, but Ella was conscious of nothing but Vadim when he lowered her onto the bed and immediately stretched out next to her. The only source of light in the room was the glow from the torch, casting shadows on the ceiling, but he found her mouth with unerring precision and covered it with his own, moving his lips on hers with feverish need and demanding a response she was powerless to deny.

Above the angry growls of thunder she could hear the ragged sound of her breathing. Her heart was pounding as her whole body was gripped with a need she could barely comprehend. The ache deep in her pelvis had become a relentless throbbing that caused her to arch her hips in a desperate invitation for Vadim to touch her and caress her…

When he finally broke the kiss and lifted his head to stare down at her she traced her tongue over her swollen lips. One kiss was not enough, she wanted more, and she slid her fingers into his thick black hair to urge him down on her. But instead of claiming her mouth he trailed his lips down her throat, to the pulse beating frenetically at its base.

'Your skin feels like satin,' he growled, his voice rough with desire. He began to unfasten the buttons that ran down the front of her dress, and Ella caught her breath when he pushed the silvery-grey silk aside to expose her high, firm breasts. 'Beautiful,' he muttered rawly. He cupped the twin mounds in his palms and revelled in their softness before he lowered his head and flicked his tongue across one nipple, so that it instantly swelled and hardened. The sensation was so exquisite that Ella could not restrain her startled cry of pleasure. No man had ever touched her as Vadim was doing, and when he transferred his attention to her other breast and drew the sensitive peak fully into his mouth she trembled with reaction.

He gave a ragged laugh when she gripped his hair and held his head against her breast, desperate for him to continue the erotic caress. 'Do you like that? I knew that beneath the ice-maiden act I'd find a sensual sex kitten,' he murmured, unable to disguise his satisfaction. Her open enjoyment of his mouth on her breasts was a massive turn-on, but it put paid to his plan for a leisurely seduction, Vadim acknowledged self-derisively. His arousal was rock-hard, and throbbing with impatience for him to spread her beneath him and plunge between her pale thighs. He had wanted her from the moment he'd laid eyes on her, but she had made him wait. It wasn't surprising that his body was taut with desire—a desire that grew more urgent when he dragged her dress over her hips to reveal her pale, slender body; naked but for the pair of grey lace knickers that hid her femininity from his gaze.

He felt the tremor that ran through her when he traced his lips down over her flat stomach and dipped his tongue into the delicate recess of her navel. He wanted to take his time exploring each delightful dip and curve, but his feverish need was clamouring to be assuaged and he continued lower, hooking his fingers in the waistband of her knickers and tugging them down her legs with one deft movement.

Ella felt a moment's panic when Vadim stared down at her body. It was the first time any man had seen her naked, and while the heat in his brilliant blue gaze was flattering, his un-disguised hunger sent a frisson of apprehension through her. She was about to give her virginity to this enigmatic, brooding man who was almost a stranger to her. Suddenly she was beset by doubts, and tensed when he slipped his hand between her legs.

Ella's neat triangle of pale blonde curls was silky soft against Vadim's fingers, and the delicate scent of her arousal inflamed his senses so that he barely registered that she had stiffened. Driven by a primitive, powerful urge, he eased her thighs apart and ran his finger lightly up and down the lips of her vagina until they swelled and slowly opened, like the petals of a flower unfolding, to reveal her moist, damp heat.

Ella gasped when she felt Vadim probe the slick wetness between her legs and her fear faded. Lost in the world of sensory pleasure he had evoked, she was beyond conscious thought, her whole being focused intently on each new sensation that he created with his wickedly inventive hands. The feather-light brush of his thumbpad across her ultra-sensitive clitoris made her cry out, her breath coming in sharp little gasps when he gently parted her and slid his finger deep into her welcoming heat.

'Please…' She did not know what she was pleading for, only that his erotic exploration with one finger, and then two, easing into her and caressing her with skilful precision, was creating a raging tumult inside her that was rapidly spiralling out of control.

Abruptly Vadim ended the mind-blowing foreplay and muttered something in Russian as he sprang up from the bed. 'I can't wait either,' he admitted harshly. She had tormented his dreams for too many nights, and the sight of her pale beauty, her hair falling in silky disarray over her shoulders, brushing against her small breasts with their swollen, dusky nipples, drove everything from his mind but his desperation to take her hard and fast and reach the sexual nirvana that he knew instinctively he would find with her.

He shrugged out of his clothes with urgent movements that lacked his usual grace, his gaze locked with Ella's as he stripped. His shirt fell carelessly to the floor, swiftly followed by his trousers. Satisfaction and a heightened sense of anticipation surged through him when he stepped out of his boxers and heard her sharply indrawn breath as she stared with flattering fascination at the jutting length of his arousal.

The only naked male body Ella had ever seen had been sculpted from marble and standing in an art gallery. Vadim's body was more beautiful than any sculpture, she thought, her mouth suddenly dry as her eyes moved over his broad chest, gleaming like polished bronze in the torchlight and overlaid with a covering of wiry black hair that arrowed down over his flat stomach. Heart pounding, she dropped her gaze lower still and felt a jolt of shock when she absorbed the awesome strength of his erection. He was all hard, muscular male, and as he walked purposefully back to the bed she tensed. What was she *doing*? the voice of doubt in her head demanded. She knew of Vadim's reputation as a playboy—she must have been mad to have allowed things to get this far.

'Are you going to live like a nun for the rest of your life?' Jenny's words taunted her. No, she denied fiercely, she did not want to remain a virgin for ever. Nor was she saving her virginity for when she fell in love. Love was an illusion. But the instant she had seen Vadim across a crowded room in Paris she had fallen in lust, and at twenty-four it was high time she discarded her innocence.

Vadim knelt on the bed, leaned over Ella and captured her lips in a hard, hungry kiss, sliding his tongue into her mouth in an erotic mimicry of how he would soon drive his throbbing shaft into the welcoming slick heat of her femininity. Next time he would take the leisurely route and taste her honeyed sweetness with his mouth, maybe tease the tight nub of her clitoris with his tongue until he brought her to the edge of ecstasy. He would encourage her to touch him too. But right now just the thought of her slender fingers encircling him intensified his arousal, so that he feared he was about to explode with the hot, pulsing need that made his entire body shake.

He broke the kiss briefly to reach into the bedside drawer, and donned protection with swift efficiency before he positioned himself over her and nudged her thighs apart. The faint wariness in her eyes made him pause for a second, but his blood was pounding through his veins, his desire for her an unstoppable force, urging him to surge forward. He slid his hands beneath her bottom, lifted her hips and entered her with one powerful thrust—and instantly stilled when he felt the tear of a fragile membrane and heard her shocked cry of pain.

For a few seconds he stared at her in stunned incomprehension which swiftly turned to anger as his brain accepted the indisputable truth. 'Your first time?' he demanded harshly. He swore savagely in Russian. 'What the devil are you playing at, Ella?'

'I'm not playing at anything,' she denied falteringly, shaken by his reaction. Perhaps naïvely, she had not expected her initiation into sex to be quite so uncomfortable. When Vadim had penetrated her untutored body she had felt a sharp, stinging pain, but already it was fading, and the restless ache in her pelvis was once more clamouring to be assuaged. She could not hide her confusion when he abruptly withdrew from her, and she tentatively placed her hand on his arm, thinking that he was angry with himself for hurting her. 'Vadim, it's all right…'

'The hell it is,' he bit out savagely. His facial muscles were so taut that he looked as though he had been carved from granite, and Ella's stomach dipped as she realised that he wasn't angry with himself, but with her. 'If I'd had any idea you were a virgin I would never have taken you to bed.'

He closed his eyes and in his mind he saw Irina. He had been her first lover, and making love to her on their wedding night had been a special experience for both of them. With Ella it was simply sex. But he was aware that her first time should have been special, with someone who cared for her, and he felt guilty that he had unwittingly stolen her virginity. She had chosen to sleep with him, he reminded himself. But he hoped she did not think his emotions were involved, because she meant nothing to him.

The heated passion in Ella's veins quickly cooled, leaving her feeling shivery, and sick with mortification. There was no hint of the hungry desire that had blazed in Vadim's eyes when he had carried her up to his bedroom, and she felt stupid and embarrassed that she hadn't warned him of her inexperience.

He rolled away from her and swung his legs over the side of the bed, raking his hand through his dark hair as he struggled to control his simmering frustration. From the moment they had first met the chemistry between them had been explosive, and her passionate response to his kisses had given no indication that she had never had a lover. He turned his head to stare at her slender body, her skin milky-pale against the blue silk bedspread and her small, pert breasts pouting at him, tempting him to close his mouth around her nipples and feel them harden against his tongue. Desire clawed in his gut but he forced himself to ignore it.

'Why did you do it?' he asked coldly.

Ella bit her lip. 'I…I didn't think it would matter. The fact that it's my first time means nothing to me.' She quickly looked away from him, stunned by the realisation that she had lied and that she had wanted him to be her first lover. She barely knew him, she thought despairingly, and this feeling that he was the other half of her soul was utterly ridiculous.

'Really?' He gave a sardonic laugh. 'Are you sure you did not think that I would somehow be honoured that you had given your virginity to me? Because if you did, I'm afraid I must disappoint you. I don't want a sacrificial lamb in my bed,' he continued harshly, ignoring her swiftly indrawn breath. 'I only bed experienced, sexually confident women, and I have neither the time nor the patience to tutor a naïve girl—especially when there is the added danger that you might fall in love with me.'

'My God—you arrogant *jerk*!' Trembling with humiliated rage, Ella sat bolt-upright, the violent movement causing her breasts to bounce provocatively, so that she quickly dragged the silk coverlet over them, her cheeks burning. 'I would never fall in love with you—' She broke off, blinking dazedly when his face was suddenly illuminated. For a second she could not understand what had happened, but then she realised that the power had been restored and the timer on the bedside lamps had been activated. The room seemed painfully bright after the dark, and the furious expression on Vadim's face made her want to weep with shame.

From outside came the sound of rain—big, heavy drops, falling slowly at first as the stormclouds broke. A gust of wind whipped in from the balcony and tugged at the curtains, and with a muttered oath Vadim got up and strode across the room to close the doors. Ella stared at the masculine beauty of his naked body, trailing her eyes over his wide shoulders and then down to his waist, hips, and finally his buttocks and long, muscular legs. Minutes ago he had lowered himself onto her and pushed her legs apart with one hair-roughened thigh, and the stark memory fanned the flames of the hot, pulsing need inside her that refused to die.

What was she going to do—beg him to take her? she asked herself raggedly. Her self-respect was in shreds, and the realisation that her body still ached for his possession, even after his scathing comments that he did not want to bed a virgin, filled her with panic. His rejection hurt, she acknowledged miserably. But she would rather die than let him see it. She had to get away from him. He had closed the doors to the balcony and was drawing the curtains across them. Any second now he would turn around… Frantically she snatched up her dress and dragged it over her head. There was no time to gather her shoes or knickers; she simply fled out of the door and down the stairs, not pausing when she heard him call her name.

The door to her part of the house was locked. She rattled the handle in frustration, remembering how she had bolted it earlier in the day, when she had discovered that Vadim was the new tenant of Kingfisher House. She heard his footsteps on the landing above and raced through the dining room and out onto the terrace. The rain was falling so hard that it stung her skin, but instead of running along the terrace to the French doors leading to her flat, she turned and sped across the lawn, desperate to put as much space between her and her tormentor as possible.

The lights from the house spilled halfway down the garden, but the decked patio beside the river was in darkness, broken only occasionally when the scudding clouds parted to allow the moon to glimmer across the water. Ella stared down at the swirling river while the rain lashed her and mingled with the angry tears streaming down her face. First thing tomorrow she would phone Jenny and ask if she could stay with her until she found somewhere to live—because she would rather die than have to face Vadim ever again.

'What are you doing out here? The rain's like a god-damned monsoon.'

His angry voice sounded behind her, and she spun round, lost her balance and almost fell into the fast-flowing river.

Uttering a curse that singed her ears, Vadim sprang forward and snatched her into his arms. 'Watch your step. You could be swept away, you little fool.'

Fury replaced the fear that had surged through him when he had seen her standing so close to the water's edge. For a second he had thought she would fall, and he knew he would have had little chance of dragging her from the swirling current before she was swept away. He could not stand another death on his conscience.

When he had first realised that Ella had run from the bedroom he'd had no intention of following her. She hadn't been honest with him, and he'd felt angry that he had been tricked into a situation he would never have chosen. He did not want the responsibility of being her first lover. But he had been tormented by the expression on her face when he had rejected her. The flash of hurt in her eyes had been uncannily similar to the look on Irina's face during one of their many arguments about how he spent too much time at work rather than with her.

Ella should have told him she was a virgin, but the knowledge that he had been unnecessarily cruel had seen him drag on his trousers and chase after her. Now, as he stared down at her rain-drenched form and felt the violent shivers that ripped through her, an indefinable feeling tugged in his chest.

Vadim's scathing tone was the last straw, and the fact that he still looked gorgeous, even when his hair was plastered to his head, the rain running in streams down his bare chest and moulding his trousers to his thighs, set fire to Ella's temper.

'I must be a fool to have had anything to do with you,' she yelled as she fought free of his hold. The memory of how he had rejected her burned like acid in her gut, and in an agony of embarrassment she lashed out at him, beating her hands against his chest until he caught both her wrists in his vice-like grip.

'Be still, you little wildcat,' he ordered harshly, snaking his other arm around her waist to haul her away from the river's edge. He was breathing hard, his nostrils flaring as he fought the urge to claim her mouth and kiss her into submission. Ella shook her head, so that her wet hair whipped across his face, and she gave a cry of frustration when she failed to free her wrists from his grasp. The driving rain had soaked through her dress so that the grey silk moulded her body like a second skin, and as she squirmed furiously against him the feel of her pebble-hard nipples dragging against his chest drove Vadim to the edge of sexual insanity.

'*Let go of me.*' Ella had to shout above the sound of the rain beating against the wooden decking, but she had spent so much of her life keeping quiet, keeping her mouth shut so as not to annoy her father, that shouting was a revelation which restored a little of her pride. She was no longer a scared little shadow, flitting about Stafford Hall, she thought as she lifted her head and glared at Vadim. She was a grown woman, and she was hurt and humiliated and as angry as hell. 'Just so you know—there's not the slightest chance I would *ever* fall in love with you,' she flung at him. 'I didn't choose you to be my first lover because I harboured some stupid idea that emotions would be involved. I *know* what kind of a man you are. You're a notorious playboy, and I would never make the mistake that your last girlfriend, Kelly Adams, made, by hoping to touch your heart, because I'm well aware that you don't have one.'

'Is that so?' he gritted, hauling her so hard against him that their bodies were welded together while the rain continued to hammer down on them. He'd had a heart once, he recalled bitterly, anger surging through him at Ella's accusation that he was an immoral womaniser, intent only on seeking his own pleasure. She had no idea that his heart had been torn apart. The pain of losing his wife and daughter had been unbearable, and he had vowed never to lay himself open to such agony ever again.

'The only reason I decided to sleep with you was because you push all the right buttons,' Ella continued wildly. 'You were right when you said the sexual chemistry between us blazed from the moment we met, and all I ever wanted from you tonight was your sexual expertise.'

She knew a moment's triumph when Vadim released her wrists, but seconds later she gasped when he lifted her off the ground and held her so tightly against him that she could feel the rock-solid length of his arousal pushing against her pelvis.

'Well, if that's really all you want, who am I to deny you, angel face?' he drawled mockingly.

'Put me down. I mean it, Vadim.' Panic sharpened her voice when he ignored her plea and strode across the decking towards the summerhouse. 'I'm tired of playing games.' Once again she tried to fight her way out of his arms, but he was too strong for her. He carried her as easily as if she were a rag-doll, and as the warmth of his body seeped into her, and his heart slammed in time with her own, the fight drained out of her. Desire flowed like molten lava through her veins as she clung to his shoulders and wrapped her legs around his thighs, so that with each step he took the jutting hardness of his erection strained against his trousers and nudged insistently between her legs.

'You're right; the time for games is over,' he growled as he shouldered the door of the summerhouse, stepped inside and immediately bent his head to capture her mouth in a devastatingly sensual kiss that drove the breath from Ella's body.

It was a statement of possession and a warning of intent, his tongue thrusting between her lips with such erotic skill that resistance was impossible. But her pride demanded that she should try. 'I thought you said you don't bed virgins?' she reminded him savagely, when he finally lifted his lips from hers.

'I'm prepared to make an exception for you.' His wicked smile revealed his white teeth and reminded her of a wolf about to devour its prey. The summerhouse was dark, but his eyes gleamed with a fierce determination as he dragged the cushions from the garden chairs, spread them on the floor and lowered her onto them.

She should push him away, Ella thought desperately. But her hands seemed to be drawn of their own volition to the muscular strength of his chest, and she brushed her fingertips through the dark whorls of hair that covered his satiny skin. Earlier he had aroused her body to the very edge of fulfilment, and the abrupt halt to their lovemaking had left her aching with a need that only he could appease.

The combination of slippery wet silk and tiny buttons running down the front of her dress tested Vadim's patience to its limits—until with a muttered oath he gripped the fragile material and ripped it to the waist, exposing her naked breasts to his hungry gaze. She was shivering with cold and intense excitement, and the first hard strokes of his tongue lashing one nipple and then the other made her cry out and arch her back, so that he drew one tight nub fully into his mouth and sucked until the pleasure was almost unendurable.

The fire inside her was burning out of control, his earlier rejection and the scalding humiliation she had felt when she had fled from him forgotten in the maelstrom of sensations he was inciting with his hands and mouth. Her heart slammed beneath her ribs when he dragged the hem of her dress up so that it bunched around her waist, but she made no attempt to stop him when he pushed her legs apart and slid his finger into her slick wetness. Her heightened state of arousal from his earlier caresses had not faded and she was instantly ready for him. But, although he was more turned on than he had ever been in his life, Vadim was determined not to rush her. She had taunted him that the reason she had chosen him as her first lover was for his sexual expertise, and he was not going to disappoint her.

Ella gave a moan of protest when Vadim lifted his mouth from her breast, and then gasped when he moved down her body and she felt his warm breath against her thigh.

'No…' Utterly shocked by the first brush of his tongue against her swollen vaginal lips, she instinctively tried to bring her legs together, but he held them firmly apart and continued the intimate caress with a ruthless efficiency that brought her to the very edge of sexual ecstasy.

By the time he lifted his head she was mindless with desire, and when his hand moved to his waist she sat up and helped him drag his wet trousers over his hips. The throbbing length of his erection filled her hands and she stroked him tentatively—until he groaned and pushed her onto her back.

'It has to be now, angel,' he muttered, drawing on all his formidable willpower to slow the pace and rub his swollen shaft gently against her, until she opened and he entered her with one slow, careful thrust.

There was no pain this time. Just an incredible feeling of fullness as Vadim slid deeper and then withdrew almost completely. For a split second Ella was terrified that he was going to leave her again, and she dug her fingers into his shoulders to anchor her to him. His rough laugh told her he understood her fear, and he surged forward and drew back, sliding deeper with each thrust as he taught her the age-old rhythm that took her higher and higher, until she felt as though she were teetering on the edge of some dark and mysterious place, trembling with desperation to discover its secrets.

He slid his hand beneath her bottom and tilted her hips, and each powerful thrust suddenly became even more intense. 'Vadim!' She cried his name and clung to him, almost afraid of the cataclysmic explosion of pleasure that ripped through her as she experienced her first orgasm. It was awesome and utterly indescribable. Nothing had prepared her for the exquisite spasms that radiated out from her central core and enveloped her entire body in a feeling of complete ecstasy. And as she arched beneath him and sobbed his name she heard the low groan that seemed to be torn from his throat and felt him tense, poised above her, his blue eyes locked with hers for timeless seconds, before he gave one final, savage thrust and threw his head back, his face a taut mask and his big body shuddering with the force of his climax.

The sound of the rain beating down on the summerhouse slowly impinged on Vadim's brain and dragged him reluctantly from his deeply relaxed state. It felt good lying here, cocooned in the soft darkness and shielded from the wild elements outside. His body was still joined with Ella's—and that felt more than good, he acknowledged ruefully. It felt amazing. The tight sheath of her vaginal muscles held him in a velvet embrace, and already he could feel himself hardening again. But he should not have made love to her without protection even once, and it would be criminally irresponsible to compound the mistake.

Ignoring the tug of regret in his gut, he withdrew from her and rolled onto his side. The rain was easing, and in the silver moonlight glimmering through the window she looked pale and ethereal, with her wet hair streaming around her shoulders. But the stunned expression in her eyes made him grimace. He had not planned to make love to her. The discovery of her innocence had put her off-limits as far as he was concerned, and his sole intention when he had chased after her was to ensure her safety. But from the second he had pulled her into his arms, away from the edge of the swirling river, and held her trembling body against him, he had been lost. No woman had ever got to him the way Ella did, nor aroused him to the point that his usual cool logic was replaced with mindless, fevered desire. Even the knowledge that she was a virgin had no longer mattered, he thought grimly. Driven by his desperate hunger for her, he had followed the dictates of his body rather than his brain as passion had overwhelmed him. But now guilt tore at him.

'Did I hurt you?' he asked roughly.

Ella's eyes flew to Vadim's face. 'No,' she said truthfully. There had been no pain this time, just a wondrous feeling of fullness as he had joined his body with hers. 'You ruined my dress, though,' she added, blushing as she dragged the grey silk across her breasts and discovered that every button was missing.

His slow smile stole her breath. 'I'll buy you a new one.' He stood up, held out his hand to help her to her feet, and then to her shock scooped her up into his arms.

'I can walk,' Ella protested as he stepped out of the summerhouse and strode up to the house, apparently unconcerned that he was stark naked. It was lucky that Kingfisher House was not overlooked by neighbours, she thought as she clung to his shoulders. Her heart lurched when he walked straight past the doors leading to her flat, on into the main house, where he climbed the stairs and carried her through the master bedroom to the *en suite* bathroom.

'I should go back to my room,' she murmured when he set her on her feet and slid her torn dress over her shoulders. The walk back to the house through the rain had cooled her skin, and shock at her wanton behaviour in the summerhouse was setting in, so that she felt a ridiculous urge to cry. In those moments when Vadim had taken her to the very pinnacle of pleasure she had felt as though their hearts had become one. But of course it was an illusion—because if Vadim had a heart he kept it under lock and key, and she would never be so foolish as to fall for a playboy who viewed women as a means of entertainment. 'I'm all in,' she whispered as her dress slithered to the floor and his brilliant blue eyes blazed over her naked body.

'I know,' he said, and the unexpected gentleness in his voice tugged at Ella's heart. Her eyes were huge in her delicate face, and she looked achingly vulnerable. He should have taken her to her room and bade her goodnight. But for reasons he refused to decipher he'd wanted her with him. She was shivering with cold, and he lifted her and carried her into the shower. 'This will warm you up, and then you can sleep,' he promised, smiling at her shocked expression when he picked up the bar of soap and began to smooth it over her breasts.

By the time Vadim had soaped every inch of her body, shampooed her hair and held her against him while the spray rinsed them both, Ella was tingling all over, and his ministrations with a towel caused molten heat to surge through her veins. The feeling of being cared for was dangerously beguiling, she acknowledged when he carried her through to the bedroom, slid into bed beside her and drew the sheet around them. They'd had fantastic sex, but it meant nothing to either of them, she reminded herself firmly. But when he drew her into his arms, so that her head was resting on his chest, a feeling of utter contentment stole over her and she fell asleep, unaware that he remained awake watching her for long into the night.

CHAPTER EIGHT

ELLA was awoken by the gentle breeze which stirred the voile curtains. The doors were ajar, revealing a cloudless blue sky, but her eyes were drawn to Vadim, who was standing on the balcony, staring out over the garden. He was dressed in a superbly tailored suit and looked devastatingly handsome, but his stern profile made him seem so remote and forbidding that it was almost impossible to believe he was the same man who had woken her just before dawn and made passionate love to her.

Just thinking about how skilfully he had aroused her with his hands and mouth made her blush, and as he turned and stepped into the bedroom she was acutely conscious that she was naked beneath the silk sheet.

'What time is it?' she murmured, wishing she knew the protocol for greeting the man you'd spent the night having great sex with, but who seemed to have turned into a stranger in the cold light of day.

He flicked back the sleeve of his jacket and glanced at his watch. 'Just after eight.'

Ella gave a yelp as reality hit with a vengeance. 'I have to be at rehearsals at nine. Gustav blows a fuse if any of the orchestra members are late.' She jerked upright, the rosy colour in her cheeks deepening as she dislodged the sheet and Vadim's eyes immediately dropped to her bare breasts.

'Where are the rehearsals?'

'Cadogan Hall, near Sloane Square,' she mumbled as she snatched the sheet around her.

Vadim strolled over to the wall of wardrobes, opened a door and selected a robe from several that were hanging inside. 'Here,' he said, walking back to the bed and handing it to her. 'It'll probably swamp you. I'm afraid I don't have anything in your petite size.'

'Thank you.' Ella took the robe and glanced across at the others in the wardrobe, startled by the realisation that he kept bathrobes in a variety of sizes—presumably for the occasions when he invited a woman to spend the night with him. It was extremely thoughtful of him, she reminded herself, trying to ignore the heavy feeling in the pit of her stomach that she was just another blonde who was passing through his bedroom.

'My offices are not far from Cadogan Hall, so I can give you a lift. What time will you finish tonight?'

'The orchestra will finish late afternoon, but I have additional rehearsals for my solo performance coming up in Paris, and I don't suppose I'll get away until at least six o'clock.'

Vadim shrugged. 'Fine. I usually work until then. I'll meet you at six-thirty for dinner. Do you want to go on somewhere afterwards? I'll ask my secretary to arrange tickets if you'd like to see a show.'

Ella's gaze flew once more to the selection of bathrobes he kept for his lovers. 'I don't think so,' she said quietly. 'In fact I think it would be better if we kept last night as a one-off. I don't want to have an…an affair with you,' she faltered, flushing when his piercing blue gaze settled thoughtfully on her face. She had the unnerving feeling that he could read the jumble of emotions whirling around her head. 'Neither of us wants to be tied down in a relationship,' she reminded him, despising herself for the way her heart rate quickened when he dropped down onto the bed and wound a few strands of her hair around his fingers.

'I agree,' he said coolly. 'But surely the very fact that we have no desire for a relationship makes us ideal candidates for an affair? There's nothing to stop us being lovers for as long as either one of us wants it to last. And besides,' he murmured, his voice dropping to a deep, sensual tone that caressed her senses, 'one night was not enough for either of us—was it, Ella?'

She gasped when he pushed her flat on her back, but the sound was smothered by his mouth as his head swooped and he claimed her lips in a fierce, hungry kiss that left her in no doubt that one night had not satisfied his desire for her. Last night had not been enough for her either, she thought despairingly. He only had to touch her and molten heat flooded through her veins, and the hot, restless ache in her pelvis made a mockery of her decision to distance herself from him.

Agreeing to an affair with him would only be dangerous if she allowed her emotions to become involved—but she would never do that, she assured herself. She knew what kind of a man he was, and that knowledge made her safe from him—so why not enjoy his sexual expertise? whispered the reckless voice in her head.

When he pushed the sheet down and bent his head to take one dusky pink nipple into his mouth she could not restrain a soft moan, and she arched her back in mute invitation, sliding her hands into his silky black hair to hold him to the task of pleasuring her.

Vadim was tempted, desire corkscrewing through him when he kissed Ella again and felt the tentative foray of her tongue into his mouth. For the first time in his life he was actually contemplating putting pleasure before business. As head of his company, he answered to no one. He could spend all morning making love to Ella and turn up at his office at lunchtime if he pleased. But the realisation that she could exert some sort of hold over him brought his brows together in a slashing frown. No woman had ever caused him to change the way he ran his life. The company he had created from nothing was the most important thing in his life, and women were merely an entertaining distraction from his hectic work schedule—even this woman, he reminded himself fiercely.

Even so, it took all of his formidable willpower to ease the pressure of his lips from the moist softness of hers, and regret tugged in his gut when he lifted his head and sat up. 'Forget going to the theatre; we'll follow dinner with an early night,' he drawled, his mouth curving into an amused smile when colour flared in her cheeks. He watched the confusion in her eyes slowly turn to frustration when she realised that the foreplay was not going to end with another mind-blowing sex session, and he felt a pang of sympathy that, like him, she was going to spend the day in a state of aching arousal. 'But right now you have twenty minutes to get ready, or you'll miss your lift,' he informed her, ignoring her yelp of protest as he flicked back the sheet.

Ella hastily thrust her arms into the robe. 'You think you're God's gift, don't you?' she snapped, incensed by his arrogance, and furious with herself for her shaming inability to resist him. She marched over to the door, but his mocking laughter followed her into the hallway.

'I know I'm the only man who turns you on, angel face. And, more to the point, you know it too,' he said softly.

* * *

Vadim's taunt stayed with Ella all day, and for first time in her life she was unable to concentrate on her music—much to the wrath of the RLO's conductor, Gustav, who expected perfection at all times.

'Are you okay?' Jenny asked her during a much-needed break. 'You look pale.'

'I didn't get much sleep last night,' Ella muttered, and then blushed scarlet at the memory of her energetic night with Vadim. Fortunately Jenny seemed not to notice.

'The storm was awful, wasn't it? Why don't you tell Gustav you're feeling unwell and need to go home?'

'No, I can't do that.' Ella shook her head. 'I'd never let the orchestra down, and anyway I need to practise for my solo concert. It's only two weeks away, and I'm already nervous.'

By sheer effort of will she managed to get through the rest of the rehearsal without incurring more of Gustav's sarcasm, but she was dismayed that Vadim had the power to affect the part of her life that she held sacrosanct. Music meant everything to her, and she could not contemplate an affair with him if it would be detrimental to her career. But when she walked out of Cadogan Hall and saw him leaning against his gunmetal grey Aston Martin, the painful jerk of her heart beneath her ribs made a mockery of her determination to play it cool with him.

'Hi,' she greeted him, striving to sound nonchalant.

The amused gleam in his eyes told her he was aware of her internal struggle. He moved with the grace of a big cat, slid his hand beneath her chin and claimed her mouth in a slow, drugging kiss that drove every thought from her mind other than the hot, pulsing need that had been simmering inside her all day. 'How did rehearsals go?'

'Badly,' she muttered tersely, resenting the way one kiss weakened her so that she had to cling to him for support.

His sensual smile stole her breath. 'My day wasn't great either,' he admitted, frowning when he recalled how memories of making love to Ella had interrupted his usually razor-sharp thought processes throughout the day. 'Perhaps we were both distracted by the same fantasies.'

'I don't know what you mean,' she said stiffly.

Vadim laughed and drew her so close against him that she could feel the tantalising hardness of his arousal nudge between her thighs. 'I'll tell you mine, and then you can tell me if yours were the same,' he drawled, and proceeded to whisper the shockingly erotic daydreams that had plagued him, even during an important board meeting, so that Ella's face was scarlet by the time he'd finished.

'Were your thoughts along the same lines?' he queried, his amused smile changing to an expression of sensual hunger when he felt the shiver of desire that ran through her. Ella couldn't answer, her mind still filled with the image of him making love to her across his desk, and with a muttered oath he opened the car door and bundled her inside. 'We'll eat at a little Italian restaurant I know. The food's excellent and, more importantly, the service is quick,' he growled, the sultry gleam in his eyes leaving Ella in no doubt that dinner would be followed by the early night he had promised that morning.

The food at the Trattoria Luciano was as good as Vadim had promised, but Ella barely tasted her chicken *cacciatore*, and, despite having only eaten a couple of apples at lunchtime, her appetite had deserted her. Throughout the meal she could not tear her eyes from Vadim, and although he did better justice to his *lasagne al forno* he did not finish it, and gulped

down his glass of red wine before he took her hand and practically dragged her from the restaurant.

He did not say a word on the drive back to Kingfisher
House, his tension so tangible that Ella began to think that she
had annoyed him in some way. But no sooner had she stepped
out of the Aston Martin than he swept her into his arms and
strode purposefully into the house.

'You have been on my mind all day,' he admitted harshly
as he took the stairs two at a time, shouldered open the door
to the bedroom and dropped her onto the bed.

He came down on top of her and captured her mouth in a
searing kiss that sent liquid heat flooding through her veins.
She was on fire for him instantly, and when she tugged at his
shirt buttons and ran her hands over the crisp dark hairs that
covered his chest she knew from the erratic thud of his heart
that he shared her desperation to experience the tumultuous
passion they had shared the previous night.

Her clothes, his, were a barrier he swiftly removed, and he
paused only to don protection before he pushed her legs apart
and found the moist heat of her femininity with unerring fingers.

'Did you think about me today, Ella?' he growled against
her skin, before he closed his lips around the taut peak of her
nipple and suckled her until she gasped with pleasure. 'Did
you think about this?'

'This' was him sliding one finger and then two deep inside
her, and caressing her until she hovered on the edge of ecstasy.
'Yes,' she groaned, knowing that it was pointless to deny it
when he could feel the slick wetness of her arousal. During
rehearsals she had struggled to concentrate on playing her
violin because her mind had insisted on reliving every glorious moment of his lovemaking the previous night. Nothing
had ever come between her and her music, and she was dis-

mayed by the level of her fascination with Vadim, but right now nothing mattered except that he should possess her.

'Please…' She gripped his silky dark hair when he lowered his head to her other breast and flicked his tongue across its dusky crest. She hadn't known that she was capable of this level of need, and she held her breath when he positioned himself over her and entered her with a hard, deep thrust that caused her vaginal muscles to convulse around him.

He was her man, and she belonged to him for all time. The words thundered in her head in time with the rhythm of his body as he drove into her again and again, and when he covered her mouth with his she responded to his kiss with an uncontrollable passion that blew his mind.

It couldn't last. His hunger for her was too intense for a leisurely seduction, and he increased his pace, thrusting deeper still and filling her so completely that she arched beneath him and cried out as pleasure crashed over her in a shattering orgasm. The feel of her internal muscles tightening around his shaft was too much for Vadim, and he fought briefly for control, lost it spectacularly, and felt a shudder run through his powerful body as it experienced the sexual release it craved.

Afterwards, when their breathing had finally slowed and he'd rolled off her, she kept her eyes tightly closed, feeling suddenly embarrassed at her wanton response to him.

His rough laughter grazed her skin. 'It's too late to be shy now, angel face. I knew the moment we met that you would be a wildcat in bed,' he added in a satisfied tone. It was the truth, Vadim mused as he swung his legs over the side of the bed and headed for the *en suite* bathroom. That night in Paris he had been shocked by his powerful attraction to Ella, and by the instinctive feeling that they were destined to be lovers. But the idea that she was his woman and his alone was a dangerous one.

He did not want a relationship with her, he reminded himself. Undoubtedly his desire for her would soon pall, and then he would walk away from her—just as he had done with his many previous mistresses. There was no place in his heart for Ella, only in his bed, and the fact that her soft grey eyes and shy smile tugged at his insides was all the more reason to remember the vow he had made after Irina had died, that he would never allow any woman to touch his emotions again.

When Vadim emerged from the bathroom Ella assumed he would rejoin her in bed, but to her disappointment he crossed to the wardrobe, took out jeans and a shirt and proceeded to dress. 'I have to work for a couple of hours,' he explained when he caught her confused expression. 'Why don't you catch up on some sleep? I'll be up later.'

His sensual smile made her heart leap, but she sensed that he had distanced himself from her—or perhaps she had imagined the feeling of closeness between them when he had made love to her? she thought bleakly. What had happened between his walking into the bathroom and returning to the bedroom that had caused him to close up, so that he was once again a brooding stranger? She wished she knew what was going on behind his brilliant blue gaze, but his face was a handsome mask, giving no clue to his thoughts.

Vadim could not have made it clearer that he saw her as his mistress and nothing more. Pride dictated that she should go back to her own flat rather than meekly wait until he wanted to have sex with her again, but he had kept her awake for much of the previous night, and his energetic lovemaking of a few minutes ago had left her exhausted. Her eyelids felt heavy, and within moments she fell into such a deep sleep that she was unaware that Vadim returned to the bedroom less than an hour later and stood by the bed, watching her sleep.

* * *

Ella was awoken in the early hours of Saturday morning by Vadim stroking his hands down her body and gently parting her thighs. Any thoughts she might have had of resisting him crumbled, as they had all week, when she saw the sultry gleam in his eyes, and with a sigh she arched her hips to welcome him into her and gave herself up to the exquisite pleasure of his lovemaking.

They spent most of the weekend in bed, or down by the river, where he made love to her beneath the weeping willow tree whose fragile branches and delicate green leaves provided a private bower. She ached in places she had not known existed, Ella thought ruefully when she woke early on Monday morning and watched the rose-pink glow of dawn spread across the sky. Later today she was flying to Paris to prepare for her solo concert, and she assured herself that the heavy feeling in her stomach was due to nerves about her performance—not because she would be away from Vadim for the next week.

Her planned programme contained several exceptionally complex pieces, particularly the compositions by Paganini, and although she had received intensive coaching from the famous Hungarian violinist Joseph Schranz, she still did not feel confident about the performance. Sleep was impossible when her mind kept running through the pieces, and although it was not yet five a.m. she was desperate to practise. She threw back the sheet, collected her violin from where—much to Vadim's amusement—she kept it beside the bed, and slipped out onto the balcony, closing the door carefully behind her so that she would not disturb him. The morning air was cool and fresh, and the feel of the smooth wood of her violin beneath her fingertips filled Ella with fierce joy. Music meant everything to her, and she was soon lost in her own world, so that when the balcony doors opened she stared at Vadim in confusion.

'Do have any idea what the time is?' he queried mildly, aware of the familiar pull of desire in his groin as he took in her slender figure in the grey silk robe he had bought her because the colour had reminded him of the smoky hue of her eyes. Her pale gold hair streamed around her shoulders, and he could not resist reaching out and winding a long, silky strand around his fingers.

'Um…early,' she mumbled guiltily. 'I'm sorry I woke you, but the taxi's picking me up at eight to take me to the airport, and I wanted to run through the Paganini compositions one more time.'

His lips twitched. 'I suppose your artistic temperament is to blame for the fact that you've woken before dawn the last couple of days?' He'd felt her increased tension, and had watched her appetite fade to the point that she'd barely eaten a thing at dinner last night. 'Are you always this nervous before a performance?'

'I'm afraid so,' Ella admitted unhappily, embarrassed colour staining her cheeks. She hated the agonising stage fright that gripped her, and had tried various remedies, including hypnotherapy, to try and control it, but she still felt ill with nerves before she gave a solo performance.

'There's no need,' he said gently, surprised by the surge of protectiveness he felt for her. 'You have a phenomenal talent and you play superbly. And if you're leaving at eight, you need to come back to bed now,' he added deeply, drawing her against him and slipping his hand inside her robe to cup her breast in his palm.

'I should get dressed,' Ella murmured, catching her breath when he tugged on her nipple until it swelled and hardened.

But he ignored her token protest and scooped her into his arms, capturing her mouth in a hard, hungry kiss as he deposited her on the bed and parted her robe before he positioned himself over her. As he slipped his hand between her legs and gently parted her, his eyes locked with hers, and somehow his intense gaze heightened the intimacy of his caresses, so that she gasped and arched her hips in mute appeal for him to continue his erotic exploration.

'Please...' She clutched his shoulders to urge him down on her, and sighed her pleasure when he entered her with one deep thrust that filled her to the hilt. Nothing mattered but this. Music, her nervousness about the concert in Paris—everything faded as she surrendered totally to Vadim's mastery.

He was a skilled lover, who knew exactly how to drive her to the edge of ecstasy and keep her teetering there until she begged for the release her body craved while he remained in complete control. But this morning she sensed a difference in him, a new urgency in each powerful thrust as he took her with an almost primitive passion that sent them both swiftly to the heights. Ella could feel the delicious little spasms begin deep within her, and she wrapped her legs around his back to incite him to thrust harder, deeper...

'Vadim...' She could not hold back her desperate plea as the spasms became powerful ripples that radiated out from her central core and engulfed her in mind-blowing pleasure. Frantically she dug her nails into his sweat-sheened shoulders, and felt a surge of feminine triumph when he gave a harsh groan and exploded within her in a shattering climax that left his big body shuddering with after-shocks.

It was ridiculous to feel as though their souls as well as their bodies had joined as one, she told herself when he lay lax on top of her, so that she could feel the thud of his heart gradually return to its normal beat. It was just good sex. But when at last he rolled off her she longed for him to hold her in his arms, and the ache in her heart when he slid out of bed and strolled into the *en suite* bathroom served as a warning sign that she was getting in too deep.

What the hell had happened there? Vadim brooded as he stepped into the shower and began to soap his body. The sex had been good. It was always good with Ella—maybe the best he'd ever had, he admitted. But he'd never lost control like that before. The truth was her passionate response had blown him away, and the knowledge that they would be apart for the next week had·intensified his desire, so that it had overwhelmed him and resulted in that spectacular climax. There was no chance he was going to miss her while she was in Paris, he assured himself. They shared fantastic sex, but that was all he wanted from her. Maybe the week apart would lessen his desire for her, and he could end their affair and move on to another pretty blonde.

The Palais Garnier was arguably the most prestigious concert hall in Paris, and with an audience capacity of over two thousand it was the largest venue where Ella had ever given a solo performance.

'It's a full house,' her publicist, Marcus, announced when he bounded into her dressing room. 'Every ticket sold out. I knew we should have arranged for you to perform for two nights rather than just one.' He paused and stared at Ella. 'Heck, you're pale. I'd better call the make-up girl back to see if she can make you look less like a ghost. How do you feel?'

'Sick,' Ella replied truthfully. She bit her lip as panic surged through her. 'I don't think I can go through with it, Marcus.'

'Nonsense,' he told her robustly. 'You always suffer from

stage fright, but the minute you start playing you'll be fine. Oh, these came for you,' he added, thrusting the bouquet he was holding into her lap.

Ella despised herself for the way her heart gave a little flip, and she fumbled to open the envelope of the attached card, disappointment swamping her when she read the good luck message from her cousin Stephanie and her family. 'They're lovely,' she murmured as she placed the flowers with the other bouquets she'd received, from her aunt and uncle, and Jenny and her family.

It was stupid to have hoped that Vadim would send her flowers, she told herself impatiently. He'd sent her red roses once, but that was when he had been trying to persuade her into his bed. Now they were lovers—or perhaps sex partners would be a better description of their relationship. She was well aware that she meant nothing to him. He'd probably forgotten about the concert tonight. Maybe he had invited another woman out to dinner while she was away? The mental image of him taking some gorgeous model back to Kingfisher House for the night evoked such searing jealousy inside her that she actually clutched her stomach, as if she had been stabbed with a knife. It shouldn't matter to her if Vadim entertained half a dozen nubile blondes in his bed, she reminded herself, swallowing the bile in her throat and taking a gulp of water, dismayed to see that her hands were shaking.

She couldn't play like this, she thought wildly. Her nervous tension was so acute that it was doubtful she would be able to hold her violin, let alone draw her bow across the strings. She had the career her mother had dreamed of, she reminded herself. But knowing that her adored Mama would have been proud of her did not ease her self-doubt nor lessen her fear at the prospect of walking onto the Palais Garnier's vast stage.

It was ridiculous to feel hurt that Vadim had not contacted her for the whole time she had been in France, and she was ashamed of the tears that stung her eyes. She'd known what she was getting into when she'd agreed to an affair with him—known what kind of man he was—so why did the fact that he had not sent her flowers make her want to bury her head in her hands and weep?

Marcus had gone—presumably to find the make-up girl. But adding some blusher to her cheeks was not going to make her feel any better, Ella thought desperately. In her ivory silk evening dress, with her hair swept up into a chignon, she resembled a wraith rather than a confident woman who was about to walk onto a stage and entertain two thousand people. With a muttered cry she yanked open the dressing room door—and slammed into the solid wall of a muscular chest.

'Isn't the stage in the other direction?' Vadim enquired lightly. 'Where are you going in such a hurry?' Ella looked like a terrified doe, her eyes huge in her white face. The shimmer of tears on her lashes evoked a curious feeling in his chest, so that without pausing to question what he was doing he drew her into his arms and held her close.

'What are you doing here?' she whispered, clutching his arms as if she feared he was an illusion who would disappear in a puff of smoke.

'Do you think I'd miss a concert by one of the world's most amazing violin virtuosos?' he said softly. 'Also, I wanted to personally deliver these,' he added, lifting a bouquet of fragrant cream roses from the table behind him and handing them to her. 'You didn't think I'd forgotten that this is your big night, did you?'

Utterly overwhelmed, Ella closed her eyes, but could not prevent a single tear from escaping and rolling down her cheek. 'I can't do it,' she said shakily. 'I know I'm going to go to pieces in front of all those people. I must have been mad to think I could ever have a successful career as a soloist when I'm paralysed with nerves before every performance.' She stared at Vadim, half expecting to see mockery in his eyes, but instead she glimpsed an expression of compassion that brought the words tumbling from her mouth. 'This is what my mother wanted for me. She devoted her life to teaching me so that I might have the career she never had. My father was right,' she said miserably. 'He said I was too shy and pathetic to make it as a musician.'

'When did he tell you that?' Vadim asked roughly, feeling again a violent surge of anger at her dead father.

'Oh, he said it every time he tried to persuade me to sell my violin. It's a Stradivarius and worth a fortune—and my father needed money,' she said bitterly. 'But my mother had left it to me in her will, and he had no claim on it. He was furious when I refused to sell it.' She broke off and bit her lip. 'He never loved me, you know. I don't know why. When I was little I tried so hard to please him—I was desperate for his approval, but I never won it,' she said huskily, unwittingly revealing a vulnerability that tugged at Vadim's insides. The image she presented to the world was of a confident, talented woman on the cusp of an astounding career, but underneath she was still the lonely little girl who had tried to win her father's love and been deeply wounded by his uninterest.

It was little wonder she was afraid of relationships. She had been hurt once, and her determination never to let anyone too close was a self-protective measure to prevent herself from being hurt again. He understood; he'd done the very same thing. The pain of losing his wife and daughter had caused him to build a wall around his heart which he had no intention of ever dismantling. But as he stared down at Ella and watched another tear slip silently down her face, some long-buried emotion inside Vadim stirred into life and he felt a fierce urge to comfort her.

'Your father was wrong,' he said deeply. 'You have a re-markable gift, and you also have an inner strength and grace that will enable you to overcome your nerves. I have abso-lutely no doubt that you can walk onto the stage tonight and blow the audience away.'

'Do you really think so?' she murmured uncertainly, feel-ing warmth begin to seep through her veins instead of the icy fear that had frozen her blood. She was suddenly acutely con-scious of the muscular strength of his thighs pressing against her, and molten heat unfurled in the pit of her stomach when he slid his hand down to her bottom and pulled her closer still, so that the hard ridge of his arousal nudged between her legs. She lifted her head and drew a sharp breath when she glimpsed the fire blazing in his eyes. After five long, lonely nights away from him her body instantly recognised its master, and when he lowered his head and captured her mouth in a searing kiss she melted against him and wound her arms around his neck, kissing him back with a fervency that drew a low groan from his throat.

Muttering something in Russian, Vadim lifted her up and strode into her dressing room. His sole intention when he had taken her in his arms had been to offer support and encour-agement, and hopefully alleviate her stage fright, but Ella was a fever in his blood, and the moment he'd touched her he'd been consumed with the savage need to possess her.

She got to him in a way no other woman ever had, he acknowledged grimly. It was a state of affairs he could not allow to continue, but at this moment he could think of nothing but assuaging the fire that raged in both of them. With shaking fingers he drew the zip of her dress down her spine and slid the narrow straps from her shoulders so that her small, firm breasts spilled into his hands. Her skin felt like satin beneath his lips as he trailed urgent kisses down her throat. He lifted her and sat her on the edge of the dressing table, arching her backwards so that he could close his lips around one dusky nipple and then its twin, sucking each crest until it swelled against his tongue.

Her sharp little breaths matched his own laboured breathing, and their mutual desire blazed out of control, so that he jerked the long skirt of her dress up to her waist and slipped his hand beneath the lacy panel of her knickers to find her slick, wet heat.

At the first stroke of his wickedly inventive fingers Ella sobbed his name, her fears about the concert swept away in the wild torrent of passion. The sexual hunger in Vadim's eyes warned her that he was dangerously out of control, but she loved the fact that his usual formidable restraint had crumbled and his need was a great as hers. With trembling fingers she unfastened his bow tie and wrenched the buttons of his white silk shirt apart. Her nerve faltered momentarily when she fumbled with the zip of his trousers, but when he deftly stepped out of them she dragged his boxers over his hips, and caught her breath when the throbbing length of his erection filled her hands.

'Hold on to me,' he commanded roughly, and she immediately clung to his broad, bronzed shoulders as he slipped his hands beneath her bottom, lifted her, and sank his swollen shaft into her with a hard thrust that drove the breath from her body.

She was dimly aware of a crash as the various jars of toiletries on the dressing table fell to the floor. Thank heaven he'd locked the door, was her last coherent thought, before she caught and matched his pagan rhythm and tilted her hips to meet each devastating thrust. Harder, faster—this was sex at its most primitive, and she gloried in the power of it, her whole being focused on reaching that magical place that was uniquely special to them. It couldn't last. She felt him tense and knew he was fighting for control, but as her body arched with the drenching pleasure of her orgasm she heard the ragged groan that was torn from his throat and felt the judders that ripped through him as he exploded in a violent climax and spilled into her.

Ella slowly came back to earth to face the realisation that they had just had wild sex on her dressing table, and that she was due to perform in front of two thousand people in ten minutes' time. Usually she would be sick with nerves by now, she thought ruefully. But Vadim had commanded her mind as well as her body, and she was still too dazed with pleasure to worry about the concert.

'You'll have to make love to me before every performance,' she quipped huskily, blushing when she saw the marks on his chest where she had raked him with her nails.

The flare of colour on her cheeks evoked a curious ache in Vadim's chest. Beneath her shy exterior she was a tigress, but he was the only man to have discovered her sensual nature and he was startled by the possessive feeling that surged through him. 'I missed you,' he admitted roughly, noting how her eyes had darkened with an emotion he did not want to define.

The moment was broken by the sound of Marcus Benning's voice from the other side of the door.

'Ella—time to go. Are you ready?'

'Almost.' A bubble of laughter rose in her throat as Vadim swiftly donned his trousers while she refastened his shirt buttons.

He slid the straps of her dress back into place, set her on her feet and grimaced as he smoothed the creases out of her skirt.

'At least you've got more colour in your cheeks,' he murmured, running his finger lightly down her flushed face. 'How are the nerves?'

'What nerves?' Her smile stole his breath. She picked up her violin and headed for the door. 'Wish me luck?'

'You don't need it, angel face. You'll wow the audience.' His eyes held hers. 'Play for me,' he said softly.

'I will.' She took a deep breath before she unlocked the door, and smiled serenely at Marcus as she swept past him and along the corridor towards the stage.

CHAPTER NINE

SHE received a standing ovation. Blinking bemusedly in the glare of the lights, Ella gave a final bow and turned to walk off the stage, the thunderous applause from the audience echoing in her ears.

'You were bloody marvellous,' Marcus greeted her buoyantly. 'I knew your nerves would disappear the minute you played the first note.'

Ella nodded weakly. She felt utterly drained, both emotionally and physically, and longed to retreat to the quiet of her dressing room, but she knew that Marcus had arranged for her to give interviews to several journalists at the after-concert party.

She spent the next hour chatting and smiling until her jaw ached. Marcus paraded her around the reception, where it seemed that everyone wanted to meet her, but although she scanned the room whenever she had the opportunity she was disappointed not to see Vadim. Perhaps he had flown back to London immediately after the concert? She knew he was negotiating an important deal in the capital, and the fact that he owned a private jet meant that he could travel whenever it suited him.

Taking advantage of a lull in conversation, she escaped to a quiet corner of the room and rubbed her brow wearily, aware of the familiar throbbing pain behind her temples that warned of the onset of a migraine.

'Do you have your painkillers with you?' Vadim materialised at her side, and she was so shocked at the sight of him, when she had convinced herself he had returned to England, that for a few seconds she could not disguise the emotion that flared in her eyes.

He was so stunningly handsome that she actually hurt inside when she looked at him, but she did not possess sufficient willpower to look away. They were back in Paris, where they had first met. She recalled vividly the feeling that she'd been struck by a lightning bolt when she had glanced across a crowded room and seen him for the first time. She had known then that he spelled trouble, she mused ruefully. She had sensed that he would be dangerous to her peace of mind and she had tried to fight the simmering sexual chemistry between them. But the truth was he fascinated her in a way no other man had ever done.

He had stated that their affair would last until either of them wanted to end it. But as her eyes locked with his brilliant blue gaze a sense of longing for something she could not explain unfurled deep inside her, and with it came a sharp stab of pain as she envisaged a time in the probably not too distant future when they would no longer be lovers. She could not be falling for him, she reassured herself frantically. She always felt emotional after a performance, and the ache in her heart was definitely not because she wished for more from her relationship with Vadim than simply great sex.

Vadim watched the play of emotions in Ella's stormy grey eyes and correctly deciphered each one. He frowned, silently debating whether it would be fair to go ahead with his plans. He did not want to hurt her. But, reasoned the voice in his head, he had made it clear from the beginning that he had no intention of allowing their affair to develop into something deeper.

He'd only ever wanted a mutually enjoyable sexual liaison, and he was infuriated that she seemed to have some sort of hold over him. He had spoken the truth when he'd told her that he had missed her during the five days—and hellish nights—that she had been in Paris, preparing for the concert. But he knew from experience that, for him, prolonged intimacy bred boredom. The best way to get her out of his system was to spend all his time with her, and that was exactly what he was going to do for the next days or weeks—however long it took for him to tire of her.

'My tablets are in my dressing room,' she told him. 'Do you think anyone will notice if I disappear from the party for a while?'

'I've already told Marcus we're leaving.' Vadim smiled at her startled expression and slipped his arm around her waist to steer her over to the door. 'I assume you've had enough of the party?'

'Heavens, yes,' she agreed fervently. 'I'm staying at the Intercontinental again. Have you booked into a hotel?' she queried when they reached her dressing room. She quickly took a couple of the strong painkillers that would hopefully prevent her headache from developing into a full-blown migraine.

'No, I'm flying out on the jet tonight—and you're coming with me.'

Ella's heart flipped at the prospect of returning to Kingfisher House with Vadim when she had expected to spend another night at her hotel, alone.

'I take it you have no argument with the arrangements?' he murmured as he drew her into his arms.

'None at all. I can't wait to go home,' she admitted, hectic colour staining her cheeks when she imagined him making love to her in his big bed back at the house she loved. 'But I'll have to stop off at the hotel to collect my things.'

'One of my staff will do that.' He claimed her mouth in a long, sensual kiss that stirred her desire back into urgent life, and when he finally released her she snatched up her handbag and followed him out to the corridor. She collected her violin from the security desk—after refusing point-blank Vadim's suggestion that his PA would arrange for its safe transportation.

'My violin stays with me at all times,' she explained.

'So I've discovered. I must admit it's a novelty to share my bedroom with a musical instrument,' Vadim said dryly, referring to her insistence on keeping her violin beside the bed at Kingfisher House.

They emerged from the Palais Garnier to be met by a barrage of flashing camera bulbs. Ella had known that her performance had attracted some media interest, but it soon became clear that the press were more curious about her relationship with playboy billionaire Vadim Aleksandrov. 'Maybe I should go back inside,' she muttered as they were jostled by the dozens of photographers who were vying to snap the best shots of the enigmatic Russian and his beautiful companion who was rapidly becoming an international star.

In reply Vadim slid his arm around her waist and shouldered his way through the crowd, seemingly unconcerned that his action had incited fevered interest among the journalists. 'Don't worry about them,' he told her when they finally reached the car, where his chauffeur was holding the door open for them to scramble inside.

'But they'll think we're…together,' Ella said uncertainly, holding up a hand to shield her eyes from the glare of the camera bulbs that continued to flash outside the car's windows. 'You know how the paparazzi exaggerate things. News that we're having a torrid affair will probably be in all tomorrow's tabloids.'

Vadim shrugged. 'What does is matter what they say? It's the truth, anyway. For now, we *are* together, angel face.'

He seemed perfectly at ease with the likelihood that their affair would soon be common knowledge, but in London Ella had noted that he had deliberately avoided places where they might have been spotted by the press, and had taken her to out-of-the-way restaurants where they had not attracted attention. Did the fact that he now seemed happy for them to be seen in public together mean that he wanted their relationship to develop into something deeper than a meaningless sexual liaison? she wondered, annoyed with herself for the little flutter of hope in her chest. Daydreams were for children, she reminded herself irritably. And since when had she decided that Vadim was her knight in shinning armour?

They took off from Charles de Gaulle Airport within minutes of boarding the Learjet. Ella had never been on a private plane before, and as she glanced around at the elegant cabin, with its cream leather sofas, cocktail bar and vast cinema screen, she appreciated for the first time how very different Vadim's world was from hers. Even the two female flight attendants looked like top models, she noted wryly, and a poisonous little voice in her head wondered if they provided in-flight entertainment when he travelled on his numerous business trips around the world.

'You look like a ghost,' Vadim murmured, frowning as he studied her pale features. 'Is your headache worse?'

'No, I'm just tired,' she replied quickly, praying that his uncanny ability to read her mind would not reveal the flare of jealousy that had ripped through her when one of the flight attendants had leaned unnecessarily close to him as she had served him his drink. 'Where are we going?' she queried in a puzzled voice, when he unfastened her seat belt and drew her to her feet.'

'Bed,' he informed her succinctly.

Her heart lurched at the wicked gleam in his eyes, and she gasped when he swung her into his arms and strode towards the back of the plane. He shouldered a door and walked into a plush sleeping compartment, complete with vast double bed. 'You certainly like to travel in comfort,' she muttered as he laid her down and removed her shoes. The idea that he was going to make love to her when they were thirty thousand feet in the air was shockingly exciting, but to her dismay he did not join her on the bed, instead drawing the cover up to her chin as if he were taking care of a small child.

'Go to sleep,' he bade her gently, wondering why her air of fragility tugged on his heart. 'I'll wake you when we're about to land in Nice.'

The moment Ella's head touched the pillows exhaustion overwhelmed her, and her sleepy brain could not comprehend Vadim's last statement. 'Don't you mean Heathrow?' she mumbled. 'We're flying to London, not Nice.'

'Actually, we're on our way to my villa in the Cap d'Antibes,' he informed her, pushing her gently back down on the mattress when she struggled to sit up. 'Nice is the closest airport.'

She shook her head in confusion. 'Do you mean we're going to France for the weekend?'

'I'm planning on us staying for a few weeks,' he informed her smoothly.

'Well, that might be your plan, but it's certainly not mine,' she snapped, annoyed by the arrogance in his tone. 'I can't just disappear to France indefinitely.'

'I checked with Marcus Benning, who told me your diary is clear for the next month. You're not scheduled to record the film score with the RLO until the end of August. Marcus actually agreed with me that it will do you good to have a holiday.'

'Oh, did he? It's nice to know the two of you have organised my life for me,' Ella said tightly, using sarcasm to disguise her panic at the prospect of spending the next few weeks with Vadim at his villa. He had changed the rules of their affair without asking her, she thought bitterly. Sharing a holiday with him and being with him twenty-four hours a day was a daunting prospect. They might drive each other mad. But far more worrying was the possibility that she would fall even deeper under his spell—and that would be just asking to have her heart broken.

She could see from the determined set of Vadim's jaw that arguing about the trip to his villa would be pointless, especially as they were already *en route* to France. But she would be on her guard against him, she assured herself as she lay back down on the pillows. And with that thought firmly in her mind she fell asleep.

The Villa Corraline was a stunning Provençal-style house, set in beautiful grounds and commanding spectacular views of the coastline of the Côte d'Azur. It was dark when they arrived, and Ella was instantly captivated by the sight of the house, lit with lamps which turned the pink walls to a deep coral colour. When she followed Vadim inside, she glimpsed various elegant, marble-floored rooms, but she was still dazed with sleep, and only made a token protest when he swept her into his arms and carried her up the sweeping staircase to the huge, circular master bedroom, which was dominated by an enormous bed.

'I only packed enough clothes for a week,' she said, when she caught sight of the small suitcase that a member of Vadim's staff must have collected from her hotel in Paris.

'You'll find everything you need in here,' he replied, pulling open one of the wardrobes to reveal a rail full of dresses and skirts in a rainbow of soft colours that would suit Ella's delicate skin-tone.

Frowning, she ran her hand along the row of clothes, noting that each item carried the label of a top design house. 'I don't understand. Who do these things belong to?' she asked, a sinking feeling in her stomach as she remembered how he kept a selection of bathrobes in his wardrobe at Kingfisher House for his lovers. If he thought she would wear clothes belonging to one of his previous mistresses, he'd better think again!

'They're yours. I gave details of your size and colouring to a personal stylist and asked her to put together a selection of outfits for you,' he explained with a shrug—as if the subject of what she would wear during their stay in France was of minimal interest.

'I can't possibly allow you to buy clothes for me,' Ella told him fiercely. She owned a few designer evening gowns which she had bought for performances, and she had a good idea how much each item hanging in the wardrobe must have cost. The idea of being beholden to any man was repugnant to her. 'I pay my own way,' she told Vadim stiffly. 'Perhaps your *personal stylist* will be able to take the clothes back and get a refund.'

Ella was the only woman he had met since he had achieved billionaire status who did not seem to think that an affair with him included unrestricted use of his credit card, Vadim noted.

His eyes narrowed on her flushed face, and for a moment Ella thought she had angered him, but then his mouth curved into a sensual smile that she found impossible to resist. 'Don't be ridiculous. You need something to wear while you're here. Many of my friends own houses along the coast, and we will do a fair amount of socialising. Although if you insist on walking around naked for the next couple of weeks I won't complain,' he promised, in a voice that was suddenly as rich and sensuous as crushed velvet.

The brush of his mouth across her lips, before he trailed a line of kisses down her throat to the pulse beating jerkily at its base, demolished her thought processes and effectively put an end to further argument about the clothes he'd bought for her. But later that night, after Ella had briefly donned a sexy black silk chemise, and he had teased and tormented her senses as he had taken his time removing it, she made a silent vow that she would only wear the clothes while she was his mistress, and would return them when their affair was over.

After a night when Vadim made love to her three times, and drove her to a shattering climax on each occasion, Ella did not stir until mid-morning. Sunlight dancing across her face finally prompted her to open her eyes, and she caught her breath at the magnificent view of the cobalt-blue Mediterranean visible through the glass walls of the circular room.

'I take it the house meets with your approval?' Vadim was propped up on one elbow beside her, amusement gleaming in his eyes when he took in her rapt expression. He looked devastatingly sexy, with a night's growth of dark stubble shading his jaw and his olive-gold skin gleaming in the sunlight, and the sheet lying low over his hips barely covered the jutting length of his arousal.

'It's wonderful.' Looking at him made her heart ache, and she quickly glanced back at the view, praying he would never guess how much he affected her.

'You haven't seen the pool yet—or the gardens, or the private beach.' Her beautiful smile tugged at Vadim's insides. Her excitement was infectious, and for the first time in years he found he was looking forward to having some time away from the punishing work schedule he imposed on himself. 'We'll spend the day exploring the house and grounds,' he promised, 'and this afternoon we can go to the beach and I'll take you out on the jet-ski.'

They quickly fell into a pattern of spending their days by the pool or on the beach, sometimes driving into Antibes town, or along the coast to Cannes and St Raphael. Occasionally Vadim retreated to his study to work during the afternoons, but more often he sat on the terrace and listened to Ella play the violin for two or three hours at a stretch.

'What are you going to serenade me with today?' he quipped late one afternoon, when they had retreated from the blazing heat of the patio to the shade of the tall pine trees that surrounded the garden.

'I thought a little Tchaikovsky to start with, followed by Brahms.' Ella turned the pages of her music score and settled her violin beneath her chin. 'I still find it strange to play wearing a bikini,' she owned with a smile.

'You could always take the bikini off,' Vadim suggested dulcetly, 'if that will help?'

She blushed at the wicked gleam in his eyes. 'I don't think that's a good idea. You know what happens when I take my clothes off.'

'Mmm, I feel duty-bound to make love to you.' Vadim trailed his eyes over Ella's slender figure in her minuscule turquoise bikini, and allowed his gaze to linger on her small, firm breasts which were barely covered by the triangles of material. Would he ever have enough of her? he wondered as he felt himself harden. She was like a fever in his blood, and he was tempted to carry her inside and sate his hunger for her for the third time that day.

'I really need to practise,' she murmured, recognising the sultry intent in his eyes.

His smile stole Ella's breath, and her heart seemed to swell in her chest until she was sure he could see it beating frantically beneath her ribs. Surely she was not imagining the close bond that she sensed was developing between them? she thought, hope soaring inside her. They had become friends as well as lovers, Vadim shared her love of music, and he was the only person she had ever met apart from her mother who seemed to understand how much it meant to her.

'Then play for me,' he bade her, leaning back on the sun lounger and folding his arms beneath his head. 'I'll conserve my energy for later.'

For the next hour Ella was utterly absorbed in her music, but at last she lowered her bow and flexed her fingers. Vadim was no longer watching her play, and instead was staring across the garden to the sea, which sparkled like a sapphire beneath the dense blue sky.

'Penny for them?' she said cheerfully, her teasing smile fading when she glimpsed an expression of raw pain in his eyes, before his urbane mask slipped back into place. 'Is—is something troubling you, Vadim?' she faltered, so shaken by what she had seen that she ignored his warning frown that he did not welcome questions about his personal life. It was not the first time she had sensed that his thoughts were far away, and when he stared at her without replying she found his brooding silence unnerving.

He shrugged laconically. 'What could be troubling me, angel face?' he drawled. 'I'm enjoying good weather, fine food and the company of a beautiful mistress in my bed every night. What more could any man ask for?'

Mistress! How she hated that word, Ella thought savagely, looking away from him so that he would not see how much his casual description of her role in his life had hurt her. Vadim was a charming and charismatic companion, and a generous lover, but she sensed that there were secrets in his past that he would never reveal to her.

'I just thought you looked bothered by something,' she muttered stiffly, telling herself that it was ridiculous to feel rejected just because he chose not to confide in her. They did not have that kind of relationship, she reminded herself. She was his temporary mistress, and all the wishing in the world would not change the situation.

'It's sweet of you to be concerned about me,' he said, in a faintly amused tone that caused a flush of embarrassment to stain her cheeks. 'But I assure you there is no need.' Vadim's conscience gnawed at him when he saw the flare of hurt in her eyes. He knew he had sounded abrupt, but he had no intention of revealing to Ella that her rendition of Mozart's exquisite *Eine Kleine Nachtmusik* had reminded him of an evening many years ago, when he had taken Irina to a concert by the Moscow State Symphony.

It had been a few months after their marriage, a celebration of the news that Irina was pregnant with their first child, and he could still recall the excitement he had felt that he was going to be a father. Why had he allowed his ambition to make money to become more important than his wife and child? he wondered bleakly. His obsession with developing his business had hurt Irina, but by the time he had realised just how much she and Klara meant to him they had already made their fateful journey to Irina's home village, and although he had followed them he had arrived too late to save them.

'Did you remember we're meeting Sergey and Lena Tarasov for dinner tonight?' He dragged his mind from the past and forced a casual tone.

'I hadn't forgotten.' Ella glanced at her watch. 'I think I'll go and shower and start getting ready now,' she muttered, needing to get away from him before she gave in to the stupid urge to burst into tears.

She had met Vadim's Russian friends the Tarasovs on several occasions. They were a charming couple, and she enjoyed their company, but if she was honest she would have preferred an intimate dinner on the terrace with Vadim, followed by a stroll along the beach in the moonlight before he swept her off to bed. When they had first arrived in Antibes they had spent many evenings alone together at the villa, but lately he had accepted invitations to social events every night, and she wondered if it was a sign that he was growing bored of her.

She'd known right from the start that their relationship would only ever be a temporary affair, she reminded herself when she stepped out of the shower, smoothed fragrant lotion onto her lightly tanned skin and returned to the bedroom to dress. She had also known that falling in love with him would be emotional suicide—but Vadim had dismantled her defences one by one, until she feared she was in danger of losing her heart to him irrevocably.

A noise from the doorway alerted her to his presence, and she pinned a smile to her face as she spun round and swept a hand over her dress. 'What do you think?'

'I think you look stunning,' Vadim said truthfully, feeling the familiar tug of sexual hunger in his groin when he studied her. The black silk strapless sheath was deceptively simple, its bodice cut low over the upper curves of her breasts, and the side split in the skirt revealing a glimpse of slender thigh encased in gossamer-fine black hose.

With her hair swept up into a chignon, she looked elegant and desirable—the perfect attributes for a mistress. She would turn heads tonight, and he knew that other men would fantasise about her slender body beneath her dress and envy him. But she belonged to him, and only him. He was surprised by the feeling of possessiveness that surged through him. She meant nothing to him, he reminded himself grimly. She was just another blonde, passing briefly through his life, and the realisation that he was becoming addicted to her company—in and out of the bedroom—was the reason he had started to accept social invitations which ensured that he spent less time alone with her.

'I have a present for you,' he said, strolling over to her and taking a slim black velvet box from his pocket.

Ella caught her breath when he extracted a glittering diamond necklace from the box and fastened it around her throat. 'I can't possibly accept it,' she faltered as she stared at her reflection in the mirror and watched how the diamonds sparkled in the golden glow of the setting sun. 'It must be worth a fortune.'

He shrugged. 'You deserve it.' Unlike his previous mistresses, Ella never expected him to lavish her with gifts. 'It pleases me to buy things for you. Don't you like it?' he murmured, his voice whispering against her skin as he traced his lips up her neck and found the sensitive spot below her ear.

'It's beautiful.' Ella said quietly, but the words 'you deserve it' echoed in her mind. Did he regard the necklace as payment for her services in the bedroom—along with the designer clothes he had bought her? She was his mistress, she reminded herself dully, and he was a billionaire who probably bought all his mistresses diamonds. She remembered the daisy chain he had made for her the previous day, when they had lain on the grass beneath the shade of the olive trees, and wondered what he would say if she told him she would rather wear the simple necklace made of flowers that was now hidden in her bedside drawer than the priceless and meaningless precious gems that felt like a weight around her neck.

Vadim's Aston Martin had been shipped to the villa a few days after their arrival. The powerful car ate up the twenty miles between Antibes and Monaco, and they drove through the Principality to the famous Grand Casino, where they met up with the Tarasovs.

'It's a spectacular place, isn't it?' Lena Tarasov murmured, after the two couples had dined in the exclusive restaurant and were strolling through the casino's opulent gaming rooms, where magnificent crystal chandeliers sparkled down on the array of glittering diamonds and gems worn by every designer-clad female guest. 'Monte Carlo is a world away from the slums of Moscow, where Sergey, Vadim and I grew up.'

Ella glanced at the beautiful dark-haired Russian woman at her side. 'Did you know Vadim when he was a child?' she asked curiously.

'No, he and Sergey became friends when they were in the army, and Vadim was best man at our wedding. When Sergey's electronics company folded a few years ago, Vadim offered him the position of company director at his Russian headquarters.' Lena smiled. 'Vadim is a good man and loyal friend. To be honest I think he was glad of the opportunity to hand over the Russian operation to someone he knew he could trust and move to Europe. Russia holds bad memories for him.'

Ella nodded, recalling Vadim's description of his unhappy childhood with his father and cruel grandmother, after his mother had abandoned him. 'Yes, he's told me about his family.'

'He has?' Lena gave her a speculative glance. 'I had not realised. As far as I know, Vadim has never spoken about his wife and daughter to anyone but his closest friends.' She appeared unaware of the shock wave that had ripped through Ella, and gave her another warm smile. 'Losing them both was such a terrible tragedy. I don't think Vadim has ever really come to terms with it. He has always maintained he would never fall in love again. But…' She shrugged her shoulders expressively. 'You are different to all his other women. I said so to Sergey the first time we met you. Maybe you can unlock Vadim's heart and make his eyes smile again?'

They had reached the salon, where the two men were already seated at the roulette table. The room was hot and busy, and buzzing with the hubbub of conversation, and Ella struggled to squeeze through the crowds thronged around the tables, trying to keep up with Lena so that she could question the Russian woman about her astounding revelation that Vadim—the most commitment-phobic playboy on the planet—had once had a wife and child.

She felt numb with shock. He'd never said a word to her in all the time they had spent together. But of course he did not regard her as one of his closest friends, she thought bitterly. She was just his temporary mistress, and he kept her shut out of his life. Contrary to what Lena thought, she certainly did not have the key to his heart.

CHAPTER TEN

'YOU'RE very quiet tonight. What's the matter?' Vadim queried as the Aston Martin sped along the road back to Antibes.

Ella shot him a lightning glance and felt her heart contract at the sight of his hard, classically sculpted features highlighted by the moonlight. 'I've got a headache. I'll take a couple of migraine tablets when we get back.' She turned away from him and stared out of the window, wondering why misery had settled like a lead weight in her stomach. What did it matter if he had been married and had had a child? His past had nothing to do with her. But during their time in Antibes she had felt closer to him than she ever had to any other human being, and, fool that she was, she had kidded herself that he was beginning to regard her as more than a convenient sex partner. The discovery that he had deliberately withheld important details about his past made a mockery of her stupid daydream that he would ever want a meaningful relationship with her.

'I have to make a call to the US,' he told her when they entered the Villa Corraline, and immediately headed for his study. 'Why don't you go up to bed? You look all in.'

As soon as she reached the bedroom, Ella stripped out of her evening dress and took off the diamond necklace. Maybe she was oversensitive, but all evening she'd felt as though the glittering gems had screamed the fact that she was Vadim's mistress, and she had been aware of speculative glances from various predatory women, clearly wondering how long she would hold on to her position.

Recalling that Vadim had dropped the velvet box that had contained the necklace into his bedside cabinet, she crossed to his side of the bed, opened the drawer and deposited the diamonds. She was about to shut the drawer again when something caught her attention.

The rag-doll was clearly old, and cheaply made. Someone had repaired the stitching on the arms and legs with a slightly darker thread, and some of the stuffing must have escaped because the doll was limp and strangely misshapen. Carefully, Ella took the doll from the drawer. Beneath it were two photographs: one of a woman with a mass of brown hair, holding a baby in her arms, the other depicting a little girl of maybe four or five, with an impish smile and a mop of blonde curls. The photos were not of particularly good quality and were curled at the edges, as if they had been held many times. They could only be of Vadim's wife and child, she realised, her heart thumping as she stared at them in fascination, unaware of the faint sound of footfall until he materialised in front of her.

Flushing guiltily, she quickly dropped the photographs into her lap. 'I'm sorry. I didn't mean to pry,' she mumbled. 'I was putting the necklace away when I saw the pictures…and I was curious.' Vadim's silence was unnerving; the expression on his hard face unreadable, and her hands shook slightly as she handed the doll and photos to him. 'Cute little girl,' she commented, striving to sound normal as she got up from the bed.

'Yes.' He finally spoke, and gave a faint shrug of his shoulders, his eyes veering from her face to the pictures. 'They're friends—in Russia.'

Ella nodded. 'I see.' She picked up her robe and headed swiftly for the *en suite* bathroom. She was not one of Vadim's closest friends; she was the woman he had sex with. There was no reason why he would confide in her, she reminded herself.

In the bathroom she removed her make-up, washed her face and released the pins from her chignon, pulling the brush through her hair with automatic strokes until she could not put off returning to the bedroom any longer. Thank God she'd made the excuse about having a headache earlier, she thought bleakly. She knew she was being stupid, but she could not bear to make love with Vadim tonight, when his lie about the identities of the woman and child in the photographs emphasised how unimportant she was to him.

He had switched off the lamps so that the room was shadowed; fingers of silvery moonlight were glimmering through the windows. Vadim had stepped outside onto the terrace. She could see him sitting on the garden bench, his shoulders slumped in an air of such utter loneliness that instead of sliding into bed she was drawn towards the open doors, her grey silk gown rustling as she hurried down the steps.

He looked up as she approached, and she caught her breath at the expression of haunted agony on his face.

'The woman in the photo was my wife,' he said harshly.

Ella's eyes flew to the photographs in his hands, and her heart contracted when she saw him stroke his finger lightly over the face of the little girl.

'And this was my daughter—Klara.' The silence trembled between them before he added in a tightly controlled voice, 'They're both dead.'

He passed his hand over his eyes, and the betraying gesture tore Ella's heart to shreds. She was stunned to see this powerful man suddenly so vulnerable. She wanted to go to him, hold him, but fear that he would reject her sympathy held her immobile.

'I'm so sorry.' She didn't know what to say, and the words seemed desperately inadequate. When Lena Tarasov had revealed that Vadim had been married, she had been bitterly hurt that he had never spoken about his past to her. But now, as she witnessed his raw pain, she hated herself for having been so childish. He had clearly been devastated by the loss of his wife and daughter, and who could blame him if he found it hard to talk about their deaths?

'What…what happened?' she asked huskily.

His throat worked, and his lashes were spiked with moisture when he lifted his head and met her startled gaze. 'They were killed in an avalanche which hit Irina's parents' village,' he explained harshly. 'Most of Rumsk was wiped out.' He stared down at the photos in his hand. 'My parents-in-law lived on the lower slopes of the mountain, and when hundreds of tons of snow hurtled down the mountainside no one in the house stood a chance. It was three days before the rescue team found Irina, and another two before they reached Klara.' His voice cracked with emotion. 'Of course it was too late. When they found Klara she was still holding her doll.'

He picked up the rag-doll and swallowed the constriction in his throat. He could sense Ella's shock, and knew she was struggling for something to say. But there was nothing to be said. Irina and Klara were gone, and no amount of words would bring them back.

Ella's throat ached with tears, but she forced herself to speak. 'When?' she whispered.

'Ten years ago.' His mouth twisted into a grimace. 'Today would have been Klara's fifteenth birthday.' The memories had been agonising today, but he had suppressed his pain in

the same way that he always did, and had arranged to socialise with friends to prevent himself from dwelling on the past.
But now the evening was over, and he could no longer banish
the images in his head of his angelic-faced little girl.

'I suppose your…wife…' Ella stumbled slightly over the
word '…had taken your daughter to visit her parents.' She fell
silent, finding it impossible to imagine how terrible it must
have been for Vadim when he'd heard news of the disaster.

Vadim stared silently across the dark garden, reliving those
harrowing hours and days when he had joined the search
teams and dug through the snow until his shoulder muscles
had burned with his frantic efforts to find Klara, so that he
could place her body with Irina's in the mortuary. Even after
ten years, the memory of finding his lifeless daughter still
ripped his heart out.

He didn't understand why he suddenly felt an overwhelming urge to confide in Ella. All he knew was that somehow
she had crept beneath his guard, so that for the first time in a
decade he found himself contemplating a relationship that en-
compassed more than mindless sex.

Ella looked ethereal and achingly fragile, with her silver-
grey gown fluttering gently in the breeze and her pale gold
hair streaming like a river of silk down her back. But her love-
liness was more than skin-deep. He had discovered that she
was funny, witty, fiercely intelligent, and she possessed a
depth of compassion that he had never found in any other
woman. He admired her strength of will as she fought her
nerves to pursue her career as a soloist, and he recognised the
vulnerability she tried so hard to disguise. She needed—
deserved—more than he could give her. He had failed in one
relationship, and that failure had resulted in unimaginable
pain. He could never risk failing again.

'If you want the truth, Irina was in Rumsk because she had walked out on our marriage,' he told her savagely, the familiar feeling of self-loathing rushing over him. 'I had been away on yet another business trip, and on my return I found a note from her explaining that she felt I didn't love her, and that she was taking Klara to stay with her parents. I knew Irina had been upset that I spent so much time at work,' he admitted heavily. 'I was determined to reassure her that she and Klara were more important to me than anything, and I raced after them, but I reached Rumsk after the avalanche had hit.'

'Oh, Vadim.' It was a cry from the heart, torn from Ella when she glimpsed the agony in his eyes. There was no thought in her head to judge him. She flew across the terrace, uncaring that she was in danger of revealing how she felt about him, intent only on trying to comfort him.

He had risen to his feet, and stiffened when she flung her arms around his waist. 'You have to understand I was not a good husband,' he said roughly. 'I was obsessed with work and establishing my company, and I did not spend enough time at home—even when Irina pleaded with me to devote more time to her and Klara.' His jaw tightened as he fought to control the emotions surging through him. 'Irina accused me of not loving her. She was wrong; I did love her—but I didn't value what I had until she had left me, and she and Klara were killed before I had the chance to tell them both what they meant to me.' He drew a ragged breath. 'I should not have married. I was selfish and driven by my determination to succeed. I put my interests first, and in that respect perhaps I am not so dissimilar to your father,' he finished grimly.

'You are nothing like my father.' Ella fiercely refuted the suggestion. When she had first met Vadim she *had* believed he was a man like her father, a heartless playboy who only cared about himself. But since they had become lovers he had treated her with kindness and respect, as if he valued her as a person and did not regard her merely as a form of entertainment in his bed.

But thoughts like those were dangerous, she conceded bleakly. Vadim might have a depth to him that she would not have believed in the early days of their relationship, but he had made it clear that an affair was all he would ever want from her. Lena Tarasov had stated that he would never fall in love again, and now she knew why. He was still in love with his dead wife, and consumed with guilt that he had somehow failed Irina and his little daughter. Falling in love with him would be emotional suicide, warned a voice in her head. But in her heart she knew the warning was too late. She loved him, and learning about the tragedy of his past made her love him more.

'The avalanche that killed Irina and Klara was a terrible accident, but you were not to blame for their deaths,' she told him gently. 'You say you feel guilty that you devoted all your time to your business, but I imagine your determination to succeed was so that you could give your wife and daughter a better life.'

'I wanted to buy a house with a garden for Klara to play in—give her the things I'd never had as a child.' He gave a grim smile. 'She loved music, and wanted to learn to play an instrument, but it was impossible in our cramped apartment.' He shook his head. 'Ironically, most of the children from the village survived. They had gone on a school trip and returned to find their school buried and many of their parents dead. I set up an orphanage and paid to have the village rebuilt, but no amount of money can rebuild shattered lives. I go back every year, but the new Rumsk is a strangely quiet place, shrouded in sadness.'

He expelled a ragged breath and gave in to the temptation to slide his arms around Ella's waist and hold her close. Her hair smelled of lemons, and he could feel the thud of her heart beneath her ribs, its steady beat strangely comforting. He turned his head and felt a curious tugging sensation in his chest when she brushed her lips over his cheek, his jaw, and finally across his mouth, in a feather-light caress that soothed his ravaged soul.

He needed her tonight; he needed her in a way he had never needed any woman—although he refused to assimilate the emotions churning inside him. Her mouth moved over his in a tentative kiss that made his stomach muscles clench, desire and some other indefinable feeling surging through him, so that with a groan he swept her up into his arms and strode back across the terrace.

She was the most generous lover he had ever known, and the sweetness of her response when he laid her on the bed and claimed her mouth with his evoked an ache around his heart. He knew every inch of her body, but he revelled in exploring every dip and curve again as he opened her robe and stroked his hands over her satin-soft skin. Her firm breasts filled his palms, and he heard her swiftly indrawn breath when he bent his head and closed his lips around her nipple, laving it with his tongue until she clutched his shoulders and twisted her hips in a mute plea for him to slide his hand between her legs.

Ella gasped at the first brush of his thumb across the ultra-sensitive nub of her clitoris, and molten heat pooled between her thighs as her body prepared for Vadim's possession. He gently parted her, slid a finger in deep to work his magic, and in response she traced her hand through the crisp dark hairs that arrowed down to his hips. She heard his low groan as she caressed the throbbing length of his arousal.

She loved him, and tonight she sensed that he needed to lose himself in the passion that, as always, had swiftly built between them. When he moved over her she arched her hips to meet him, and held his gaze as he entered her with one deep thrust that joined their bodies as one. He was haunted by his past, but if he was able to forget the pain of his loss in these moments when they soared to the heights of sexual pleasure then she was glad, and she matched his rhythm, urging him to find solace in the explosive ecstasy of their mutual climax and holding him close against her heart when they slowly came back down to earth.

For long moments afterwards he lay lax on top of her, his face buried in her throat. Ella's heart contracted when she felt wetness on her skin, and with shaking fingers she touched his cheek, wanting to weep at the evidence of his grief. How could she ever have thought him heartless? Despite his unhappy childhood, and the brutal years he had spent in the Russian army, he had loved his wife and child. But losing them had been a shattering blow; it was little wonder that he had built a wall around his heart, and if Lena Tarasov was right he would never allow any woman to break through his defences.

When Ella opened her eyes the following morning she was alone, the faint indentation on the pillow the only evidence that Vadim had slept beside her. She rolled onto his side of the bed and breathed in the evocative scent of his cologne that lingered on the sheets. Last night, his decision to confide the details of his marriage to her had given her confidence that they had passed a cornerstone in their relationship. But in the clear light of day she could not escape the stark realisation that he was still in love with his dead wife.

The fact that he had opened up his heart to her must mean

something, she thought wistfully as she slid out of bed and wrapped her robe around her. His ravaged expression when he had spoken of Irina and Klara was indisputable proof that, far from being the heartless playboy she had once believed, he was capable of deep emotions. But the possibility that he could ever fall in love with her seemed as remote as ever. Vadim was tied to his past—not simply by the love he felt for his wife and child, but by guilt because he felt that he had not been a good husband and father.

Could he ever be persuaded to take another chance on love? She cast her mind over the happy times they had spent together since they had come to Antibes. The closeness they had shared had not only been in her imagination, she thought, feeling a fragile flame of hope spark inside her. They had become friends as well as lovers, and in choosing to reveal the secrets of his past to her Vadim had shown that he trusted her.

She walked down the stairs and out to the terrace, her heart clenching when she saw him sitting at the breakfast table. It was important that she encouraged him to talk more about Irina and Klara, she decided. He had kept his pain locked away for far too long, but now he had lowered his barriers she wanted to help him come to terms with his past.

'Good morning, angel face.' Vadim lowered his newspaper when Ella approached, and gave her a cool smile that bore no hint of the raw emotions that had overwhelmed him the previous night. 'Did you sleep well?'

'I…yes, thank you,' she murmured, trying to hide her confusion that he was acting as if the events of last night had never taken place. His face was once more a handsome mask, his eyes concealed behind designer shades so that she had no clue to his thoughts. She dropped into a chair opposite him, and poured herself a glass of orange juice while she assembled the words she wanted to say. 'How are you feeling this morning?' She bit her lip when his dark brows winged upwards, and continued in a rush, 'I realise that last night it must have been very difficult for you to tell me about your wife and little girl, but I just want you to know that I…I'm here if you need to talk some more.'

'You mean you are offering to be…what, exactly? My counsellor?' Vadim suggested sardonically.

The faint mockery in his voice caused Ella's heart to dip, and she stared at him, searching his face desperately for some sign of the man who had opened his emotions to her the previous night.

'I'm offering my support,' she told him quietly. 'You've bottled up your grief about Irina and Klara for far too long and I want to help you.'

A nerve jumped in Vadim's cheek as he stared at Ella's beautiful face. She was so very lovely. His eyes strayed to her pale gold hair that fell in a silky curtain around her shoulders. He had never felt as close to any other human being as he did to this woman, but his every instinct was to fight the feelings she evoked in him. He did not fear any man, but emotions scared the hell out of him, he acknowledged grimly. He bitterly regretted revealing his past to her. It made him feel vulnerable and exposed, and the look of pity in her eyes made him want to weep, as if he were once again the small boy who had prayed every night that his mother would come back to him.

'I don't need your help, or your support,' he said abruptly. 'The past is gone, and no amount of talking will bring Irina and Klara back. You are my mistress, Ella—nothing more—and all I want from you is mind-blowing sex.'

Ella flinched as if he had slapped her, and she blinked hard in a desperate attempt to dispel the tears that blurred her vision. Vadim could not have made it plainer that she meant nothing more to him than a convenient sex partner. She had entered into an affair with him confident that her emotions would not get involved, but, fool that she was, she had repeated the mistake her mother had made and fallen in love with a man who did not love her. Unlike her father, who had been incapable of love, Vadim had proved that his emotions ran deep, but his heart belonged to his dead wife.

The sheer hopelessness of loving him swept over her; and with it a feeling of nausea that made her jump to her feet, terrified that she was actually going to be sick in front of him. She had felt queasy for the past few days, and had lost her appetite—classic symptoms that a migraine was brewing.

Vadim was watching her through narrowed eyes. She could not bear for him to realise how much he had hurt her and she forced a brittle smile. 'Well, I'm glad you've clarified my role in your life. If you'll excuse me, I need to take a couple of headache tablets,' she said coolly, before she hurried back into the house.

Vadim walked into the bedroom an hour later and found Ella sitting on the balcony, apparently engrossed in her book. He stared intently at her pale face, and she was glad that her sunglasses hid her red-rimmed eyes.

'Something has come up,' he said abruptly. 'I have to go to Prague for an urgent business meeting. The maid has packed a case for you. I thought we'd spend a few days there and play tourist. Have you ever been to Prague?'

'I performed there once,' Ella replied slowly, 'but I didn't get a chance to look around the city.' She hesitated, feeling her heart splinter. Earlier, she had fled from Vadim in tears, and after an hour of soul-searching she had reached the conclusion that she could not continue her relationship with him knowing that, while he was the love of her life, his heart belonged to Irina.

Why not enjoy one last trip with him? whispered a voice in her head. She would love to go to Prague with him—but then she'd happily fly to the moon with him if he asked her, she acknowledged heavily. She had always known their affair couldn't last, but she hadn't envisaged that ending it would feel as though her heart was being ripped out.

'As a matter of fact I really need to go back to London. Marcus phoned yesterday evening while you were in the shower,' she explained, flushing as she uttered the lie. 'He told me that rehearsals for the film score we will be recording have been brought forward.'

Vadim's eyes narrowed on the twin spots of colour that flared briefly on her pale face before they faded again, leaving her looking like a fragile ghost. She had seemed unwell for the last few days, but had dismissed his concern, saying merely that she was tired. It was a reasonable explanation, considering that they frequently made love several times a night, he conceded. But it wouldn't hurt to insist that she see a doctor.

'Why didn't you mention your conversation with Marcus last night?' he queried.

'I…I forgot.' Ella dropped her eyes from his. 'Give me ten minutes to pack and I'll catch a lift to the airport with you. I'm sure I'll be able to book a last-minute flight home.'

'I told you—the maid has packed a case for you.'

The edge of impatience in Vadim's voice exacerbated Ella's tension, but she forced herself to meet his gaze. 'I need to pack my own clothes, that I brought with me.' She paused and then said quietly, 'I've been in touch with Uncle Rex. He's found a flat big enough for me to keep my piano, and I intend to move out of Kingfisher House as soon as I get back to London.'

Vadim regarded her silently for long, tense moments which stretched her nerves to snapping point. 'This is all very sudden,' he drawled. 'What has triggered this unexpected urgency to return to London, Ella?'

'I've been thinking about it for a few days,' she mumbled untruthfully.

'Really? So every time we made love recently you were plotting to leave me?' he queried coldly.

'It's time we moved on,' Ella said desperately, when anger blazed in Vadim's eyes. 'Our affair was only ever a temporary arrangement, to last as long as either of us wanted it to.' She reminded him of his words when they had first become lovers.

Vadim could feel his heart slamming against his ribs. Sure, he remembered what he had said when he'd laid down the rules of their relationship, but he had never expected that he would want to change those rules—and he'd certainly never contemplated that Ella would be the one to call time on their affair.

'You know as well as I do that this isn't over,' he said harshly. He pulled her to her feet and wrenched the edges of her robe apart, ignoring her startled cry as he stared down at her naked body. 'Do you want me to prove it to you?' he demanded, moving his hand to his belt. 'I could make love to you right now, Ella, and you wouldn't stop me.'

'No!' The flash of fear in her eyes stopped him in his tracks, and he flung her from him, frustration boiling up inside him.

'Why?' he bit out, nostrils flaring as he sought to control his temper and suppress the fear churning in his stomach. He didn't want to lose her. Hell—where had that thought come from? he asked himself as he raked a hand through his hair.

'Being here with you has been…fun,' she told him, praying

he would not hear the tremor in her voice. 'But music is my life, and I need to focus exclusively on my playing to succeed in my career. I don't have time for distractions. I thought you would understand,' she said tremulously when his jaw tightened. 'You admitted that you felt the same drive and determination when you were building your company.'

It was the truth, but he did not like having the tables turned on him, Vadim thought grimly. Ella had a fantastic career ahead of her, and to achieve the success she deserved she *would* need to dedicate herself utterly to her music. He had no right to try and interfere with the life she had mapped out. But the thought of letting her go tore at his insides. These past weeks at the villa had been the happiest of his life, and he was shocked to realise how much he had enjoyed the time away from his work schedule. He had finally mastered the art of delegation, and had handed tasks over to his chief executives so that he could spend more time with Ella. It was bitterly ironic that she was citing the demands of her career as the reason why she wanted to end their relationship.

But if she thought he would beg her to stay with him she could think again. They'd had a good time, but she was right: it was time to move on. It was not as though their affair could ever have been more than a brief fling. He had proved that he was no good at relationships, and he had no intention of going down that road again.

He swung back to face her, and felt a hand squeeze his heart when he saw the glimmer of tears in her eyes. She was so very lovely, but she clearly had her own agenda—and beautiful blondes were ten a penny for a playboy billionaire. 'If that's really what you want, you'd better pack whatever you want to take with you,' he said coolly, forcing himself to turn and walk away from her. 'I'll meet you downstairs in fifteen minutes. Do you want me to phone the airport and see if I can book you a flight to London?'

'Please.' Somehow Ella managed to articulate the word, but the minute he walked out of the bedroom she raced into the bathroom and was violently sick.

It was over. And, from his faintly bored attitude, Vadim clearly did not give a damn. Those times when he had made love to her with tenderness as well as passion, whispering words to her in Russian as he cradled her in his arms, had meant nothing to him, and she had been a fool to hope that he was beginning to care for her.

Somehow she dragged herself back into the bedroom, dressed quickly in the clothes she had brought with her from Paris and packed her few belongings. Her violin was in its case next to the bed, and she picked it up and hurried out of the room, tears burning the back of her throat when she glanced back at the bed where every night Vadim had taken her to that magical place she had believed was uniquely theirs. Doubtless he would soon replace her with another mistress, she thought bleakly. Images of him making love to another woman lacerated her heart, and she flew down the stairs and across the hall to the front door of the villa.

He was lowering the roof of the Aston Martin while talking on his mobile phone. Maybe he was arranging her flight home? Misery swept through her as she faced the devastating reality that he would never hold her in his arms again. She felt dizzy with grief, and as she walked down the front steps she lost her footing. Her startled cry rent the air, and she heard Vadim swear violently, saw him move towards her—and then there was nothing.

She came round to find that Vadim had laid her on the back seat of his car. She lifted her lashes and stared groggily at him, shocked by how grey he looked beneath his tan. His jaw was rigid, and for a moment something blazed in his eyes, before he moved away from her and leapt into the driver's seat.

'My violin!' she cried, staring back at her violin and her suitcase, lying on the driveway as the car sped away. 'Vadim, I can't go to the airport without it.'

'We're not going to the airport,' he informed her tersely. 'I'm taking you to the local hospital.'

'The hosp…? I fainted, that's all.' She sat up, and the wind whipped her hair across her face.

'Women do not faint without a reason,' he said grimly. 'You're as pale as death, you've barely eaten a thing all week, and you collapsed and would have fallen down a set of stone steps if I hadn't caught you. I have a friend who is a doctor. Claude will check you out, and if he says you're well enough to travel, then I'll take you to the airport.'

His implacable tone warned Ella that arguing would be futile. How could she tell him that she had suffered an extreme physical reaction to the mental anguish she felt at the ending of their affair? He would guess that she was in love with him, and then her pride as well as her heart would be in tatters.

At the hospital they were met by a nurse, who whisked Ella off to check her blood pressure and requested a urine sample before ushering her into the doctor's office.

Claude Arnot stood up from his desk and indicated that she should take a seat. She glared at Vadim when he dropped into the chair next to her, but his hard smile told her that he was staying for her consultation with the doctor.

'Vadim tells me you have lost your appetite recently, Mademoiselle Stafford. Do know why that could be?'

She shrugged. 'I've been feeling a bit nauseous, but I suffer from occasional migraines, and I suspect I'm going to be hit by one any day soon.'

The doctor nodded. 'Is everything else normal? Your periods, for instance? When was the date of your last one?'

'I don't really know.' Ella frowned, trying to remember, and feeling ridiculously embarrassed at discussing something so personal in front of Vadim. 'They've never been regular. In fact my GP told me it's possible that I will need fertility treatment if I ever want children. But the demands of my career mean that I will probably never choose to have a family,' she explained, with a faint catch in her voice.

They were interrupted by the arrival of the nurse, who handed the doctor some notes. He skimmed through them in silence. He would probably say that she was anaemic, Ella decided. She had forgotten to mention that her GP had prescribed a course of iron pills last year, when a blood test had shown that she was suffering from an iron deficiency. She wished he would hurry up. Sitting next to Vadim, breathing in the familiar sandalwood scent of his cologne, was torture, and she was in danger of flinging herself at him and begging him to take her to Prague with him.

She gave a start when Claude Arnot cleared his throat, and looked across the desk at him, puzzled by his sympathetic smile.

'I hope your career is not *too* demanding, Mademoiselle Stafford,' the doctor said gently, 'because you are pregnant.'

CHAPTER ELEVEN

AFTERWARDS, Ella had no clear recollection of walking out of the consulting room. On the periphery of her shell-shocked mind she heard Vadim's terse voice, asking if the test indicated when she might have conceived, and heard the doctor's reply that she was about six weeks into her pregnancy.

It must have happened at Kingfisher House, right at the beginning of their affair, she thought dazedly, as Vadim gripped her elbow and whisked her back to the car. His thoughts were obviously on the same track, and as he fired the engine he said harshly, 'That first time in the summerhouse, during the storm—I didn't use protection. I assumed, since you did not say anything, that there had been no repercussions after my carelessness, but clearly that is not the case.'

He was white-lipped with shock, and Ella sank back in her seat as they sped back to the villa, trembling with reaction to the astounding news that she was carrying Vadim's baby. The possibility had not crossed her mind. As she had explained to Dr Arnot, her periods had never been regular, but she had not bothered to seek a reason because she had assumed that, as she never planned to get married, she would never have children.

From the look of fury on Vadim's face it was clear he did not welcome the news that she was expecting his child. A wave of protectiveness flooded through her, so strong that she placed her hands on her flat stomach. Poor baby! At this early stage it was technically only a cluster of cells, but to Ella it was a child that she and Vadim had created. Could their baby possibly know that it was unwelcome? The idea was so unbearable that tears filled her eyes, and love swept through her with the force of a tidal wave; love for the baby she had never expected to conceive, but who already aroused such a fierce maternal instinct within her that she knew she would give her life for her child.

But what was she going to do? How would she manage as a single mother? She could not realistically pursue a career as a soloist when it would mean dragging a young child around the world each time she toured, she acknowledged heavily. Lost in her thoughts, she did not notice that they had driven through the gates of the Villa Corraline until Vadim cut the engine, and her heart thudded frantically in her chest when he led the way into the house in a grim silence that shredded her nerves.

He had no right to be so angry, she thought rebelliously when he ushered her into the sitting room and followed her inside, closing the door with an ominous thud. He had admitted that her pregnancy was due to *his* mistake. He was probably furious because he believed she would demand a huge maintenance agreement for their child—but he had no need to worry, she thought fiercely. She wanted nothing from him. Somehow she would manage to bring up her child alone.

Vadim crossed to the bar and poured himself a large vodka, uncaring that it was only eleven a.m. His hand shook as he lifted the glass to his lips, and he gulped the clear liquid down in one, feeling the alcohol warm the blood that had frozen in his veins. Ella had moved to stand by the window and sunlight danced over her hair, turning it into a river of gold that flowed down her back. She was so beautiful—but he could not bear to look at her, and he gripped the glass in his hand so tightly that it was in danger of shattering.

'No wonder you were so desperate to leave France and go back to London,' he bit out savagely. 'I assume you weren't going to tell me you are carrying my child.'

Startled by the accusation, Ella shook her head. 'I had no idea I was pregnant,' she defended herself.

'How could you not have known?' Vadim demanded blisteringly. 'You *must* have known, and that's why, out of the blue, you announced that you wanted to end our affair—because you didn't want me to find out.' He drew a ragged breath and fought to control the emotions that had been building inside him since the shocking revelation that Ella had conceived his baby.

'*Push me higher on the swing, Papa...*' Klara's sweet voice echoed in his mind, and for a moment he saw her face with such crystal clarity that he felt he could almost reach out and touch her, hold her wriggling little body in his arms and tell her she was his princess. Grief pierced him like an arrow through the heart. Klara had gone, and he would never hear her laughter again. But now, amazingly, there would be another child—not a replacement for the child he had lost, but a precious gift he would treasure, a second chance at fatherhood that he would not fail.

He stared at Ella, recalling the several occasions when she had stated that she did not plan to have children because she wanted to concentrate on her career, and a sickening suspicion crept into his mind. 'Do you intend to go ahead with the pregnancy?' he demanded coldly. 'Or was the reason for your sudden decision to rush back to England so that you could have a termination?' He ignored her shocked gasp and continued harshly, '*You* might not want this baby, but I do. I realise that nine months of pregnancy will interrupt your career, but I will compensate you financially, and from the moment the baby is born I will take charge of it. You will be able to have your life back.'

Ella opened her mouth, but her vocal cords had been strangled and no sound emerged. 'You're offering to...to *buy* the baby from me?' she faltered at last, shock swiftly replaced by searing rage. 'How dare you make the appalling suggestion that I would even *think* about ending my pregnancy?' Her emotions were on a rollercoaster, and her anger died as quickly as it had come as hurt unfurled inside her. How could she ever have believed that she and Vadim were growing close when he could think that of her? It proved that he did not know her at all, she thought miserably.

But in truth his reaction to the news of her pregnancy had taken her by surprise. She had not expected him to want this baby. But she had seen the pain in his eyes when he had told her about the tragic loss of his daughter—she should have known that he would feel protective of the child she was carrying.

'I might not have planned to have children, but I want this baby, and I will love it and be the best mother I possibly can,' she said shakily. 'If you want to be involved in our child's upbringing, then I'm sure we can work out arrangements for shared access and...and visiting rights,' she pushed on, her voice wavering slightly when Vadim's brows drew together in a thunderous frown.

'I have no intention of *visiting* my child,' he grated. 'I want to be a proper, hands-on father.' The kind of father he should have been to Klara, instead of spending long hours at his office.

'But...what will we do?' Ella queried uncertainly, wondering if Vadim would demand that their baby should spend a few weeks, or even months, living with each of them in turn. An arrangement along those lines might enable her to continue with her career, she acknowledged. But she knew instantly that she would not be able to bear being parted from her child for even a day, and compared to being a mother her career was no longer the most important thing in her life.

'I'm not sure how we'll sort out the details,' Vadim admitted. 'All I know is that I am determined to take an active role in my child's upbringing. Maybe we could continue with the arrangement to share Kingfisher House, so that the baby lives with both of us?'

Ella frowned, wondering if he meant that she and the baby would live in the caretaker flat, enabling him to see his child regularly while he maintained his bachelor lifestyle in the main part of the house. He had made it clear that he wanted his baby, but had made no mention of how he saw *her* future role in his life. He might bring other women back for the night, she thought, blanching at the idea of living next door to him, knowing that he was making love to a new mistress in the master bedroom where he had once made love to her.

'That would be unbearable!' she burst out, feeling sick with misery. 'I want to live in my own house and lead my own life.'

Did the new life she suddenly seemed so keen on include dating other men? Vadim wondered furiously. He felt as though he had been kicked in the gut by her adamant refusal to share Kingfisher House with him. It seemed the obvious solution, which would enable them to both care for the baby, but Ella had sounded horrified by the suggestion.

What if she had a relationship with some guy and invited him to stay the night—or even move in with her? Jealousy burned like acid in his stomach as he imagined another man making love to her, and perhaps acting as a father figure to his child. The prospect was intolerable, and his resolve hardened.

'I should warn you that if we cannot reach an amicable agreement on shared care then I will fight for sole custody of our child—and I will win,' he said harshly.

Ella paled. He was deadly serious, she realised shakily. She had always known that beneath his charisma there was a ruthless side to him, and here now was proof of his lethal power. 'You wouldn't…' she said shakily.

'I can afford the best lawyers; and I can give our child a stable home, an excellent education—everything that money can buy,' he listed harshly. 'Whereas you…' He raked his eyes over her slender figure. 'You have admitted that you need to practise your violin for five or six hours a day, and playing with an orchestra means that you would be at work in the evenings. What do you propose to do with our child then? Leave him or her in the care of a babysitter? And what about when you are on tour—will you drag the baby around Europe with you?'

'*I don't know!*' she cried, hating him for voicing exactly the same problems she had foreseen. 'Despite what you think, finding out that I'm pregnant was a complete shock, and right now my world feels as though it has been turned upside down,' she admitted huskily, brushing her hand across her eyes to wipe away her tears.

The betraying gesture tugged on Vadim's conscience and his anger drained away—to be replaced with a strong urge to haul her into his arms and simply hold her, tell her that he would take care of her and their baby. But she had made it clear that she did not want his care. Pain lanced him, and he moved away from her, needing to put some space between them while he brought his emotions back under control. He who prided himself on having dismissed emotions from his life! That was a laugh, he thought savagely. Ella had got him so stirred up that he couldn't think straight, and his normal cool logic had been replaced with a seething mass of emotions.

Ella was right. The news of her pregnancy had been a shock for both of them, and if she felt anything like him then she was beyond rational thought right now. They needed a breathing space, and whatever else was happening in his life the logical part of his brain reminded him that he still needed to go to Prague. His dedication to his business was still total, and iron self-discipline won over the urge to send one of his executives to the meeting so that he could remain at the villa with Ella.

'We'll continue with this discussion in a couple of days, when I get back from my trip,' he told her brusquely, silently acknowledging that there was nothing to discuss. He had not expected to be a father again, but Ella had conceived his baby, and he was utterly determined to bring his child up and be the best father he could.

'You need to sit down before you fall down,' he growled, concern flooding through him when she swayed on her feet. She looked like a wraith; all wide, bruised eyes in a face the colour of parchment, and with a muttered oath he lifted her into his arms and strode out of the room and up the stairs. 'I'll tell Hortense to bring you something to eat,' he told her, re-ferring to the good-natured housekeeper and cook who worked at the villa. 'Rest for a while—for the baby's sake,' he reminded her when she opened her mouth to argue, and took advantage of her parted lips to bestow a brief, stinging kiss that drew Ella's instant response and left her full of despair as she watched him stride out of the room, the taste of him lingering on her skin.

Minutes later she heard the Aston Martin roar down the

drive. The dramatic events of the morning had left her physically and emotionally drained, and she lay lethargically on the bed, feeling too weak to move.

She was still stunned that she was going to have a baby. It was unexpected and unplanned, but as the news sank in she felt a piercing joy at the prospect of being a mother. Her mind turned to Vadim's threat that he would fight for custody of the baby, and her happiness dissolved. She sat up and instinctively placed her hand on her stomach, as if to protect the tiny speck of life within her.

As Vadim had pointed out, he could afford to hire the best lawyers, and there was a strong possibility he would win a court battle. Panic swept through her, destroying all rational thought. She would never hand over her child—never. All she could think of was to leave the villa before he got back from Prague and flee back to England. She would move out of Kingfisher House and go away somewhere, cover her tracks so that he could not find her, she decided frantically. And, filled with a sudden energy born of desperation, she jumped up, grabbed her violin and the suitcase that the maid must have rescued from the driveway after Vadim had driven her to the hospital, and raced down the stairs.

Vadim strode through the hotel lobby, trying to focus his mind on the take-over bid of a media company that he was about to clinch. The deal was an important one, hence his decision to personally attend the meeting to hammer out the last remaining details. But instead of profit margins all he could think about was Ella.

Ella and his baby. Thoughts of his unborn child eased the ache in his heart caused by the death of his little daughter so many years ago. He had mourned his wife too, but his grief at losing Irina had been mingled with a feeling of guilt that he had not loved her as deeply as she had loved him. He had cared for her, and had tried to do his best for her, but he had not felt the earth-shattering, volcanic eruption of emotion that the poets described as love.

In all honesty he had not believed that such a powerful love even existed, and if it did he had always been certain that he was not capable of it. But now, as he stood on the steps of the hotel and stared across the ancient city of Prague, he realised that his life was a series of dull black and white images without Ella.

If she had been with him they would have explored Prague together. She loved history, and would have been fascinated by the castle, and the beautiful Basilica of St George. Maybe they would have taken a boat trip down the River Vltava, and then eaten in one of the charming little restaurants in the Old Town before returning to their hotel to make love with a passion that touched his soul.

He missed her, he acknowledged, feeling the ache in his chest grow and expand until it seemed to encompass his whole body. He wanted to be with her. The thought drummed through his veins, and suddenly it seemed as if a curtain had lifted in his mind and he saw what a blind fool he had been.

During the weeks they had spent together in Antibes he had refused to admit that he was falling in love with her. He had been afraid of the emotions she stirred in him, and determined to fight his feelings. But now it hit him that what he really had to fear was a life without Ella. His heart was beating too fast, and his skin felt clammy as the emotions he had tried so hard to deny surged through him with the unstoppable force of a tidal wave. Prague looked beautiful in the sunshine, but he turned his back on the city and strode back into the hotel, to inform the receptionist that he was curtailing his visit.

In the taxi to the airport he phoned his PA and asked her to postpone the meeting, and then he called his chief executive and ordered him to catch the next flight to Prague. The delay meant there was a danger they would lose the deal, but for the first time in his life he had something he cared about more than business—his one thought was to get back to the Villa Corraline as quickly as possible.

He should not have left Ella alone. Especially when she was in a state of shock after finding out that she was pregnant. He believed now that she had not known she was expecting his baby. Unlike many women he had met she was not a clever actress, and the expression of stunned disbelief on her face when the doctor had given her the news had been real. He could not believe he had made that crass accusation that she had planned to get rid of the baby. The Ella he had come to know was simply not capable of such an action. But, having accepted that fact, he also had to accept that she had announced she was going back to London because she wanted to end their relationship.

Guilt clawed in his gut when he recalled their last explosive confrontation. They both wanted their child, but instead of having a rational discussion about how best they could bring up the baby he had threatened her with a custody battle. No wonder he had glimpsed real fear in her eyes. In her mind he must seem as much of a bully as her father had been—that same father who, when she was a child, had locked her in the tower room of the family mansion, knowing that she was terrified the place was haunted.

He could not blame her if she refused to have anything more to do with him, he thought bleakly, cursing the traffic that clogged the roads leading to the airport. He could only pray that she would give him another chance and allow him to explain just what she meant to him.

* * *

Silver moonlight danced across the waves which gently lapped the shore. The beach was silent, the air warm and still, and the fine white sand felt soft beneath Ella's feet as she strolled along by the water's edge.

For the first time since she had learned that she was pregnant with Vadim's baby a sense of calm had settled over her, and she knew that her decision to remain in France and wait for him had been the right one. She had been in the taxi, on the way to the airport, when she had come to her senses and accepted that running away was not the answer. She couldn't live as a fugitive for the rest of her life, and, more importantly, she accepted that she could not deny Vadim his child.

Back at the villa she had tried to remain calm, and for the baby's sake had forced herself to eat something. But tonight sleep had proved impossible, and after tossing restlessly in the big lonely bed for over an hour she had finally got up, slipped on her grey silk robe and walked down to the beach.

She missed Vadim, she acknowledged as she stared up at the crescent moon and the stars that studded the sky like diamonds on a velvet backdrop. Apart from the few days when she had been in Paris, this was the first night they had spent apart since they had become lovers. It was such a short time, really, yet her life seemed to have been entwined with his for ever, and she could not imagine living without him.

Now that she was over the shock of discovering that she was pregnant, she was able to think rationally again. Vadim's threat to fight for custody of their child was understandable when she knew that he still grieved for the daughter he had lost. But she was certain he would never force her to hand over her baby.

It all came down to trust, she mused as she turned to walk back towards the house. Her father had been a cruel man, who had delighted in hurting her and her mother, but Vadim was nothing like him. She could not deny him his chance to be a father again, and when he returned from Prague she would tell him that she accepted his proposal to share Kingfisher House, so that they could bring up the baby together. It would not be easy, living close to him yet being shut out of his life. But she loved him so much that she was prepared to sacrifice her happiness for his.

Lost in her thoughts, she gave a start when she heard her name being called across the dark beach. Vadim was calling her. But Vadim was in Prague. She gave herself a mental shake, convinced that she had imagined his voice. Loving him was turning her into a madwoman, she thought ruefully.

'*Ella…*'

A figure came running out of the shadows, tearing across the sand towards her. 'Vadim?' Even from a distance she sensed his urgency, and without thinking of anything but her need to be with him she began to run too.

He reached her and swept her into his arms, crushing her against his chest so that the breath was driven from her body. The expression on his face was tortured, his brilliant blue eyes blazing with an emotion that made her heart miss a beat. She could not imagine why he was there, and she stared up at him in confusion when she felt a shudder run through his big body. What could have happened to cause him to look so *shattered*?

'I thought you had gone—that I had driven you away…' His voice was muffled against her throat, and her heart turned over when she felt wetness against her skin.

'Why are you here?' she asked shakily. 'Why aren't you in Prague, finalising your deal?'

'I suddenly realised what was truly important to me.' His Russian accent was very pronounced, his voice as deep and haunting as the notes of a cello. 'I thought I had terrified the life out of you with my unforgivable threat to fight you for custody of the baby. I was sure you had decided to leave me, and when I arrived at the villa and saw your violin was missing I knew I had been the biggest fool on the planet.'

The expression blazing in his eyes made Ella tremble, but she was afraid that her mind was playing tricks, seeing what it wanted to see. 'I had planned to leave,' she admitted, 'but halfway to Nice I realised that I couldn't go. Our baby needs both its parents,' she said huskily.

Vadim closed his eyes briefly and sent up a silent prayer. His heart was slamming beneath his ribs as he tightened his arms around Ella and pressed his lips to her brow, utterly undone by the emotions storming through him. 'When I walked into the empty house I was afraid that I had left it too late to tell you—' He broke off, his throat convulsing, and Ella stroked a trembling hand over his face.

'Tell me what?' she whispered.

Her hair smelled of lemons. He would carry the evocative scent to his grave—a tangible reminder of the woman who had stolen his heart. Taking a deep breath, he stared down into her smoke-soft eyes. 'That I love you,' he said unsteadily. 'With all my heart and everything I am, *angel moy*.' He gave a faint smile at her stunned expression. 'You are my world, Ella, and I am nothing without you.'

'Vadim...' Tears blurred her eyes and she placed a trembling finger across his lips, no thought in her head to hold back the words she had wanted to say for so long. 'I love you too— desperately—and I will do so for ever,' she added fiercely, realising from his stunned expression that he needed convincing of the depth of her love for him.

'Then why did you say that living at Kingfisher House with me would be unbearable?' he demanded raggedly.

She blushed. 'Because I knew that I loved you, and I couldn't stand the thought of sharing the house but not your life.'

'I only said I would fight you for the baby because I hated the idea of you living away from me and having other relationships,' Vadim admitted, tangling his fingers in her long blonde hair and tipping her face to his. 'I refused to admit how much you meant to me until I went to Prague and it finally hit me how goddamned miserable I was without you.'

His tension suddenly eased, and he stared down at her, his blue eyes blazing with such tenderness, such love, that tears blurred Ella's vision.

'I want to spend the rest of my life with you, Ella,' he said softly. 'Will you marry me, my angel?'

He felt her tremble, and mistook her joy for apprehension. 'I know you have bad memories of your parents' marriage, but I would never do anything to hurt you. I intend to spend the rest of my life taking care of you, and the baby, and any other children we might have.'

Ella's heart turned over at the urgency in his voice. 'I think we'd better concentrate on one baby at a time,' she teased gently. She hesitated, and then said huskily, 'I thought you had buried your heart with Irina.'

Vadim shook his head. 'I loved her, but I'm ashamed to say that I took her for granted. I was ambitious, and often I was so busy chasing deals that I put her second to my business. When I met you, you dominated my thoughts from the start— and I knew I was in trouble when I realised I would rather spend time with you than at work. I thought I could have an affair with you and then dismiss you from my life, but deep down I think I always recognised that you are the other half of my soul, *angel moy*, and I will love you until I die.'

He cupped her chin and lowered his mouth to hers, claiming her lips in an evocative kiss that made her feel as though fireworks were exploding inside her. 'I was determined not to fall in love with you,' she whispered. 'But I couldn't resist you. And eventually I was forced to admit that I didn't want to run from you, but to you. You are my life, my love…'

'My wife?' he queried gently.

'Yes.' Another tear trickled down her face and he caught it with his mouth, so that she tasted the salt on his lips when he kissed her again, this time with a sensual passion that sent fire coursing through her veins. He was the love of her life, and she told him so when he parted her silvery robe and it whispered to the ground. She stood before him, pale and ethereal in the moonlight. She told him again when he kissed her mouth and throat and breasts, catching her breath when he caressed each dusky nipple with his tongue before he knelt to press hungry kisses over her flat stomach, where their baby lay, and down to the cluster of gold curls between her thighs.

The sensation of his wickedly inventive tongue probing her slick wetness made her cry out, and she curled her fingers into his thick black hair as the intimate caress sent her close to the edge. He stripped out of his clothes with an uncharacteristic lack of grace that made her love him more, and then he spread her on the sand and moved over her, his brilliant blue eyes locked with hers as he entered her and made them one.

'I thought it was just good sex,' she said shyly, her eyes widening until they reflected the silvery gleam of the moon as he set a rhythm that drove them both higher.

'It was *never* just sex with you, angel,' he groaned, feeling the first delicious spasms of her orgasm close around him.

'Every time I made love to you it was with my heart as well as my body—I just didn't want to admit that you had such a hold on me.'

He moved inside her, and suddenly there was no need for words when their bodies could express the deep and abiding love they felt for each other. It was a love that would last a lifetime and beyond, Vadim vowed, and was finally able to translate the Russian words he had whispered to her every time they had made love, so that she was in no doubt as to how much she meant to him.

EPILOGUE

THEY were married a month later, in a simple but moving ceremony in the grounds of the Villa Corraline. Vadim's close friend Sergey Tarasov acted as best man, and Jenny flew over to be Ella's maid of honour. At the reception, Lena Tarasov commented that she had always suspected Vadim had fallen for Ella like a ton of bricks, and the love that blazed in Vadim's eyes when he looked at his new wife supported her theory.

They returned to London so that Ella could continue to play with the RLO, but, much to Marcus Benning's disappointment, she announced that she no longer intended to pursue a solo career now that she was going to be a mother.

Their baby daughter was born the following spring, when the cherry blossom trees in the garden at Kingfisher House were in full bloom. They named her Odette, because in the womb she had kicked hardest every time Ella played Tchaikovsky's score from *Swan Lake*, and from birth she was instantly pacified by the sound of the violin.

'Perhaps she'll grow up to be a famous virtuoso,' Ella mused one evening as Vadim cradled his newborn daughter, who was refusing to go to sleep and squawked a protest every time her mother put down her bow. 'Although, of course, she might be a genius business tycoon like her father.'

'Whatever she chooses to do in the future, she will always know that she is loved,' Vadim replied deeply. 'Just as I hope her mother knows that she is the love of my life.'

He lifted his head and trapped her gaze, the tenderness and love in his brilliant blue eyes filling Ella with joy. 'As you are mine,' she promised him fervently. 'Now and for always, my love.'

MILLS & BOON®

The Italians Collection!

2 BOOKS FREE!

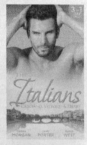

Irresistibly Hot Italians

You'll soon be dreaming of Italy with this scorching six-book collection. Each book is filled with three seductive stories full of sexy Italian men! Plus, if you order the collection today, you'll receive two books free!

This offer is just too good to miss!

Order your complete collection today at
www.millsandboon.co.uk/italians

0815_ST17

MILLS & BOON®

It Started With...Collection!

1 BOOK FREE!

Be seduced with this passionate four-book collection
from top author Miranda Lee. Each book contains
3-in-1 stories brimming with passion and intensely
sexy heroes. Plus, if you order today, you'll get
one book free!

**Order yours at
www.millsandboon.co.uk/startedwith**

715_ST15

MILLS & BOON®

The Rising Stars Collection!

1 BOOK FREE!

This fabulous four-book collection features 3-in-1 stories from some of our talented writers who are the stars of the future! Feel the temperature rise this summer with our ultra-sexy and powerful heroes. Don't miss this great offer—buy the collection today to get one book free!

**Order yours at
www.millsandboon.co.uk/risingstars**

0715_ST16

MILLS & BOON®

It's Got to be Perfect

IT'S GOT
TO BE
Perfect

UNCORRECTED
PROOF COPY

HALEY HILL

* cover in development

When Ellie Rigby throws her three-carat engagement ring into the gutter, she is certain of only one thing. She has yet to know true love!

Fed up with disastrous internet dates and conflicting advice from her friends, Ellie decides to take matters into her own hands. Starting a dating agency, Ellie becomes an expert in love. Well, that is until a match with one of her clients, charming, infuriating Nick, has her questioning everything she's ever thought about love…

Order yours today at
www.millsandboon.co.uk

MILLS & BOON®
By Request

RELIVE THE ROMANCE WITH THE BEST OF THE BEST

A sneak peek at next month's titles...

In stores from 21st August 2015:

- **His Virgin Bride** – Melanie Milburne, Maggie Cox & Margaret Mayo

- **In Bed With the Enemy** – Natalie Anderson, Aimee Carson & Tawny Weber

In stores from 4th September 2015:

- **The Jarrods: Inheritance** – Maxine Sullivan, Emilie Rose & Heidi Betts

- **Undressed by the Rebel** – Alison Roberts

Available at WHSmith, Tesco, Asda, Eason, Amazon and Apple

Just can't wait?
Buy our books online a month before they hit the shops!
visit www.millsandboon.co.uk

These books are also available in eBook format!